CONSIDER THE DRAGONFLY

ALSO BY MALCOLM IVEY

With Arms Unbound

On the Shoulders of Giants

Sticks & Stones

www.MalcolmIvey.com

CONSIDER THE DRAGONFLY

MALCOLM IVEY

tempus fugit *amor manet*
ASTRAL PIPELINE BOOKS | ORLANDO ⋆ PENSACOLA ⋆ SAN DIEGO

First Astral Pipeline Books Edition, October 2020

Astral Pipeline Books LLC
1317 Edgewater Dr., Ste 2023
Orlando, Florida 32804

astralpipelinebooks.com

ISBN: 978-1-953519-00-9 (paperback)
ISBN: 978-1-953519-01-6 (ebook)

Library of Congress Control Number: 2020944636

Interior dragonfly artwork by Michelene Phillips.
Cover dragonfly artwork by Natalya Aksenova.

For Mom

Prologue

AUGUST 1991

He tracked the roach with bloodshot eyes, imagining he could hear its tiny barbed legs scurrying across the bedroom wall. Distant engines revved and faded beyond the swaying curtains of his window. The alarm clock on the nightstand blinked *12:00.*

From the crack beneath the door he could vaguely make out the murmuring voices of news correspondents on the television in the living room. Slowly, he leaned back on the bed and unbuttoned his jeans.

The bag was crushed purple velvet with the words *Crown Royal* stitched across the front. Its gold-colored drawstring was looped through the opening of his boxers and secured by a tight double knot. He watched the door as he worked it free.

A far-off siren wailed. He glanced over at the ashtray on the nightstand and selected a decent-sized butt, then dug in his pocket for a light. The drag and crackle of the match flaring to life was loud in his ears. Once upon a time he used to hide his smoking from his parents. He no longer bothered. He had since graduated to darker secrets than cigarettes.

The purple pouch was heavy in his hand. He weighed it thoughtfully for a moment before emptying its contents on the bed. A gold rope chain with a diamond-crusted San Lazaro was tangled around a wad of twenties. There was other jewelry too: rings, bracelets, earrings, a watch. He wasn't nearly as excited by any of it as he used to be.

The gun was another story. Chrome and compact with a black rubber handle, it lay flat against the backdrop of money and jewelry like the cover of a gangsta rap album. He bit down on the filter of the stale Newport as he reached for it.

Images flooded his mind as he gripped the handle . . . of bullies and sell-outs and liars . . . of people that ignored him and laughed at him and brushed him aside. He twirled the pistol on his finger then rolled across the bed and aimed it skyward locking in on the roach making its pilgrimage across the popcorn ceiling. *Freeze!*

The apartment floor began to creak and groan. Footsteps were approaching. He gathered the money and jewelry and raked them back into the pouch along with the pistol. He ripped open the nightstand drawer and shoved the purple bag into the back corner, then slammed it shut.

He lay back in the bed just as the doorknob turned. His father's huge frame filled the doorway. Although it was after midnight and despite the fact that his dad hadn't been out of the apartment in months, he still wore a tweed suit and tie.

"You know your mother doesn't like you smoking."

He took a last drag from the butt and stuck it in the ashtray.

His father glanced back over his shoulder and shuffled his feet. "So. . . do you . . . is there anything?"

He studied his old man for a moment before reaching into the front pocket of his jeans and seizing the dime bag he had bought earlier at the Metrorail station. He tossed it across the bed and his father almost tripped as he hurried to scoop it up.

He smiled with childlike glee as he held the baggie up to the light. "Bless you, my son," he said, turning to leave, "bless you."

PART ONE

1988

"We either make ourselves miserable,
or we make ourselves strong.
The amount of work is the same."

—Carlos Castaneda

Chapter 1

The sun forced its way through the blinds, exploding from the tiny cracks in pencil-thin beams of brilliant white.

CJ McCallister flexed as he stood shirtless in front of the mirror. He turned left and right, examining his skinny body for any signs of progress. He *felt* a little taller, a little heavier, a little stronger, but it was just so difficult to tell.

He looked hard into his own eyes, then began bouncing lightly on the balls of his feet. He threw a jab at his reflection, then another, then a hook.

"CJ. Get up, baby." His mom's voice came through his bedroom door. *Knock knock knock.* "CJ? Are you up? Breakfast is ready."

"I'm up, Mom," he said, taking a last look in the mirror before grabbing his t-shirt and opening the door. He ran sideways down the stairs.

The McCallisters lived in a lower-middle-class apartment complex in South Miami. They moved there from Mobile, Alabama, when CJ was in the third grade. His mother had gotten a promotion and since his father was unemployed, they jumped at the opportunity for a new start in sunny Miami.

His mother was sitting at the table smiling at him when he reached the kitchen. "Hurry up and eat. We're running late."

He sat down at the table and shoved a half-piece of toast into his mouth while she poured milk in his Froot Loops. He glanced over his mother's shoulder into the living room, where his father lay snoring on the couch. The coffee table was full of overflowing ashtrays, empty two-liter bottles of Chek Cola, and pizza boxes from the night before. Suddenly his snoring pattern was disrupted by one of those half-snore-half-choke deals that always threatens to wake the snorer, but he only mumbled something unintelligible and settled back into his cacophonous rhythm.

"Lung-shot grizzly bear," CJ said, referring to a long-standing family joke about the thunderous volume of his father's snoring.

His mother smiled and sipped her coffee. CJ was secretly ashamed of his dad. He even hated his own nickname. His name was Paul McCallister. If anything, his name should be "P.M." or "P-Mac" or "Pauley," but shortly after his birth, his Uncle Marcus and Aunt Karen came down from Virginia Beach and christened him "CJ"—Christopher Junior, because in their opinion, he looked "just like his father." That story always amused CJ. How could he NOT look like his father at one month old? He was fat, white, and baldheaded. Half the babies in the country looked like his father, but they weren't named "CJ."

"Ready to go?" his mother asked, eyeing him as he raised the cereal bowl to his mouth and drained the remainder of the milk.

"Yep," he replied, standing and slinging his backpack over his shoulder.

They walked through the living room, where the snoring had picked up a few decibels, overpowering the man on television rambling about the upcoming presidential election between Bush and Dukakis. "That shit would put me to sleep too," CJ mumbled under his breath as he closed the door behind him and stepped out into the South Florida sunshine.

It took three attempts for the rusty old Toyota to crank up. When it finally burst into life with a massive plume of black smoke coughing from the exhaust pipe, his mom patted the dash and said "good girl" as if she were talking to a small child. CJ rolled his eyes and looked out the window. She always did that. It didn't matter if it was a car, a plant, a stray animal, or even a couch or some other inanimate object.

They pulled out of the Southwinds apartment complex into the heavy Monday morning traffic and slowly made their way to South Miami Junior High.

The car slowed to a stop in front of a house about a block away from his school. His mother looked at him.

"Don't skip," she pleaded.

"I won't, Momma," he said, kissing her on the cheek and opening the car door. He grabbed his backpack off the floorboard while she dug in her purse.

"Here's some lunch money," she said as she handed him three one-dollar bills.

He thanked her and shut the door. She made a U-turn and waved to him in the rearview mirror as she drove away. He watched her car disappear down the street before he reached into his backpack and fished out a crumpled pack of Newports. He shook one out, pulled the matches from the cellophane, fired it up, and took a deep drag before walking slowly toward the school.

There was a stark contrast between the quiet suburban street where his mom dropped him off and the hub of activity just around the corner. CJ walked along the endless line of school buses with their flashing red and yellow lights attached to retractable stop signs that jutted from their sides. The cars driven by parents who insisted on dropping their kids off at the front doors crept slowly by in a long procession of Escorts, Cavaliers, and Cutlasses, while the students on bikes and skateboards wove their way in and out of traffic.

South Miami Junior High school was built like all South Florida schools should be built: outdoors and airy with lots of plants and murals everywhere. It consisted of three long, two-story structures that ran parallel to each other with outdoor hallways and classrooms that seated over forty students. On either side of the middle structure were the auditorium and the cafeteria, and behind the school were basketball courts and football, baseball and soccer fields.

CJ was still a relatively new kid at South Miami. He enrolled at the end of his seventh-grade year and was now midway through the first semester of his eighth. This was his first "real" junior high. Two years ago, as a sixth grader at Radford Elementary, he stole a joint from his dad's stash to impress some friends and got busted smoking it in the boy's bathroom. The principal and guidance counselor called his mother and agreed not to press charges if she got him some help for his "drug problem." That's how he landed at the Longwood Center, where he finished sixth grade and started the seventh.

He fell in among the others making their way through the entrance. The crowd diverged at the end of the breezeway as each student made his or her way to their first-period class. CJ walked in the direction of Room 216, where Señora Salazar taught Spanish I. Spanish was a requirement in the Dade County Public School System, but CJ would have taken it regardless. It was his favorite class for many reasons. First, Señora Salazar smelled awesome, and you could sometimes see down her shirt whenever she came to your desk to help you, which was often in CJ's case. Second, he actually liked learning how to conjugate verbs according to their tenses *y practicar con trabalenguas.* And finally, everyone he knew spoke Spanish, and it annoyed the hell out of him that they could speak two languages and he couldn't. Even when he skipped, first period was mandatory.

The hallways were thinning as he emerged from the stairwell. Most of the second-floor classroom doors were already closed and he could hear some teachers in the process of calling roll as he passed them. He was midway between 214 and 215 when he saw her. He froze. Everything did. Except her. She continued walking toward him and smiled at his obvious attention. Was that the wind that was blowing her hair back and creating the illusion of some supermodel photo shoot? Where was the glitter coming from? And that light? Were those harps he was hearing or wind chimes? Her smile was intimate. Personal. A special gift from her to him. Sparkling white teeth behind pouty red lips. Her eyelashes curled out from her liquid brown eyes, and when she blinked it was like a fist squeezing his heart. She wore a white miniskirt and a pink top that tied at the shoulders, revealing much of her back. Her long brown hair was up today and she wore large hoop earrings and a small chain with a heart locket. Her skin was golden silk, and when she walked by he could smell her shampoo . . . strawberries. She was Andrea Marcos, the most beautiful girl at South Miami Junior High and in the world for that matter, as far as he was concerned.

He turned and stared as she glided down the hall. Other students looked at him funny as they stepped around him on their way to class. He was a statue in the hallway. An island in the channel. He wouldn't be released from this trance-like paralysis until she was out of sight. Suddenly her lovely form was eclipsed by a monstrous, hulking frame and the light went out of the hall like the sun sliding behind an ominous storm cloud. Two of them to be exact. The Barocela twins. Joey and Hector, the school bullies. They were identical in appearance as well as viciousness and looked more like NFL offensive linemen than teenage schoolchildren. CJ, who was moments ago paralyzed by lust, was now suffering from another form of paralysis: fear.

It seemed as if the very foundation of the building trembled beneath their heavy footsteps as they made their way toward him. CJ warily eyed their approach the way a bound, convicted criminal eyes his executioner. He was still praying they would walk by when they came to a stop directly in front of him. Many of the other students stopped as well.

Joey Barocela held out his catcher's-mitt-sized hand and sneered malevolently down at CJ. "Lunch money, *gringito.*" Though neither of the twins was known for his intellect, Joey was considered the smarter of the two and did most of the talking. Hector rarely spoke and when he did it was via hand gestures, grunting, and monosyllabic Spanish. CJ was still frozen in place when Joey's proffered hand wound back and slapped the shit out of him. His head bounced sharply off the wall and a bell in his head began clanging incessantly. Where was he? School? Who pulled the fire alarm? Hector stepped behind him and caught him before he could fall, sliding his own arms under CJ's and clasping them around the back of his neck in a full nelson, lifting him off his feet. Joey quickly dug in his pockets and seized the three dollar bills his mother had given him for lunch and held them in the air triumphantly. Hector the halfwit smiled adoringly at his brother, who ostentatiously pocketed the money and then slammed his huge fist into CJ's abdomen before sidestepping him and walking off. Hector released him from his hold and turned to follow his brother. CJ fell to the floor in a pitiful heap.

The hallway traffic sprang back to life as if someone had flipped a switch, whispering excitedly about the spectacle they had just witnessed while ignoring the pathetic figure at their feet clutching his stomach. CJ lay there dazed, the left side of his face throbbing and vomit threatening to erupt from his churning stomach. He willed it back down and sat up. As his brain began to clear, bits and pieces of what just transpired came back to him. He was manhandled, slapped, robbed, and dumped unceremoniously on the concrete floor. Rage and humiliation battled for supremacy in his head. *Assholes!* he thought, the rage winning for the moment.

A hand touched his shoulder. "*Pobrecito,* are you okay?" Andrea Marcos was kneeling next to him and she was on the verge of tears. She reached out and stroked his face and for a moment he forgot about everything else. He smiled at her and she laughed and smiled back. Then a thought struck him. She might have seen everything. *Oh my God!* He was overcome with shame. He just got his ass beat in front of the girl of his dreams. He had never felt so small in his life. He stood abruptly and her hand fell away as he rose. He scooped his backpack off the floor and walked quickly to the stairwell.

He took the steps two at a time and slung the bottom door open with such force that it ricocheted off the wall with a loud bang, sending the birds congregating in the hallway into immediate flight. He walked briskly down the hall to the nearest exit and emerged into the quiet street in front of the school that was bustling with activity fifteen minutes ago. It was now desolate. He was halfway across the street when he heard "HEY!" He turned to see the school cop walking in his direction and motioning for him to come back. He slid his free arm through the other strap on his backpack, took one more look behind him, and hit it. He flew down the sidewalk, leaving the flailing protests of the truant officer in his wake. He ran through the nearby neighborhood, cutting through backyards and hopping fences, putting as much distance as possible between himself and the school.

Dogs chased him, disgruntled old homeowners shook their fists, and one lady even sprayed him with a hose. He sprinted over canals, through parking lots and parks, and finally through the small patch of woods that shielded the railroad tracks that ran behind his apartment complex. He fired up a Newport and started walking.

~

Mr. McCallister was dancing. He'd had a pretty productive morning thus far. He dumped the ashtrays, threw away the pizza boxes, took out the trash, washed the dishes, and even swept and mopped the kitchen. He didn't mind cleaning. It was the least he could do. He hoped that later on that night when his wife got home she'd be impressed enough by his efforts to give him a twenty. That way he could get an eighth from Zach. If that bastard would ever pick up the damn phone. He'd been running low for a couple of days now and needed to re-up before he ran out. He dreaded running out. He needed marijuana like an asthma patient needed his inhaler. He literally couldn't breathe without it. He was aware of how "unaddictive" it was supposed to be, which made him feel all the more weak. What kind of idiotic schmuck becomes hopelessly addicted to a drug that's not even habit forming? Well, regardless of what the studies, tests, and experts said, he needed it. Needed it to face his wife, needed it to face his son, needed it to face the world and, most of all, needed it to face himself. When he looked in the mirror, he saw a fat, bald, ugly, weak, unemployed man who was losing his family. Marijuana softened that reality, or at least temporarily distracted him from it.

He turned up the stereo. Neil Diamond was singing the breakdown of "Cracklin' Rosie." He did his signature move. He was by far the best dancer at his Jesuit High in his glory days. When the girls from Lourdes came to the gym for the monthly dances, it was Chris McCallister they wanted to dance with, and even though he was overweight, he always ended up making out with the prettiest girl at the end of the night. *Ahhhh,* he thought, *the good old days.* And look at him now. Dancing in his boxers in a dark apartment living room, stoned out of his mind while his wife, along with the rest of the world, worked.

He stopped dancing and looked at the folded classified pages on the coffee table. He could see column after column of openings with their respective descriptions and phone numbers. His next job was in there somewhere. All he had to do was pick up the phone, turn on the charm, and line up some interviews, and he *intended* to. Later. He stood there pondering the word "intention" and marveling on how many of those he'd had that never came to fruition, especially since he started smoking pot. *Wow,* he thought, *how many goals have I set and forgotten over the last few years? How many good ideas have I not acted upon?* The correlation between smoking pot and unfulfilled intentions was crystallizing in his smoke-filled mind. He could see it. He was having an epiphany! A revelation! *Whoa,* he thought. *Wait, what the hell was I just thinking about?*

He was yanked from his reverie by the staccato ringing of the kitchen phone. He wondered who could be calling at—he looked at his watch—9:30 in the morning. Probably Cheryl asking if he had found anything promising on the job front. He loved his wife, but sometimes she could aggravate the piss out of him. The phone continued to ring furiously.

"Okay, okay," he muttered as he walked through the living room to answer it. He hated the downstairs phone. Upstairs was the phone he got free with a subscription to *LIFE* magazine. Its ringtone was a sequence of polite beeps. The kitchen phone was the exact opposite. It rang with such loud urgency and sonic force that it threatened to leap from its cradle on its own and dangle from the cord.

He snatched it up, mid-ring. "Y'ello."

"Is this the McCallister residence?" an official-sounding female voice inquired from the other end of the line.

He hesitated. *Who the hell was this?* Had he already made some calls about job openings this morning and forgotten? He didn't think so, but his short-term memory was fried. He dialed up his most professional-sounding adult voice just in case. "This is Chris McCallister. How may I help you?" he asked in a rich baritone.

"I'm calling from South Miami Junior High," she said. He could hear other voices and the click-clacking of typewriters in the background. "Are you related to a Paul McCallister?"

Chris began to worry. "He's my son," he answered, hoping that CJ was okay.

"Are you aware that he is absent from school today?"

He frowned. CJ and Cheryl left over two hours ago. He was feigning sleep when they walked out the door. The last thing he saw was CJ's red backpack. He was definitely going to school.

"Ma'am," Mr. McCallister began, making an uncharacteristically quick decision, "my son has a 102-degree temperature with tonsils the size of Swedish meatballs. He's in his bed right now. I was planning on calling you, but I guess that is unnecessary now. We hope to have him back in school in a couple of days."

"Oh," she replied, obviously disappointed at his response. "Well, we hope he feels better soon."

"Thank you," he said and hung up. He walked slowly back to the living room, lost in thought. *CJ is acting up again,* he mused, *trouble.* He reached beneath the couch and pulled out the wooden tray that was littered with seeds and stems, as well as a tiny mountain of green little buds waiting to be broken up and rolled into one of the loose Zig-Zag papers in the corner. He lit up a Camel and took a deep, satisfying drag before setting it in the ashtray and getting down to business. That school bitch had blown his high. It was time to refresh.

~

Mrs. Sinclair hung up the phone and reached for her tea. She took a sip and glanced across her desk at Officer Pratt, who was looking at her with raised eyebrows.

"Well?" he asked.

"He's sick," she said, straightening a few loose files on her otherwise immaculate desk. Pratt made her nervous. Every conversation with him, no matter how trivial, felt like an interrogation.

"Sick," he echoed.

"That's what his father said," she shot back. Her body language and tone were clearly dismissive.

Officer Steven Pratt sat back in his chair and reviewed the facts: approximately ten minutes ago he observed a student leaving school property well after the first-period bell had sounded. He instructed him to stop but the perp fled into a nearby neighborhood. He pursued on foot but lost sight of him after he cut through a backyard. A member of his safety patrol force had positively identified the perp as Paul "CJ" McCallister, whom she sat next to in her fifth-period English class. Now the father was saying the boy was sick in bed. If, in fact, the person Sinclair had spoken with was actually the father.

"Hand me his emergency contact card." He looked at the information listed: In case of emergency contact Chris and Cheryl McCallister, 305-555-3849, 6749 SE Southwinds Circle, Apt. 318C. He knew the Southwinds. It was part of his old beat. He did some figuring in his head. Those apartments were roughly three miles from the school. Unless the kid was an Olympic track star, there was no way he could have made it home on foot yet.

"I think I'll get visual confirmation on our sick little friend," said Truant Officer Pratt, standing and adjusting his belt. He instinctively patted his holster, a habit forged during his twenty-year tour in the field. He frowned when he remembered it was no longer a part of his uniform and looked at Mrs. Sinclair, who was still nervously tidying her desk. "Just in case," he said, and headed for his car.

~

Andrea Marcos sat in first-period social studies, trying unsuccessfully to pay attention. She couldn't. Her thoughts kept returning to the boy in the hall.

She knew who he was, CJ McCallister, an eighth grader who transferred to South Miami at the end of last year. She first became aware of him the second week of school when she caught him staring at her in the cafeteria. She thought she had food on her face and made a quick exit from the lunchroom to inspect. Nothing. The next day at lunch she caught him looking again. The following day she decided to change tables and studied him intently as he frantically scanned the cafeteria. When he finally saw her, he quickly looked away, but it was obvious he had found the object of his search.

What was his problem? She knew she was a little too tall and sometimes clumsy and awkward, she was probably a little overweight, especially in the back, her neck was too long, her mouth too wide, her feet too big, her breasts too small, and her face too plain, with ordinary brown eyes and average brown hair, and on top of all that, her mother made most of her clothes. She knew there was nothing special about her, but was she so hideous, such a novelty circus freak show act, that people stared at her in stunned horror?

It wasn't until he bowled over poor Mr. Kaplan in the hallway that she realized his staring was not rooted in disgust. It was actually just the opposite. He had a crush on her! She smiled at the memory.

Three weeks ago she was walking from algebra to drama class when she sensed eyes upon her. She looked across the median to the second floor of the adjacent building and noticed CJ keeping pace with her. His facial expression wasn't one of curiosity at her ugliness or pity. The look on his face as he stared down at her was pure adoration. Worship. Love. He stared at her hopelessly with a goofy grin that made her blush. She became hyper-aware of every step she took and added a little more switch to her walk just for him. She could literally feel him holding her with his eyes, kissing her, loving her. She cocked her head to the side and aimed a sweet smile up in his direction just as he was colliding with her sixth-period science teacher. He never tore his gaze from her. Even as he was going down, she could see him craning his neck for one last look.

She shook her head and giggled. A friend of hers sat next to him in English and told her his name but smirked at her apparent interest in him. After all, he was short and skinny, with baggy clothes, a gap between his front teeth, and freckles on his nose. Andrea didn't care. She loved the way he looked at her. It made her feel pretty.

They had never spoken, but this morning when she saw those *gemelos estupidos* hurting him, she had to go back. She wanted so much to cradle his face in her hands, but in the end opted to touch his shoulder lightly. When he looked up and saw her, a smile formed on his face like the sun breaking free from the clouds; then just as quickly, the clouds came back and he leapt to his feet and took off. She chewed on her bottom lip as her teacher rambled on about population growth. She hoped he was okay.

~

Cheryl McCallister was crying again. She could still type seventy words a minute, even with tears streaming down her face, but she knew her running mascara must look pitiful as well as unprofessional to the various department heads and other employees that came looking for her boss throughout the day.

There were over five hundred employees at the Essex Hotel and all of them had seen her cry. From Housekeeping to Engineering to Food & Beverage, including all the waiters and cooks in its three restaurants, everyone in the Accounting Department, Security, the grounds crew, and Registration; hell, even the airport shuttle drivers and lowly bellhops had all seen Cheryl McCallister crying at one point or another.

She normally cried because her husband was not the man she married or because her son was growing up, but not being *raised* or because money was tight or because she was so far away from her momma and sisters in Alabama, but today she cried for a different reason altogether. The man who taught her the hotel business in Mobile and promoted her to his executive secretary when he was called upon to open the Essex in Miami, Mr. Mizell, was transferring to the

Capitol Essex in D.C. He was told he couldn't take any of the department heads with him, and that included Cheryl McCallister.

As if on cue, Mr. Mizell walked past her desk. He stopped and looked at her. "Jeff Steele and his wife are flying in tomorrow." Steele was CEO of the company that actually owned the hotel. It was only staffed and managed by Essex. "Reserve him a room at Beachside and make sure he is upgraded."

"Yes sir," she said, picking up the phone. Essex Beachside was over on Collins Avenue. It was the sister hotel of the Airport Essex, where she worked. She called and spoke to their front desk manager and reserved him a nicer room at a lower rate. It was an "upgrade" in hotel lingo. It was no big deal. If someone in a management position had called her, she would have done it without thinking. It fell under professional courtesy and was done all the time.

She hung up the phone and sat back in her chair, looking through the blinds out into the palatial lobby of the Essex. It was an indoor paradise, with marble columns, waterfalls, tropical birds, and a domed ceiling. She realized that her brow was furrowed and her face was scrunched. She took a deep breath and allowed her facial muscles to go completely slack. Then she realized her neck and shoulders were just as tense, so she rolled her head around a few times before mentally commanding her entire upper body to relax. She felt the tension melting away as her shoulders slumped.

The executive offices were quiet and serene. Only she was there. She almost hated to disturb the tranquility with her machine-gun typewriter, but she had to finish a memo. Her thoughts flicked to CJ. She hoped he made it home from school okay and that he got enough to eat, and that his father surrendered the television long enough for him to watch *Family Ties* and *The Cosby Show.* He would be asleep by the time she got home. Because she worked such long hours, she wasn't able to spend any time with him anymore. This morning he seemed taller or was that just her imagination? She was missing his life, but she had no choice. Someone had to pay the bills. *Maybe Chris lined up some job interviews today,* she thought. *Lord knows we need the money. Christmas is right around the corner and—* Her phone rang.

"Airport Essex and Marina, this is Cheryl speaking, how may I help you?" she said, conjuring her bubbliest tone.

"Is this the same Cheryl that instructed MY front desk manager to give someone a discount?" roared an angry, heavily accented voice. "I am resident manager of this hotel. Me, Jose Ramos, and I will not tolerate you or anyone else from that hotel demanding complimentary rooms from my employees. Do I make myself clear?"

"Sir," she stated calmly, "the room is for an Essex VIP at the request of the general manager and I didn't demand anything. I asked for an upgrade, but please forgive me if I—"

"DON'T YOU EVER, EVER call this hotel again unless you call to speak with me! Do you understand?" His volume rose and his speed increased so much that by the end of his sentence it sounded like one long, extremely loud word followed by a hollow silence. "DO YOU?"

She stood up behind her desk. "Look, Jose, I don't work for you and if the man I DO work for says to call the front desk again, then that is exactly what I'll do. Good-bye." She slammed the phone down. And started crying again.

~

The Southwinds apartment complex was originally designed and priced to attract upper-middle-class families, corporate bachelors, and University of Miami post-grad students. It was conveniently located close to the University, the mall, and the hospital, and it boasted two pools, two saunas, and a tennis court. The units were all two stories with private patios, trellises, and L-shaped balconies that could be reached from both bedrooms through sliding glass doors.

Management and ownership changed many times during the late '70s and early '80s. Paint started to peel, holes began appearing in the wooden privacy fence that surrounded the place, and the guard booth at the entrance was soon abandoned. Then graffiti started popping up on the walls, the saunas began to reek of urine, and the once beautiful pools were filled with murky water and home to thousands of frogs as well as sticks, discarded clothes, and floating trash. By 1988 you could rent an apartment at the Southwinds for a fourth of the rental price in the '70s, even though inflation and the cost of living had skyrocketed.

CJ ducked through a hole in the fence that separated the railroad tracks from his apartment complex. He stopped as a low-riding Cutlass made its way over the speed bump in front of him. He could hear MC A.D.E.'s "Hit Hard" vibrating through the trunk. He raised his chin slightly as it passed, but the windows were too tinted to know if he was acknowledged or not. He stepped off the curb and crossed the road, cut through the foul-smelling pool area, walked along the broken sidewalk that snaked between A and B buildings, and high-stepped through the overgrown grass that was once a courtyard before arriving at the back side of Building C.

He hoped his dad was stoned or still asleep. He didn't feel like talking. When he rounded the corner, he immediately saw the police car in the parking lot. No sirens. *PRATT!* CJ could hear him pounding on the front door.

"Police! Open up!"

Officer Pratt was a joke. He was nicknamed Tackleberry at South Miami based on the super-serious gun-loving idiot cop from the *Police Academy* movies. Until today CJ had managed to elude his radar, but apparently those days were over. CJ ducked behind an air-conditioning unit to listen as he pounded on the door again.

~

Mr. McCallister was having a serious meltdown in the living room. *The fucking cops are outside!* He had just finished twisting a doobie when the front door began to rattle and he caught a glimpse of the uniform. *SHIT!* He immediately began to panic. First he ran toward the kitchen, then slid to a stop, reversing his course and running full speed back into the living room before stopping on a dime and reversing course again. He finally sat down hard on the living room floor, holding his head in his hands as the banging continued.

"I see you moving in there. Open up!"

He was busted. Time to surrender. He slid the wooden tray holding his last bit of reefer back under the couch, hoping they'd miss it in their inevitable search, but he knew it was all over for him. "Father," he prayed while doing all the necessary rocking, shifting, and straining required of a man his size to remove himself from the floor, "if you help me out of this one, I will NEVER smoke pot again." He went to the door, slid the chain lock in place, and cracked it open.

"Do you have a warrant, sir?"

"My name is Steve Pratt. I'm the truant officer at South Miami Junior High School."

I'm going to KILL CJ for this, Chris McCallister thought.

"Mr. McCallister, minutes ago Mrs. Sinclair from the principal's office spoke with you, and you indicated that your son was sick. I was wondering if I could have a word with him?" said Pratt, watching him suspiciously through the crack in the door.

"Well, he, uh . . . actually he's . . . sleeping," said Chris. His initial relief that the man was only a school cop looking for CJ and not a REAL cop quickly morphed back into fear when he realized he was busted in a lie.

~

CJ stopped listening. He knew what he had to do. He stood on the AC unit and it roared to life just as he reached for the patio wall and pulled himself up. Good, he thought, he could use the noise as cover. He saw Pratt at the front door arrogantly rocking back and forth on his heels. Even though his back was to CJ, he could imagine the smug look on his face as his dad stammered behind the door.

He stepped on the rotting wooden trellis, hoping it wouldn't choose now to collapse, and reached for the balcony railing, swinging his 115 pounds over it quickly and landing lightly on his feet in front of the sliding glass door. He could have done this blindfolded. He had probably snuck in and out of their apartment a thousand times since they moved there. He quietly slid the door open and closed it behind him.

"I'm really going to have to insist on seeing him," Pratt was saying through the chained door as CJ reached the middle landing of their stairwell. His hair was mussed. His eyes were hooded and a little red, and all he had on were his underwear and a blanket wrapped around him.

"I just don't think he . . . uh . . . I mean he was up all night vomiting and . . ." His father was a visible wreck. CJ could see his legs shaking as he reached the bottom step.

"Dad," CJ said from behind him in a sick little boy voice. "Who's here?"

Chris McCallister whirled around and beheld his son in amazement. "Hallelujah!" he cried before recovering nicely. "I mean, you're up and walking. What a blessing." He unchained the door and presented him to Officer Pratt, who looked at CJ with open hostility. He knew he had been played, but he couldn't prove it.

"Paul McCallister?" CJ nodded his head and stared at him. His mouth said, "I hope you are feeling better," but his eyes said, *This means war.* He turned around and headed off to his car. CJ watched him disappear from view before shutting the door and locking it.

"Thank you," his father said, reaching under the couch for his stash, "and fuck you," he added with a smile.

Chapter 2

Rudy lay awake in his bed and tried his best to ignore the sounds coming through the bedroom wall; the raucous laughter, the grunting and moaning, the furious pounding of headboard against drywall. Thirty minutes ago he heard the clicking of stilettos on the pavement accompanied by an unfamiliar Hispanic voice attempting to sing "Pedro Nevaja," followed by the jangling of keys, the slamming of the front door, the opening and shutting of the refrigerator, the sound of bottles and glasses clinking, heavy footsteps on the staircase, and now, the climactic end of his mother's evening ritual.

His mother was a *puta.* Of course, if anyone else said that he'd break their fucking jaw, but he knew it was true. The mornings were the worst part. Waiting in the hallway to wash his face and brush his teeth before school while some stranger took a shit in HIS bathroom. His father had taught him to always look a man in the eye, but it was tough to do that when the man in question was walking down the hallway of your own apartment after fucking your mom and shitting in your toilet. Things were a lot different when his father was around, but that was a long time ago.

Rudy rolled over and looked at his alarm clock. It was almost one in the morning. The loud knocking against his bedroom wall was driving him crazy. He had to get out of there. He threw on his shorts and a t-shirt and bolted barefooted down the stairs and out the front door. He heard his mother cry out from behind the swaying curtains of her bedroom window as he walked down the winding sidewalk. He hoped the neighbors didn't hear her.

He continued walking until he came to the courtyard in the middle of his apartment complex. The only sounds he could hear now were coming from the cars passing on the Palmetto and crickets harmonizing in the overgrown grass. For a moment, he considered marching back to the apartment, kicking his mother's bedroom door open, snatching whoever was in there off of her, throwing him down the stairs and out into the parking lot. He could do it too. Although he was only fifteen years old, he was, physically, already a man at five-feet-ten-inches tall and 190 pounds. He still saw the same old Rudy when he looked in the mirror, but he could tell he was growing by the way men, and women for that matter, had been looking at him lately . . . or looking away in some cases. He picked up a few small pebbles from under a picnic table and headed in the direction of Building C.

~

CJ sat in the dark on his bedroom floor, using the light coming under his door from the hallway to read over what he had written so far.

Dear Andrea,

Hi. You probably don't know who I am, but my name is CJ.

He was stuck right there. How do you tell a girl you think she's pretty without sounding like a chump? He thought about it for a few minutes, then wrote:

I think you're really pretty.

That was easy, he thought, and then added:

I hope you don't have a boyfriend, but even if you do, I'd still like to be friends with you.

And now the clincher:

Maybe we could get something to eat after school one day, if you're down . . .

He finished with:

Write me back.

♡ CJ

He sat back and admired his work. *It was perfect.* Now he just had to grow some balls and hand it to her. This was probably the tenth love letter he had written to her. All the others had been flushed by fourth period the next day. *Not this time,* he thought. *I'm gonna walk right up to her and hand her this one.*

He thought back to a couple of months ago when the Barocela twins had caught him in the hall. She touched him that day. She even smiled at him. He should have spoken to her then, but he was so ashamed of being manhandled like that in front of her that he took off. He wished that day would have never happened. Now Pratt was on his ass, he imagined other kids whispering and snickering behind his back in class, and worst of all, his dealing with the whole situation in such a cowardly manner was killing his self-esteem. But what other choice did he have? The twins were a combined six hundred pounds, with fists the size of softballs and they both knew how to use them. CJ had been in two fights in his life and both were one-sided losses. He just sucked at fighting. And it wasn't even the pain involved with having a black eye, a bloody nose, or a fat lip that he feared. It was the humiliation that comes with being overpowered and stomped on in front of your peers, seeing their cheering faces blur as you go down, then watching the circle disperse, sometimes even stepping over you, but always talking excitedly about the ass-whipping they just witnessed.

CJ had no appetite to relive those types of experiences, so he was basically relegated to checking hallways and bathrooms before he entered them, sticking close to faculty members, and occasionally busting a quick U-turn or even ducking into an empty classroom to hide. He knew it was a spineless way to live, but it beat the alternative. Suddenly his thoughts were broken up by a sharp *TAP!* against his window. *TAP! TAP!* He looked back over his shoulder as two more pebbles made contact. *Rudy!*

Below, Rudy was standing on the sidewalk, looking up at his bedroom window. CJ held up a finger, then ran to his bed to grab his cigarettes and lighter before returning to the window. He opened it and walked out on the balcony, closing it softly behind him. Then, in a sudden burst of energy, he swung himself over the rail, landing lightly on the trellis, which he danced across quickly before leaping in the air, and touching down nimbly on the patio wall. He then leapt into the grass below, capping his performance with a series of chops and kicks before bringing his hands together in a praying position and bowing before his best friend.

"You're gonna break your neck one day," said Rudy, smiling at him.

CJ shook two cigarettes from his pack and passed one to Rudy. They had been friends since CJ moved to Miami in the summer of the third grade. They built forts together, watched movies together, and even formed a breakdancing crew called the RC Express—the RC standing for Rudy and CJ. They both went to Radford Elementary for the fourth, fifth, and sixth grades before CJ got in trouble and had to go away for a while and Rudy started private school. They knew things about each other that only best friends would know, like how CJ hated onions and thought they resembled toenails in his food, or how Rudy had a major crush on Blair from *The Facts of Life* and, of course, they also knew the deeper, darker secrets like the fact that Mr. McCallister was a lazy pothead with psychological issues and that Rudy's dad was one of the infamous River Cops currently serving thirty years in federal prison for using his uniform and department-issued pistol to jack drug traffickers along the Miami River in the early '80s.

The only secret CJ kept from Rudy was that he thought his mom was hot, and that was only because CJ knew how sensitive Rudy was about his mother. The fact that they now attended different schools made it harder to see each other as often, but that made little difference to them. They were as close as two boys could be.

They walked and smoked in silence until they came to the pool area. There they saw two men sitting under a ragged, weather-beaten umbrella, drinking beer and passing something between them that required the constant use of a lighter. *Why wouldn't it stay lit?* CJ wondered as he and Rudy emerged from the shadows. The men suddenly looked up, reminding CJ of the way wild animals act on *National Geographic* when they sense that humans are nearby. They watched CJ and Rudy from across the filthy pool. CJ noticed how gaunt their faces were and the way the skin seemed to hang from the sharp bones. They were both doing something odd with their jaws, which slid back and forth across the bottoms of their faces as if they were chewing on something, but the strangest thing about them was their eyes. They were as round as saucers, and even though they glowed brightly, they still managed to convey a sense of hopelessness and emptiness that caused CJ to stop short and look uncertainly at Rudy. He had no idea what the men were doing, but he instinctively understood that he was in the presence of evil, and he was glad he had his friend along.

"Hey kid," one rasped, "lemme see your lighter." CJ walked over to where they were sitting and held out his Bic. The man nearest him snatched it greedily from his hand and flicked it, checking the height of the flame, and quickly adjusted it to his preferred setting. He then reached between his legs and produced a dirty glass tube about the length of a pen and stuck it squarely between his lips. When he ignited the lighter again, it illuminated his face the way CJ's dad used to do with a flashlight against his chin at Halloween. CJ watched as white smoke began to swirl around the inside of the pipe, first in wisps, then gathering quickly until a torrent of clouds filled the cylinder. He became aware of a sizzling, popping sound just as the smoke disappeared from the glass and into the man's lungs. He sat back in his chair blissfully and blew a humongous mushroom cloud of smoke into the air, absently extending the pipe to CJ, who held out his palm to receive it in a trancelike state.

Rudy had seen enough. He reached out and slapped CJ's hand hard, sending the hot pipe spiraling toward the concrete, where it exploded on impact.

"What the fuck is your problem?" the other crackhead hissed, rising to his feet. Rudy met him in two quick steps, grabbing him by the throat and slinging him over the lounge chair he was just sitting in. He looked over at the other one, who was still somewhere in the stratosphere, and held his hand out. "Lighter," he quietly demanded. The man held it out in a bony, quivering hand. "Crackheads," Rudy said scornfully, pushing CJ into the shadows and away from the foul-smelling pool.

Once they were a safe distance away, Rudy stopped walking and looked searchingly at CJ. "Man, you were actually gonna try that shit, weren't you?"

"Sure, why not?" CJ answered, fishing out his last cigarette and balling up the empty package. "Gimme a light."

"Why not?" Rudy asked incredulously. "For real? CJ, that was crack they were smoking back there! Did you get a good look at those guys? Their skin? Their teeth? Their eyes? That shit is poison, man!"

"Okay, I got it. Now can I have my lighter, please?"

Rudy stared at him for a few long seconds, adrenaline still pumping through his body from the confrontation by the pool. He shakily produced the lighter and struck it, cupping the flame in his hand. CJ learned forward and lit his cigarette. They started walking again.

"Drugs are drugs," said CJ. "We smoke green all the time, and what about all that acid we were dropping last summer when those college kids moved in next door to you? Remember? Shit, we even bought that coke at the Metrorail station that time, or at least we thought it was coke," CJ said with a smile. "I bet they laughed at our dumb asses all the way back to the hood."

"Crack's different," Rudy said, coming to a stop in front of CJ's apartment. He lowered his voice and spoke through clenched teeth. "I want your word that you will never fuck with it." He looked at CJ intensely, as if he could burn his point home through sheer force of will.

CJ finally looked away. "I give you my word," he said, taking a last drag from his cigarette before passing the short to his friend.

"As a brother?" Rudy asked.

"As a brother."

"Bueno," Rudy said, a smile spreading across his face. "Now go get your beauty sleep. Andrea is waiting."

They bumped fists and CJ was up the wall, across the trellis, and over the balcony in seconds.

Damn! he thought, spinning quickly, *my lighter,* but Rudy was already gone.

~

Chris McCallister was miserable. He hated it when Cheryl got in one of her moods.

". . . and what are you doing all day while I'm working my fingers to the bone? Nothing! That's what."

He didn't even try to put up a defense. It was futile anyway. He just sat there, head down, shoulders slumped, and wore it.

"I can't take it anymore, Chris. I'm sorry. I just can't. Pat says I'm codependent and that I'm enabling you."

Shit, he thought, *not Pat again.* He hated Pat. He didn't actually *know* Pat, didn't even know if Pat was male or female since Pat was one of those *ambidextrous* names that could go either way like . . . well, like Chris. What he DID know was that Pat's name always seemed to pop up when his wife started talking about things like rehab, separation, and him having to work. *Why the hell is Pat always meddling in my marriage?*

". . . so tomorrow, you're going to drop me and CJ off at work and school and then you're going to drive all over Miami until you find a job, and at eight o'clock when you pick me up from the hotel, you're going to tell me all about your new place of employment. Otherwise, and believe me when I say this, you can have the apartment because CJ and I will be moving out. Do you understand?"

He looked at her. She was still wearing the outfit she wore to work that day, even though it was after one in the morning. He remembered when she bought that dress. It was the one she got from Penney's just before they left Alabama. He remembered her modeling it proudly for him and little CJ in their living room. *Wow,* he thought, suddenly stone-cold sober. *She's really gonna leave.*

"Do you understand, Christopher?" she asked, her tears doing nothing to soften the steel in her voice.

He nodded slowly.

~

CJ was stunned when he reached the bottom of the staircase and saw his father sitting at the table in a suit, sipping coffee, with the classified ads open in front of him.

"Hey, buddy," his dad said with a smile. "Ready?" He wore a navy blue polyester suit with a white shirt and a fat red tie with diagonal blue stripes winding their way around it. He had finally shaved that scruffy-looking, nicotine-stained beard and mustache. CJ smiled. He knew the only reason his father had grown the beard in the first place was to disguise the extra chin which now dangled nakedly from his round, hairless face. The entire downstairs reeked of his favorite aftershave, Aqua Velva.

"Mmmm." His mom beamed, coming down the stairs. "I'd hire you on the spot just for smelling like that."

CJ's dad winked at him and stood, stuffing the classifieds in his enormous jacket pocket as he moved toward the door. "Let's go."

CJ climbed in the backseat of the Corolla and his mom sat in the passenger seat. His father reached below the driver's seat and yanked the lever upward while pushing hard against the seat itself, forcing it as far back as possible. He sat down and slammed the door, already sweating profusely. He stuck the key in the ignition—tick tick tick tick tick. "Son of a bitch," he muttered. Cheryl looked away. He tried again—tick tick tick tick tick. "Come on, you asshole."

Cheryl patted the armrest reassuringly. "It's okay, girl," she said to the car in what was barely a whisper. He tried again, pushing the key hard—tick tick tick tick tick.

"YOU SORRY ASS PIECE OF SHIT!" he erupted, slamming his fist into the steering wheel violently.

"Honey!" his mom exclaimed in a shocked tone. She was now openly consoling the car, rubbing the sun-cracked dash and talking to it like a small child. "Give her a little gas and try again." He did as she instructed and the car finally roared to life in its usual spastic, smoke-shooting way. "Good girl," Cheryl said, patting the dash again as they pulled out of the parking lot.

~

Mr. McCallister did not understand why CJ wanted to be dropped off down the street and was adamant about giving him front door service. CJ argued vehemently from the backseat, but his words were drowned out by The Supremes' "Baby Love," which blared from the oldies station his father insisted on setting the radio to whenever he drove. In the end, his mom saved the day by touching her husband on the knee and simply saying, "Stop." She opened her door and CJ stumbled from the backseat feeling the way people must feel after a near-death experience. If his father had pulled to the front of the school blasting "Baby Love" in that rusty piece of shit, the fallout for CJ would have been catastrophic, especially if Andrea had been in the area. He patted his pocket as he turned toward the school, feeling the edges of the note through the material of his jeans.

"Hey," his mom said through the window of the running car, "no kiss?" He smiled and turned back to the car, giving his mom a peck on the cheek.

"See ya, champ," his father said before turning the car around and heading off in the other direction.

CJ walked quickly up the street, cutting between cars and buses until he reached the sidewalk. He scanned the swarm of humanity making their way to the entrance. He was looking for Andrea but didn't see her. Who he DID see was Officer Pratt leaning against the flagpole, arms folded, sneering at him with a match in his mouth like Stallone in *Cobra.* CJ didn't know what to do, having already made eye contact, so he forced an uncomfortable wave at the officer, acknowledging his presence, but it was only stared at disdainfully in return. He dropped his hand and hurried past him, imagining lasers on the back of his neck. He was glad when he finally made it through the entrance, just to be out of Pratt's line of vision, but now a new danger lurked: the

Barocela twins. He didn't see them but he knew they were somewhere in the hallways of the school, like two fat-ass hyenas waiting on a stray injured cub to pounce upon. He would never let that happen again. He moved stealthily through the hall, alert, aware, and ready.

He took the stairs two at a time and stepped tentatively into the upstairs hallway. This was always dangerous territory. They had caught him up here the last time, but it was also the route he knew Andrea took to her first-period class. He surveyed the corridor and saw neither Andrea nor the twins, so he began his trek to first-period Spanish, where Señora Salazar awaited him.

The crowd parted and there she was, moving regally through a sea of adoring onlookers, oblivious to the attention she was getting, oblivious even to her own perfection. She hugged a three-ring binder and book to her chest and smiled prettily at everyone with whom she made eye contact. CJ stared. When her eyes met his, she quickly looked away. His feet were cinder blocks. He stood there nailed to the ground, frozen in ice, watching helplessly as she passed. Then, he remembered the note.

"Hey," he said to her back, the word dying immediately in the hundreds of other voices that filled the hall. She continued walking away.

He took a deep breath and pushed his vocal cords harder. "HEY," he shouted. Everyone stopped. *Whoops,* he thought, *too loud.* She was looking back at him questioningly. He was committed now. The five steps it took to reach her felt like five thousand as every eye in that hallway watched him curiously. When he came to where she was standing, he said, "May I talk with you?" She fell in step beside him and the hallway came back to life.

"I'm CJ," he began.

"Andrea," she replied. "Nice to meet you."

It was so good to be near her, he momentarily forgot all about the note. They walked together in silence, one occasionally grinning at the other.

"Well," she said, stopping in front of a door. "This is my class."

Watching her lips make words up close was a new experience for CJ and he was temporarily dumbstruck yet again, but he broke the spell by digging in his pocket and presenting her with the note. "Somebody told me to give this to you."

She reached out and plucked it from his hand, brushing his fingers as she did. "Somebody?" she said, looking into his eyes.

He was now officially lost. He nodded dumbly.

"Oh," she said, disappointed. "I was hoping it was from you." She closed the classroom door behind her, and he stared at it for a moment, digesting her words. Then a smile spread across his face and he leapt into the air, raising a clenched fist before hitting the ground in a flurry of breakdancing moves. The few students remaining in the hall stopped to watch. He came to an abrupt halt when a thought came screaming into his mind like a flashing red warning: *THE TWINS!* He jumped to his feet and looked left and right before spotting them at the end of the hallway. He turned in the other direction and bolted for the safety of Señora Salazar's Spanish class, closing the door behind him just as the bell rang.

"Buenos dias," he said.

~

Chris McCallister was running out of daylight. He'd been to two banks, a department store, and a photography company so far and was politely turned down by each. He knew the problem wasn't in his credentials, references, or ability. He was a former bank president with a lengthy résumé full of former employers and coworkers who would vouch for his professionalism. He had read books by people like Hill, Peale, and Carnegie, and even took courses on their management techniques. He was intelligent, articulate, and highly motivated once he got into whatever the job required. None of that was the problem, he thought as he fired up a Camel and pulled out onto U.S. 1. The problem was that he was a fat, baldheaded guy who only spoke English in a city where English was the second language.

He looked at his watch. It was 2:30. *Damn,* he thought, *not much time left.* He remembered the long drive this morning to the hotel where his wife worked. They had turned the radio down and talked about everything. It was just like the old days, laughing together and holding hands. She even laid her head on his shoulder at one point, but when he pulled into her hotel, things turned serious.

"Chris," she said, looking into his eyes, "I meant what I said last night. I love you with all my heart and I always will, but I can't do this anymore. I've waited on you for weeks and months and years. No more excuses. If you don't get a job today, CJ and I are moving out." She closed the car door without saying good-bye and disappeared through the electronic sliding glass doors without looking back. She was serious this time. He knew it.

~

CJ got back to the apartment just before four o'clock. His father was still gone. He reached under the flower pot and found the spare key. When he opened the door, he dropped his backpack on the floor and headed straight for the kitchen. His mom always made sure he had plenty of Little Debbie Brownies and Fudge Rounds for after school, but she had to be creative in her hiding places because once his father smoked a joint, he would disassemble the entire kitchen in search of munchies. CJ reached far back in a cabinet full of Tupperware and moved his hand around until he heard the crackling of wrappers and came away with two brownies. He poured a tall glass of milk and went into the living room.

When the phone rang, he thought it was probably his mom making sure he made it home from school. He hopped off the couch and ran to the kitchen to answer it, sliding full speed across the linoleum floor in his socks.

"Hello."

"May I speak to CJ please?" asked a youngish, lightly accented female voice.

CJ frowned. *Who in the world?* "This is CJ. Who's this?"

"It's Andrea."

CJ was suddenly aware of his heart thumping against his chest. "Wow," he said, trying to sound casual. "How did you get my number?"

"It wasn't that hard. There's not many McCallisters in the phone book so I just dialed the one closest to the school and found you on the first try."

CJ was flattered. He had never had a girl show this much interest in him, and never in his wildest dreams did he imagine the prettiest girl in school would be calling him.

"Anyway," she was saying, "I just wanted you to know that . . . that I thought your note was really sweet, and I would love to hang out with you after school one day, but it will have to be on a Friday because my mother works late on Fridays. She's kinda funny about me talking to boys." She laughed nervously.

"Okay," CJ said, desperately searching for something cool to say. There was a long, pregnant silence.

"Well," she finally said, "I guess I'll see you at school then."

"Definitely," CJ managed to say. *C'mon, dumbass!* he thought, *say something!*

"Bye, CJ."

"Bye," he echoed, but she had already hung up.

CJ slowly set down the receiver. He was thrilled. Andrea Marcos had just called him! He needed a cigarette. He grabbed a pack of his father's Camel non-filters from the freezer and tore off the cellophane with his teeth. He turned the stove burner on high and waited for the rings to heat up. He wished he could have thought of something funny or witty to say at the end of the call but, as usual, he froze up. Then an idea came to him. He remembered a trick Rudy had shown him when he was getting prank calls last summer. It was a new service offered by the phone company. In addition to features like call waiting and three-way calling, you could always find out the last number that called your residence by simply dialing *69. He picked up the phone and tried it. "The number is," the automated female-sounding voice began, "area code 3-0-5 5-5-5 2-7-5-8."

CJ smiled. *Got her,* he thought and quickly dialed her number.

"Hello."

"Andrea?"

"CJ? How did you get MY number?"

"Magic. Listen, you never told me whether you had a boyfriend or not."

"No!" she whispered. He could hear someone calling her name in the background. "CJ, you can't call here. My mom doesn't let me talk to boys." She sounded scared.

"Well, it's a good thing that I'm a man, then. Friday?"

"Yes," she said, laughing, "Bye!" and hung up.

Now that, CJ thought with a smile, *is more like it.* He walked over to the now red-hot stove burner and lit his cigarette, then strutted back into the living room.

~

It was after four in the afternoon and Chris McCallister was panicking. Most businesses were going to be closing for the day in less than an hour and were no longer seeing applicants. He had circled eight potential jobs that morning, driven to each, and been sent away by every one. He was running out of cigarettes, running out of gas, and running out of time.

He pulled into a Zayre parking lot in the Grove and spread the classifieds over the steering wheel, his eyes darting from column to column: nursing homes, pet stores, art supply stores. He found the nearest address and threw the Toyota in gear, tires screeching as he flew out of the parking lot.

Damn her, he thought. *How the hell am I s'posed to get a job in one day? She is setting me up for failure. She probably wants to haul ass, probably has a boyfriend at that damn hotel. Fuckin' suits,* he scowled as he shifted into second, *tryin' to take my wife.* He saw a sign that said Pet Heaven and yanked the wheel hard, skidding into the parking lot, almost running over a lady with a birdcage.

Great, he thought, jumping out of the car and straightening his tie as he raced toward the entrance. The door jangled violently as he pushed it open way too hard, startling the inhabitants. His eyes bulged from his face and he was sweating heavily.

"Hi," he said in his most professional-sounding voice. "I'm here about the position. May I speak to the manager please?"

The bored-looking teenager behind the desk quit smacking her gum, smiled sweetly and said, "Ah, that would be the lady you just almost killed in the parking lot."

~

Cheryl McCallister was having trouble concentrating. She tried her best to focus on the mounting pile of paperwork on her desk, but her thoughts kept returning to her husband. Was she being too hard? Was the "one day" deadline pushing it? But it wasn't really "one day," she thought. It had been years. Sure, he had made a few token attempts and even held down that office supply sales job for a few weeks, but the majority of his time in Miami so far had been spent on the couch smoking pot. She hated marijuana. Hated the smell of it in her home. Hated the way it made him giggle over the stupidest things and seriously hated that blank, red-eyed facial expression he got when he was smoking it. She was so grateful that he had quit. Or had he? She wasn't really sure, but she hoped so.

He wasn't always like this. The man she married sixteen years ago was funny, romantic, and believed in hard work. She thought back to when she met him. She was training to be a teller at the First Alabama National Bank in Mobile, and he was the vice president. He made his interest in her known immediately. She didn't know what to think. She was a country girl from a big family in rural Alabama. He was a 325-pound banking executive who smoked cigarettes and told dirty jokes. He was also very sweet to her and the first man to ever show so much interest. She could have done way better. She was young and pretty and just stepping out into the world, but she fell for Chris McCallister. Hard.

They were married at the county courthouse in 1972. She wore a miniskirt and he wore a leisure suit. Things were great in the beginning and got even better in '74 when he was promoted to president of the bank and she gave birth to CJ. She took her baby's entire first year off work and got a better paying job at the Mobile Essex in '75.

She didn't pay much attention to money in those days. Chris was responsible for the finances and she never doubted or second-guessed his money management skills. He was a bank president. If there was one thing in this world he knew, it was money. They rarely ate at home back then. He preferred to frequent the lavish steak houses and fine dining establishments on the Alabama and Florida Gulf Coast. Everything was paid for with plastic. No problem.

Then in 1981, he went crazy. She knew he was dabbling with pot at the time, but to this day, she wasn't sure if he got hold of something more dangerous or if it was a true psychotic episode that changed their lives forever. She had just begun her new job at the Essex when she came home to find their living room full of recording equipment: high-tech tape recorders, reel-to-reels, microphones.

"What's all this?" she asked.

"They're watching me," he replied, busy unraveling a cord.

"Who?"

"You know," he said, smiling up at her, the light of insanity in his eyes.

The episode lasted less than a month, and he slowly came out of it, but he had quit his job and the bills were mounting. That was when he began lying on the couch all day and smoking pot and watching TV. She and little CJ stopped having friends over, and he quickly became the family secret. She worked her ass off to keep them afloat, sometimes working two and even three jobs during Christmas, but by 1982 she had no other option but to file bankruptcy. It was the most humiliating experience of her life, but she was stubborn and a fighter and refused to admit that her marriage was a failure. When she was offered the promotion to the Miami Essex, she really believed that a new start in a new city was all he needed. Six years had passed since they moved to Miami and nothing had changed.

She stiffened her resolve and willed the doubt out of her heart. *No,* she thought, *NO! This is what is best. For me, for CJ, and for him.* She had already spoken to Mr. Mizell about using a hotel room for a couple of weeks until she and CJ could find a new place. She knew he wasn't going to get a job. He probably wasn't even looking. She began to cry.

~

Yolanda Spencer was the night manager of the Wendy's on 67th Avenue. Business was slow which was a good thing because Eddie had just called in. She would have to run the fries. It was all good. She was used to it.

She was staring out at the empty parking lot when an ugly little red hooptie pulled in. She watched as a fat white man exited the vehicle. *Uh-oh,* she thought, *time to get to work.*

As soon as he approached the counter, she noticed how distressed he was. She smiled at him.

"Welcome to Wendy's," she said. "May I take your order please?"

He shook his head. "No, ma'am, I need to speak with the manager," he said, looking behind her.

"That would be me," she said. "What can I do for you?"

He broke down on the counter, sobbing heavily. She looked back over her shoulder for help, but no one was there. She couldn't quite make out what he was saying; something about a pet store, the president, and his wife. She watched him helplessly.

"Hold on," she said, coming around the side and patting his ample back. "Let's go sit down."

Her touch seemed to make him weep even harder, but finally he settled down and told her his story.

"So you see," he said at the end, "if I don't have a job when I go pick her up, she's gonna take my son and leave me."

"Well, you're kinda overqualified, don't you think?"

"I don't care, I don't care. I just need a job. I'll do anything."

She stared at him for a while. *What the hell,* she thought. *At least I'll be saving a marriage.* "Okay," she said, finally. "You've got it."

"I've got the job? Really?"

"Yes. Be here at three tomorrow afternoon."

He shook her hand and wiggled out of the booth. "Oh! Thank you so much," he looked at her name tag, "Yolanda."

She nodded and smiled.

He was almost to the door when he turned back. "Hey, is there any way I can get a small advance on my first check?"

She raised an eyebrow. "You serious?"

"Yeah, I'm starving. I need a cheeseburger!"

She smiled and went back behind the counter.

~

He waited in the car, sandwiched between a limo and a shuttle van at the hotel entrance. Some little fellow in a maroon uniform and hat kept telling him he had to move, but he ignored him. His wife worked for the general manager. He'd move whenever she got there and not before. He sat there listening to talk radio while periodically checking the rearview mirror for Cheryl. When she finally arrived and got in the car, the man in the uniform glared at him. He resisted the urge to give him the finger on the way out. He knew his wife would not be pleased if he did.

They rode in silence. The lights of roadside restaurants, gas stations, pawn shops, and liquor stores flashed across their faces as they made their way down the highway.

"Well?" she asked, finally.

"I got one."

"Where?" she asked, turning toward him in her seat.

"Wendy's," he said, glancing at her.

She smiled all the way home.

Chapter 3

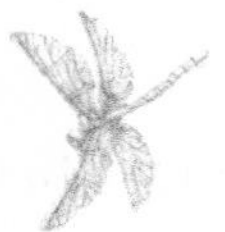

It was a week of firsts for Chris McCallister. The first time he ever rode a city bus, the first time he took orders from a teenager, and the first time he ever worked at a fast-food joint. It was humbling for him, but he made the best of it, and in a way, it was fun. He'd been in that dark living room so long, confined to the couch, wasted, with the majority of his conversation coming from the flickering images on the television set. *No way to live,* he thought while lowering another batch of fries into the sizzling grease.

He wore black polyester pants and a white short-sleeved button-down shirt. He was still waiting on his real uniform, which had to be custom ordered because of the size. His bald head was encompassed by a visor that said "Wendy's" and it sported a huge round pin that read "Where's the beef?" on the bill. He knew he looked like an idiot, and his blistered feet hurt like hell, but at least his family was still together, and he was earning money.

He couldn't wait until that first check! It was going to be so nice not to have to beg his wife for a twenty so he could buy a sack. He was sick of lying and groveling, manipulating grocery lists so that he could cuff a few dollars for some smoke. *Those days are over,* he thought as he raised the deep fryer and shook it. Of course, he couldn't let her know he was still smoking, but it would be much easier to hide once he was buying it with his own money. Now, he just needed a new connection. His old one, Zach, had disappeared last month. On Monday he saw a "For Rent" sign in front of his apartment. He was thinking about asking one of his co-workers where he could score some, but he was still too new to try that. It wouldn't be long though. He was already winning them over. They loved the way he danced around the restaurant and sang Elvis at closing time. He was way older than everyone who worked there, and it cracked them up to see the fat, bald, middle-aged new guy dancing around with a mop. Even his boss, Yolanda, clapped along with his performances.

To say he actually enjoyed being on his feet all day behind a thousand-degree deep fryer surrounded by acne-faced teenagers would be an obvious lie but, he had to admit, it was gratifying to join the human race again after so many years of exile. He felt pretty damn good. Now he just needed a joint.

~

Cheryl McCallister sat at her typewriter putting the finishing touches on a letter that needed to be sent to the New York Essex that day. Things were finally looking up in her world. Her husband was working, her son was doing well, and she was choosing to view her boss's transfer as an opportunity for growth rather than a situation to lament. Mr. Mizell would be leaving for Washington in two weeks and though no one knew the name of his replacement, she was optimistic that the universe had something special in store for her.

She was lost in thought when her office door swung open and Brett Wagner swept in along with his ever-present entourage. He lowered his chin and wiggled his fingers at her.

"Cherie," he said breathlessly, "you look fantabulous as usual." He spoke in a feminine Deep South drawl. She always thought that his voice better suited the wife of some plantation owner in 1800s Georgia, rather than his six-foot-two-inch frame.

"Hi, Brett," she said, smiling, then added, "Jaquez, Li, Pedro," nodding in turn at each.

Brett Wagner was the interior decorator of the Essex. He was originally from Charleston, South Carolina, where his father served on the police force and his mother did hair. He began his career after dropping out of community college in 1975 and begging his mom and dad for a small loan. He never looked back. His rise to the top of the decorating world was both meteoric and legendary. By 1982 he could basically write his own ticket. He had become the most sought after interior decorator in the country. Brett Wagner called everyone "darling," spoke with sweeping, flamboyant hand gestures, and was never seen without Pedro, his Chihuahua, cradled in his arm. Jaquez and Li were his assistants. Jaquez was a bald, jet-black Haitian with a pencil-thin mustache and a beret, who never stopped smiling. Li was a tiny Vietnamese girl who chain-smoked and wore fishnet.

Brett surveyed her office. He was always at work, constantly measuring, imagining, enhancing. He wrinkled his nose at a painting her boss had hung on the wall and scanned the titles of the books behind her desk while Jaquez and Li spread out and inspected the crown molding and furniture respectively.

"Darling," he said, sitting on the corner of her desk, "how are you?"

"Things are good, Brett," she smiled, "really good."

"CJ?" he inquired while picking the lint from his pants.

"Doing well. He has a love interest. A Spanish girl named Andrea. He never misses school anymore."

"And Chris?" he said disdainfully.

"He's doing fine."

"I know you're going to miss Mizell," he said, referring to her boss by last name, as always.

"Of course," she said softly.

"Oh darling," he said, reaching for her hand, "don't worry. You are simply going to *l-o-v-e* working for Jose Ramos."

The blood drained from her face. "WHO?" she stammered, feeling sick.

~

CJ waited in the breezeway with his back and foot against the wall. He had already observed the twins getting on their bus, so that was one problem he didn't have to deal with. Now he just hoped Andrea showed up. *Of course she'll be here,* he told himself. *Why wouldn't she?* He had been saving the lunch money his mom had been giving him since Tuesday and now had a bankroll of twelve dollars in his pocket. There was a pizza place that sold slices a few blocks in one direction and there were a few fast-food spots down the road the other way. He really didn't care where they went. He was just excited about being close to her. Alone. He wondered if she would let him kiss her . . . or more. He had put on a little extra Drakar that morning just in case.

Suddenly her laugh filled the hallway, transforming it from cold concrete into a vibrant echo chamber. She was walking with a friend, but they stopped when they saw CJ. They exchanged a couple of sentences in Spanish and giggled again before her friend waved to him and walked out into the sunshine, leaving CJ and Andrea in the quiet hallway. She looked at him expectantly, hugging her books to her chest and resting her chin on top of them. He pushed himself off the wall and approached her.

"Que vola?" he asked, using a slang term for "what's up" that Rudy had taught him.

"Hablas Español?" she asked him, surprised.

"Estoy apreniendo. I'm learning. Are you ready?"

She nodded and they left the hallway for the sidewalk.

"Hand me your books," he said, stopping to unzip his backpack and sliding them inside before slinging it over his shoulder and continuing. He forced himself to talk.

"Andrea, Andrea, Andrea," he heard himself saying, "what's it like being the finest girl at South Miami?" He looked at her pretty face and waited for a response.

She rolled her eyes. "I'm definitely not the finest girl at South Miami," she paused and glanced over at him, "but thank you."

She was serious, he thought. *She has no idea how perfect she is.* When they came to the end of the street, he asked her where she wanted to eat.

"I'm not really hungry, but I live this way," she said, tilting her head in the direction of the fast-food places a few blocks down. "I've got about two hours before my mom gets home."

"Your mom is a little strict, huh?" he asked, smiling.

"Ooh, you have no idea! Have you ever had a Cuban girlfriend?" she asked innocently.

CJ shook his head. He'd never had any girlfriend, but there was no need to tell her that.

"Well, Cuban mothers are the most overprotective women on the planet. I love my mother to death, but she can be so stubborn and impossible. This one time when I was in . . ."

CJ relaxed, watching her talk animatedly about her mom. He couldn't believe he was actually alone with her. He had dreamed about this day since he first started South Miami. She was even prettier up close. He loved the way she repeatedly licked her lips when she spoke, the way her hair cascaded over her tan, delicate shoulders, the way her pretty brown eyes looked when she blinked, the way her . . .

". . . don't you think?" she was asking. "CJ! You're not listening!" She attempted to give him a quick slap on the arm, but he caught her hand and didn't let it go.

"Sorry," he said, "you make it hard to concentrate."

She smiled and laced her fingers through his, swinging their hands lightly back and forth while they walked. The signs of the gas stations and restaurants up ahead began to peek out of the trees and over the rooftops as they made their way to the intersection.

"So what do you want to eat?" he asked again.

"Let's go to Wendy's. I love Frostys."

He couldn't believe he was holding Andrea Marcos's hand and she was holding his! He could get hit by a car today and die a happy man. He was so lost in love that it wasn't until he was holding the door open for her that a thought hit him like a sucker punch: *WENDY'S! DAD! OH SHIT!*

He hadn't seen his father in a while, hadn't even thought about him really. One morning he had asked his mom why he wasn't camped out on the couch like usual and she smiled with obvious pride, explaining to him that he had gotten a job. At Wendy's. He thought she said it was the one near the school but he couldn't remember. He was only half paying attention at the time. He hoped not. Prayed not. If so, maybe it was his day off, or maybe he was on break, or called in, or . . .

"CJ!" he heard his dad exclaim as they approached the counter. He smiled nervously and glanced at Andrea.

"I think that man back there is trying to get your attention," she said, motioning to where his father stood smiling and waving enthusiastically from behind the steel food shoot.

"Yolanda!" he heard his father yell to someone in the back. "Come here a sec. I want you to meet CJ!" His father rounded the corner, beaming. He wore an apron that barely covered a fourth of his huge belly, black pants, a white shirt, and a visor turned backwards on his sweaty bald head. A pretty black woman came from the back and stood beside him. "This is my boy," he told her proudly, "CJ."

"Nice to meet you, CJ," she said, extending a manicured hand that sported gold on every finger. "I've heard a lot about you." CJ shook her hand and she smiled at his father before disappearing back into the kitchen.

"Who's this beautiful girl?" his father asked, looking directly at Andrea. CJ noticed that she was blushing.

"This is my . . . friend, Andrea." Then looking at her, "Andrea, this is my father."

Mr. McCallister nodded at her. "Well, I know y'all didn't come up here to hang out with me, and I've got work to do anyway. Andrea, look out for my son. He's a little wild." He smiled before turning to the girl behind the counter. "I'll take care of whatever they order. Bye, CJ. Nice meeting you, Andrea."

CJ continued to hold Andrea's hand as his father went back to his station in the kitchen. "Your father seems pretty cool," she said, looking at him.

"Yeah. He's all right."

~

Kevin Mizell strolled through the lobby of the Essex. As usual, he was impeccably dressed in a Brooks Brothers suit, Gucci loafers, and a tie he bought in Milan. His white teeth glistened in contrast to his deep, South Beach tan, and a Presidential Rolex peeked from under his sleeve.

He walked slowly among the arriving and departing guests, nodding crisply at any employee who happened to make eye contact with him. The Miami Essex was *his* hotel. He was here when there was nothing but a couple of trailers on the property. He had built it, staffed it, opened it, and now he was leaving it.

He produced a cigar from the inside pocket of his coat and stuck it in his mouth. He stopped lighting them nine years ago, but he still felt he did his best thinking with one clenched in his teeth. He looked up at the chandeliers, the mezzanine, and the beautiful domed ceiling, then over at the waterfalls, the huge aquariums which were part of the walls, and finally down at the carpet that he had selected himself. This was *his* castle. He spun slowly in a full circle. *He* built this monument to luxury and comfort in the middle of paradise. *Him.* But like all the other hotels he had opened in this tenure with Essex, he had to leave it all behind and start anew. *Such is life,* he thought as he passed the elevators and headed toward his office.

When he opened the door, he was instantly aware that something was wrong. Brett Wagner and his two assistants were wringing their hands and shifting about uncertainly in front of the copy room door.

The copy room wasn't really a room at all. It was just a small closet that housed a Xerox machine and a few office supplies. Mr. Mizell looked at the small ensemble of fashionistas and raised his eyebrows.

"Problem?" he asked, looking directly at his interior decorator and longtime friend.

Brett Wagner merely cocked his head in the direction of the copy room. Mizell looked at him curiously for a moment before hesitantly approaching the door. There was a hushed silence as he gripped the knob. Every eye in the room was upon him. Even Pedro the Chihuahua sat up straight in the crook of Brett's arm and watched in rapt interest as the general manager suddenly flung the door open. He was greeted by a red-faced, swollen-eyed Cheryl McCallister, whose mascara was running so much that she resembled a member of the band KISS. She released a mournful, high-pitched wail and he reflexively slammed the door shut before she could reach her hysterical crescendo. He turned back to Brett and took the unlit cigar from his mouth.

"What happened?"

Wagner shrugged his shoulders innocently. "I don't know. I only mentioned that she was going to enjoy working for Jose Ramos from over at Beachside and she flipped out."

"Good job," Kevin Mizell said in a voice that dripped with sarcasm before adding, "Asshole." He slammed his office door behind him and headed straight for the decanter of scotch in the cabinet.

Pedro barked once in protest.

~

CJ and Andrea sat in a corner booth by the window and talked nonstop for over an hour. He decided he'd rather sit next to her than across from her when they selected their table, so he gave her a firm bump with his hip when she sat down and she scooted over to make room, laughing. They discussed important matters like middle names, favorite colors, lucky numbers, and music. The time flew as they talked, and she eventually gave him a sad smile.

"I need to go," she said, touching his hand. He instinctively leaned over and kissed her cheek. He hesitated for a moment, then softly kissed her lips. When he pulled away, her eyes were still shut, so he gently touched her face and began kissing her some more. She wrapped her arms around him and pulled him closer and they stayed that way for a while before she finally released him.

"I really need to go."

CJ kissed her once more and stood weakly, holding out his hand to help her up.

"Can I walk you home?"

"Not all the way. My neighbor and my mom are best friends."

"Okay. How far is it?"

"Not far," she said, reaching for his hand again as they crossed the busy street.

A passing car honked twice and swerved into the gas station in front of them. It was a silver Monte Carlo, Rudy's mom's car. The tinted window rolled down to reveal his best friend's smiling face.

"*Oye,* CJ! *Que vola,* brother?"

CJ smiled back and pulled Andrea toward the car.

"Andrea, this is my best friend Rudy Rodriquez. Rudy, this is Andrea Marcos."

Rudy nodded. "I've heard a lot about you, Andrea." He reached over to open the passenger door. "Get in, I'll give you a ride."

Andrea looked hesitantly at CJ, but he pulled her to the car and said, "C'mon, it's cool."

They climbed in the front seat next to Rudy and slammed the door. He had the AC on high and Stevie B. on the radio. Rudy turned the car around and pulled back out into traffic. He nodded his head to the backseat.

"I need to drop these groceries off at home real quick and then I'll take you wherever you want."

CJ looked over at Andrea. "Do we have time?"

"How far away is it?" she asked, looking a little nervous.

"Southwinds," Rudy said, already heading in that direction.

"I've got about thirty minutes."

"No problem," he responded, stepping on the gas. They rode in silence for the next five minutes, speeding through South Miami's backstreets while Andrea squeezed CJ's hand tightly. Soon they were rolling over the faded yellow speed bumps of the Southwinds. Rudy stopped in front of his building and left the engine running.

"Be right back," he said, grabbing the two bags of groceries from the backseat and sprinting up the sidewalk. CJ and Andrea watched him disappear behind the patio wall of his apartment.

"He seems nice," she said.

CJ couldn't resist stealing a quick kiss before saying, "Yeah," *another kiss,* "we've been down since" *another kiss,* "the third grade." *Another kiss.* This was the best day of CJ McCallister's life! He was kissing Andrea Marcos! A lot!

Rudy jumped back in the car and put it in drive. "Okay, where to?"

"Just go back to the gas station where you picked us up and I'll show you from there," she said.

They were back at the gas station in a few minutes, and after a few lefts and rights, the car rolled to a stop on the curb of a quiet suburban street. She told Rudy it was nice to meet him and kissed CJ on the cheek before exiting the vehicle.

"Oh yeah," she said, smiling at CJ, "my books."

He grabbed them out of his backpack and handed them to her through the open door.

"Bye," CJ said, watching her every move.

"Bye." She shut the car door behind her. They sat there for a minute and watched her go. Rudy gave a low whistle as she turned around and waved once more.

"Damn, bro," he said, smiling, "you sure you can handle that?"

CJ punched his arm. "Please tell me you've got a cigarette," he said, watching Andrea walk up the steps to a house about a block down the street. "I'm nickin' my ass off."

~

The next couple of weeks of CJ McCallister's life can only be described as kick-ass. He was living his own dream. For so long he had watched

Andrea and adored her from afar, almost to the point of stalking, but he never thought he'd actually be eating lunch with her every day in the cafeteria or walking her to class or talking to her on the phone or making out with her under the bleachers. He looked up at the clock in his fifth-period English class and willed it to move faster. Today at lunch she told him she might skip sixth period and hang out with him since she had a substitute teacher in science all week. The bleachers were the best blind spot at South Miami. They were located at the very back of the school by the football field and the only people who ever ventured under them were looking for the same thing CJ and Andrea were: privacy.

The bell finally rang and kids from every class spilled out into the hallway. CJ moved as stealthily as possible through the flood of humanity. They were supposed to meet at the library, but she told him that he shouldn't wait for her if she wasn't already there when he arrived. He could tell she was having second thoughts. She told him she had never skipped class in her life. In a way, he felt guilty for being a bad influence on her, but his hormones were more powerful than his conscience.

He smiled when he saw her down the hall by the library. She was trying her best to appear cool and nonchalant, but he knew her well enough by now to see that she was scared and unsure. The fact that she even showed up at all made CJ's heart soar. She was taking a huge risk just to be alone with him.

"Hey!" he said when he finally reached the place where she was standing.

"CJ, are you sure?" she asked, biting her lip and looking at him searchingly.

He smiled and took her hand. "Come on."

She dragged her feet at first, but the thrill of risk-taking soon overtook her and by the time the late bell rang, she was practically skipping.

"Are you sure you wanna go under the bleachers?" she asked. "It's kinda yuck down there."

"Where d'ya wanna go then, the bathroom?" he asked innocently, laughing when she wrinkled her nose and pushed him. "Wait, I know a place. The auditorium. We can hang out on the balcony."

They quickly changed directions. The auditorium was at the other end of the school and they had a lot of ground to cover. It was dangerous for them to be roaming the halls together after the late bell had sounded. If a teacher, counselor, or someone else from the administrative office caught them, they'd be considered truant and given detention or maybe even suspended. CJ couldn't let that happen. Andrea's mom would shit. She giggled and held his hand while he peeked around corners to make sure the coast was clear before they proceeded. At one point he jerked her into a janitor's closet when they heard heels clicking against the concrete. He held her tight and kissed her hungrily until the footsteps dissipated down the hall. CJ then released her and waited a few heartbeats before cracking the door. If anyone had been looking at that particular moment, they would have seen two seriously disheveled teenagers exiting the hall closet. Silently, they crept down the empty corridor that led to the entrance of the auditorium. CJ looked over at her and smiled, then reached back and shocked her by grabbing a handful of her butt. She squeaked and jumped in the air before scowling at him and popping him in the arm. He held it in mock pain and she laughed, pushing him toward the double doors of the auditorium.

"Ai, que lindo," a gruff Spanish voice said. *How sweet.*

CJ and Andrea both spun around, surprised that anyone else was near. There, side by side in the hallway stood Joey and Hector Barocela. Andrea inched closer to CJ, clutching his hand.

"El gringito y la princesa," Joey said. *The white boy and the princess.* His words were coated in derision and he sneered when he said them. Hector blew bubbles impassively and watched. Suddenly they burst into action. Hector grabbed CJ by the throat and slammed him hard to the ground, pinning him there by planting an immense foot on his chest and continuing to smack his gum while he watched his brother. Joey lunged for Andrea and caught her by the waist, spinning her around to

face Hector and CJ and holding her firmly against him. She began to cry.

"Did *mama* leave us three dollars today?" Joey asked CJ.

He dug in his pocket and produced two crumpled bills. "Here, man, it's all I have. Let her go."

Hector reached down and plucked the money from CJ's hand, but his heavy foot remained on his chest, immobilizing him. He smiled at his brother.

"I don't know, bro," Joey said, snaking a hand over Andrea's breast and smelling her hair, "she's pretty fine." Andrea began struggling violently and Joey finally tired of restraining her and slung her viciously in the grass where she tumbled and slid, staining her white jeans. *"Puta,"* he said over his shoulder before walking over to where CJ watched helplessly from the ground. As he approached, CJ felt a tsunami of hatred and rage fill him. He began to shake uncontrollably. Everything slowed down. He heard Joey say "Pussy," and saw white leather coming toward his face. Then the world exploded in colors and lights.

He heard them walk off and he rolled over on his stomach, pushing himself up on his hands and knees. Blood dripped from his face to the concrete. He looked over at the area in the grass where Andrea went down. He didn't see her. Something was wrong with his vision. Everything looked fuzzy, watery, and doubled.

"You're hurt," Andrea said from behind him. He climbed to his feet unsteadily and leaned against the wall.

"I'm okay," he said, staring at the green and brown stains on her knees, feeling weak and impotent for not being able to protect her. "What time is it?"

"Almost two."

"Go to P.E." Physical Education was her seventh-period class, the last of the day. "Can you wear your gym clothes home?"

She nodded and wiped the still falling tears from her cheeks. He turned and started down the hallway, using the wall for balance.

"Where are you going?" she asked to his back.

"Home," he answered without turning around.

~

Chris McCallister exhaled an acrid plume of smoke and coughed heavily, leaning back into the couch. He smiled blissfully as the THC began to swim through his bloodstream. He was already feeling the initial effects of the high. *This is some good shit,* he thought.

On the table were five thumb-sized manila envelopes loosely packed with weed. Each envelope bore a stamp in red ink that said "confo" with a star underneath. One of the envelopes was open with green buds spilling out onto the tray.

He wasn't accustomed to buying his dope in dime bags. He generally preferred to buy it by the weight; mostly eights, quarters, and halfs, maybe an ounce occasionally, if his finances allowed, but he was quickly learning that things didn't work that way in the hood.

One of the girls at work, Tasha, lived in the nearby South Miami projects called "the creek." Last week in an act of desperation, he clumsily asked her if she could get him some weed. She looked at him funny and said, "You ain't the PO-lice are you, baby?"

"Hell no."

"How much you want?"

"What'll fifty get me?" he shot back, excited.

"Give it here," she said, holding out her hand. She stuck it in her bra and went back to work.

He was a little worried about handing over fifty dollars of his hard-earned cash to someone he barely knew, but it'd been over a month since he'd gotten his head right and he was desperate.

Later on in the shift a white Eldorado came through the drive-thru with the bass up so loud that the entire restaurant rattled. Yolanda hollered from her office in the back, "Tasha, tell his ass to turn that bullshit down!"

The driver turned out to be Tasha's boyfriend. She leaned out the window and talked to him awhile, but the cars started to line up behind him so he took off. An hour later the car returned. He was trying his best not to be nosy, but he sure hoped that Tasha's man was bringing him a little somethin'-somethin'.

That night during cleanup, Tasha dropped the five envelopes in his apron pocket.

"You welcome, fat boy," she said and walked away smiling.

Last night he had copped five more. He hoped to make these last another ten days. That way he still had enough for cigarettes and bus fare with close to a hundred left over to give his wife for bills and shit.

He stopped to take another deep, cough-inducing hit. He kept forgetting to buy rolling papers, so he was forced to use his own homemade smoking apparatus. This consisted of an empty plastic two-liter bottle with a crude hole the size of a quarter punched in its middle using a steak knife, and a piece of aluminum foil, which was placed over the hole with its ends taped to the bottle. The center of the foil was depressed to fashion a "bowl" and he used a tack to punch a few small holes in it. He could then drop in a few buds, hold the bottle upright, place it against his mouth, add fire, inhale, and *voila!* Instant buzz. It was either that or use the thin paper wrappers on his wife's tampons, and he suspected she was on to him regarding that.

He looked over at the clock on the VCR and sighed. It was time to catch the Metrobus to work. He stuck his stash under the couch, hid his bong behind a speaker, grabbed his visor and apron, and hauled ass out the door.

~

CJ made it all the way to the railroad tracks before he started crying. It was still hard for him to see, and the tears made it almost impossible. He stumbled and fell to his knees. His stomach tightened and vomit spewed from his mouth onto the rocks below. It was as if even his body was appalled at what he just went through and was rejecting it the same way it would a virus or bacteria. The remaining pieces of his self-control fell away and he howled up at the sky in broken agony.

"MOTHERFUCKERS!" he screamed. His voice bounced off the backside of a nearby supermarket and echoed back at him. He picked up a rock and fired it in the direction of the echo. Then another. And another. And another. He continued hurling rocks until his arm was completely spent while uttering every single insult he had ever heard from "Cocksucker!" to "Faggot Bitch!" Finally he sat down on the rusty tracks. His left eye was swollen shut. His face was a mess of sweat, snot, blood, and vomit. And worst of all, what little bit of dignity he had left was now shattered. The shittiest part was watching helplessly as that asshole manhandled Andrea. He even felt her up! What kind of man lets that happen to his woman?

As he sat there, exhausted, a strange calm washed over him and a thought sprang to life in his mind. At first it was like a distant point of light that he struggled to see, but the more he focused on it, the quicker it approached, growing and expanding until it illuminated his entire mind. A smile crept across his swollen face as he stood and started toward home.

~

It was after 10 p.m. by the time Cheryl made it home. She glanced up at CJ's window on her way to the front door. His light was out. She unlocked the door and walked inside the quiet apartment, immediately kicking off her high heels. The downstairs was a mess. There were overflowing ashtrays and several dirty glasses. A half-eaten sandwich sat stale on a plate awaiting roaches, and there were clothes strewn about the coffee table and living room floor.

She let out a deep breath and started cleaning up. She hummed softly to herself as she took the dirty dishes to the kitchen and emptied the ashtrays. She collected the clothes and threw them in a hamper before dampening a rag and wiping down the filthy coffee table. She saw the month's worth of dust that had settled on top of the television and began to wipe that off too. She noticed an empty plastic two-liter bottle behind the stereo speaker and shook her head. *There's trash everywhere in this filthy apartment,* she thought as she leaned over to grab it. She was halfway back to the kitchen when a foul-smelling odor penetrated her thoughts. She looked down at the bottle she was holding and saw the charred aluminum foil. She wasn't the most street smart person in the world, but she knew a drug pipe when she saw one. *Damn it, Chris!* she thought, suddenly holding the offensive bottle like a dead rat. She placed it on the table and sat down heavily on the couch, glancing at her watch.

He got off at midnight. She'd wait.

~

CJ lay awake in his bed and listened to his parents argue downstairs. He looked over at the clock radio on his dresser. It was 12:42 a.m.

"What is the meaning of this?" he heard his mother ask.

"I have no idea," said his father innocently.

"Chris, I'm not going to put up with this. It's bad enough that CJ comes home to an empty apartment every afternoon, but I refuse to allow him to grow up in a drug-filled environment. What if he had found this pipe and experimented with it? Don't you even care?"

"Isn't mine."

"You promised me you would quit," she pleaded. "Is your word worth so little?"

"I did quit," he responded blankly.

And on and on the conversation went, with his mother continuing to launch attacks and his father calmly defending and denying. Of course, they'd had thousands of similar confrontations such as this throughout their marriage and knew their roles well. CJ could guess accurately what each would say during the course of the argument.

"Chris, don't let drugs destroy our family," she was saying.

"I'm not using drugs."

"I don't want to leave you. I love you. But CJ's future is at stake. He's already smoking cigarettes. It's only a matter of time, especially if you're getting high. You're his father, Chris. He looks up to you."

"I'm not getting high," he said robotically.

"Stop that!" she snapped. "You know damn well that . . . *thing* is yours."

Silence.

"Whose is it, then? CJ's?"

"No."

"Whose then?"

"It's Rudy's," his father finally said.

CJ sat straight up and looked at the door. *Did he just say Rudy?*

"Rudy," his mother said flatly. Then he heard the couch squeak and the sound of footsteps on the stairs. He rolled over on his side and pretended to sleep.

His mother first knocked on the door, then opened it.

"CJ?" she said, followed by "CJ!"

"What?" he asked in a sleepy voice.

"How dare you allow your friends to bring drugs in this house!" she said angrily. "You know your father is trying to quit!" She turned on the lamp next to his bed and sat on the edge.

He quickly pulled the pillow over his head.

"CJ, look at me. Look at me, damn it!"

Oh well, he thought, *she's gonna see it tomorrow anyway.* He took the pillow off his head and rolled over to face her.

"Oh my God, baby!" she cried. "Who did this to you?" She forgot all about the pipe and began lightly rubbing his hair.

"It's okay, Mom. I got into a fight at school. It's over now."

His father suddenly appeared at the door. "Did you win?"

"It was a tie," CJ said.

His father nodded, looking closely at CJ's eye. It was black, purple, and swollen shut. "I'll get some ice."

"Let's take him to the ER," his mom wept.

"He's okay," his dad said. "He just needs some ice."

"Well, I'm calling that damn school tomorrow," his mom insisted.

CJ cringed.

"No, you won't," his father said. "Don't embarrass him, honey. Look at him. He's had a tough enough time already. Let's not make it any harder."

CJ silently thanked his father, who disappeared down the stairs to make him an ice pack.

"Mom, are you mad?" he asked her.

"At you? Absolutely not," she said, kissing his face and turning off the light. She walked out of his room and down the hall.

"Here you go, buddy," his father said, holding a Ziploc bag full of ice. CJ looked up at him standing there in the dark in his Wendy's outfit. "Rudy, huh?"

His dad shrugged. "Sorry."

His mom came back in with a Tylenol and a glass of water. "Take this."

He looked up at the silhouettes of his parents, backlit by the hallway light. His mom was still crying and his father was patting her back consolingly.

"Good night," he said and rolled over.

Chapter 4

CJ leaned toward the bathroom mirror and tentatively prodded the skin surrounding his left eye. The swelling was already subsiding, but it still looked terrible. He reached in his pocket for the sunglasses and gently slid them on. They weren't much, but at least they covered the area he was trying to conceal. He had gotten them at the Dade County Youth Fair two years ago. Rudy had a pair too. They were the standard made-in-Taiwan dark boys that came in a stapled plastic wrapper and sported a circular sticker on the lens. In fact, the sticker was still there. CJ pried it off with his thumbnail and flicked it in the toilet.

"CJ," his mom called up the stairs, "come eat."

He looked at himself once more before backing out of the bathroom. Hopefully his teachers wouldn't force him to remove the shades.

His mom was standing at the stove when he came down the stairs. "I'm not eating," he said. "I'll be in the car."

"CJ . . ." she began to protest, but he was already out the door.

The car was unlocked. He quickly jumped in the passenger side and opened the glove compartment. It was crammed with papers and maps. He pulled it all out, handful after handful, until he finally spotted what he was looking for. It was buried deep in the back. He grabbed it and shoved it in his pocket, checking to see if his mom was coming.

He hastily began jamming everything back in the glove box. When he finished, he tried to close it, but it wouldn't shut. He slammed it over and over, but the flap seemed intent on hanging limply from the dash. In a last-ditch effort, he pressed his feet against it while holding the sides of the seat, concentrating all of his 115 pounds behind the thrust. He was finally rewarded for his efforts by an audible click, just as his mom was opening the door.

"What are you doing, silly?" she asked. He shrugged. She sat down in the driver's seat and shut the door. "Can I see?" she gently inquired, reaching for his sunglasses.

He instinctively pushed her hand away and slunk back against the window.

"Come on, CJ. I'm worried about you."

He relented and lifted the shades to his forehead, allowing her to inspect.

"Poor baby," she said, softly touching his face. "Are you sure you don't want to miss a few days? You could come to work with me."

CJ was tempted. He loved going to the Essex. They had a huge pool with waterfalls, a marina with jet skis, and an arcade with all the new games in it. He knew everyone who worked there because of his mom and they were all really nice to him. He hesitated before finally shaking his head. He knew that if he didn't act quickly in response to what happened yesterday, his resolve would eventually weaken and he'd end up backing down. He needed to make a stand, not only for himself, but for Andrea as well. That bastard slung her to the ground and made her cry. He had to act now.

His mom stared at him for a few more seconds before smiling sadly and saying, "Okay." She slid her key in the ignition and the car started right up for once. "Good girl," she mumbled softly before backing out into the parking lot.

"So," she said, once they were on the road, "how's Andrea?"

"Mom," he answered, "I don't want to hurt your feelings, but I really don't feel like talking this morning."

She looked at him sharply, but said nothing. They rode the rest of the way in silence. When they finally arrived on the side street where she usually dropped him off, she passed him a five-dollar bill without looking at him. He leaned over and kissed her cheek.

"I'm proud of you, CJ," she said. "You're a good boy."

He closed the door behind him and watched her drive away before starting toward the school.

~

CJ reached in his pocket and carefully extracted the cylindrical object he had placed there earlier. He looked down at it. If you weren't really paying attention, you could easily mistake it for one of those fat markers graffiti artists use to tag bus stops. CJ knew better. He learned that lesson in the fourth grade.

His grandmother was named Maybell Raines, but everybody in Loxley, Alabama, knew her as Mema. She was a God-fearing, gun-loving, card-carrying Republican who truly believed that the state of Alabama was being infiltrated by Communists. The fact that her oldest daughter was living in a big city like Mobile scared her but when his mom informed her that she was moving to Miami, Mema almost shit on herself. She tried everything to stop her. First, she simply forbade it. Then she tried crying. When that didn't work, she faked life-threatening cancer, but her daughter was as stubborn as she was. In the end, she conceded to "allow" her to move IF she took a shotgun with her. His mom eventually talked her down to a canister of Mace.

As a kid CJ loved rifling through the contents of his parents' closet and chest of drawers. His dad in particular had a wealth of interesting things tucked within the nooks and crannies of their room: pocket-knives, arrowheads, buffalo nickels, and even a magazine with naked women in it. CJ was always getting spanked or punished for his secret missions into their bedroom, but that only raised the stakes of the adventure for him. It was on one of these very missions that he stumbled upon the Mace.

His father was dozing on the couch. The Masters Golf Tournament was on. Golf always put his dad to sleep because the commentators insisted on speaking in hushed tones. CJ could hear them mumbling quietly from his parents' closet between his father's chainsaw snores.

His mother was out grocery shopping. He had managed to pull down a shoe box from the top of the closet and was sitting on the floor exploring the contents of his find. There was a calculator, a set of dice, a compass, a bent spoon, and what appeared to be a black Magic Marker. CJ shook it first, and then tried to twist off the cap. Nothing. He was puzzled. He brought it to eye level for a closer look and tried the press-twist technique that unlocked most of the medicine bottles in the bathroom. Suddenly a vaporous blast erupted from the nozzle and covered his face in liquid fire. He screamed. When his father finally made it up the stairs, he found CJ gyrating on the carpet, clawing wildly at his face and begging for help. He saw the Mace canister on the floor and called 9-1-1. The operator instructed him to put CJ in the shower until the effects wore off.

He remembered that day vividly. The burning had spread from his eyes to his armpits, then even down to his nuts and asshole. Two years later he spotted the canister in the glove box and treated it with respect and trepidation. There was excruciating pain inside that little can. He didn't even know why it was still around. His horrifying experience with it was one he would not even wish on his worst enemy.

Unless, of course, that enemy happened to be named Barocela.

CJ's plan wasn't complex. It actually wasn't a plan at all. He just knew he couldn't beat either of the twins in a fistfight, so he needed some type of equalizer to level the playing field. That's where the Mace came in. He figured they'd approach him at some point in the day, especially if he made himself available. They'd probably be looking to make fun of him about his eye and take his money again. He'd give them the bonus plan. Of course, there was a huge difference between fantasizing about spraying them and actually doing it. The thought of confrontation made his knees shake as he entered the school. His rage from yesterday was slowly giving way to fear and he made himself focus on Joey feeling on Andrea in order to revitalize his intensity. *Assholes!* he thought while walking up the stairwell to the second floor.

The hallway was crowded with students making their way to first period. The classroom doors were open and many teachers stood by them, greeting the kids who entered. CJ saw Andrea immediately. He dreaded having to face her with the stupid sunglasses on, and his hatred for Joey and Hector began to swell with every humiliating step he took in her direction. She gave him a sad smile, which he mistook for condescension. He cringed inwardly.

"Are you okay?" she asked.

"Yeah," he answered, dying behind his shades. "You?"

She nodded, and then quickly glanced over CJ's shoulder. Her eyes narrowed and she groped for his hand. He imagined two giant shadows falling over them as he turned to face the twins.

"Nice sunglasses, *gringito,*" said Joey Barocela, smiling cruelly down at CJ. Hector watched impassively.

CJ reached in his pocket with his free hand and seized the canister of Mace. *NOW!* his mind was screaming, but his body wasn't cooperating. He could only look dumbly up at their snarling faces and tremble.

Joey looked briefly at a nearby teacher in the hall, then back at CJ. "Maybe I'll take those shades later on," he said, glancing over at his brother, "for Hector."

"Mine!" Hector echoed happily.

Joey leered at Andrea and licked his lips suggestively before continuing down the hall with Hector in tow. Andrea curled her upper lip in disgust.

They stood there in silence, holding hands and watching the twins strut down the hall. CJ cocked his head to the side when Hector abruptly veered off into a classroom and watched with interest as Joey made his way to the boys' bathroom and disappeared inside.

CJ made up his mind. He gave Andrea a quick peck on her cheek and left her standing in the hallway. He moved quickly down the corridor, weaving through traffic and sidestepping teachers, students, and open doors on the way.

When he reached the boys' room, he cracked the door and peeked in to make sure Joey wasn't at a urinal or sink. He wasn't. CJ slid inside the quiet bathroom and closed the door behind him. He could see Joey

Barocela's tight Edwin jeans bunched down around his ankles and resting atop his Lotto sneakers. His heart was hammering in his chest as he reached in his pocket for the Mace. The bathroom stall doors at South Miami had no locking mechanisms on them. All CJ had to do was rip the door open and blast his ass. Still he hesitated. *What if he's immune to this shit?* he thought frantically. *What if the nozzle is broken or something else goes wrong?* His thoughts were interrupted by the wet, sloshy, farting sounds of shit gushing from the bully's intestines down into the toilet. CJ took a deep breath, gripped the handle, and slung the door open.

"What the fuck?" Joey shouted angrily, but his protest was cut short by the chemicals being splashed across his face. He was instantly blinded. He couldn't breathe.

CJ reached down between his ankles and clutched a handful of his jeans. He yanked violently and snatched the panic-stricken twin, feet first, off the toilet and out of the stall, cracking the back of his head on the porcelain. Joey howled like a wounded animal and began kicking his legs wildly, trying to break free of CJ's grip on his jeans. It was no use. They were too tight. A puddle of blood was quickly growing under his head from where it had banged against the toilet. Joey pounded his fists on the floor in frustration and began to cry.

"Somebody help me!" he pleaded in anguish. CJ responded by spraying his flopping genitals with Mace and pulling his writhing body to the door, tossing the can in the trash on his way out.

Everyone in the hallway was watching in stunned silence as he burst through the bathroom door dragging a half-naked, kicking and screaming Joey Barocela behind him. He pulled him ten feet down the hall, leaving a streak of shit and blood before finally coming to a stop. He let go of his jeans, and his feet fell to the floor with a thud.

"Oh God! Please!" Joey wailed desperately, with one hand clutching his burning testicles and the other trying futilely to wipe the gas from his face using the sleeve of his t-shirt. When he couldn't get any relief and the pain grew more intense, he thrashed on the ground violently, causing the crowd in the hall to take a step back. Joey finally settled into the fetal position with CJ standing over him like a modern-day version of David and Goliath. He ignored his sobbing and looked into the faces of the crowd. His eyes came to rest on Andrea, still standing where he left her. She looked at him sadly. His mind suddenly flashed back to the day before, when Joey Barocela squeezed her breast and slung her in the grass. Still looking at Andrea, CJ brought his right foot back and with all the power he could muster, launched a savage kick squarely into the face of the bully. Joey roared in agony and frustration, then braced himself for the next blow. There was none. CJ left him balled up and bleeding in the middle of the hallway with his jeans still wrapped around his ankles.

He looked at the spot where Andrea was just standing, but she was already gone. He walked through the door of his first-period Spanish class and sat down at his desk to wait.

~

Cheryl McCallister pulled into the employee parking lot of the Essex and found a decent spot near the entrance. She checked her makeup in the rearview mirror before exiting the vehicle. Kevin Mizell had already left for Washington and it would be at least another week before Jose Ramos came over from the Essex Beachside. IF he came at all. She was praying he wouldn't. Although the move from Resident Manager to General Manager was technically a promotion, the Beachside was a much more glamorous and renowned resort. When celebrities and members of the international jet set came to Miami, they reserved rooms there. Maybe he would opt to stay put until the G.M. position of that hotel came open. She hoped so.

Her thoughts turned back to CJ. She was worried about her son. He wasn't a fighter. He just wasn't raised that way. CJ made friends with everybody from little old ladies and janitors to the handicapped girl who used to live a few apartments down. It was hard for her to imagine him balling up his fist and striking someone, and the idea of anyone hurting him nauseated her. She really wanted to call the principal of South Miami, but Chris was adamant about her not doing so.

"Boys go through these kinds of things," he had told her. "It's like a rite of passage. He's growing up, Cheryl. You can't keep interfering every time he runs into problems. If he needs us, he'll ask for help. Until then, no matter how bad it hurts, we need to let him find his way."

Well, she thought, *at least in this area, he probably knows best.* But that didn't stop her from worrying. A tear slid down her cheek as she remembered his swollen little face. She hoped his teachers allowed him to wear his sunglasses in class, but she doubted they would.

When she entered her office, there was a man behind her desk examining the pictures on her bookshelf. He had a swarthy complexion and his head was shaved completely bald. He turned expectantly at the sound of the door and raised a questioning eyebrow at her. "Cheryl McCallister?" he asked in heavily accented English.

She nodded and sized him up. He wasn't much taller than CJ, but he was powerfully built, with a barrel chest and immense shoulders straining against the material of his Italian suit.

"I'm Jose Ramos," he said, crossing his arms. "You work for me now."

~

Señora Salazar looked up from her desk as CJ entered the classroom. She paused and tapped a pen against her calendar as he walked by. Paul McCallister, or CJ as he called himself, was one of her more interesting students. He was loaded with potential. He had a phenomenal memory, a natural aptitude for language, and seemed to learn effortlessly while many of his peers struggled to grasp the same concepts. Unfortunately, like other talented students who had traveled through her classroom over the years, he exhibited many of the warning signs she associated with a teen on the verge of going down the wrong path. Many times she observed him staring listlessly out the window. He often carried the pungent odor of cigarette smoke in his clothes and hair. Now, today, he was testing the limits of her patience by wearing sunglasses in her classroom. Sunglasses! She considered admonishing him in front of the class but decided against it. Instead, she jotted a note on her calendar to request a parent/teacher conference. He was obviously at a crossroads in his young life. She considered the position of teacher to be more than just giving tests and homework. She would save a life whenever she thought it was possible. She felt obligated to do so. Caring was part of her job.

She stood and reached for her lesson plan while clearing her throat. The murmurs in the class immediately fell silent as she approached the chalkboard and began to write. Suddenly her classroom door flew open and Officer Pratt strode in, followed by the principal, the assistant principal, the guidance counselor, and the hulking new gym teacher who had transferred from Broward. Pratt surveyed the curious faces of the kids in the class. The assistant principal walked over to Señora Salazar and said, "This will only take a minute."

"Mr. McCallister," Pratt said from the end of CJ's aisle. "Place your hands where I can see them."

Everyone turned in their desks to gawk as CJ slowly lifted his hands.

Pratt walked stiffly down the aisle of desks, moving slowly and deliberately until he came to a stop in front of CJ.

"Get up," he ordered, "and take those stupid sunglasses off. Where do you think you're at? South Beach?"

CJ stood but didn't remove the shades. Pratt studied him for a moment before reaching out and snatching them off his face. The class erupted with a collective gasp. His left eye was purple, swollen, and oozing liquid. Pratt opened, then shut his mouth before impatiently motioning with his arm for CJ to walk in front of him. He quickly turned on his heel and followed.

"What's going on?" Señora Salazar asked as they were filing out the door. The principal silenced her with a look.

That's okay, she thought. *I'll find out.* She walked over to her desk and drew a red circle around the parent/teacher conference she had just noted on her calendar a few minutes ago. Make that *ASAP.*

~

Chris McCallister walked gingerly down the carpeted staircase wearing an Essex robe with a tampon lodged behind his ear. His feet, still unaccustomed to standing for so long, hurt like hell, but at least the blisters were healing. He was really beginning to hate working at Wendy's. He forced himself to look on the bright side: free cheeseburgers, money for dope, and someone to spend it with as well. *Things could be worse,* he thought as he hit the power button on the living room stereo and turned it to the oldies station. The high-pitched voices of the Everly Brothers wafted harmoniously from the speakers. They were singing about dreams. He hummed along.

He was grateful at least to be working the four-to-twelve shift. It allowed him to sleep in and have the apartment to himself during the day. He sat down heavily on the couch, causing it to squeak in protest. He reached beneath it and felt for the lip of his wooden dope tray, but couldn't find it. He immediately began to panic, groping wildly and berating himself for being so careless. His wife had found his stash! He said a small prayer, finishing with his customary sign of the cross.

He got down on his knees between the couch and the coffee table. He laid his head flat on the carpet with his eye parallel to the space beneath the sofa. All he saw was blackness. He lifted it up a couple of inches to allow some light in and exhaled with relief when he spotted the rectangular shape of the tray back near the wall. He must have inadvertently pushed it back a little further than usual last night. "Thank God," he said, meaning it.

When he finally managed to extract his dope from beneath the couch, he set the tray on the coffee table and quickly tore into one of the envelopes. He dumped its contents in a small pile in front of him and began the process of breaking up the compact little red-haired nuggets.

The phone rang. He didn't even look up. What he was doing was far more important than anything anyone could be calling about. A thought flashed across the screen of his mind around the eighth ring:

What if it was Ed McMahon calling to tell him he won the Publishers Clearinghouse Sweepstakes? He paused and looked in the kitchen, where the phone continued to ring violently in its cradle. Then it was quiet. He shrugged and got back down to business, removing the tampon from behind his ear. He considered it one of life's little ironies that Tampax actually packaged their product in what was basically rolling paper. It was as if the manufacturer was saying, "Here, men of the world, you're probably going to need this." He laughed at his own wittiness as he found the end of the tiny string and pulled it slowly along the perforated seam, carefully tearing it in the straightest line possible. A perfectly executed tear resulted in enough paper for two small joints. The phone began to ring again. "Fuck off, Ed," he said, sprinkling the tiny buds along the paper. "I'm busy right now."

~

CJ sat quietly in a straight-back chair in Officer Pratt's cubicle. His hands were folded in his lap and his eyes were trained on the carpet in front of him. Every few seconds his line of vision was obscured by the navy blue cuffs of Pratt's uniform pants swishing across his polished shoes as he paced back and forth. CJ focused on his own reflection in their glossy shine each time he passed.

His outward demeanor betrayed none of the emotional fireworks erupting behind the calm, disinterested mask he was wearing. He fought back the desire to raise his fists in the air, throw his head back, and laugh maniacally. He had just humbled the biggest bully in the school. He wished he could remember more of it. He wanted to replay the entire scene over and over in his head for the rest of his life, but unfortunately he could recall only bits and pieces. He remembered snatching the stall door open and spraying Joey in the face, but everything after that was vague. One thing was for sure, the conversations in the cafeteria, the hallways, the classrooms, and the school buses would be dominated by one topic for a while—him. CJ McCallister, giant slayer. He suppressed a smile. Never again would he be considered weak or a coward. Today he had permanently altered the course of his own destiny by standing up. Today he looked fear in the eye and spat. Today he became a man. He wondered what Andrea thought of his heroics. He knew he had a good make-out session coming for this, maybe even some second-base action. He frowned when an ugly thought crept into his mind: How would he ever see her if he was expelled from South Miami? Especially with her mother being so strict. *We'll work it out,* he thought.

Pratt's shoes stopped pacing and came to rest directly in front of him. CJ didn't bother to look up.

"Who gave you that ugly shiner?" he asked. "Was it your pothead father?"

CJ flinched.

"What's wrong, scumbag," he asked, squatting down to eye level with him. "You didn't think I knew your fat, lazy dad was a druggie? I smelled that shit the second I stepped foot on your ugly porch. You thought you were so smart that day, didn't you?" He sneered at CJ malevolently. "I knew I'd have the last laugh. Your sorry excuse of a father can't cover for you this time, boy. That poor kid you assaulted is in the hospital! Traumatized. He's probably still screaming his balls off from that shit you sprayed all over him, not to mention the stitches he's gonna need in his head. And," he lowered his voice conspiratorially, "why were his pants around his ankles? Were you trying to do something naughty to him?"

CJ had heard enough. "I want an attorney," he said. He'd seen enough episodes of *Miami Vice* and *Hill Street Blues* to at least have a rudimentary understanding of his Miranda rights.

"An attorney?" Pratt laughed. "You're gonna need a lot more than that where you're going. They're gonna have some fun with your little narrow white ass in juvie." He winked suggestively. "Bank on it."

Juvie? a voice shrieked in CJ's mind. He hadn't considered that possibility. Now he was getting scared. He figured he'd probably be suspended and more likely expelled, with some type of program or maybe alternative school, but Juvenile Hall? That's where they sent criminals. He wasn't a criminal. Pratt was just bullshitting him. *What an asshole,* CJ thought.

His thoughts were interrupted by the appearance of two men in suits at the entrance of Pratt's cubicle.

"Is that him?" one asked.

Pratt nodded.

"What the hell happened to his eye?" asked the other one.

Pratt shrugged. "He won't talk."

"Get up, kid," the first one ordered, producing a pair of cuffs and clicking them loudly.

CJ obeyed.

"You have the right to remain silent," he said, cuffing him. "Anything you say can and will be used against you in a court of law. You have the right to an attorney. If you cannot afford . . ." His words droned on.

They escorted CJ to an unmarked car out front. He looked up at the school as they pushed his head down and maneuvered him into the backseat, slamming the door behind him. He could see teachers writing on chalkboards and addressing their classrooms through the windows. Suddenly he longed to be in Señora Salazar's Spanish class again, conjugating verbs and writing notes to Andrea. Then, the Crown Vic roared to life and pulled out into the deserted street, leaving South Miami Junior High, and a chapter of CJ McCallister's life in the rearview.

~

Cheryl sat across from Mr. Ramos in what used to be the office of Kevin Mizell. She glanced up at the wall. Gone were the numerous pictures of him shaking hands with presidents, entertainers, and foreign dignitaries. All the rock memorabilia had been removed as well. The only evidence that they were ever there at all were tiny slivers of yellowish tape and puncture wounds in the drywall.

"Can you take dictation?" he asked.

She nodded curtly. She was already defensive as hell because of their battle on the phone a few weeks ago, and she assumed he was challenging her secretarial skills. She produced a notebook and pen and flipped the cover back, looking at him in anticipation of the first word.

"Before we start," he said in heavily accented English, "as you can see, my English is no perfect. I depend on you to make the *necesario* changes in my letters and memos in order for them to . . . how do you say . . . 'flow.' Okay?"

"Yes sir."

"*Bueno.* This morning I need to send letter to Sharon Spears to thank her for booking electronics convention here next month. Ready?" he asked, standing and beginning to pace back and forth behind his desk.

"Ready, sir."

"*Estimada* Mrs. Spears," he began.

She looked up abruptly. *"Estimada?"* she asked, unfamiliar with the word. "Don't you mean 'dear'?"

"Forgive me," he said, "we Cubanos reserve words like 'dear' and 'love' only for people who are truly special to us. We do not use these words . . . how do you say . . . 'freely,' but in this case, you are right. I was meaning to say Dear Mrs. Spears."

Her office line began ringing. She looked up at him.

"Go ahead."

She walked into her office, picked up her phone and pressed the blinking button.

"Miami Airport Essex and Marina, this is Cheryl."

"Cheryl McCallister?" a female voice asked.

"Speaking."

"This is Renee Sinclair. I'm calling from South Miami Junior High."

Cheryl swallowed and gripped the phone tighter. "Yes," she said quietly.

"Ma'am, your son, Paul McCallister, was just arrested for assault and removed from the premises by the Metro-Dade Police Department. I'm sure they'll be contacting you shortly. Regardless of the—"

"Assault? CJ? There must be some mistake!"

"Regardless of the outcome in his criminal proceedings, he is hereby expelled from South Miami—"

"But someone assaulted HIM! Have you seen his eye?"

". . . effective immediately."

Cheryl was trembling with rage and worry. She was oblivious to the tears now running down her cheeks or even to her new boss watching from the doorway of his office. Her maternal instincts began to boil within her. Yesterday someone at that school had beaten her son's precious face to a pulp and now today she was being told that the police had arrested him?

"Where is my son?" she said through clenched teeth.

"I told you he's in police custody," the voice came back in a clipped, condescending tone.

"Look, bitch," Cheryl exploded, "you've got five minutes to call me back with a name and a number where I can reach my son. Otherwise my attorney will be there demanding answers from your principal. I drop him off at that school every day, trusting that you will provide a safe learning environment for him. Yesterday he came home with a black swollen eye! Where was your snotty phone call then? For all I know YOU could be the one abusing my child, or one of your faculty members—"

"Mrs. McCallister," she began, sputtering, "I'm truly sorry if—"

"Five minutes," Cheryl said icily, and hung up.

Mr. Ramos stood behind her, his voice hesitant. "Can I help?" he asked gently.

She shook her head before laying it on her desk to cry.

Five minutes later her phone line lit up again. She forced herself to answer professionally in case it was a hotel exec or customer calling her.

"Airport Essex and Marina, this is Cheryl."

"Mom?"

"CJ! Where are you?"

"The police station. I'm sorry."

"What happened, baby?"

"Nothing. They want to talk to you—"

"Ma'am," an official-sounding voice came on. "Detective Whitehead, Miami-Dade Police. Sorry to inconvenience you at work like this."

"What happened?"

"From what we can tell, your son was being bullied by another kid at school. Someone much bigger than him. I'm sure you've seen his eye—"

"Yes, he came home with it yesterday."

"Well, apparently your son decided enough was enough and brought a can of Mace to school with him today."

Cheryl cringed, remembering the canister in the glove box that should have been thrown away after CJ's first experience with it.

"The details are sketchy," he continued, "and your son won't talk, but the victim is known as a bully, and after seeing your son's eye it didn't take a rocket scientist to figure out what happened."

"Is he okay?"

"He's fine," the detective said, "but he's not helping himself by being uncooperative. He's being charged with assault with a weapon, a single count. We'll be taking him to the Juvenile Justice Center this afternoon. He'll have a court appearance in the morning. You should be there if you can."

"Where is it?" she asked, crying again.

"It's over on 27th Avenue. The phone number for the center is 555-0775. If you give it a few hours before you call, they should be able to tell you everything you need to know."

"How long will he be locked in there?" she asked in a small voice, hurting for her son.

"I don't know, ma'am," he answered. "He may be released tomorrow. There are a lot of variables at play—what judge he gets, what mood that judge is in, victim input, remorse on your son's part, etcetera."

"Okay," she said in a daze. "Thank you."

"Mrs. McCallister?" he added. "Don't worry too much, he'll be okay."

She set the phone in its cradle and stared at a point above the door, heartbroken. The thought of CJ in a cage was like a knife in her stomach. He was such a picky eater, what would he eat? Would those criminals in there hurt him? Would the staff be abusive? She laid her head on her desk and began to cry again, the sobs racking her shoulders. She had never felt so helpless in her life.

~

CJ's first night in juvie was uneventful. After the cops dropped him off, he was interviewed by a pretty lady in an office for a couple of hours and had to answer all kinds of stupid questions. Was he addicted to drugs? No. Did he feel like hurting himself? No. Had he ever before? No. Did he hear voices? No. Was he gay? What? Hell no! After the million questions, there were a million more papers to sign, and then he got to call his mom again. She was crying so hard that he barely understood anything she said. By the time it was all over, he was looking forward to a nice quiet cell. He had had a long day and just wanted to lie down for a while.

The pretty lady turned him over to a muscle-bound black dude in baggy jeans and a polo shirt. He was escorted through three secure doors and up a flight of steps before coming to a place called "Unit One." It was there that he was turned over to another black dude who wore a red Kangol hat and a beeper.

"What's up, Whitebread?" he asked, smiling.

CJ nodded and looked at the floor.

"You hungry?" he asked, reaching over in a crate of bag lunches. "Here, take two. You gonna need to get your weight up anyhow."

CJ took the bags and looked around. He was standing in an office with a metal desk and chairs. There were two windows that looked down two sterile-looking hallways lined with steel doors and Plexiglas windows.

"This your first time?" the man asked.

CJ nodded.

"Your last too, I s'pose?"

CJ nodded again.

"That's the number one song in here, little brother." He smiled again. "Let's get you an apartment."

He grabbed a bedroll and a Ziploc bag with a bar of soap, a comb, toothpaste, and a toothbrush and walked down the hall humming an Anita Baker song CJ recognized from the video jukebox network. Most of the cells were empty. He stopped at a door and stuck an enormous key in the lock, pushing it open with a sweeping gesture.

"Your palace," he said.

CJ walked in and looked around. It wasn't much. There was a stainless steel toilet connected to a sink in the corner, a window that was impossible to see out of, and an eight-foot concrete block jutting from the wall with a thin green plastic mat lying on top of it.

"This is just Intake. You'll either go home tomorrow or," he nodded back over his shoulder, "you'll go down to the compound. Now eat that food."

He placed the bedroll and Ziploc on the cell floor. He then slammed the door behind CJ and checked to make sure it was locked before walking back down the hall. A few minutes later he returned with a folded khaki outfit, some flip-flops, and a brown bag. He opened the flap on CJ's door and pushed the items through.

"Okay Killer, take off all your clothes and put 'em in this bag." He paused for a moment and looked at CJ speculatively. "You ain't got lice or crabs, do ya?"

CJ shook his head.

"Didn't think so. We gonna bypass the shower tonight and let you get some rest. I'll put the 'Do Not Disturb' sign on your door," he said with a smile, revealing four gold bottom teeth. He looked down at his beeper and said, "Be right back. Go 'head and change."

CJ placed his personal clothes in the bag and set them on the flap, then slid on the khaki jumpsuit. When the man came back he found CJ dressed and sitting on his bed. He took the brown bag and pushed CJ's Reeboks back through the flap.

"You can keep these. If you need anything, just holla. Here's something for you to read." He set a Bible on the flap and CJ got up to grab it. "You gonna be all right, Champ. My name is Mr. Jackson, by the way, but most everybody just calls me Jack. What they call you?"

"CJ."

"All right, CJ. Get you some sleep. You probably be outta here in the mornin'." He shut the flap and walked back down the hall.

CJ lay down on the hard mat and used his bedroll as a pillow. He stared up at the ceiling and let his mind go. His thoughts ran wild. From the day's events, to his dad at Wendy's, to his mom crying on the phone, to Andrea, to Señora Salazar, to the twins, to Rudy, to Pratt, back to Andrea, his dad again, Joey Barocela again. The thoughts were whipping around and twisting in his mind like a tornado, swirling faster and faster, gaining momentum each time around until CJ realized he was white-knuckle gripping the sides of his mat. He took a deep breath and shook his head in an attempt to clear his mind. He looked down at the Bible lying beside him and impulsively grabbed it, flipping through the pages in search of a good story. He smiled and settled back when he recognized the story of David, son of Jesse, and Goliath, champion of the Philistines.

~

Business was slow at the Wendy's on 67th Avenue. One of the girls in the back turned the radio up and began to sing along with the music. Chris McCallister recognized the song. He thought it was called "After the Pain," but he wasn't sure. Some chick sang it who reminded him of his wife. It wasn't that she sounded like Cheryl, and he doubted she looked anything like her either. It was her insistence on sticking with her man, Mr. Charlie, no matter what, that made him think of Cheryl. He nodded his head to the music. He was familiar with most of the songs by now. The radio at work was locked on "Starforce 99," the local R&B and soul station. He didn't like it at first, but he had to admit it was growing on him. After a month of eight-hour shifts, he really had no choice; it was either adapt or lose his fucking mind.

He looked at his watch. It was 8:00 p.m. He grabbed a half-full garbage can and held it up so that Yolanda could see it from her office window. She was talking animatedly with someone on the phone and motioned for him to go ahead with a quick nod. He walked out the back door toward the dumpsters, which were enclosed by a square section of wooden fence.

Once he reached the blind spot of the dumpster area, he set down the trash can and reached in his pocket for his cigarettes. He quickly shook out the second of the two joints he had rolled earlier and stuck it in his mouth.

Suddenly, an authoritative female voice pierced the night air. "Don't move."

He jumped and turned quickly. It was Tasha, the diminutive drive-thru girl who scored his dope for him. He sagged in relief.

"Whatchu doin', fat boy?"

"What's it look like?" he shot back, firing up the joint and taking a deep pull. He held it for a few seconds and then exhaled, feeling instantly warm.

"Lemme hit it," she said, impatiently clicking together the purple nails of her thumb and index finger.

He took another drag before hesitantly extending his hand. He hated sharing, but this was Tasha, his only connection. He needed to stay on her good side.

She expertly withdrew the pinner from his fat fingers and casually glanced at it before doing a double take and zeroing in on the pink letters running down its side. The "A" and "X" had disappeared as a result of his first two hits, but there was still enough of the word left for her to know what he was using for his rolling paper.

"Crazy-ass white boy!" She laughed, handing him the joint back without hitting it and walking back to the restaurant shaking her head. He shrugged and finished it off in a few more pulls. Then he dumped the trash and headed across the parking lot to the back door of the kitchen, making his own lyrics to the song that was playing.

He was already good and toasted. *These next four hours should fly,* he thought.

He washed his hands before going to his station and emptying a bag of french fries into the deep fryer in anticipation of the small surge of customers that always came in between 8:00 and 9:00 p.m.

He looked out through the food shoot and saw a pretty lady waiting at the counter. *Wow,* he thought, *she looks just like Cheryl.* The lady looked up and made eye contact with him. Her lips were moving. Between the fan, the music, and the deep fryer, he had no idea what she was saying. *Man, I'm wasted,* he thought, wondering if Cheryl's twin was really out there at all or if he was hallucinating. Her face reddened and she became irate, gesturing wildly with her hands and pointing at him. He laughed. *This is some good shit,* he thought.

Finally Tasha rounded the corner and began yanking on his sleeve. "Hey fat boy," she said, snapping him out of it, "that lady out there's looking for you."

Oh shit! he thought, momentarily considering hiding somewhere before thinking better of it. *It IS her!* He took a deep breath before walking around to meet her.

"Can you get off early?" she asked.

He nodded, looking at her. She had been crying. Something was wrong. He hoped like hell he hadn't left any evidence lying around the apartment.

"It's CJ. He's in the Juvenile Detention Center. We need to be at the courthouse tomorrow morning at eight."

Chapter 5

The long line of boys was herded like cattle through a series of hallways, doors, and stairs. The burly staff members who escorted them laughed and talked among themselves, occasionally stopping to wave up at a camera, which apparently was the signal to pop yet another steel door. The procession continued until they reached a narrow corridor with a long bench that ran along the wall. The boys sat down and waited. Many had been through this so many times that it was merely a formality to them, an inconvenient but unavoidable part of life, like a trip to the dentist or the doctor's office. Others, like CJ, were there for the first time and had no idea what to expect. All were quiet, each lost in his own thoughts, hoping, and in many cases, praying, to be released that day. Some prayers would be answered. Some would be ignored.

CJ stared at the huge polished oak door across the hall. There were six of them in all, each about twenty steps apart. The one in front of CJ suddenly cracked open and a slick-looking guy in a suit slid into the hallway. He smiled at the line of boys who looked at him expectantly.

"Washington?" he said, surveying their faces.

A tall kid toward the end stood. The suit approached him and extended a hand.

"I'm from the public defender's office," he began while maneuvering him down the hall and out of earshot of the other boys and staff.

Eventually the other doors began to quietly peek open too, and more suits drifted in and out of the hallway in search of their respective clients. They huddled in groups of two and murmured softly. Hands were shaken, backs were patted, briefcases were popped, and papers were signed. CJ watched it all from his spot on the bench. Some of his fellow prisoners followed the suits through the big wooden doors, and then returned twenty or thirty minutes later. Many of them came back smiling but not all; one boy about his size returned crying softly. He sat down on the bench and everyone inched away from him as if whatever was causing his misfortune was contagious. CJ felt bad for him. He wondered if some bully had pushed him over the edge too.

"McCallister," a voice said, causing him to look up.

A diminutive man in a shabby brown suit held a hand out toward CJ. He had yellow protruding teeth and wore a yarmulke. CJ slowly lifted his arm to shake hands with him, wondering how the man knew who he was.

"Your eye," the little lawyer said, reading his thoughts, "makes you stick out like a turd in a punch bowl." He laughed. "I'm Joe Levin. The court has appointed me to represent you. I've already spoken to your parents." He jerked his head in the direction of the door behind him. "Nice people. You qualify for home detention. I should be able to get you out of here today. Okay?"

CJ nodded.

"This judge," he said, lowering his voice, "is sort of an asshole." He paused and adjusted the collar of CJ's uniform, centering it. "Make sure you say 'yes sir' and 'no sir' in there and," he winked, "let him get a good look at that eye. Should score us a few sympathy points, if nothing else."

"Yes sir," CJ said, suddenly grasping the seriousness of what was about to happen behind one of those gigantic doors. His freedom was at stake. And what exactly was freedom? Freedom was Andrea. Freedom was a cigarette. Freedom was steak and fried chicken and watching *Miami Vice* with his mom on the weekends. The adrenaline rush from his episode in the bathroom with Joey Barocela and the subsequent events had finally worn off. He wanted to go home.

Joe Levin straightened his tie and pressed his yarmulke down on his head. He smiled at CJ, who watched him curiously.

"I'm Jewish," he said, pointing to the yarmulke. "But I'm also losing my hair, and this," he removed the cap with a flourish, exposing a wispy, sparse section of scalp at the crown of his head, "provides some good cover."

CJ forced a smile.

"Follow me," Joe Levin said and turned toward the door. He opened it slightly and motioned for him to come through. CJ took a deep breath and entered the courtroom.

The contrast of the two worlds existing on either side of the door was staggering. One was a narrow, dimly lit space where fear and anxiety seemed to be a part of the very oxygen he breathed, where public defenders feigned concern and told corny jokes while the kid next to him cried like a baby. CJ searched his memory for anywhere he'd ever been that could rival the desperate, hopeless vibe of that hallway. A funeral home? The nursing home in Biloxi where his grandfather died? The psych wing at the Longwood Center? All were depressing in their own way, but at that moment, he believed that none of those places could match the hollow, foreboding feeling that hung over that back corridor like a thick layer of smog.

On the other side of the mammoth oak door, vibrant life pulsed. Babies cried. People craned their necks to catch a glimpse of their loved ones still waiting in the hallway. The stenographer was laughing at something another professional-looking lady was saying. The rows of seats were packed with people there to speak on behalf of their sons, nephews, little brothers, and neighbors. Even the colors of their clothes were indicative of the fact that THIS was the land of the living. This was where CJ belonged: the free world.

He spotted his mom and dad standing against the back wall. There were no vacant seats. His dad raised his chin and CJ nodded back. His mom tried to smile, but the effect was more like a nervous wince than a grin. Her eyes were red and puffy and he could see her digging her middle fingernail into the flesh of her thumb like she always did when she was worried.

"Have a seat," Levin said, ushering him into the jury box, where a few other boys waited in their baggy DJJC khakis. His public defender then walked over to a table where a tall, pale man with bushy eyebrows sat cross-legged and doodled on a yellow pad of paper. A small wooden plaque on the table read "State Attorney".

When Joe Levin reached him, he looked up briefly, then went back to his doodling. Neither offended nor perturbed by the obvious snub, CJ's lawyer continued to talk. The man stopped writing and looked over at CJ. His eyes were cold and disinterested. It took him a second to realize that the man was actually smirking. After a few moments, the man looked back up at the still-rambling Levin, shook his head, then returned to his doodling. CJ was relieved when he finally looked away. He hated stare-downs. He wondered what the man with bushy eyebrows was thinking. His understanding of the law was extremely vanilla and limited to what he learned from courtroom dramas on TV. But he knew the public defender, Joe Levin, wanted him to go home, and the state attorney, Bushy Eyebrows, wanted him to stay, and the judge, wherever he was, would have the final say. He hoped Levin was good.

CJ looked back over at his parents. His father's mouth was moving while he stared back blankly at his son. *What is he saying?* CJ wondered, attempting to read his lips. But the words kept coming. Finally he caught a glimpse of the rosary beads dangling from his father's hand and understood.

A bailiff shouted, "All rise," and a small gray man in a black robe entered through a side door. The conversation in the room quickly died off and everyone stood as he made his way up the side of his towering bench and settled into his chair.

"All right, who's up?" he said, putting on his glasses and looking over at the clerk.

"State versus Paul McCallister, Your Honor," she said.

CJ stood uncertainly and knifed his way between the knees of his fellow offenders and the wooden frame of the jury box. He walked across the courtroom to join Mr. Levin at the podium facing the judge. A ripple went through the crowd as Cheryl and Chris McCallister made their way down the aisle and came to stand behind them. CJ felt his father's large hand settle on his shoulder and was comforted by it. The judge smiled politely at them before shooting a withering glance at the state attorney.

"Are you planning on joining us, Mr. Bass?" asked the judge in a tone dripping with sarcasm.

"Sorry, Your Honor," he said, scooping up the loose papers spread across his table and hurrying to the podium opposite Joe Levin and the McCallisters.

The judge looked back at CJ. "Son, you didn't receive that while you were in custody, did you?" referring to his eye.

"No sir," CJ responded.

"Good," the judge said, obviously relieved by his answer. His gaze lingered on CJ for a few more uncomfortable moments before he shifted his focus back to the clerk.

"Case number?"

"89-6105, Your Honor."

"Mr. Bass?"

Bushy Eyebrows cleared his throat. "The defendant is charged with assault with a weapon. The incident happened on school grounds and the young victim is said to be traumatized. Due to the violent nature of the crime, the state recommends that Mr. McCallister be held in custody while more information is gathered."

The judge grunted and quickly dabbed his finger on his tongue, turning the page of a stapled packet of papers in front of him before looking over at Joe Levin. "Defense?"

"Your Honor, my client has never been in trouble before. As you can see, he has the benefit of two loving, supportive parents and a structured home life. There is much more to this case than the statement of facts listed in the arrest report. Mr. McCallister, himself, is a victim, Your Honor," Joe Levin began to pace behind the podium. "A victim of one of the most severe cases of bullying I've ever seen. Just look at his eye! He—"

"Objection!" bellowed the state attorney. His once pale face was now an angry violet, and those bushy eyebrows were almost touching. "We're not in trial!"

"Sustained," said the judge, stifling a laugh. "Mr. Levin, please just stick to the facts. We'll determine innocence or guilt at a later date. Now, how does your client plead?"

"Not guilty," said Levin.

"What does non-secure recommend?" asked the judge. Non-secure detention was a pre-trial release program for juveniles, allowing them to await their court date at home as opposed to behind bars.

"We'll accept him, Your Honor," said a female voice from behind a stack of files on a desk. "He qualifies."

"Would the parents like to say anything before I make my decision?" the judge asked.

His mom stepped forward. "Your Honor," she began, wiping a tear from her cheek, "we just ask that you have mercy on our son. We're not sure what happened, but this is completely out of character for him. He's a good boy, smart, obedient, respectful. If you let him come home today, I promise he will be present at all his future court dates." She lost it right there and began sobbing heavily. "In a suit," she managed to squeak out before his dad placed an arm around her and she sank her face into the lapel of his suit. He patted her back consolingly.

"Anyone else?" the judge asked.

"Yes sir," a voice called from the back of the courtroom.

The McCallisters, Joe Levin, the clerk, and the judge all looked in the direction of the voice. "Excuse me. Excuse me. Please step aside, sir," they heard as the crowd reluctantly parted and allowed the starched, polished, uniformed police officer through.

OH SHIT! CJ thought, feeling the walls around him begin to close in. *PRATT!*

He took large steps across the floor of the courtroom and came to a stop at the podium next to Mr. Bass. Anyone paying attention would have noticed the way he clicked his heels together upon reaching his destination. He stood ramrod straight with arms behind his back, right hand clutching left wrist.

"Your Honor, my name is Officer Steven Pratt and my post is the school where this incident took place. I am very familiar with the defendant," he said, nodding his head in the direction of CJ, "as well as the victim in this case, a fifteen-year-old boy. With regret to Mrs. McCallister, I feel it's my duty as a law enforcement officer to point out that this is not, in fact, young Mr. McCallister's first brush with trouble. Truancy has been an ongoing problem with him, and he was also caught with marijuana on school grounds a few years back."

How did he find out about that? CJ wondered, remembering his counselor's insistence that his record would be sealed upon completion of the program. He wasn't even a student at South Miami when that happened.

"In light of the seriousness of the offense, the fact that it occurred on school grounds, and the possibility of even more harm being done to the victim, I feel it's in the best interest of both boys, the school, and society that he remain in custody until this issue is resolved." He stepped back from the podium but maintained the look of concern that he held on his face throughout his speech.

The judge frowned and stared at Pratt for a few moments before removing his glasses and pinching the bridge of his nose.

"Okay," he said, "here's what we're going to do. I'm going to remand Mr. McCallister into the custody of the Juvenile Justice Center for twenty-one days. After three weeks, we'll all get back together and see where things stand. Fair enough?"

Pratt was the only one to break the stunned silence. "Yes sir."

"Good," said the judge, banging his gavel. "Who is next?"

CJ felt numb as he was escorted back across the courtroom and through the oak door that led to the holding chamber. He looked back once before the door closed and caught a glimpse of his father guiding his grief-stricken mother through the crowd. Then the door clicked shut and he fought back the tears as he found a secluded spot on the end of the bench to sit and wait.

~

The McCallisters rode home in silence. Occasionally Chris reached over and patted Cheryl's knee reassuringly. She didn't respond. She merely stared out the window at the passing city of Miami, numb and defeated.

What just happened? she asked herself. CJ's public defender seemed so certain earlier that day when they met with him. *"Don't worry,"* he had said. *". . . just a formality . . . we'll have him out of here today. I've represented literally thousands of kids. I see this type of thing all the time." LIAR!* she thought. *Who the hell appointed this guy to represent my son anyway? Maybe I should hire an attorney.* She looked sharply at her husband, who sensed her movement and glanced over at her from the driver's seat. *With what money?* she asked herself, looking resignedly through the dirty love-bug splattered window of their Corolla while newspaper hawkers, barefoot teenage fruit salesmen, and old women with buckets of flowers roamed the median peddling their wares.

They pulled past the long-abandoned guard shack at the entrance of the apartment complex and wove their way through the maze of cross- roads, past the dead brown palms that lined the streets, over the faded yellow speed bumps, and into the heart of the Southwinds. Suddenly it was 1984 and a ten-year-old CJ surged past the passenger window of their car on his blue Huffy, waving enthusiastically and shouting, "Watch this, Momma!" She smiled wistfully as he raced ahead, rocking his bike from side to side, gaining momentum, before hitting a speed bump and going airborne. He landed shakily and skidded to a stop in the nearby grass, smiling his gap-tooth grin as the car rolled by; then he quickly evaporated back into the past. She smiled sadly at the memory. *Why would anyone want to lock up such a sweet little boy in a cage?* she wondered for the hundredth time.

They pulled to a stop in front of Building C. Three young girls were in the parking lot skipping rope and they waved to her as she got out of the car. She waved back halfheartedly. Her husband had just opened his car door and was in the process of prying his large body from the small sedan when the ringing started. There was no mistaking the ear-piercing shrill of their downstairs phone. *CJ!* Cheryl's mind screamed. She immediately burst into a full sprint toward their patio door and overlooked the cement parking bumper, which sent her sprawling across the asphalt, scraping her hands and knees and ruining her pantyhose. Before her shocked husband could come to her aid, she was back on her feet and flying toward the apartment. She flung the patio door open, impervious to the bloody handprint she left on the knob, and blitzed the front door like an outside linebacker. She barely broke stride to swoop her hand down inside the flowerpot before coming away cleanly with the spare key, spinning on her heel, and plunging it into the keyhole. She pushed the door open, rounded the corner, and knocked over a chair en route to the phone, snatching it forcefully from the cradle and answering loudly before the receiver was even against her ear.

"Hello!" she said desperately, only to be met by a dial tone. She had missed him. She quietly set the phone back in its cradle and sat down on the kitchen floor to cry. She was suddenly aware of the blood on her hands and knees, the pain settling in and overtaking the initial surge of adrenaline. She heard the door close and her husband's footsteps approaching. He stood in front of her and held out a hand, deep lines of worry etched across his bald, sweaty head. He opened his mouth to say something just as the phone sprang back to life with its violent fire alarm clanging, startling them both. Her arm shot out and snatched it up.

"Hello! CJ?"

"Is this the McCallister residence?" a female voice asked.

"Yes," she said dejectedly, "this is Cheryl McCallister."

"My name is Maria Salazar. I'm calling about Paul. He's in my Spanish class. I had planned on calling you about a possible conference before all of this happened. I'm still very concerned about him and I'd like to speak with you in person if I may."

Cheryl looked up at Chris, who was watching her with a questioning look on his face before she sighed and said, "Sure. When?"

"Is Saturday around 5:00 p.m. okay?"

"Yes," said Cheryl, again looking at her husband.

"Do you mind if I come there?"

"That's fine," said Cheryl. "We live in the Southwinds Apartments. 318C."

"I'll be there," she said, then hesitated. "Mrs. McCallister, I'm truly sorry about your son."

"Thank you," Cheryl managed to choke out before the floodgates opened. She didn't even bother to hang up the phone. She just laid it on the floor and allowed the tears to overtake her. Chris tried to help her up, but she resisted his efforts by inching under the kitchen table. She lay in the fetal position on the linoleum floor as her body convulsed with sobs.

When she was a little girl she imagined she would grow up to marry a strong, handsome, hardworking man and raise kids who were happy, safe, and had all the things that she and her sisters missed out on as children in rural southwest Alabama. The fact that her husband was unreliable, irresponsible, and a drug user was depressing, but the idea of her only son spending the next twenty-one days in what amounted to a juvenile jail was unbearable. As she lay there crying on the floor, a single repeating thought spun continuously around her mind like a Hindu mantra: She had failed CJ.

Life wasn't supposed to be like this.

~

The ragtag group of teenage boys shuffled haphazardly down the sidewalk just as the morning sun began to spray the eastern sky with streaks of purple and orange. They were dressed in navy blue jumpsuits with the number eight stenciled above the chest pocket. Across the courtyard, the gray uniforms of Unit 2 were exiting the chow hall and making their way back to their dormitory.

The Dade Juvenile Detention Center did a superb job at camouflaging reality. There was no razor wire surrounding the property, there wasn't even a fence. The prisoners were confined by a large, concrete, rectangular configuration of dorms, classrooms, and other buildings like the chow hall and the gym. The walls were high, flat, and unclimbable. Each side was adorned with murals of everything from beach scenes to civil rights leaders. In the center was a sprawling green courtyard where the inmates were allowed to hang out in the evenings and on weekends. But the inmates were never referred to as "inmates." For some reason, here, even the vernacular was altered in a feeble attempt to file down the pointy edges of truth. So the inmates were called "clients," the cell-blocks were known as "units," the cells themselves were simply "rooms," and the guards, who all wore jeans and t-shirts, were referred to as "staff." CJ wasn't fooled. This was a jail, he was a prisoner, those were guards, and freedom lay shimmering just over that wall. Calling a shark a goldfish wouldn't change the reality of its identity, nor would it lessen the danger it presented.

The boys from Unit 8 entered the double doors of the chow hall and formed a line that wrapped around walls. They moved slowly along as each boy came to the stainless steel serving line and grabbed a tray. The hair-netted cafeteria ladies dipped their ladles deep into pans of oatmeal and eggs, heaping generous portions on the passing trays followed by two pieces of toast, a frozen, unspreadable dab of butter, a cup of juice, and a small carton of milk. The boys left the serving line in single file and were directed by a staff member to a vacant row of tables where they broke off in groups of four and sat down to eat. Talking, trading food, and switching tables were all strictly prohibited.

CJ ate quickly, then settled back in his chair to scan the other tables in search of a familiar face. There was none. Three other units shared the chow hall with CJ's Unit 8, each identifiable by the color of their uniforms. Unit 4 wore orange, Unit 7 wore brown, and Unit 9 wore a faded, washed-out black. Juvenile Hall consisted of a total of twelve units and each had its own color.

"Unit 8! Pick 'em up!" said Mr. Royce, the staff member who worked midnights in CJ's dorm. He was jet black with a bald head and a goatee. He wore a gold hoop in his left ear like Michael Jordan, military fatigues, and a tight black t-shirt.

The young men from Unit 8 slowly filed out of the chow hall, dumping their trays as they left. They lined up on the sidewalk and waited for Mr. Royce to say "Go." Birds lined the top of the wall just above the mural of Dr. Martin Luther King and watched the boys curiously as they walked by. Occasionally one would burst into flight, darting quickly over their heads, causing the others to chirp excitedly. CJ couldn't help but wonder if the birds were aware that they were hanging out in a jail.

Once they returned to their unit, the doors were popped and each boy was expected to go to his room and shut the door behind him, which automatically locked. Ten minutes later Mr. Royce made his final round before shift change to ensure that each door was secure. They would be locked down for an hour, then the doors would pop and they would line up for school. After school was lunch, then gym class, then another hour of lockdown during shift change, then dinner, then a couple of hours on the yard, then three hours of free time in the unit to shower, play cards, and watch TV, then a snack, and then they would be locked down for the night. The next day they'd wake up and do it all over again. The only difference between weekends and weekdays was that school was substituted by visitation for those who actually had family out there who cared enough to come visit them. Many didn't. Visiting hours were from 9:00 a.m. to 11:00 a.m. Units 1 through 6 went on Saturday, and 7 through 12 on Sunday.

The last time CJ had spoken to his mom, she had assured him that both she and his dad would be there. He was looking forward to it. It would be nice to relax around people he loved and trusted for a little while. It seemed as though everyone he made eye contact with in this place greeted him with a hard look, but he had managed to avoid trouble so far by keeping to himself. He had sixteen days left until he went back to court. He learned from listening to other conversations that twenty-one days was usually the longest anyone stayed except for those who were waiting to go up the road. "Up the road" meant one of the actual prison-like juvenile camps such as Chobee or Dozier. CJ doubted he qualified for those places since he had no criminal record. He was almost positive he'd be going home in less than two and a half weeks. He just hoped he could make it to that date without incident.

In spite of all the structure and the college campus grounds with manicured grass and colorful paintings on the walls, the juvenile detention center was a violent, scary place. In his first days he'd witnessed five fistfights, plus gang confrontations, jumpings, initiations, and retaliations. Many of the staff were abusive as well and those who weren't were simply indifferent. He'd even heard rumors of rapes. That thought made him shudder. He quickly turned his mind to memories of Andrea and shut out the fear. *Sixteen days,* he thought, flopping down on his bunk and staring up at the vent above his door, *I can do this.*

~

Cheryl McCallister looked at herself in the bathroom mirror. She was wearing a faded blue t-shirt that said "Forty Isn't Old . . . If You're a Tree" across the front in white peeling letters. CJ had bought it for her two years ago on her birthday. She smiled at the memory. The face smiling back at her looked haggard and worn and a lot older than forty-two. She sighed and pulled her hair back in a scrunchy before turning off the light and heading downstairs.

It was five o'clock. CJ's teacher would be there any minute. She was almost to the foot of the stairs when she noticed her husband. He was sitting in the living room chair, one leg over the other in one of his four-pocketed Cuban shirts and black polyester pants from the "Big and Tall" shop. A Camel non-filter burned slowly in the ashtray while the flickering images of a black-and-white movie illuminated the side of his fleshy face. It was then that she noticed he was wearing a pair of large, square-framed tortoiseshell bifocals. In their seventeen years of marriage, she had never known him to wear glasses. She wasn't even aware there were any in their apartment.

"What's with the glasses?" she asked, wrinkling her nose as she rounded his chair to snuff out the still smoking cigarette in the ashtray.

"Impressions," he stated simply, cocking his head to the side and gracing her with a scholarly look.

She rolled her eyes and walked into the kitchen. *He's high again,* she thought. There was a knock at the door. Her husband immediately stood up, brushed off his shirt and pants, and moved to answer it. She joined him.

"Mrs. Salazar?" she asked, opening the door.

"Maria," the woman corrected with a smile. She was a pretty, late thirtyish Latina dressed in espadrilles, jeans, and a t-shirt.

"I'm Cheryl and this is my husband, Chris." Señora Salazar bowed her head slightly and Chris nodded. "Please come in."

"I love your home," she said politely, before getting down to business. "May I sit?" She did not wait for an answer. The McCallisters joined her at the kitchen table.

"I'm here," she began, "because your son is at a crossroads. He was already exhibiting all the warning signs before this last incident occurred. One of the privileges of teaching young teens is that occasionally you get to make a difference in someone's life and witness them turn back from the brink and go on to find success and happiness. Of course, that's a double-edged sword because once you've done all you can, you're forced to stand idly by while they continue to spiral out of control and self-destruct. The hardest part is seeing them on street corners or the evening news or worse, reading their obituaries." She paused momentarily and leveled her gaze at each of them, allowing the weight of what she had just said to settle in. "I don't want that to happen to your son."

Cheryl was immediately hooked. "What can we do?" she asked breathlessly, leaning forward in anticipation of Señora Salazar's answer.

Chris reached for his Camels and fired one up, blowing a thick stream of smoke up toward the light.

"The number one thing is to spend time with him, pay attention to his friends, and monitor his coming and going closely. Be firm with him when he begins veering off course and show pride in him whenever he does well. Prisons are full of young men whose parents were 'their friends' growing up. He needs discipline. I doubt he'll be returning to South Miami, but whatever school he ends up attending, make it a point to encourage him and motivate him to learn. I'm sure you already know this, but your son is a brilliant kid with tons of potential."

Cheryl took notes in shorthand, scribbling furiously as the woman spoke, while her husband looked over her shoulder at the black-and-white movie still playing in the living room.

"If he is experimenting with drugs or being bullied, as he was at South Miami, or acting out or skipping class or whatever, stay on him and with him until he works through the problem and, believe me, he will. Be firm but fair, and above all—"

"Are you done yet?" Chris blurted, still staring into the living room.

"Honey!" Cheryl exclaimed.

"Excuse me?" Señora Salazar asked.

"All CJ needs," Chris McCallister said simply, "is love."

Señora Salazar sat there a moment longer before finally shrugging and saying, "Okay." She stood silently. "I'll let myself out."

Cheryl glared at her husband as the front door closed.

~

The McCallisters sat in the packed cafeteria and struggled to hear each other over the noise. CJ was on one side of the table and his parents were sitting across from him. Staff walked up and down the aisles smiling at the visitors, occasionally stopping to joke with a family before moving on. Many of the staff were from the same communities as the clients and their families. Many of the clients were the sons, little brothers, and nephews of big-time dope boys who ran their neighborhoods with iron fists and could order hits the way other people order pizza. Needless to say the staff was extremely respectful on visiting days.

CJ's father spent most of the visit looking around at the other visitors while his mom leaned as far forward as possible.

"Are you eating enough?" she asked.

He nodded and smiled.

"Do you share your room?"

"No ma'am."

"What's school like?"

"Fun. They've got computers."

"Your eye looks good," she said, reaching out and stroking his face.

"C'mon, Mom!" He looked around to see if anyone was watching.

"Sorry," she said, drawing her hand back and smiling at him. His eye did look good. The black and purple had faded to a light yellow. It would probably be completely gone in a few more days.

"Has Andrea called?" he asked.

"No," she said, shaking her head. "Why don't you call her?"

"Can't," he answered vaguely, lost in his own thoughts. He could only use the phone after 7:00 p.m. and her mom was always home by then.

"I like your haircut, son," his father interjected. "You look like a Marine."

Since the fourth grade, CJ had always worn his hair the same way: long in the back, short on the sides, spiky up top, with bangs. But when the barber came to Unit 8, CJ impulsively decided to let it go and requested a No. 1. Long hair drew attention and made him stand out. That was the last thing he needed. It felt strange for him to touch his stubbly head, but he didn't regret his decision. He just needed to blend in for a couple of weeks, then he could leave this shithole and never return.

"Time to wrap it up!" a voice bellowed from the front of the room.

"Already?" his mom protested, looking around.

Families were rising from their seats and hugging their loved ones before slowly filing toward the front.

His father hugged him and said, "Pray to Saint Jude. He'll help you."

His mother pushed his dad out of the way and embraced him. He could feel her shoulders moving as she sobbed.

"Be good," she said as his father grabbed her hand and began gently pulling her toward the exit.

"Clients, have a seat," said a heavyset staff member in a t-shirt that read Newport across the front in big green letters.

Damn, CJ thought as he sat down, *I wish I could have a Newport.*

"Did Mommy come and see her little boy today?" asked a voice from across the aisle. The question was delivered in a tone reserved for babies and small children. It dripped with sarcasm. CJ slowly turned toward the source, hoping it was directed at someone else. It wasn't. There, at the next table, languishing in their chairs with their arms slung lazily over the backs and their uniform collars popped, were two black dudes and a Chico he recognized from his unit. They were all laughing at him.

He knew they were trouble the first night he moved to Unit 8. After his ordeal with the Barocela twins, CJ considered himself an expert on bullies. These three definitely qualified. The biggest one, Duke, was obviously the leader. He looked like a man among boys whenever they lined up for school or chow. He was jet black with a hi-top fade and his teeth were all gold as far as CJ could tell. His muscles bulged from his uniform, and even when he was laughing and smiling there was always a heavy undercurrent of danger and violence that surrounded him. His nastiness was especially evident on the basketball court, where he was constantly shooting bows, hard fouling, and even punching opponents in the face when he got frustrated.

The other two were commonly thought of as Duke's lackeys, but CJ didn't underestimate them. He had overheard a kid from Unit 4 at school say that Kiki, the Hispanic one, had stabbed someone in the face with a pen his last time in and that was why pens were now banned on the units. The other one was named Pep, but CJ didn't know much about him other than the fact he thought he could rap and was mistaken.

"You smoke, cracker?" Duke asked him.

CJ hesitated, measuring his words. "What, weed?" he finally asked, wishing like hell Rudy was with him.

"Or cigarettes," Duke said. "Whatever you want."

"I don't have any money," CJ finally said, hoping that would close the discussion.

"Your mama does," he shot back. "She could slide it to my brother next visit or just drop it by the crib, or," he leaned further back in his chair and laced his fingers behind his head, "you could just work it off in here."

CJ was lost. He could tell he missed a joke by the way Kiki and Pep burst out laughing. He had no idea what was so funny or how he could possibly work for cigarettes, but what he DID know was that these guys were trouble and even though he was dying for a smoke, getting involved with them would be a mistake.

"I'm all right," CJ said, "thanks anyway."

"Unit 8, on the wall!" yelled Mr. Dupree, bailing CJ out.

The boys in the dark blue uniforms were quickly patted down before being escorted out of the chow hall, across the courtyard, and back to Unit 8. CJ made sure to hang back in the line in order to put some space between himself and Duke's little crew. He eyed them warily as they strode confidently across the yard.

The words his father whispered in his ear before his parents left sprang into his mind. *"Pray to Saint Jude. He'll help you."* Catholics had saints for everything. Saint Anthony helped you find shit, Saint Christopher helped travelers, and Saint Jude was the patron saint of hopeless causes. CJ looked ahead once more and saw the huge muscles rippling along Duke's shoulders as he walked. He impulsively made the sign of the cross and swallowed hard.

Saint Jude, he began, *I've got a problem.*

CJ was sitting in the grass with his back against the Unit 8 wall watching a soccer game in the courtyard. The Mexicans and Colombians were playing the Haitians and Jamaicans. It was a brutal game where legitimate battles for the ball, or even position, sporadically erupted into flurries of blows which flared up and quickly faded throughout the course of the game. The goals were marked by balled-up t-shirts ten paces apart. There were no out-of-bounds markers, meaning that sometimes heated competitions for the ball drifted as far as the basketball court or the sidewalk by the chow hall. It was a good game. The dreads had just tied it up, two to two, on a pass that got behind a bulky Colombian defender and was then powered through the Mexican goalie along with a lowered shoulder that sent him sprawling in the grass.

"Damn!" said a voice from CJ's left side.

He snapped his head sharply in that direction, instantly alert. The voice came from a black kid about CJ's size wearing the dark blue uniform of Unit 8. CJ remembered him from the hallway behind the courtroom. He was the one crying, but he didn't realize they were on the same unit. He was probably trying to keep a low profile.

"This is a good game," he said.

"Real good," CJ agreed.

"You play?"

"A little. You?"

"Nah," he said, sitting down next to him. "I'm Rick." He held out a hand.

CJ accepted it. "I'm CJ."

So at dusk on that spring evening in 1989, while the sound of bouncing basketballs echoed off the high walls of the yard, an alliance was formed.

Chapter 6

The Metrobus roared down 67th Avenue, peppering cars, pedestrians, and the occasional cyclist with thick, black diesel smoke. The ride from the Southwinds to the intersection closest to Wendy's was only about twenty minutes, but Chris McCallister had recently begun to relish this part of the day. The thunderous rumble of the bus engine relaxed him and he got a slight voyeuristic thrill from looking down through the tinted windows into people's cars. As he neared his stop he stood to grab the thick cable that ran down both sides of the bus. He yanked it twice and was rewarded by a "ding" signaling the bus driver to pull over at the next stop. When the bus slowed to a halt, he made his way to the front and nodded at the driver before stepping down onto the curb. The doors shut behind him followed by a hydraulic hiss as the bus rose up and rumbled back into traffic.

Fat raindrops began to fall as he made his way through the parking lot. They momentarily sizzled, then evaporated into the hot asphalt like someone flicking water against a cast-iron frying pan. He stepped under the shelter of the awning and fired up a Camel, his last before break. Tasha was already inside and hard at work wiping down the trademark newspaper print tables that filled the dining area. She looked pissed. She wouldn't even make eye contact with him. He hoped she wasn't fighting with her boyfriend again. She was his only connection and when they had these little spats, his stash suffered. He flicked his cigarette out into the rain and swung the door open.

"Good afternoon, my love," he declared with arms slightly raised and extended as if waiting on a hug. "Did you miss me?"

"Yo-Yo wanna see you," she said.

"What's up?"

She only shrugged and moved on to the next section, wiping fiercely. He put his visor on and walked around the counter, waving at the day shift prep cook as he made his way through the kitchen to the office in the back. He knocked on the wooden door and waited.

"Come on," he heard Yolanda say.

He opened the door and stepped inside the small room. He was hoping this little meeting was to inform him he had been selected as Employee of the Month—Cheryl would love that—but one look at her troubled face shattered any hope he had about receiving some good news.

"Sit down," she said.

He glanced at the frail little chair in front of her desk and shook his head. "I'll stand."

"I don't know how to say this," she began. "The regional manager called today. He wants two positions cut, one on each shift. The most recent hires. That means you . . ." Her voice trailed off.

He nodded and removed his visor, setting it on her desk. He stared numbly at the red "Where's the Beef?" pin on the bill. His wife was gonna shit. No wonder Tasha wouldn't look at him.

"It's been a pleasure knowing you and working with you," she said. "I've got your number. If a position opens, and you still want it, you'll be the first person I call." She got up and came around the desk, impulsively wrapping her arms around his ample body.

"I'm sorry, Chris," she said, mumbling the words into his chest.

"It's all right. I was getting too fat around all them fries, anyway."

"Is your wife gonna leave you?"

"Nah," he said, reaching for the door, "we need each other."

"Bye, Chris."

"Bye." He closed the door behind him and headed for the kitchen exit. How was it that he, a former bank president and Rotary Club member, could not even hold down a job at a fast-food joint? His pride was in tatters. He ducked out the back door and stepped out into the rain, grateful that no one stopped him to say good-bye. He walked slowly back to the bus stop on 67th, looking forward to what awaited him under the couch back at the apartment.

~

Cheryl McCallister sat at the red light on the corner of Bird Road and 67th Avenue, restlessly tapping her fingers against the steering wheel. She hoped she hadn't already missed CJ's call. He normally called between 8:00 and 8:30 p.m. She glanced impatiently at the small watch on her wrist. It was 8:10.

She looked over at the small vase of white daises propped carefully against the passenger seat and smiled. They were from her boss and his wife. A flicker of a smile crossed her face when she thought of the words that were neatly printed across the small card in perfect English.

> Dear Cheryl,
>
> Even though we got off to a rocky start, I just wanted you to know that it's been a pleasure working with you so far. You are an asset, not only to me as an assistant, but also to the Essex Hotel Corporation as a whole.
>
> I know you're going through some tough times at the moment. Please know that *my* family is praying for *yours.*
>
> Love,
>
> Jose Ramos

He had underlined the words "Dear" and "Love." She thought back to their first meeting almost two weeks earlier when he explained to her that Cubans didn't use those words as liberally as Americans, that they were reserved for those people in their lives who were truly special. She remembered crying in the closet the day Brett Wagner had let it slip that Jose Ramos was going to be the new general manager. She had almost resigned then and there. She was glad she didn't. Jose Ramos was strict, intense, and a no-nonsense dictator when it came to running the hotel, but he was also proving to be fair, generous, and kind. Mizell had never given her flowers. It felt good to be appreciated.

A barrage of heavy raindrops suddenly exploded against the windows of the Corolla just as the light turned green. She flipped the windshield wipers on and accelerated into the storm, focusing intently on the wet brake lights of the car in front of her.

By the time she reached the Southwinds it was raining so hard that she could barely see ten feet in front of the car, even with the high beams on. She slowly made her way through the labyrinthine complex with its multitude of speed bumps before finally arriving at the designated parking lot for Building C.

She turned the car engine off and reached for her purse and the flowers in the passenger seat while mentally preparing herself for the inevitable dousing she was about to receive. She took a deep breath and stepped out into the rain, slamming the car door behind her. She walked quickly but carefully through the parking lot. The lacerations on her hands and knees were not yet healed and served as reminders of her last attempt at running on this same surface when it wasn't raining.

She was drenched by the time she reached their patio door, which had been left open and was crashing repeatedly against the wall in the high wind and rain. She shut it firmly behind her and darted across the porch to the shelter provided by the balcony overhang. It was then that she noticed all the lights were on and . . . *was that Elvis's "Suspicious Minds" she heard on the stereo?* Chris was at work and wouldn't be home until after midnight. Someone's in our apartment, she thought, holding her breath as she inserted the key. She turned the knob and pushed slightly; the living room light and Elvis instantly filled the small crack. She peeked inside and there, on the couch, naked and oblivious, sat her husband.

She walked in and shut the door behind her, noting the tin foil and empty Pepsi bottle on the coffee table as she took the four quick steps to the record player and silenced Elvis with one long *scrraaatch!*

Chris McCallister looked over at his wife, who stood there dripping on the living room carpet holding a bouquet of flowers. The beginnings of a smile tugged at the corners of his dry mouth and slowly spread across his face before reaching the twin lanterns of his bloodshot eyes.

"Are those for *me?*" he asked hazily.

~

Rick Robinson was far from a pussy. The rumors of him crying in court were whispered behind his back everywhere he went, accompanied by snickering and slick remarks, but he ignored them. He really didn't give a fuck what other people said about him. He had way bigger problems than that. In the courtroom, his mother had told him, via his attorney, that his oldest brother had been shot in the back and was in critical condition at Jackson Memorial. He really didn't understand where the tears came from; he had hated Ty his whole life. Maybe it was seeing his mother looking broken and old in that courtroom, or maybe somewhere in his subconscious he knew there was a high probability that he too would someday experience the horror of hot lead penetrating his own flesh, or maybe the reason was simpler than that. Maybe deep inside he truly loved Ty despite the uncountable beatings he suffered at his hands, not to mention the attempted drownings, the loaded pistols against his head, and the numerous times he was humiliated by his big brother in front of his friends and especially the girls in their Perrine neighborhood. He wasn't sure where the tears came from or why, but a bunch of dumb motherfuckers in juvie gossiping about him were the least of his worries. *Fuck what they thought.*

Rick was the youngest of three children born to Alicia and Ray Robinson. He had never met his father, who was in the county jail when he was born and was now somewhere in the Florida prison system serving life. People were always sympathetic toward him when they heard about his father, but they were really astonished when they learned that he truly didn't give a shit. It wasn't that he resented his father's absence, it was just that he had never experienced his *presence* and it was hard for him to miss something he never had. He was indifferent.

His mother had never remarried or even dated as far as Rick knew. He had heard people say it was because she was still in love with Ray, but the truth was that he had beaten her so badly and so often that once he was finally gone for good, she felt no desire to sign up for that again. Plus, between raising three boys, driving the school bus, and volunteering at church, her life was full.

His oldest brother, Ty, was twenty years old and had been selling dope on their block for as long as Rick could remember. He was constantly fighting anyone and everyone. It didn't matter to Ty, especially when he was drinking and snorting. It wasn't surprising that someone had shot him. At all. The only question was why? Dope? Dice? Money? A woman? All Rick knew was that whoever did it better hope that Ty didn't make it out of the hospital because if that happened, there was gonna be blood.

His other brother, Mario, was an athlete. At seventeen, he was already an inch taller than Ty at six-foot-four and could flat-out fly on the football field. He was a junior at Palmetto who played wide receiver and defensive end. His best 40-time was a 4.37, but he played even faster, causing scouts from all over the country to occupy the stands on Friday nights.

Rick was nothing like Ty or Mario. He had no interest in selling dope and he sucked at sports. Mario used to tease him about being the "mailman's baby" because he was short and red while both his brothers were dark skinned and well over six feet tall. Rick's thing was cars. When he was eleven, his neighbor, Sap, started bringing around a Chico named Nica. One night Rick smoked a joint with them and ended up tagging along on a mission to a nearby apartment complex. He looked on in amazement as Nica disabled a car alarm, entered the vehicle, and had it running in under five minutes. Rick was hooked ever since. He quickly absorbed and digested everything Nica knew, then improved upon his methods. All he really needed was a dent puller and a flathead screwdriver and any car could be his in a couple of minutes. His first splack was an I-Roc, but within a year he had easily stolen twenty-five cars, and by the time he was fourteen, he was jumping them for a grand apiece, minimum, at a chop shop in Homestead.

Although he had been in numerous high-speed chases, he had never been caught. Until now. And he would have gotten away this time if that hero hadn't tripped and tackled him when he jumped out. Being in juvie sucked, but having to crash the Buick Grand National he had been scoping for six months was agony.

~

The clients on Unit 8 were having *free time.* A group of boys sat on plastic chairs positioned loosely around a television set watching *Diff'rent Strokes. "What comes from the sea, shall return to the sea!" Arnold announced in a loud, ostentatious voice before dropping a dead goldfish into the toilet and flushing it.*

CJ and Rick loved *Diff'rent Strokes* and had been watching it together every weeknight since they became friends.

"Is Andrea finer than Kimberly?" Rick asked, referring to Willis and Arnold's adopted sister.

"Seriously?" CJ asked. "Way finer, man."

"Finer than Lisa-Lisa?"

"Oh yeah."

"Brooke Shields?"

"Definitely."

"Janet Jackson?"

"No contest."

"Come on now. Ain't nobody finer than Janet!"

"Andrea is."

"How 'bout Karyn White?"

"Who?" said CJ, looking over at him.

"Never mind. Sometimes I forget you still just a white boy." A few of the other boys sitting around them laughed at their conversation.

Suddenly the TV screen was obstructed by Duke's gigantic back as he changed the channel. He then sauntered over to the spade table where his homeboys awaited him.

Before CJ could stop him, Rick mumbled "fuck that" and switched the channel back to *Diff'rent Strokes.* The tension in the room was instantly palpable. Duke looked back over his shoulder as if someone had just called his mom a whore. He shot up from the card table and moved quickly to the TV area, kicking chairs out of the way as he went. The staff member in the bubble looked up from his phone call, saw that it was Duke, and spun his chair in the other direction, intentionally not seeing.

"Who touched the TV?" Duke growled.

"I did," said Rick, attempting to stand, but before the words were even out of his mouth, Duke slapped him so hard that he crashed over three chairs and landed on the carpet in a dazed heap.

"You want some, cracker?" Duke asked CJ.

CJ looked away.

"I thought so."

Mr. Dupree came out of the bubble and announced it was time to lock down for the night. "Everything cool?" he asked Duke with a smile.

"Yeah," Duke said, nodding over at Rick, who was slowly getting up off the carpet.

"All right. Let's go. Let's go. Let's go!" Dupree said. "Everybody to their rooms. Lock the doors behind you. Bedtime, fellas. Let's go!"

CJ slowly got up and made his way to his room, trying not to look at Rick still struggling to stand over by the TV. When he got there he softly clicked the door shut behind him; the locking mechanism slammed home loudly, echoing the irrevocable finality of his actions. It was official. He was a coward. Again.

He sat on his bunk for close to an hour, belittling himself for his treasonous actions. The lights went out and he barely even noticed. *You're a bitch,* he told himself. *Rick stood up and you left him hanging.* CJ wished he could get a do-over, maybe slow things down a little. A knock on his door interrupted his thoughts.

"Check this out, *Blanco,*" said a muffled voice.

CJ got up and walked to the door. Kiki was smiling through the Plexiglas, holding a broom. "Look," he said, motioning to a supply closet across the hall.

CJ saw Pep holding Rick's arms behind his back while Duke smashed his fist into his abdomen and nuts over and over. Finally, Mr. Dupree walked over and stopped them. Shifts were changing soon and they all needed to be locked in their rooms. Duke laid into him once more before they finally dragged him from the closet to his room, dumped him in his bunk, and shut the door behind them. They all laughed and high-fived each other before heading off to their own rooms.

"You next," Kiki said, giggling and walking away. His door slammed behind him and Unit 8 was finally silent. Except for the bass drum pounding in CJ's chest.

~

The following morning was uneventful. The doors popped and the clients trickled out of their rooms to line up for breakfast. CJ was surprised when Rick fell in behind him. Duke and his minions were up front as usual. They walked across the courtyard at dawn, passing the exiting Unit 3 as they entered the chow hall and wrapped around the wall.

Since Duke, Pep, and Kiki were at the front of the line, they were already seated and eating when CJ and Rick walked past them carrying their trays.

"How's your stomach feelin', bitch?" Duke said to Rick as they passed. "We gonna fuck up your little white homegirl tonight." The table erupted into a chorus of laughter at his statement, causing a patrolling staff member two rows over to bark, "Shut the fuck up!"

CJ and Rick sat down to eat. There were four to a table, two facing two. Unfortunately, every time the kid in front of CJ lowered his head to slurp his oatmeal, he opened up a direct line of vision between CJ and a scowling Duke. He couldn't even eat. He nibbled on a piece of toast, removed his milk, and slid the rest of his tray over to Rick, who looked at him like he was crazy.

"You sick or something?" Rick asked.

CJ shook his head.

"You sure, man?"

CJ gave a curt nod, still trying to ignore the intimidating baleful stare of Duke, two tables in front of him, while his friend made short work of the extra food. Rick was acting as if last night never happened. *If he's pissed off,* CJ thought, *he's doing a kick-ass job at hiding it.*

"Unit 8, pick 'em up!" a staff member yelled, just as Rick was shoveling the last spoonful of eggs into his mouth.

"Bet that up," he said, sliding the tray back to CJ and rising from the table.

The line of boys from Unit 8 exited the chow hall and walked back to their dormitory. Once inside, each drifted to his own room and within five minutes every door was locked for shift change.

~

CJ sat quietly at his desk, converting fractions to decimals while his teacher nodded off and his classmates talked excitedly about the heavyweight champion of the world, Mike Tyson, and his latest knock-out victim.

An open *Tiger Beat* magazine was slapped down on his desk showing a pretty light-skinned black woman under a caption that read: "She's not your superwoman" in bold letters. He looked up to see Rick standing above his desk.

"Karyn White," Rick said.

"Oh."

"Well? Who's finer?" Rick asked, picking up on their conversation from the night before.

"Andrea," CJ said, smiling for the first time that day, "all day long."

"Now I know you full of shit, white boy," Rick said, laughing and sitting down in the desk next to him.

CJ stopped smiling and looked at his friend. "Last night was fucked up."

Rick stared at him for a moment. "Yeah."

"You don't seem hurt. Or fazed."

Rick looked over at the snoring teacher, who was now drooling on his shirt sleeve. "My oldest brother, Ty, is in the hospital," he confided. "Shot in the spine. Doctors are sayin' he'll never walk again."

"Damn, man, I'm sorry."

"Oh, I hate the motherfucker," Rick stated calmly. "He's been dish-raggin' me my whole life. Punchin' me, kickin' me, chokin' me out, cuttin' me, pointin' pistols at me, lockin' me in closets. Fuck Ty!" he said, a storm flaring in his eyes.

CJ was speechless.

"But as bad as I hate my brother, he kinda helped me out in a way, cuz after years of dealin' with his crazy ass, that bullshit in the closet last night with that faggot-ass Duke wasn't nothin'. I ate every single one of those powder puffs he was throwin' and slept like a baby."

"I feel like shit for not standing up with you," CJ said, seeing his friend differently now after hearing about his brother. "I just froze up."

"You good, C," he said, before leaning toward him, "but you better not freeze up tonight. They comin'. You ready?"

CJ sagged. He wasn't ready at all. He was scared shitless. This was a completely different situation than the twins at South Miami. There was nowhere to run and nowhere to turn. He was trapped.

"Well, whatever happens," Rick said, reaching to grab his magazine, "I got your back."

CJ watched him walk back across the carpeted hallway to his own class area. "Thanks, man," he mumbled, too low for him to hear. CJ again wished he had Rudy with him. He was grateful to have someone like Rick on his side, but he was only five-feet-six at the most and couldn't weigh more than 120 pounds. Duke was a giant by comparison. Even his do boys, Kiki and Pep, outweighed them both, and it wasn't like there was any Mace lying around to even the odds. The worst part was that even the staff seemed to be friendly with Duke—at least Mr. Dupree was—and allowed shit like last night to happen. That much was clear. So going to a staff member wasn't an option, not that it ever was anyway. Although CJ was relatively green to institution life, he instinctively understood that snitching was weak and cowardly. He'd rather be smashed by Duke and his little posse than be labeled a rat.

He'd fight if he had to, he just didn't want to.

~

"Attention in the Unit, attention in the Unit," a voice said over the PA system. "Report to your rooms and lock down for shift change."

The boys were still filing in through the large steel door with a black "8" stenciled over it when the announcement came. They were talking animatedly about a fight they had just witnessed in the gym between some kids in Unit 2. CJ missed the beginning, but he'd never forget how it ended. The two boys were rolling around on the floor of the weight cage, knocking over benches and crashing against mirrors, neither gaining an advantage until the bigger kid finally pinned the smaller one on his back and began battering his face with blow after blow spurred on by the cheers of encouragement from the bloodthirsty spectators.

Then an Hispanic kid about CJ's size stepped through the crowd, grabbed a twenty-five-pound dumbbell off the rack, and buried it in the bigger kid's head, crushing his skull. Fight over. The crowd became instantly silent as the would-be winner's body collapsed atop his still struggling opponent and the mysterious Hispanic kid melted back into the crowd. Moments later, three staff members came pushing their way through. Two of them went rigid at the sight of the grisly scene on the floor while the other made a beeline for the emergency phone on the wall. It was obviously too late.

That incident only served to heighten the gravity of CJ's own situation. This wasn't the Southwinds or South Miami or even the

Longwood Center, which he actually thought was pretty dangerous at the time. This was the Dade Juvenile Detention Center, home to some of the most brutal, violent teenagers Miami had to offer. Mr. Dupree would be working next shift and Duke and his boys would, no doubt, be coming for him. Time was running out.

"Hey, white boy," said a deep voice from behind him, just as he was entering his room. He already knew who it was. He turned slowly to face Duke.

"Check this out," he said with a smile that revealed at least sixteen gold teeth that were dingy and unpolished from months of using state toothpaste. "We ain't gotta go through all this bullshit."

CJ's hopes soared. Maybe he wouldn't have to fight, after all.

"All you really gotta do," he said, grabbing his dick through his uniform pants, "is suck on this for a minute and we even."

"Fuck you," CJ said, turning back toward his door when suddenly Duke's size-12 Nike caught him squarely in the ass and sent him flying into the back wall of his room. Duke slammed the door shut behind him, but CJ could still hear the entire unit laughing. He got up off the floor and walked slowly back to his cell door. He looked out of the Plexiglas across the unit and saw Rick staring at him through the window of his own door. Rick slowly raised both his arms in the air as if to say, *"What's up? Let's handle this."* CJ nodded at him and sat down on his bunk to wait.

~

The doors popped and Mr. Dupree's voice came over the PA system. "Line it up for chow, fellas, let's go!"

CJ stood slowly and took a deep breath before approaching his cracked cell door. He was overcome by the urge to empty his bladder and turned back toward the toilet before leaving. He had to look over his shoulder while he was pissing, just in case. He finished quickly and washed his hands, splashing a little cold water in his face for an extra jolt. He had no idea what to expect or what he was going to do, but he knew he needed to stay on his toes.

He immediately located Duke, Pep, and Kiki at the front of the line when he exited his room. Rick was standing about halfway back watching him. CJ slid behind him just as the unit door opened and a blast of hot air filled the dorm. The line was moving.

"We gotta straighten that," Rick said out of the side of his mouth, low enough for only CJ to hear.

"I know," said CJ.

"When?"

"I don't know." It was only a little after 4:00. They still had chow and evening rec before they were locked in the unit for the night. *IF* they had evening rec. Nothing was guaranteed after what happened in the weight cage that afternoon.

The industrial-sized fans in the chow hall kept the hot air circulating, but there was nothing to combat the hundreds of flies that continuously dive-bombed the food and buzzed annoyingly around the sweaty faces of the clients. Rick, then CJ, lifted a thin tray from the stack at the beginning of the serving line and pushed them along while the cafeteria women argued about soap operas and loaded their slots with heaping piles of steaming food. CJ wasn't hungry.

He followed Rick down the aisle between the tables of boys wearing Unit 8 blue. Everyone was immersed in stuffing their faces while simultaneously fighting off the stubborn flies. As they carried their trays, CJ spotted Duke's hulking back and shoulders just ahead, seated on the aisle side nearest him and facing Pep, who was obviously notifying him of their advance.

As they were passing, Duke called out to Rick. "Hey, butterscotch," he spat, alluding to Rick's light complexion, "let me borrow your bitch tonight." He emphasized his statement by reaching out and slapping CJ on the ass as he walked by.

At that moment, all the fear and indecision in CJ's mind quickly gave way to howling rage. CJ was two steps past him when he pivoted and swung his tray like a baseball bat into Duke's eye socket, the hard, thin fiberglass exploding against his orbital bone and shattering it on contact. His spaghetti-covered face rocked back in confused horror just as the tray came whistling through the air again, this time catching him in the throat and crushing his larynx. He tried to scream as CJ dropped the tray and pulled him out of his chair by the collar of his uniform, slinging his colossal body to the food-smeared floor and kicking him repeatedly in the face and stomach as the onlookers stood and cheered him on.

Pep finally unfroze and stood to come to the aid of his friend, but Rick was waiting. "Nah, bitch," he said, unleashing a devastating flurry of punches that culminated with a haymaker that lifted Pep off his feet and sent him sprawling in the aisle. "Hold my arms now, motherfucker!" shouted Rick, quickly going after him again, and like CJ, kicking him ferociously until his cowering body was too far under the table to make any more significant contact with. They stopped and faced each other in the aisle, surrounded by more than a hundred fist-pumping, cheering kids who stood on tables and chairs and roared wildly in approval of the violence they just witnessed. CJ was covered in food and blood and breathing so heavily that his entire upper body rolled forward with every exhalation. Rick was staring back at him, alternately opening and closing his right hand.

"Good job, white boy," he said over the noise.

CJ smiled at his friend and took an awkward step toward him when a breach opened in the crowd and a massive staff member came barreling through, slamming into CJ's body from behind and tackling him. There was a commotion behind Rick too and he turned just as another staff member came knifing through on his side, planting a shoulder in his skinny back and driving him forcibly to the floor.

The crowd dispersed as the huge staff members lumbered to their feet, pulling CJ and Rick up with them. They shoved them roughly out of the chow hall just as backup and the medical team was arriving. In the chaos, CJ spotted Dupree, leaning against the building smoking, as more and more staff arrived. They locked eyes for a second and a hint of a smile briefly passed over his face before he flicked his cigarette in the hedges and walked back inside.

Both CJ and Rick were due to appear in court in six days. This incident wasn't going to look good on their files. At that moment, the memory of slamming the tray into Duke's throat flashed across CJ's mind like a bolt of lightning. *Oh shit,* he thought, swallowing hard, *did I kill him?*

By the time they got to lockdown, CJ was a nervous wreck. As soon as the door slammed behind him, he fell to his knees and began praying fervently for Duke's life, the tears rolling down his face and exploding on the dirty concrete beneath him.

"Your name is CJ, right?" said a voice through the door. He turned to see Mr. Jackson, or "Jack" as he called himself, shaking his head and smiling through the Plexiglas.

CJ nodded.

"Thought so. I never forget a name. You stepped in a little shit, huh?"

CJ nodded again, and a stray, solitary tear raced down the side of his face.

"Well, you're doing the right thing. Just stay on those knees and keep asking Him for help. He ain't never let me down yet."

"I thought you worked on Unit 1," CJ said, wiping his eyes.

"I do. Seven years now."

It was then that CJ realized he *was* back on Unit 1. *This must be the other wing,* he thought, looking up at the graffiti on the walls. A sense of relief began to wash over him. He was safe in this solitary cell on Unit 1; no Dukes, no Mr. Duprees, no Kikis, no Peps, no twenty-five-pound dumbbells to crush his skull. He'd do the rest of his time right here if he could.

"This where they put the gangstas," said Jack, placing a worn NIV Bible on the floor and pushing it under the door. "I gave your homeboy, Robinson, the room across the hall. Y'all may be here a minute. Try and hold the noise down, okay?"

"Yes sir," said CJ.

He tapped the door once before walking off.

"Hey, Jack!" CJ called out.

He came back to the Plexiglas with raised eyebrows.

"Thanks."

~

CJ lay on the thin green mattress and counted the cinder blocks on the wall again. He already knew how many there were: 107 on the wall across from his bunk, eighty-five behind him, sixty-six surrounding the stainless steel toilet/sink at the back of his cell, and forty-eight framing the door for a grand total of 306 blocks. None was unblemished. Some sported gang signs and others declarations of love to God. There were also 'hoods, nicknames, and crude drawings of naked women. The blocks that were unmarred by graffiti were dotted with spitballs, boogers, and suspicious-looking brown streaks located on the wall next to the toilet. The day shift staff was supposed to bring around cleaning supplies today, but he didn't really care if they showed up or not because tomorrow marked his twenty-first day in juvie. He had court in the morning.

He had spent the last four days doing push-ups, praying, reading the Bible, and talking to Rick through the window on his cell door. Through necessity and boredom, they developed a new form of communication that was a blend of charades, hand gestures, lip reading, and yelling when all else failed. Rick was a good dude. CJ was glad they were friends. He had underestimated him before their incident in the chow hall. Pep never had a chance. He hoped they both were released tomorrow. Rick never said anything else about his brother, but CJ could tell it was on his mind.

Duke didn't die. According to Jack he was already back from the hospital and being housed in the medical unit until he healed enough to be released back into population. The doctors had to perform a tracheotomy on him for the damage to his windpipe as well as reconstructive facial surgery on the area surrounding his right eye. CJ hoped they never crossed paths again. He knew he had made a lifelong enemy.

On the phone his mother told him she had obtained character references from a few of her coworkers at the Essex who had known him since he was in the third grade. CJ knew she was doing everything in her power to get him home. His dad had briefly picked up the extension toward the end of the call and reiterated his need to appeal to Saint Jude. He rolled his eyes at the memory.

His thoughts turned to Andrea. Had it been twenty days since he'd last seen her? It felt like twenty years. Sometimes at night he was haunted by the image of her standing in the hallway, just beyond the crowd, watching him with big brown eyes as he delivered that final kick into Joey Barocela's face. He had wanted to call her many times over the last three weeks, but he could never use the phone before 7:00 p.m. and he knew her mom would kill her if a boy called their house. He couldn't wait to kiss her again. *Maybe tomorrow,* he thought with a smile, pulling his pillow to his chest and imagining it was her, before drifting back to sleep.

~

"Robinson, McCallister, let's go," came a voice from the hallway, followed by the sharp, metallic sounds of their doors unlocking.

They both emerged from their cells at the same time, silently bumping fists before turning and walking side by side down the polished hallway toward the waiting staff member. When they reached him, he looked up at a camera and said "One." After a few seconds, the door in front of them hissed and slid open.

The staff member jingled his keys as he led them through the myriad of hallways, doors, and stairwells that eventually led to the ominous corridor where that particular day's group of boys nervously awaited their fates. Since CJ and Rick were on lockdown, they were escorted separately. As they walked down the hall, past the massive oak doors, most of the kids they made eye contact with nodded at them. Although none of the faces were familiar, some of them called their names as they walked by. Apparently they were now celebrities due to their little episode in the chow hall. They found a spot to sit near the end of the bench.

"We're famous," CJ said, staring at the door in front of him.

Rick smiled. "Shit, we've *been* famous, they just now figurin' it out."

Door number three opened and Joe Levin slid into the narrow hallway. CJ watched him scan the faces apprehensively for a few moments.

"Is McCallister back here?" he finally asked.

CJ stood.

The slight attorney looked at CJ suspiciously before approaching him.

"You look different," he said. "Did you get a haircut?"

CJ nodded and glanced over at Rick, who rolled his eyes.

"Something else, too." Levin examined him closely through the small square-framed glasses perched on the edge of his nose. "Ah yes, the black eye is gone."

He draped a polyester-clad arm over CJ's shoulders and guided him toward the courtroom. "You got in a little trouble back there, huh?"

"Yes sir," CJ answered dejectedly.

"That's not going to help our cause," Levin said, opening the huge door.

There was a blanket of silence hanging over the courtroom as they entered. All eyes were on him. The judge was already seated. The gaunt state attorney stood alone at his podium while, across the floor, CJ's mother was wiping tears from her face and smiling at him sadly as his father patted her back. CJ's heart sank. He was in deep shit.

"Young man," the judge began, "it has come to the attention of this court that you have recently been displaying some very violent and anti-social tendencies."

CJ bowed his head. *Violent? Him?* He had never felt so misunderstood in his life. He wanted to explain that he hated fighting, that he was actually terrified of violence and bullies, but he felt overwhelmed by all the authority in the room. Judges, cops, lawyers, adults. He couldn't speak.

"The State of Florida simply will not tolerate this type of behavior," said the judge, glancing at his mom. "Your mother makes a very convincing case on your behalf. She obviously loves you very much. Unfortunately, sometimes love is not enough. There comes a time where discipline is necessary, which is why we're all here today."

CJ looked over at his dad and immediately thought of Saint Jude, the patron saint of hopeless causes. He tried sending up a quick prayer now, although he knew he was screwed. *Please help me, Saint Jude,* he prayed. *I just want to go home.*

"So, the court hereby refers you to TASC. If you successfully fulfill all that's required of you, I will consider expunging this from your record at a later date. Good luck, young man," he said, dismissing him before asking the clerk, "Who's up next?"

CJ was numb. He didn't even look over at his parents. Joe Levin guided him slowly out of the courtroom and shut the door behind them.

"Well, Mr. McCallister," Levin said with a smile. "I hope we never meet again."

CJ slumped heavily on the bench, trying his hardest not to break down.

"What's wrong?" his attorney asked, confused by his somber mood.

"I just wanted to go home," he finally said in a small voice.

Levin burst out laughing. "That's where you're going. He sentenced you to TASC—Treatment Alternatives to Street Crime. It's basically probation with a class here and there. You're going home, man!"

CJ lifted his head slowly and stared at him wide-eyed. "Today?"

"Today," Levin said, patting his knee and getting up. "Don't come back," he added, then walked away.

He disappeared through the door of Courtroom Three just as Rick was exiting Courtroom Five. CJ was unable to contain his excitement.

He shot off the bench and ran over to his friend.

"I'm outta here!" he said, way too loud. A staff member on the bench admonished him with a scowl.

"That's good," Rick said.

CJ noticed the lack of enthusiasm in his response. "What happened with you?"

"Set me off," he said, "twenty-one more days."

"Damn. I'm . . ." He noticed the smile spreading across his friend's face.

"Sike," Rick said, laughing.

"Asshole!" CJ exploded, pounding fists with him and laughing gleefully before remembering the nearby staff member. "Sorry," he mouthed before collapsing next to Rick on the bench.

~

The rusty Corolla turned slowly off 67th into the Southwinds. His mom chattered happily from the front seat, constantly glancing at CJ in the rearview while his father hummed along with Buddy Holly on the radio. CJ had just eaten the last delicious french fry from his first meal as a free man—Burger King—and was now slurping noisily from the straw in his Coke. He looked up as they rolled over a speed bump. *Home sweet home,* he thought.

When they reached 318C and opened the door, he quickly shot up the stairs to his room. It was just like he left it three weeks ago when he decided he was going to seek revenge on the Barocelas. He needed a cigarette. *Rudy!* he thought, getting up and going back down the stairs. His father was lying on the couch.

"I'm going to Rudy's," he said.

His mother frowned at him from the kitchen. "Don't stay too long. We've got some things to talk about."

"Yes, ma'am," he answered, closing the door behind him and almost sprinting to Rudy's apartment building.

He heard salsa music wafting through the upstairs window as he knocked on the door. He waited a few moments and was about to knock again when the door opened and Mrs. Rodriquez stood in front of him with shiny, wet black hair and wearing a silky robe.

"CJ!" she said, reaching out to hug him. "We've missed you."

"Thanks," he said, a little lightheaded from her hug.

"Rudy's no here," she said in a thick Cuban accent. "He took the car to get oil."

"Okay, tell him I came by."

She nodded and smiled, closing the door. He walked off their porch and was about to take the sidewalk leading back to Building C when he noticed Rudy's mom's Monte Carlo in the parking lot. *He took the car to get oil,* she said. CJ smiled and walked over to the car. He could hear Rudy's Stevie B tape playing from outside the car.

He paused. Rudy had a girl in the car with him and they were making out pretty heavily. CJ shook his head. Rudy had it made when it came to girls. He knew he should just walk off, but he was mesmerized by the scene in front of him. The embrace was so passionate, it was as if they were clinging to each other for dear life, and their kiss was so deep. There was something familiar about the girl. Had he met her before? He could only see her hair and the side of her face, but he felt as if he *knew* her. Then he saw the heart-shaped locket hanging from her neck and he knew exactly who she was.

Before he could think, he was banging his fist against the passenger window. They whipped their heads around in shock. CJ's eyes darted back and forth between his best friend and his girl. Rudy stared straight ahead defiantly while Andrea looked away. He stared at them a moment longer, searing the memory into his brain before turning and heading back to his building.

PART TWO

1991

"He who makes a beast out of himself,
gets rid of the pain of being a man."

— Dr. Samuel Johnson

Chapter 7

Hibiscus Street was dead by 10:00 a.m. as were most of the other courts, lanes, and circles that made up the small area of Coral Gables near the Bakery Center. The colorful procession of minivans and Volvos had long ago bled out into the U.S. 1 traffic, temporarily surrendering the neighborhood to the chirping birds overhead and the occasional darting squirrel. Other than the whirring of a few sprinkler systems and a distant barking dog, the street was blanketed in silence.

"This one?" CJ asked, motioning his head to a two-story stucco home with a red Spanish barrel-tiled roof.

Rick shrugged and they turned up the driveway toward the twin palms that formed an archway over the front door. They stopped at the small raised platform that served as a porch/doorstep and CJ reached out to ring the doorbell. They heard it chime throughout the house as they stood there waiting. *Ding dong.* CJ gave it a full minute before sinking his thumb into the orange lit button again, twice this time. *Ding dong ding dong.*

When still no response came, he looked over at Rick and raised his eyebrows. Rick responded by attempting to look through the window for any signs of life, then rapping his knuckles against the large wooden door. Nothing.

Satisfied that no one was home, they stepped off the porch and quickly walked around the side of the house, hopping the privacy fence to gain entrance into the seclusion of the backyard. They'd done this a hundred times. If someone had answered the door, CJ would have said they were late for school and asked permission to cut through their yard. Then they'd have to cut over a few more streets and find another house. Not this morning.

They walked around the pool and onto the screened patio, both still listening for any sounds coming from within the house. CJ's heart was pounding now. This was part of the rush. They both shimmied out of their backpacks and unzipped them to remove their gloves. Rick walked over to the back door and checked to see if it was unlocked, noting the alarm sticker on the glass. When the knob wouldn't turn, he reached inside the collar of his shirt and removed his necklace, a thin string tied around a chunk of porcelain that was beaten off a spark plug. CJ stood behind him, ready. Bracing himself for the fire-truck-clanging of the alarm system.

Rick looped his finger around the string and swung the tooth-sized nugget of porcelain into the large glass window on the door. There was no sound, only a barely audible *pfft* as the tiny piece of china shot through the glass, causing it to spiderweb. Rick then pushed out a small section of the shattered window, prompting the tiny pieces to rain down on the tile floor. He reached through it to unlock the door, then carefully removed his hand and looked at CJ. He didn't have to say anything. If the alarm sounded, they'd have about three minutes, long enough to hit the jewelry box in the master bedroom and do a quick check for guns and cash. If not, then they could take their time.

CJ held his breath as Rick slowly turned the knob. A shattered window rarely set off an alarm; it was when they actually opened that window or door that they were blasted by the shrill sirens and loud ringing of the security system. Rick finally pushed the door open. *Click.* Silence. CJ smiled. They were in.

They moved quietly through the kitchen into the living room, noting the expensive leather furniture and entertainment center on the way. As a rule, they never took anything that wouldn't fit in their backpacks, for obvious reasons. Walking down 57th Avenue carrying a home stereo system would probably look suspicious.

CJ quickly darted up the stairs to find the master bedroom, leaving Rick to roam the hallways of the bottom floor in search of an office. Two months earlier he happened upon four one-hundred-dollar bills stuffed in a desk drawer and had been shaking down home offices ever since.

CJ walked toward the room at the end of the hall with his backpack slung loosely over one shoulder. He gave no thought to the possibility of a homeowner popping from behind one of the closed doors and blowing his brains out. That never crossed his mind. The miniscule amount of fear he did feel was more in relation to the small chance of the house being surrounded by cops while he was inside. But for the most part he felt only adrenaline and, of course, excitement at the possibility of a big payday.

He stepped inside the doorway of the master bedroom. The first thing he noticed was the huge waterbed jutting from the far wall and the mirror hovering over it from the ceiling. The second thing he noticed was a small mountain of cocaine sitting next to a razor blade in a silver platter on the nightstand. *Fuck!* thought CJ as he moved quickly back through the hall and down the stairs. *Out of all the houses I could have chosen to hit, we end up robbing Scarface.* He began rifling through the cupboards and kitchen drawers until he found a box of sandwich bags. He snatched out a few and hurried back upstairs.

It was time to move now. He'd wasted enough time as it was. He deftly transferred the coke from the tray to the baggy and stuffed it in his pocket before moving to the dresser. He barely glanced at the jewelry he was dumping in his backpack, but there was a lot of it. Two jewelry boxes full of chains, rings, watches, and bracelets. It looked and felt real. He hoped so. He spotted a rectangular wooden box near the end of the dresser and flipped it open. Inside was a folded stack of bills in a money clip, which he dropped in the bag. Then he saw the black leather wallet. *Damn,* he thought, reaching for it, *this is our lucky day.* He flipped it open and revealed the gleaming silver Metro-Dade police badge. "Oh shit," he said out loud, tossing it back in the box and thinking about the bag of coke in his jeans. *A crooked fuckin' cop!* He was ready to go and he had barely looked around yet.

Rick appeared in the doorway. "Anything good?"

CJ responded by throwing him his backpack.

"Whoa," Rick said in a low voice while looking down into the bag. "Best lick yet, huh?"

"Yeah. He had some coke too. A grip of it. I thought we were jackin' Tony Montana at first, until I found the badge."

"Aw shit," Rick groaned. "Let's go, man."

CJ was looking down into an open drawer in the dresser. "Check this out."

Rick walked over and swallowed hard when he saw the small arsenal of weapons meticulously arranged in the drawer: 38s, 357s, 380s, 45s, 25s, nine-millimeters, and a few others he couldn't even identify. Rick knew pistols. It was impossible to grow up in the same house as Ty Robinson and not. He set the backpack on the dresser.

"What's this?" CJ asked, grabbing a black plastic box with two metal prongs protruding from the end. He flipped it over in his hand and found a button on the bottom side. He impulsively mashed it and a crackling blue bolt of electricity danced between the prongs.

"Cool," he whispered, mesmerized.

"Let's go. Fuck the guns."

"No way! There's five grand in that drawer, easy!"

"Yeah," Rick shot back, "and when one of them motherfuckers we sell 'em to gets busted with a cop's stolen pistol and they tell on us, that five grand ain't gonna mean shit."

CJ looked down at the guns regretfully. "I guess you're right," he conceded, but still slipped the stun gun into his pocket. If he couldn't take the *real* fire with him, he'd at least allow himself a small consolation prize.

Rick looked over at the silver platter on the nightstand, which was smeared with the white powdery residue. "How much coke was there?"

CJ responded by producing the baggy from his pocket and holding it out.

"Damn," Rick said. "At least an ounce, maybe more." He stuck a finger in the bag to taste it. "It's gas too." He nodded approvingly. "I wonder if there's more."

CJ shut the gun drawer and ripped open the next one, throwing clothes on the floor behind him while looking for the hidden drugs. Rick flew to the closet and began yanking down shoe boxes and suitcases.

The sound of an approaching car penetrated their senses. CJ became deathly still and Rick craned his neck out of the closet to listen. The car drew nearer. *Come on, keep going, keep going,* CJ silently willed as he walked over to peek out the blinds. He watched the car pull to the curb and a large, bald Hispanic man got out, slamming the door behind him.

Rick was already rounding the bed when CJ said, "Let's go!" He was halfway down the hall when he realized his backpack wasn't on his shoulder. He quickly reversed course and shot back to the bedroom, scooping it off the dresser where Rick left it, and sprinted back toward the staircase. He was almost down when he heard the keys jingle and the door crack. Dust-filled daylight illuminated the living room.

The man's face rapidly transformed from confused shock to blistering rage as CJ went airborne for the last five steps. He bolted through the living room, hurdling a coffee table with the homeowner right behind him shouting murderous threats. As he flew into the kitchen, he could see Rick ahead of him, half over the fence behind the pool, legs dangling.

The man lunged just as he reached the back door. He caught CJ by the loose strap hanging from his backpack as he was falling.

"I've got you now, you little fuck!" his voice thundered.

CJ was terrified. He was just about to shrug off the backpack when he remembered the stun gun. He frantically dug in his pocket, gripped the black box, and spun back into his pursuer, pressing it forcefully into his fleshy face while jamming the button forward with his thumb and filling him with electricity. The man released the bag and fell limply onto the tiles, immobilized but conscious. CJ momentarily locked eyes with him while he wiggled his free arm through the loose strap on his backpack, then turned to run after Rick.

~

The Messiah Complex does not appear in the *Diagnostic and Statistical Manual of Mental Disorders.* Nonetheless, it is a well-documented, if rare, psychological phenomenon known to many experts in the field, as well as the families of those who suffer from it.

Like any other psychosis, there are different forms and degrees of this particular mental illness, but in extreme cases the subject comes to believe that he or she is the savior of the world or *the Messiah* in Biblical terms.

Chris McCallister sat Indian style on the floor of their apartment surrounded by flickering candles. He knew that any day now he was going to be summoned to a secret meeting of world leaders; it was just a question of when. He had no idea what he was going to say, but he trusted his Father, who had sent him, to put the appropriate words in his heart when the time came.

He breathed deeply and allowed his eyes to flutter shut. The last year and a half had been tumultuous to say the least. He sank into a deep depression when he lost his job at Wendy's. He spent months on the couch staring listlessly at the television, only getting up to eat and relieve himself. His wife had decided they would move to a more affordable apartment last year and he barely noticed. He just rode across town to the new place with CJ and Cheryl and took up his post on the couch while the movers shuffled back and forth through the door with their furniture in tow. His weight had ballooned to almost four hundred pounds and he was constantly under attack from a barrage of voices in his head urging him to take his life and reminding him of what a fat, ugly, worthless failure he was. It wasn't until later that he recognized those voices from two thousand years ago, when Lucifer led him to the highest point of a temple in Jerusalem and shouted, *"If you are the Son of God, throw yourself down from here!"*

He smiled at the memory of the day the scales fell from his eyes, like Paul on the road to Damascus.

He was sitting on the couch in his boxers, with popcorn kernels and cigarette ashes tangled in his chest hair when the opening notes of the theme music from ABC World News Tonight *blared from the television. Peter Jennings opened the program with the top news story of the day, a piece on big pharmaceutical companies. Chris was only half listening as Jennings continued to drone on and on, when suddenly something miraculous happened. In the middle of his monologue, Peter Jennings spun his chair so that he was looking directly into the McCallister living room and began speaking candidly to Chris about the mysteries of the universe and his role in the war of the end times. At first, he thought he was dreaming, but Peter assured him that he wasn't. Then he tried blowing him off, saying he was "too fat to save the world," but Peter only looked at him soberly and said, "Your Father is counting on you." He then spun his chair back to the anchor desk and resumed the program as if nothing had happened.*

Chris sat on the couch for a few heartbeats before falling to his knees and blubbering like a child. After almost an hour of fervent praying, he opened his eyes to a new reality. He looked around the tiny living room in wonder; everything seemed so . . . mystical, from the lampshade to the ratty old couch he'd been lying on for the last seven years. When he noticed the monstrous gobs of flesh hanging from his pasty-white body, he resolved to never let Peter Jennings see him in that manner again. He was the Messiah. *He had a reputation to protect. So from that day forward, he shaved and got dressed to watch the news.*

That was in August of 1990. He glanced down at his ever-diminishing girth illuminated in the candlelight. It was now February of '91. His mind was clear, his heart was pure, and he was weighing in at 330. *Fightin' shape.* Today marked the third and final day of his latest fast.

He took a deep breath through his nose and exhaled through his mouth before making the sign of the cross and extinguishing the candles. Then, using the coffee table for leverage, he slowly climbed to his feet. It was almost time for the news and he wanted to be dressed and ready when Peter—or *Petras* as he had taken to calling him lately—made his appearance. He hadn't been talking to him much recently, but that was fine. He understood how a mere man could feel uncomfortable conversing with him while knowing the truth of his identity. He smiled compassionately and shook his head as he walked down the hall to the shower.

~

CJ leaned forward and looked hard down the empty Metrorail terminal, making sure they were still alone before dipping Rick's house key deep into the plastic baggy and shoveling out a fat bump. He carefully raised it to his nose, balancing the powder on the tip while mashing his left nostril shut. He began snorting just as the loaded key was rising past his mouth so that by the time it reached his nose, the powder had already disappeared up through his nasal passage and into his bloodstream. His eyes instantly dilated and his hand slightly trembled as he plunged the key back down into the sack to service his other nostril.

"Whoa," he uttered, leaning his head back and sniffing a few more times to ensure nothing was left in his nose.

Rick tapped him impatiently. "Hand me that."

CJ slowly set the bag and key on the bench between them.

Rick glanced over at him again and burst out laughing. "Fix your nose, man," he said, while expertly fishing a mountainous pile of coke from the bag and quickly hoovering every granule.

CJ absently licked the tips of his thumb and middle finger and rubbed them against his nostrils as he looked down at the traffic on 27th Avenue. There was a man shadowboxing in the median with a rose in his mouth. He was there every time they took the train up to Liberty City to sell their jewelry to the Arabs in the flea market. One of the thousand simultaneous thoughts racing through his amphetamine-saturated brain leapt to the surface: *What happened in that man's life to make him wanna stick a flower in his mouth and go shadowbox on 27th Avenue every day?* Then, just as quickly, it evaporated. He realized his heart was pounding in his chest. He snorted deeply, attempting to clear his coke-clogged nasal passages again, and was rewarded for his efforts with an ether-laden glob of mucus filling his throat and causing his tongue and gums to go completely numb. He could not stop grinding his teeth. This happened the last time he did coke too. He would try to use his willpower to stop grinding them, and it worked for about thirty seconds. Then he'd forget all about it, start thinking about something else, and realize he was grinding them again.

He reached in his pocket and clutched the knot of twenties, fifties, and hundreds. It felt good to have money. After everything was sold, the entire take was $4,580. They split the $4,500 down the middle, $2,250 each. The remaining eighty dollars would be used to get something to eat and for a few sacks of weed once they got to the Overtown Station on the way back to South Miami. They did each keep one item of jewelry. Rick selected a gold Omega watch and CJ chose a diamond-crusted tennis bracelet for April.

The coke was now fully working its magic. CJ felt like a character in the movies. He had a stun gun in one pocket, a wad of cash in the other, he had just hours ago narrowly escaped arrest, or possibly an even worse fate. Now he was sitting in an empty Metrorail station, high above 27th Avenue, watching the sun set on Miami with a big sack of coke next to him, and of course, Rick.

Rick was CJ's ace. He was a *way* better friend than that sellout Rudy would ever be. They had fought together, robbed together, done time together, and forged an unlikely bond while the swirling winds of turmoil and dysfunction swept all around them. The fact that Rick was black and CJ was white was as trivial and insignificant as their differing shoe sizes. They were family. Period.

A slight tremor in the concrete caused them to look down the tracks in the direction of Hialeah. The silver train rounded the final corner in its approach and sped toward them.

"May I have your attention, please?" A polite, automated male voice echoed throughout the Northside Metrorail Station. *"A train is now approaching. Please step back from the platform edge and allow passengers to disembark before boarding."*

The message was repeated as the train quietly glided to a stop in front of them and the doors hissed open. A group of black teenage girls was getting off the train as they were getting on. They were all giggling and casting sidelong glances at Rick as they passed, ignoring CJ for the most part, until the fat one in the group wiggled her fingers at him and said, "Hey, white boy," causing her friends to erupt in laughter. CJ was too geeked to respond and the doors slid shut before he could even force a smile.

The train shot smoothly out of the Northside Station and within moments they were flying over Liberty City headed southwest, past the 24-hour pawn shops and shitty motels that lined 27th Avenue, over the project courts where kids shot ball and sold dope, and above the badass graffiti that was spray-painted on the walls of Jackson High and nearby business rooftops. CJ had been a big fan of street art ever since he saw the movie *Beat Street* when he was eleven. He thought back to a time in the fifth grade when his mom drove him all over Miami taking pictures of different graffiti pieces throughout the city. He smiled at the memory.

He and Rick were the lone passengers in the car. Not many people rode the rail at this time of day, at least not this far north. CJ leaned forward and pressed his head against the door, watching the city blur beneath him. The rapidly moving view meshed perfectly with the thoughts racing through his head. He was fucked up. He couldn't remember ever being so high. His heart felt like it was going to burst.

He knew his young life was quickly unraveling. It was almost as if unseen forces too powerful to resist were kicking him down the road of destiny.

When he was released from juvie almost two years ago and discovered Rudy and Andrea making out in the parking lot, he was devastated. Hot tears were streaming down his face before he was halfway back down the sidewalk. Neither of them followed. He was thankful for that. He couldn't imagine anything worse than a fumbling attempt at an explanation or pitiful consolation from either of them.

Once he made it to the apartment, he walked straight upstairs to his room, shut the door behind him, lay on the floor, and cried like a baby. When his mom came up later and found him there, she sat down next to him and lovingly rubbed his hair, asking him what was wrong. He ignored her. After midnight, he heard the sharp, familiar taps of pebbles against his window. Rudy was out there. Fuck you, he thought and rolled over to face the wall until they stopped.

In his life, CJ had been tormented and beaten by bullies. He'd experienced being snubbed by the popular kids at school, suffered the loss of his grandfather, been ignored and blown off by his dad for long stretches of time, and had just gone through twenty-one days in juvie, but he'd never had his heart broken before. This was a whole different type of hurt.

The following morning, after his mother reluctantly left for work, his father came up to his room and sat on the edge of his bed. CJ looked up at him from where he lay on the floor. He had fallen asleep there. His dad fired up a joint and took a deep hit. His massive belly jumped spastically as he struggled to stifle the smoke trapped in his lungs for as long as possible. When he finally released a thick cloud into the air, he inspected the joint for any potential runs, then slowly extended it to CJ, who responded by throwing his arm over his eyes in a dismissive manner, pretending to go back to sleep. He watched his father shrug and take another deep hit through the tiny crack of space beneath his forearm. Suddenly, he reconsidered. His right hand rocketed out like a jab to accept the spiff while his left arm continued to lie motionless across his eyes.

That was the first time he got high with his dad.

Out of nowhere a train screamed by, headed in the other direction, momentarily blocking the setting sun and causing the light in their car to dim. And just as quickly, it was gone.

Rick glanced behind him at the disappearing train, then looked questioningly at CJ. "You all right, man?"

"Yeah," CJ said, swallowing another ether-drenched ball of snot and flinching at the medicinal taste.

Rick smiled and shook his head. "Drainin' good, huh? This shit is fire." He reached in his pocket for the bag and offered it to CJ.

CJ surveyed the empty car out of habit before accepting the coke and doing two quick bumps in succession, spilling a little on his lap in the process. He passed the bag back across the aisle to Rick and leaned back in his seat, lost in his thoughts.

"Overtown," the polite voice announced from the train's PA system as it pulled to a stop next to the Miami Arena.

The doors slid open and the two boys stepped out on the platform. "I'll be right back," Rick said as he reached in his pocket for his half of the money. He separated four twenty-dollar bills from the knot and handed the rest to CJ.

"Put it in your underwear," Rick said over his shoulder on the way to the escalator, "just in case."

Overtown was a dangerous section. They had been robbed here once before. That's why CJ didn't go with Rick to cop anymore. A white boy in Overtown was like waving a red flag in the faces of the police and the jack-boys. Way too conspicuous. But the weed over on 11th was the best in Miami, so Rick usually took the risk to go get it since he could blend right in.

CJ stilled his sliding cocaine jaw and looked up and down the station before sticking Rick's and his own money deep in his tighty-whiteys. He then sat down on the bench to wait.

Shortly after that fateful morning in 1989, his mom decided they would move to a cheaper apartment since his father was unemployed again. It was a shithole, but at least he didn't have to worry about bumping into Rudy anymore. He satisfied the requirements of his TASC officer by attending anger management classes, keeping a curfew, and enrolling in alternative school. The winds of fate must have been at his back because he spotted Rick in the hallway on his first day. It wasn't long before they were skipping class together and getting high.

That summer CJ tagged along on a mission with Rick to steal a car. A black Vette. He was amazed at the speed and skill Rick exhibited in taking it and was instantly hooked on the adrenaline rush that was Grand Theft Auto. They had some tense moments when the steering column locked up on them while they were flying down the Palmetto, but that only heightened the adventure for CJ. The best part of that day was riding down Andrea's street with the system up and stopping in front of her house. When she walked out on the porch along with an older woman in an apron—her mom, he assumed—he rolled the tinted window down halfway and locked eyes with her. "Punch it," he told Rick, still holding her gaze. The tires screeched and she was in the rearview. Case closed, he thought.

And so began his love affair with crime and living dangerously. Just as marijuana can lead to cocaine and other hardcore chemicals, so, too, can car theft lead to burglary and more serious crimes. CJ never acted out of malice. He was not in it to vandalize or deface property, and he really never even considered the long line of nameless, faceless victims he left in his wake. He was simply getting money and riding the tornado of his life wherever it spun.

Suddenly Rick's smiling face appeared at the top of the escalator. He ran up the last few steps just as the next train was pulling in.

"Touchdown," he said.

~

Cheryl McCallister sat across from Dr. Villanueva in his small office, clutching her purse and staring at the floor. She was extremely uncomfortable airing her family's dirty laundry to a complete stranger. Talking to a shrink initially sounded like a good idea when her boss, Mr. Ramos, mentioned that a childhood friend of his was a psychologist. Now she wasn't so sure.

"Mrs. McCallister," he gently prodded in a soothing tone, "I know this is hard. Just try to relax."

His voice reminded her of one of those painters who used to come on PBS in the afternoons when she was pregnant with CJ. *What was that guy's name? Ross?*

"Try not to think of me as a doctor." *First you take your number seven brush.* "Think of me as a professional listener." *Dip it in your opaque white.* "A confidential advisor, if you will." *And put what I like to call . . . 'just a whisper.'* "A friend." *Happy little strokes.*

Dr. Villanueva was tall and gaunt, with a salt-and-pepper mustache and kind, intelligent eyes. His office, although small, was pleasant and unpretentious. The walls were a pastel green and bare, save for a framed poster of a vibrant waterfall behind his desk. In suspicious absence were the obligatory plaques and certificates that normally adorn the walls of doctors' offices. Also in absence, thankfully so, was the proverbial couch. For some reason Cheryl had an irrational fear that she was going to be met at the door and instructed to lie down and answer a litany of questions centered around her relationship with her mother. On his desk was a wooden "U" painted green and orange, and a framed picture of a smiling little girl.

He saw her looking.

"That's my Mara," he said. "She was six in that picture. She turns eight next Tuesday."

Her mind instantly flashed to CJ at eight years old: all freckles, missing teeth, and skinned knees, smiling at her from across the booth at Burger King. She wished she could go back. Tears flooded her eyes and she fought in vain to withhold them.

"It's okay," he said softly, reaching for the box of Kleenex on his desk and passing it to her. When she took a deep breath and looked tentatively up into his eyes, he gently inquired, "Now, what's troubling you?"

"My son," she sniffled, "and my husband."

"Tell me."

"CJ is seventeen," she began. "He is a good boy, and I'm not just saying that because he's my child. He truly is a good person. Smart. Warm. Funny. Kind. But over the last few years he's been acting out. He spent twenty-one days in the Juvenile Detention Center a couple of years ago for assaulting a bully who had blackened his eye in school, and it seems like he's been spiraling out of control ever since." She paused to wipe a stray tear from her cheek. "He dropped out of school last year. He stays out all night. He doesn't work, but he's constantly coming up with new outfits and sneakers. I think he may be selling drugs."

"Have you confronted him?"

She nodded. "I've tried. He's just so distant. Plus with my work schedule, I barely even see him anymore."

"Have you ever considered entering him into some type of treatment center?"

"No," she said flatly. "I couldn't do that to him."

"It could save his life."

She simply stared at him. Dumping CJ off in some institution was out of the question.

"How about your husband? He can't get through to him either?"

She looked down at her hands. "My husband is a drug addict," she said in a small voice, "who believes he is Jesus Christ."

He gave her a funny look. "In what way?"

"In the 'Son of God' way," she answered, embarrassed as hell.

"What type of drug is he *using?"* he asked, leaning forward.

"Just marijuana, as far as I know."

"How long has he . . . harbored this belief?"

"I don't know. A few months."

"Is this the first time that he's . . ."

"Gone crazy?" she volunteered. "No. It's the second time, but he wasn't so religious back then. Just paranoid. And weird."

"Is he violent?"

"Never," she said softly. "He's the most docile human being in the world."

"He needs help," Dr. Villanueva said.

"I know," she replied, crying again, "we all do. That's why I'm here."

He tapped his thumb against the button on his pen as he stared at her. "Are you familiar with Prozac?"

She blew her nose loudly and shook her head.

"Well, there's this new drug on the market."

~

After a delicious meal of spare ribs and fries at Tony Roma's, the two boys divided the remainder of the coke and weed before going their separate ways. Rick caught the Metrobus headed south toward his

Perrine neighborhood, and CJ walked across the parking lot to April's apartment building.

He met her last summer while roaming the aisles of the Peaches Music Store where she worked. CJ loved thumbing through the endless crates of twelve-inch records and albums at Peaches. He could get lost for hours in the world of music. The store closed at midnight on weekends, and often that was *still* too soon for CJ, who would have to be tapped on the back by an employee to be roused from his trance-like state. It was on one of those very weekend nights that he became aware of someone standing behind him, peering over his shoulder at the record he was holding: *N.W.A., 100 Miles And Runnin'.*

"You like that shit?" a distinct female voice challenged him from behind. He looked over his shoulder into the greenest eyes he'd ever seen.

She raised an eyebrow as if to say "I'm waiting."

"Yeah," he said, turning to face her. "Who doesn't like Easy-E?"

"I don't," she announced, wrinkling her nose. "I hate rap." She stubbornly folded her arms in front of her and waited on his reply.

He silently willed himself to hold her gaze, but there were things going on below her neck that demanded his attention. His eyes quickly flicked to her breasts, which seemed to be straining against the material of her shirt, then back to her face.

"Well," he said in a voice he hoped didn't sound too shaky, "what do you like?" She wasn't pretty in the standard Miami-exotic-Latina way. Her hair was brown and shoulder length, her eyes were wide set, and her nose was slightly pointy and presided over a small, dainty mouth. The cumulative effect was a sharp, angular face that was by no means beautiful but strangely captivating. Then she smiled and forced him to reassess his initial impression.

"Come on," she said, holding out her hand. "I'll show you."

CJ was at Peaches every night after that. He began walking her home from work in the evenings and before long he was hanging out in the apartment she shared with her older sister. April had four years on CJ, but neither of them paid much attention to age. They just clicked. She introduced him to Zeppelin, Floyd, and the Guns 'N Roses *Appetite For*

Destruction album. He introduced her to some of the best weed in Miami.

It was during one of those hazy smoke-filled nights in her apartment that it happened. It wasn't forced or planned. He really had no idea it was even coming. One minute they were laughing their asses off to Eddie Murphy Raw and the next they were looking into each other's eyes as their lips met. He kept waiting for her to stop him as he hungrily tested her limits, but she never did and they ended up having sex on her couch. It was mostly a clumsy, grasping, short-lived ordeal, but she was patient with his inexperience and he suspected she was secretly empowered by the taking of his virginity. Once they were done, she stood and led him down the hall to her bedroom, where he spent the rest of the night learning how to please her. He would never forget sitting on her balcony, wrapped in a blanket, sharing a cigarette, listening to Led Zeppelin's "Kashmir" as the sun came up the next morning . . . his first as a man.

They were not a couple and definitely not "in love," at least not in the traditional sense. They were simply good friends who kept their physicality a secret from the rest of the world. April had even dated a few men over the last couple of months, one of whom CJ actually met. She'd introduced him as her "little cousin." Later that night when he was slamming into her, their bodies covered in sweat, he kept asking her: "'Little cousin, huh? 'Little'?" He smiled at the memory. Remaining emotionally detached was not always that simple for him. April was sexy and funny and a trip to be around. She also had a delicious, curvy body with penetrating green eyes and a voracious sexual appetite. He could have easily fallen for her had she not warned him early on about being jealous or trying to control her. And falling in love wasn't exactly at the top of his priority list either after being burned the first time.

CJ could hear the familiar bass line of *In Bloom* vibrating through the wall of her apartment as he walked up to the door. Nirvana was April's favorite new band. He liked them too. There was something about their sound that made all the other music on the radio sound phony and calculated by comparison.

He knocked loudly and stared at the peephole expectantly. The music stopped and he heard footsteps approaching the door.

"Hold on a sec, CJ," April's voice came through. He fired up a cigarette and leaned against the wall across from her door. It had been a long day. First the arduous trek through Coral Gables in search of a house to hit. Then, the ensuing burglary and near-death experience, the stun gun, the getaway, the Metrorail ride to Liberty City, the haggling with the Arabs who bought the jewelry, and the train ride back, trying to keep up with Rick's insatiable appetite for all things powdery. He wasn't complaining. It was a good day. A kickass day. He had a pocket full of money and some killer dope. He was free and full and . . . The door opened and April was standing before him wearing only a pair of black lace panties. A smile spread across his face. His day just got even better.

...

"Hey, little cousin," she said, pulling him inside and slamming the door behind him. They made love on her living room floor. Her intention was really to shock and tease him a little by opening the door in her panties, but she was quickly swept away in his relentless animalistic lust for her, and before she knew it, he was between her thighs, driving deeper and deeper, holding her tight and sucking her nipples with his hot mouth. She could feel him exploding inside of her as she threw her arms around him and held him close until the last wave dissipated. She was taken aback by his ravenous hunger for her. She had been having sex since she was a teenager and had been with more men than she'd ever admit, but she'd never been made love to with such passionate intensity and desire. She could feel his desperate longing in the way he clung to her, in his fingertips, in his hungry mouth, in his powerful thrusts. She lay there on the floor watching him as he struggled to his feet, noting the sweat droplets that had appeared on his brow and upper lip. His jawline seemed stronger than it was last summer, more pronounced. He was growing up. Fast. She glanced quickly at the swollen red member hanging between his legs. He caught her looking and smiled.

"Not bad for a white boy, huh?"

"I've had bigger," she said, extending her hand up toward him to be helped off the carpet.

"Seriously?" he asked, obviously crushed.

They'd had this conversation before. She was his first and only lover and he wanted to know where he ranked on the penis scale. The truth was he was a little above average; not mammoth but definitely not microscopic either. He was actually perfect for her, but she'd never let him know that. She kept it intentionally vague, which worked out well for her because he was always trying to top his last performance in order to impress her.

CJ lifted her from the floor and she led him down the hall to the bathroom, where they made love again in the shower. He was tender and gentle this time, kissing and touching her in all the secret places on her body that she had taught him about on that fateful summer night a lifetime ago. He was sixteen then, she was almost twenty-one. She was lonely and bored and thought it would be fun to seduce the mysterious-looking kid with the haunted blue eyes and the baggy clothes who had recently taken up residence in the Rap section of her store. She never regretted it.

She looked back over her shoulder as he brushed her wet, soapy nipples with his fingertips. His eyes were shut. He wasn't only a dedicated lover, he made her laugh. He told her about his crazy father and other personal things that she knew he didn't share with others. He listened to her, he valued her opinion, he babied her when she was sick and massaged her when she was sore. She couldn't put her finger on exactly when it happened, but somewhere along the way she stopped seeing him as a gullible kid. Lately she had found herself thinking about him at work and even when she was out with other men. She placed her hands against the shower wall and braced herself as he slid in and out of her wet body, rotating his finger on the tip of her pleasure center while crashing into her over and over. She moaned aloud as she was carried off by powerful orgasmic waves.

She watched him as he stepped out of the shower and dried off with his favorite towel, the big pink one that belonged to her sister. She would be pissed when she got off work and found it wet and balled up in the hamper again. He disappeared through the doorway and walked noisily down the hall. She smiled when she heard the opening notes of *Lithium* coming from the stereo in her bedroom, his favorite Nirvana song. She was proud of the fact that she had succeeded in opening his eyes to good music. *Real music,* she thought as she stepped out of the shower. She caught a glimpse of herself in the mirror and did a double take when she realized the silly grin on her reflection. The smile died immediately. *Oh fuck,* she thought.

When she walked into her room, she found CJ lying spread-eagle on her bed with something gold and shiny coiled around his flaccid penis.

"I've got a present for you," he said, smiling.

She came closer to inspect the thing on his dick. It looked like a chain. No, a bracelet. A gold bracelet littered with what appeared to be diamonds.

"Is it real?" she whispered, climbing toward him on the bed.

CJ nodded, watching her.

It was beautiful. She watched it sparkle in the light for a few seconds, hypnotized by its magic. No one had ever given her anything so lovely. She was blown away and touched and amazed and heartbroken. She reached out to untangle it from where it swirled around the shaft of CJ's silky limp penis. Suddenly a blue bolt of crackling electricity appeared just inches from her face. ZAP!

"Oh!" she screamed, recoiling in shocked horror and almost falling off the bed.

"Gotcha," said CJ, laughing his ass off.

"Dick!" she replied, plopping down next to him and quickly freeing the diamond bracelet from his cock.

"It's beautiful," she said, kissing his cheek. "Thank you."

"I've got another surprise too."

"*Another* one?"

"Hand me that CD case," he said, motioning his head toward the stereo.

She leaned over and grabbed it as he reached for his jeans and dug out a bag of white powder from the pocket.

She silently handed him the CD case—Nirvana, *Nevermind*—and he poured a pile of cocaine over the image of the naked, swimming baby on the cover.

"You got something to chop this with?"

She got up and grabbed a laminated Blockbuster Video card out of her purse.

"Where'd you get all this?" she asked, nestling up close to him as he focused on reducing the rocky clumps of powder to a fine talc.

"I found it," he said, carving out four long white lines on the CD case.

She rolled her eyes as he again dug in the pocket, this time producing a large wad of bills and peeling off a hundred.

"Seriously, CJ, what's going on?"

"Do you want a line or not?" he asked, offering her the case and the rolled-up hundred-dollar bill.

She hesitated a second before accepting it. "Hold my hair back."

~

CJ slunk along the backstreets in the direction of his family's apartment. It was about a thirty-minute walk from April's place. The city was mostly asleep at that time of the morning. The only cars on the road were cops and taxis. He hid whenever he saw headlights, just to be safe. Other than an occasional stray cat and dumpster-rummaging wino, he had the streets to himself.

There was a light mist in the air that coincided perfectly with his mood. He wished he could have stayed the entire night with April, but her sister got off at 3:00 a.m. and he couldn't be there when she arrived home.

His noisy mind was at its most abusive and belittling as he trudged home in the early morning mist. He was a shitty son, a loser, a coward, a thief, a druggie, a nobody. It was like this every time he came down off cocaine. The high was exhilarating, but in the end he always paid the price in the form of the crushing lows.

Up ahead he saw the weather-worn sign indicating the entrance to the crumbling roach-infested tenement where he lived. The actual name of the place was Sherbourne Manor, but he affectionately christened it "Shithole Manor" when they first moved in, for obvious reasons. The dilapidated Southwinds was an island resort by comparison.

He fired up a Newport before attacking the five flights of steps that led to his floor. He could hear the murmuring voices of CNN reporters through the door as he reached the apartment. He took a deep drag from his cigarette and blew a lungful of smoke at the naked yellow hallway light, causing the circling gnats to momentarily disperse, before flicking it over the railing. He tried the knob. The door was open. He slid inside and quietly shut it behind him. His father was lying on the couch in a suit, staring blankly at the television as the talking heads behind the news desk babbled away. CJ reached in his pocket and dug out the last sack of weed.

"Here you go, Jesus," he said, flicking the fat, thumb-sized manila envelope high in the air. They both watched as it turned end over end across the living room, arching its way over the coffee table and landing safely in his father's outstretched palm. Chris looked at the confo stamp and smiled excitedly at CJ.

"Bless you, my son," he said.

He nodded and walked down the hall toward his tiny bedroom. He noticed his mom's light was on as he passed. He peeked inside her door. Her hands were folded over an open book that lay on her chest. She wasn't snoring, but there was a soft clicking sound with every breath she took. On the chair next to the bed were her work clothes for the following day, neatly arranged all the way down to the shoes.

A single tear slid down CJ's face. Something about the sight of his sleeping mother caused his heart to ache. Maybe it was his guilty conscience, or it could have just been the lingering effects of his comedown from the coke. Maybe it was a combination of both or maybe it was neither. Maybe his future self was somehow looking back in time through the eyes of his present self and yearning for something precious that was forever lost. Whatever it was, it burned like hell.

CJ carefully shut the door behind him and walked quietly down the hall to his room.

Chapter 8

Chris McCallister was sweating profusely as he pushed the shopping cart down the produce aisle of the Publix in South Miami. His wife didn't wander too far off. He was thankful for that. He was beginning to regret his spur-of-the-moment decision to join her on this shopping trip. It had been a long time since he'd ventured out into the world. It felt dangerous to him. Hostile. He nodded at an elderly man with a cane as his wife returned to the cart with a head of lettuce.

He didn't know what to expect when he followed her out into the sunlight that afternoon. *Would President Bush be waiting in their apartment parking lot? Surely he wouldn't send Dan Quayle for something so important. Would he? Would Petras be waiting in a limo? Pope John Paul? Would there be a parade? A rally? Riots? Would he be greeted by the masses with loaves and fish? Could he pull that off again? How did he do it the first time? Oh shit, he couldn't remember!* He was so relieved when he stepped out of the stairwell and saw the deserted parking lot that he almost fell to his knees and thanked his Father. He was well aware that his revelation was inevitable and that he was only prolonging the inexorable, but he was grateful that it wasn't going down today.

A short Mexican woman pushing a little boy in her cart smiled at the McCallisters as their paths crossed. Chris looked nervously over his shoulder at her retreating backside before leaning into his wife.

"Am I supposed to be blessing these people?" he whispered.

She rolled her eyes. "Bless them to yourself," she admonished through clenched teeth.

...

This is a mistake, Cheryl thought. She had been trying to coax him into leaving the apartment for months now. Her thinking was that a field trip out into the real world might somehow shatter the bubble of his current psychosis and make him normal again. She knew it would eventually break. Just like a fever. The same way it did ten years ago in Mobile when he thought people were watching him. Dr. Villanueva's latest recommendation was that she take CJ, load up the car, and go. She just couldn't bring herself to do it, nor could she bring herself to take those crazy pills he kept bringing up. *Antidepressants,* he called them. She guessed she was just old-school like that, Maybell Raines' daughter to the core. She would not abandon her family, she would not break her wedding vows, she would not run from her problems, and she would absolutely not take any magic pills to make everything seem hunky-dory. She hated drugs anyway. Drugs were the reason her family was falling apart at the seams right now. Why the hell would she contribute to the avalanche by joining the fray? Someone had to remain levelheaded.

They stood at the checkout counter waiting as their groceries were totaled up and bagged. Chris watched in rapt interest as each item was slid over the dark red x while Cheryl absently scanned the magazine headlines.

"That'll be $52.11," the checkout girl said.

Cheryl counted out the money as Chris silently blessed her.

"Thank you," she said, looking directly at him.

He took two steps and stopped in his tracks. A smile spread across his face as he turned back to her.

"You *know,*" he said.

"Excuse me?" the girl asked, clearly confused.

"You could *hear* me!" he said, barely able to contain himself.

"Yes sir," she frowned. "I hear you fine."

"I'm sorry," Cheryl said, pulling him toward the door as heads began to turn.

"But honey," he was saying excitedly as she escorted him out of the store, "she knew!"

~

They met at dusk. CJ was sitting on the curb smoking when he spotted Rick crossing the street. He stood. Upon reaching the mall parking lot, Rick leaned his head back and scanned the storefronts from under the bill of his Raiders cap, which was pulled down so ridiculously low that only his bottom lip and chin were visible. CJ often marveled that he never got nailed by a car or walked into a light pole. He waved his arms in the air and Rick angled toward him.

"Did you bring Tony?" he asked as he stepped up on the sidewalk.

CJ nodded. Then, unsure if Rick could even see his head, he tapped his front pocket. The corners of Rick's mouth climbed up under the bill of his cap in what CJ imagined was a huge smile. "Tony" was the nickname they had given the stun gun CJ had stolen and used on the coke-head cop during the Coral Gables burglary. It was sort of a joke/tribute to Tony Montana from the movie *Scarface.*

"Man, lose that hat," CJ implored as they began walking toward Kendall Drive. "You're gonna get us knocked off before we even do anything."

Rick removed his cap and shoved the bill down the back of his jeans. CJ glanced over at him. His eyes were both dilated and bloodshot. It looked like he hadn't slept in a week.

"Damn," CJ muttered, followed by a nervous laugh, "you look fucked up, Rick. You sure you're up for this?"

The truth was it was CJ who was having major second thoughts. Hittin' cribs and splackin' cars were one thing. They didn't have to actually face the victim, unless, of course, they were unknowingly happened upon during the crime. This was a whole other ball game. Robbery implied force, confrontation, violence. CJ was scared, although he'd never admit it to Rick.

Sensing CJ's fear, Rick said, "I'm straight, Cee, don't worry. This ain't nothin'." He added with a hollow smile. "Like taking candy from a baby."

"Babies scream when you do that."

"Not when you electrify their ass first!" Rick laughed.

The plan was simple. Wait in the bushes until some unsuspecting rich sucker pulled up to the glass-enclosed ATM station and hopped out of their car to make a withdrawal. Then hit 'em with the stun gun when they returned and relieve them of their wallet, purse, and any expensive jewelry they might be wearing while they lay there incapacitated.

They arrived at their destination just after nightfall. It was an isolated location in a poorly lit strip mall parking lot close to the hospital. Perfect. They ducked behind the hedges to wait. CJ sucked nervously on a cigarette and stared out through the leafy latticework of bushes at the passing headlights on busy Kendall Drive. A few cars had already pulled up to the ATM, but judging by their appearance, they were not the wealthy victims they were anticipating. As time wore on, he began to hope they never showed. He noticed his hand was trembling as he brought the Newport to his lips for a last drag. *Fuck this,* he thought as the sweat from his armpits streamed down his sides. His job—his only job—was to make contact with the stun gun. Rick would handle the rest. Then, they'd run like hell. If they got split up, they'd meet back at the Peaches where April worked. Simple.

A white Jag pulled quickly to a stop in front of them and an older woman with a Louis Vuitton purse popped out and headed for the ATM machine. Rick and CJ looked at each other as the sound of her heels clicked sharply on the asphalt.

"Let's go!" Rick whispered.

They stood slowly and looked around before abandoning the safety of the thick hedges. CJ reached in his pocket and gripped the stun gun tightly. He was committed now. *Candy from a baby. Candy from a baby.* He kept repeating the phrase in an attempt to amp himself up. He focused on the woman's back as he crossed the parking lot. She was pressing numbers into the machine. He gripped the flat rectangular box in his pocket even harder as he approached her car. *She could easily be your mom,* his conscience defiantly pointed out. He stubbornly set his jaw and fought back the voice as he began to slide the stun gun from his jeans pocket. Rick had his hat on again. Suddenly—zzzzzzz—he was looking up at the sky.

"CJ, get up," somebody was saying, "come on, man, get the fuck up!"

He couldn't respond or move or do anything. His leg felt like it was on fire and although he was consumed by the maddening urge to rub it, he couldn't lift a finger. He was paralyzed. *Why?* his brain screamed.

Rick's terror-stricken face swam into view above him. "Come on, Cee! Snap out of it!" he urged, shaking him violently.

"Hey!" a woman's voice shrieked. "Get off him!" It was the lady with the Jag, the lady they were about to rob. He felt Rick digging in his pockets.

"Somebody help!" she screamed as a few storeowners came out of their shops to see what all the noise was about. "This man's being ROBBED!"

Rick shot off into the night, leaving CJ motionless on the concrete as the sounds of far-off sirens drew near.

The woman knelt down next to him and smiled consolingly. "It's okay, darling," she cooed while reaching out to stroke his horrified face. "I saw the whole thing. The police will be here any minute."

~

It was 4:00 a.m. when Kim Curlac turned off U.S. 1 into her apartment complex. She was exhausted from spending the last eight hours on her feet behind the bar at Loco Pete's. The luster of working on Miami Beach had faded long ago, but the money was good so she couldn't complain. Enrolling in bartending school was one of the best decisions she had ever made; it sure beat the shit out of working at a convenience store like she used to, or making peanuts at a record store like April.

She backed into a parking space and cut the engine on her Jetta. Her open car door began its monotonous dinging while she used the overhead light to search for her purse and apron, which had fallen on the passenger floorboard at a red light. The draft on her ass and thighs told her that her miniskirt had ridden way up as she bent over the center console to gather her things from the floor. She was too tired to care.

"Hey, Kim," came a voice from behind her.

Shit, she thought, quickly reaching back to snatch her skirt down. *Mike.*

Mike Lozano was an off-duty cop who made extra money by moonlighting as apartment security. He lived in the building adjacent to Kim and April with his wife and daughter. He was tall and handsome, with dark, wavy hair and a deep tan. They had first met at the pool last year. She and April were exploring the grounds of their new residence when they came upon him swimming laps. They purposely hung around the area until he was finished, taking their time to inspect the sauna, the weight room, and the racquetball court. They both froze as he exited the pool, shaking the water from his hair as he emerged. His black swimming trunks clung to his muscular legs and left little to the imagination as the water rolled down his chest and abs. He glanced in their direction and smiled. April batted her lashes and whispered, "Yum." Kim shyly looked away.

"Hi, Mike," she said as she stepped out of the Volkswagen and locked the door. She had to squeeze between him and the car to cross the parking lot to her building. Of course, he did this intentionally. It was a little game he played. She smiled slightly and avoided eye contact as she slid by. The air was strong with the scent of his Calvin Klein Obsession cologne.

Kimberly Curlac thought Mike Lozano was a first-class dickhead. Her initial attraction to his golden Adonis body was quickly overshadowed by his game show host smile. She had seen his type line the stools at her bar night after night since she began working there over a year ago. The phony grins, the exaggerated leers, the chest hair and gold chains, the lame pickup lines, and the invitations to after-parties or to quiet hotel rooms on the beach. She had met over a thousand Mike Lozanos during her career at Loco Pete's and even more before that. What disgusted her most about him was the idea of his adoring, devoted wife asleep in their bed while he lathered up in cologne and roamed the parking lot until she showed.

The thought of him seeing her skirt hiked up made her skin crawl. The only real benefit to his thinly disguised stalking was the police escort to her front door. Miami could be a dangerous place at 4:00 a.m. and she had to admit she felt safe with his dumb ass swaggering along next to her as she walked to her apartment.

"How was work?" he asked smoothly.

"Tiring."

"A massage would probably be just what the doctor ordered."

She completely ignored that one.

He tried again. "When was the last time you went skinny dipping?"

"Mike, I'm really tired," she said, jamming her key in the door and opening it, "and you're really married," she couldn't resist adding, before closing it in his face.

She turned into the living room and stopped short. The ashtray was overflowing with cigarette butts as well as marijuana roaches, a half-bottle of Jack sat on the coffee table next to a few empty baggies containing what looked like cocaine residue, and a bra was slung lazily over the back of the couch. Her eyes narrowed. She knew who was responsible for this: the same little bastard that had been sleeping with her sister, eating out of her fridge, and leaving pubic hair stuck in her bath towel. She had met him once and disliked him instantly. A little baby-faced street kid in baggy jeans and a starter jersey. She could overlook the suspiciously expensive diamond bracelet April now wore, and the fact that they were having sex was none of her concern; April was a big girl. She could even turn a blind eye to the weed and the liquor as she had been doing for months now. It was the cocaine that made her stomach turn. She had to do something before things got out of hand. She bit down on her bottom lip in consternation before making a decision. She turned quickly and opened the front door again, half expecting to see Mike still standing on the doormat. He wasn't. She looked down the hall and caught sight of him near the stairwell door.

"Mike!" she whispered loudly down the corridor.

He turned slowly at the sound of her voice; an arrogant smile was plastered across his tan face.

"I need a big favor from you," she said, meeting him halfway down the hall.

"Anything."

"Well, there's this kid who's been hanging around the apartment lately. You may have noticed him . . ."

~

Rick Robinson lived in a shotgun house just off South Dixie Highway in a neighborhood called Perrine. It was the only place he had ever lived besides juvie. There was an old rusty Nova sitting on bricks in the high grass of the front yard. It used to belong to his brother, Ty, before he was shot in the spine and paralyzed from the waist down. Nino, his cousin Mike-Mike's pit bull, barked viciously at the dope boys on the corner and occasionally flung himself violently against the fence in frustration when they refused to acknowledge him. Jaundice-eyed crackheads staggered up the block while an 808 bass line rumbled in the distance.

Although the outside of the house was a ramshackle collection of rotting wood, grimy windows, and old green paint, the inside was just the opposite: clean and neat with dark leather furniture and a massive entertainment center. The TV showed live images of rowdy football fans in Georgia Bulldog jerseys shouting into the camera and holding up their index fingers defiantly.

No one in the room paid the television any attention. They were all listening to CJ recount the details of his and Rick's botched ATM robbery the other night. Mike-Mike, Rick's Uncle Dave, Nica, Re-Rock,

Flex, Yvonne, even his brother Ty, who was normally grumpy and aloof, all hung on his every word.

"Well, what happened next?" Rick asked.

"The cops came," CJ responded, "right after you left. Ambulances too."

"So what'd you tell 'em?" Rick probed.

"Shit," said CJ, surprised by the question. "I told 'em you robbed me."

The room burst into laughter. Rick slapped him on the back and shook his head. Mike-Mike passed him the joint he was smoking and turned up the volume on the TV. Even Ty fought back a gold-toothed grin.

". . . and back to return the kick," the play-by-play announcer was saying, "Mario Robinson, number twenty-seven, the sophomore out of Miami, Florida."

"Y'all shut up!" Mike-Mike said. "It's Mario!"

Everyone in the room paused except Ty, who wheeled his wheelchair closer to get a good look at his brother returning the opening kick against the Gators on national television. The kicker approached the tee flanked by five of his teammates on either side. He laid into the ball and sent it flying end over end to the other side of the field as his coverage team rushed headlong into the teeth of the Georgia wedge. Mario pulled the ball to his body five yards deep in the end zone, then shot up field as if he'd been fired from a rocket launcher. He flew past his wall of blockers and made the few remaining defenders look foolish as they clumsily grasped at air in his wake. He put an exclamation point on the electrifying run by hurdling the onrushing kicker and prancing untouched into the opposing end zone. The stadium erupted, the entire state of Georgia cheered and the Perrine community that raised Mario Robinson ran out on their lawns to celebrate. Mike-Mike and Re-Rock even fired their pistols in the air until Ty silenced them with a look. CJ was always amazed by the fact that Ty Robinson ran his block from a wheelchair and no one challenged him. He walked over to where Rick was standing on the porch.

"Hey, butterscotch," CJ said, using the name Duke had given him in the detention center.

"You better dig your mouth, cracker," Rick snarled.

CJ laughed and held up his hands. "My bad. I forgot how sensitive you are."

"Fuck you." Rick smiled.

"You got my shit?" CJ asked.

"What shit?"

"Come on, man, don't play, you know what shit. Tony, my money, I think I had a sack too."

"I smoked it."

"That's cool."

"I borrowed sixty dollars from you too."

"Damn, man," CJ scowled, "anything else?"

"I'll be right back," Rick replied, going back in the house. When he returned he handed him Tony and a wad of bills. "I can't believe you shocked yourself," Rick said with a huge smile. "Crazy-ass white boy."

CJ counted his money. "Hey," he said, confused. "You didn't take sixty bucks. There's two hundred extra in here."

"I know," Rick smiled, "that's from Ty. For not snitchin'."

"Snitchin'?" CJ looked at him funny. "I would never snitch. On you or anyone else."

"Come on, Cee, that goes without sayin'," he said, looking a little uncomfortable, "but they don't know that. Plus you *are* a white boy."

"Who gives a fuck?" CJ bristled.

"Uh oh," Rick grinned, "now we both sensitive, huh?"

CJ laughed and the tension melted as quickly as it surfaced. "You gonna chill for a while?" Rick asked him.

"Nah. I promised April I'd come by."

"You want anything before you go?" Rick raised an eyebrow. "Unc got some fire today."

"Yeah," said CJ, peeling off the two hundreds from Ty and handing them to him.

"Whatchu want, white or green?"

"Half and half," CJ answered, rubbing his hands together. Rick's Uncle Dave always had the best of the best. He fired up a Newport and leaned against the porch railing to wait.

~

The churn and snarl of a distorted guitar reverberated through the stereo system. April reached over and turned the volume down a little. She noticed the clock. It was almost three in the morning. CJ was sitting in the center of her bed breaking up a bud. They had been going at it heavy since six, alternating between smoking, snorting, and having sex. Their time together had a surreal quality to it, as if her bedroom was an independent universe. A trippy, dimly lit world where she and CJ lazily floated around in space, occasionally crashing into each other in desperate, hungry sexual collisions before separating and floating off again. CJ especially seemed to attack every line, every joint, every kiss, and every thrust with a gluttonous voracity as if it was in danger of being his last. *Was he always like this?* she wondered. It seemed like once upon a time *she* was in control, dating other men, playing on his insecurities, toying with him, beckoning him when she was bored, and sending him away when it suited her. Sure, she was using him. And he was using her. That was the agreement. That was the beauty of their "no strings" relationship. Unfortunately, the reason these types of relationships rarely work is because one of the two parties eventually becomes attached. A year ago she would have never thought it possible, but she could no longer hide from the truth: she needed him. The question was how did he feel about her?

She lay her head on his leg and looked up at him as he held the rolling paper lined with weed in one hand and used the other to saturate the tiny green nuggets in the white rocky powder he sprinkled from the coke sack. He nodded his head hypnotically to the music.

"CJ," she asked sweetly, "can you imagine having any woman you wanted? Anywhere you went?"

"Uh-uh," he responded, only half listening as he finished twisting the dirty and stuck it between his lips. He used a lit candle on her nightstand to fire it up.

"I mean," she said, watching him closely from the corner of her eye, "everywhere you go, people are wondering who you'll take home that night, hoping it's them. Hoping they'll be the one you choose to kiss and hold and make love to, but only you know who it's going to be . . ."

CJ took a deep pull.

". . . and who it's going to be is entirely up to you. You can have anyone you want." She continued to watch him carefully. "Can you imagine what that would be like?"

He shook his head.

"Because that's what it's like for me, every day."

He released a monstrous plume of smoke into the air and looked down at her before replying, "Awesome."

She responded by punching him in the ankle and rolling over to face the huge Marilyn Monroe poster on her closet door. CJ smoothed her hair back from her face, which was still resting on his leg. *"Asshole,"* she mumbled.

...

CJ stared down at April. She was confusing when he was sober, but when he was wasted? *Forget it.*

"Did you want to hit this?" he asked, holding the joint in front of her face.

She answered by grabbing his wrist and bringing his fingers to her lips, smoking from his hand. Once she exhaled, she rolled back over to face him. Her green eyes sparkled in the candlelight.

"Give me a shotgun," she demanded.

He dutifully stuck the cherry end of the joint in his mouth so that only the back end protruded from his lips. He then lowered this head while blowing out a volcanic stream of smoke which she opened her mouth and accepted. Their lips touched as she inhaled. He continued to absently stroke her face and hair as he lifted his head and removed the joint from his mouth.

"Want one?" she asked, blowing out the smoke.

He nodded and handed it to her, watching dazedly as she put it in her mouth and sent a laser stream of smoke up toward him. He again covered her mouth with his, this time on the receiving end.

CJ became acutely aware of a rapidly approaching *wom wom wom* sound in the apartment. It continued to grow in bass and volume until the whole room seemed to tremble under its magnitude. April looked up at him, perplexed. He was becoming frantic.

"What's that sound?!?" he shouted.

Suddenly there was no sound, only the dying echo of his voice in their heads. They were beyond trashed.

"Shhh," April whispered, stifling a giggle. Then CJ began to laugh too, realizing the sound he heard was only in his head.

"Whoa," he said, causing her to laugh harder, which, in turn, made him crack up again and on it went, building and building, until they both lay on her bed holding their sides and giggling uncontrollably.

She climbed on top of him and pinned his hands to the bed. His laughter trailed off when he saw the serious look on her pretty face.

"Do you have other girls?"

"Huh?" he responded blankly, still trying to adjust to the rapid change of mood in the room.

"Girls," April persisted, "how many are there?"

CJ was confused. There were no other girls. Only her, but *was she jealous?* He wondered. *Impossible,* he thought, frowning up at her. For once he wished he wasn't so ripped. Then maybe he could better process the situation. At the moment, she had him at an extreme disadvantage, and one thing he had learned from her was that it was all about who had the advantage. So he did what he knew she would do in his situation; he delayed.

"Why?" he asked.

She shoved her knee in his crotch. "Don't play with me, CJ." Her eyes narrowed. "I want the truth."

"Okay, okay." He laughed. *She is jealous,* he thought. "Three," he said, straight-faced.

"Three?" she asked incredulously before slumping against his chest, deflated.

As much as his ego was enjoying this uncharacteristic and clearly drug-induced outward display of emotion from her, he couldn't let her suffer any longer.

"April," he said softly.

"What?" she mumbled into his chest.

"Just you."

"Liar," she pouted, raising her head slightly to look at him again.

"You're the only girl I've ever been with and the only one I want," he said, the words flowing out of him now. "I like what we have, and not just the sex part. I mean, don't get me wrong, the sex is perfect. You're perfect. But it's not just that. You're my best friend. Really, my *only* friend, besides Rick."

She was staring searchingly into his soul through tear-filled eyes. "Oh, CJ," she said, collapsing on his chest again and holding him tight.

He allowed himself to languish in her affection for one sweet moment before acknowledging the fact that they were really high and this was April and tomorrow things would probably be different.

"Oh my God!" she exclaimed, noticing the clock. "It's almost four! Kim will be home any minute. Get dressed!"

"Damn," said CJ, grabbing his jeans off the floor and slipping them on. "I thought we were gonna get to cuddle for a while."

"Shut up," she said, smiling, "you know damn well you weren't planning on cuddling, perv."

She walked him to the front door and opened it. He stepped out into the hall and looked around before pulling her to him and kissing her deeply once more.

"Bye," he said throatily, after reluctantly breaking away. She held onto his hand.

"Come back tomorrow."

"Definitely." He smiled, not knowing if it was the drugs or her kiss that had him so dizzy.

"I love you," she whispered, finally releasing his hand and shutting the door before he could respond.

He stared at the closed door a moment longer, then turned and walked slowly down the hall, replaying the last hour over and over in his head, wondering if any of it was real. *Am I dreaming?* he asked himself. *Hallucinating? Maybe I'm really at home in bed asleep. Oh shit!* he thought, *I didn't accidently stun myself again, did I? Wait! Is that cologne I'm smelling?*

"Hey, dirtbag," a voice called out of the shadows by the stairwell, jerking him back to reality. "I've got a question for you."

CJ stood motionless as a man with a flashlight emerged from the darkness.

"How does a pathetic-looking loser like you bag a hot chick like April Curlac, hmm?"

He was tall, at least a foot taller than CJ, with blow-dried hair and a superhero chin. He aimed his Maglite in CJ's face as he ambled toward him.

"Is it your muscular build?" he asked sarcastically. "Your sparkling personality? I know. It's your monster cock, right?" He flicked the beam down at CJ's crotch before quickly shining it in his eyes again. "I doubt it."

CJ eased his hand toward his pocket for Tony. He could feel the flat box resting against his leg through his jeans. He didn't feel high anymore.

"Know what I think?" Blow-dryer asked him. "I think she just likes your drugs, asshole. Keep your hands where I can see 'em! Get 'em up! That's better. Now, you got any drugs on you, dirtbag?"

Fuck, CJ's mind screamed, *a cop!* He rapidly processed the situation. He had dope on him, not to mention a stun gun he'd stolen from a cop's house. If he let Blow-dryer pat him down, he was going to jail. The problem was that the only way out was down the stairs, and unfortunately the cop had positioned himself between them and CJ.

He had to somehow get around him, or go through him. He obviously wasn't carrying a gun; otherwise, it would be pointed in CJ's face. *Maybe he's not a real cop,* CJ thought.

"Don't even think about running, punk," he threatened, "you'll regret it."

Definitely a cop, he concluded. CJ made a quick decision. He'd run right at full speed and try to get by. If he was grabbed, he'd surprise him with Tony in the scuffle. He just needed to avoid getting bashed with the Maglite.

He didn't plan on yelling, but as he exploded into motion, a loud roar erupted from his vocal cords, catching Mike Lozano completely off guard. CJ had committed to his right side, but the cop had already recovered and was swinging his flashlight as he approached so CJ feinted left and threw him off balance before going low and scurrying between his long legs.

By the time Lozano whirled around, CJ was halfway down the first flight of stairs. When he reached the landing, he never slowed; he just grabbed the railing and swung his 125 pounds in a half-circle, landing in stride on the next flight and picking up speed. But Mike's steps equaled two of CJ's and he closed the distance quickly. Their loud rumbling down the stairwell could be heard throughout the building. When CJ approached the final flight, Mike was ten steps behind him on the next landing. He angrily flung his heavy flashlight at CJ's head, hoping to slow or stop him. It tomahawked down through the air and glanced harmlessly off his shoulder, clanging noisily on the metal steps in his wake. Mike took two steps and leapt to the landing as CJ burst through the exit door.

Kim Curlac never saw it coming. One second she was at the door of her building and the next, she was flat on her back.

The collision caught CJ by surprise too, and the recoil of the blow sent him stumbling, allowing Mike the opportunity to close the final few steps and slam him into the concrete while his brain was still rattled.

Before CJ could even think straight, he was face down and tightly cuffed with the cop's knee in his back. He laid his cheek on the concrete and looked over at the lady sitting on the sidewalk as the cop rifled forcefully through his pockets, removing the dope, his money, and the stun gun.

"You okay, Kim?" the cop asked over his shoulder. It was then that CJ realized it was April's sister he'd pancaked.

She nodded unsteadily.

"You're under arrest, asshole!" the cop shouted in his ear.

Chapter 9

CJ sat stoically in the dusty windowless room, staring up at the wanted posters and miscellaneous memos tacked on the bulletin board. The handcuffs chewed mercilessly into the thin layer of flesh surrounding his bony wrists, causing him to constantly shift their position in search of relief. There was none. Besides himself and the folding chair he was parked in, the only other objects in the room were the rickety table in front of him, a few old metal filing cabinets in the corner, and an empty coffeepot on a small stand by the door. Since there were no windows, he instinctively glanced up at the ceiling for a potential escape route, then scoffed at his own naiveté. *Come on, man, you ain't going nowhere in these tight-ass handcuffs.* He sank an inch in the chair as that reality set in. He was somewhere in the bowels of the Metro-Dade Police Station. He had no idea what time it was or how long he'd been there. He wasn't even sure what he was being charged with. No one had told him shit. He assumed it was going to be some type of drug possession deal and a weapons charge for the stun gun; maybe they'd throw in a resisting arrest just to be assholes. *Fuck it,* he thought. *Just get me to juvie. I wonder if Mr. Jackson is still working Unit 1. He's gonna be disappointed. I hope I don't get that same public defender. What was his name? Levin? He sucked.*

His thoughts were disturbed by muffled voices in the hall along with the approaching clicking of loafers on tile. The mention of his own name made him strain to hear what they were saying.

". . . contacted DYS about the McCallister kid?" A high-pitched New York accent came into focus.

"Not yet," answered a gruff voice that matched that of the detective who dumped him in the dusty office.

"Why not?" asked New York.

"I'm waiting on Alvorado," said McGruff as they clicked past the room where CJ was handcuffed.

"Alvorado?" asked New York, sounding confused. "For what?"

"Well," McGruff began as they turned a corner, "it's just that I'd like Al to have the . . ." Their voices faded out of earshot as the receding taps of their footsteps disappeared down the hallway.

CJ contemplated the new information, what little there was. McGruff wore a suit. *Obviously a detective,* CJ deduced, *but what field? Narcotics?* He knew that DYS was Division of Youth Services, but he wondered who Alvorado was and why they were delaying contacting juvie until he came.

More time went by and his apprehension slowly gave way to exhaustion. He slumped in the chair. He had been awake for longer than twenty-four hours and the cocaine, as good as it was, had long ago worn off. He kept dreaming that he was still in April's room; she had him pinned to the bed and was interrogating him about other girls. Just when he got to the point where she said she loved him, the weight of his head dropped down, causing his chin to bounce off his chest and his eyes to open alertly. He looked around the dingy little office once more, got his bearings, attempted to alleviate the pain and numbness in his hands by adjusting the cuffs, then drifted back to sleep, initiating the entire process again.

It went on like that for hours: nod off, same dream, chin meets chest, eyes pop open, look around room, adjust cuffs, nod off again. It was somewhere deep into the rotation of this pattern that his eyes popped open to find a man across the table with thick muscle-corded forearms folded across his chest. He was smiling. There was something vaguely familiar about him, but CJ couldn't place it.

"Good morning, Sunshine," he said. "Remember me?"

CJ slowly shook his head as his brain frantically flicked through faces from the past, seeking a match. His mind shuffled through an endless stack of mental Polaroids—snapshots of former neighbors, teachers, his mom's coworkers from the Essex, staff from juvie, and even the Longwood Center. He didn't know him.

Then he remembered. There was no smile on *that* face. It was red. Purple, even. His eyes flashed and his teeth were bared as he flew through his living room in pursuit of CJ. The same face was frozen in rage as he filled it with a thousand volts of electricity and hauled ass out the back door. Yeah, he remembered him. He was the crooked cop from Coral Gables, and CJ was in deep shit.

~

Cheryl McCallister knocked softly on CJ's bedroom door before opening it slightly and peeking in. She rarely saw her son anymore and she enjoyed looking in on him sleeping in the mornings before she left for work.

His unmade bed was empty. She opened the door wider and surveyed the small, unkempt bedroom. No CJ. She looked back over her shoulder at the open bathroom door. The light was out. He wasn't in there either. She glanced at her watch, a thin gold Relic given to her by her husband in happier times. It was almost 6:00 a.m. She needed to leave for work. She walked into the living room where Chris laid sleeping in a tweed suit she remembered from his bank president days in the early '70s. He snored lightly for a change. She grabbed her keys off the coffee table and jingled them noisily. He didn't stir.

"Chris," she said loudly, resolving to keep the contempt from her face. He opened one eye and peered up at her. "Have you seen CJ?"

He sat up and shook his head slowly. CJ did the exact same thing whenever he attempted to answer a question while his mind was somewhere far away. She paused and stared at her husband of nineteen years.

The resemblance was uncanny. In the center of all that extra flesh that framed his face—beneath his shining bald head but above his thickly layered neck and chin—his eyes, nose, and mouth offered the world indisputable proof of the child he had helped produce.

"Well, when he comes home, tell him to wait here until I get off work tonight. It's been a long time since we've all been in the same room together and I'd like to have dinner as a family."

"A trinity," he whispered mystically.

She rolled her eyes. "No, asshole." He winced at her uncharacteristic profanity. "Not a trinity," she growled, "a family. *Your* family. The one that's been falling apart ever since you took off for la-la land!"

His eyes followed her across the living room to the front door.

She turned back toward him as she opened it. "You know," she said acidly, "it's funny how you consider yourself the savior of the world, yet you can't even save your own family." She punctuated her sentence by slamming the door.

~

"So," Detective Alvorado probed as he circled CJ, "where the fuck is my jewelry?"

"I think you've got the wrong—" CJ couldn't even complete the sentence before a lightning quick hand shot out and bounced his head off the table.

"Wrong answer, douchebag!" snarled Alvorado, continuing to circle him.

CJ's brain was momentarily scrambled from the blow. It was as if someone was pressing a strobe light against his eye. When his ears stopped ringing he became aware of the cop's voice behind him.

". . . my jewelry, my wife's jewelry, my cash, my watch." He leaned in close and whispered, "My coke."

CJ was terrified. "I want an attorney," he said shakily.

Alvorado snapped. He snatched CJ out of his chair by the collar and flung him into the file cabinets across the room. He would have been no match for the burly Alvorado even without the handcuffs, but at least he could have broken the fall. With his hands locked behind his back, he was forced to lead with his face, which exploded on impact against the metal file cabinets. He fell to the floor in a heap, the iron taste of blood filling his mouth. He rolled slowly up on his knees, his forehead pressed against the cold floor in a puddle of blood. He heard footsteps, then felt a sharp explosion of pain in his ribs, *crack!* as Alvorado planted a boot in his stomach. Then another. And another. Suddenly CJ's survival instincts kicked in. He was going to die in this room if he didn't do something. It wasn't really a decision, he just panicked out of fear and pain, and the will to live took over. He released a primal scream as he rolled to his back and launched his body, feet first, into the groin of Alvorado's tight jeans.

It was probably CJ's scream that saved his life. After stumbling back in shock, Alvorado quickly regrouped and charged him again. "Motherfucker," he spat, rushing straight into CJ's kicking feet and falling on top of him, huge hands clasped around his neck, crushing him with his weight while choking the life out of him and banging his head against the floor.

There was a flurry of motion and a voice yelled, "Alvorado! Cut it out!"

Then the lights flickered and dimmed to pitch blackness.

~

CJ woke up handcuffed to a bed in Jackson Memorial Hospital. A nurse stood over him fidgeting with a tube that ran from his nose to what looked like an oxygen tank, while a uniformed cop sat at the foot of his bed watching a cooking show on TV.

CJ glanced down at his wrist, where more tubes connected him to beeping machines and monitors beside the bed. He found a few more taped to his chest and, after looking below the sheet, he was shocked to find one running out of the head of his penis.

The nurse smiled at his reaction. "Don't worry, we'll remove it this afternoon. We were just waiting on you to wake up. Welcome back."

CJ touched his face. It felt funny. "Do you have a mirror?"

The nurse looked over at the officer sitting at the foot of the bed, as if he might object. When he didn't, she shrugged and walked into the small bathroom, returning with a mirror and holding it in front of CJ.

He laughed out loud, causing the nurse to frown. Even the cop glanced back at him curiously. He couldn't help it. The reflection in the mirror reminded him of a movie his dad had taken him to see when he was a kid in Alabama. He looked like the elephant man. His entire head was swollen, misshapen, knotted, bruised, stitched, and completely unrecognizable. Apparently Detective Alvorado was still a little angry about being robbed and blasted in the face with his own stun gun. CJ laughed again. Laughing hurt like hell and the nurse was looking at him like he was a psychopath, but he didn't care. He was alive! He knew he was in a shitload of trouble and had made a powerful enemy, but he was also aware that he came very close to dying down in that office and the fact that he was lying here, handcuffed to the bed, with a tube in his dick and an elephant man head was nothing short of a miracle.

Like most kids, CJ was caught up in the illusion of his own invincibility. This was most evident in the reckless way he lived his life. Death happened to other people. *Older* people. And "older" was a long way off. But nothing can bring a man to terms with his own mortality faster than a brush with death, and what happened earlier this morning with Alvorado definitely qualified. *That was this morning, wasn't it?* He looked sharply at the nurse.

"How long have I been here?"

"Let's see," she said, walking to the door and checking a clipboard, "three days."

"Wow, I've been out for three days?"

"Pretty much."

"Was I in a coma?"

The officer scowled at them and mumbled something unintelligible as he stood to adjust the volume on the television.

"No," answered the nurse, "but you had some head trauma and that, combined with the drugs you were coming down from, in addition to what the doctor prescribed, knocked you out for a while."

It hurt to breathe. "Are my ribs broken?"

"Cracked. They'll heal and you'll be fine," she glanced over at the officer before adding, "I mean, you know, health wise."

CJ glanced at him too. "Does my mom know I'm here?"

"Oh yeah." She smiled. "She's been calling nonstop since Monday. Unfortunately this is a secure ward and visiting is prohibited, but I wouldn't doubt it if she was on the phone with the governor right now trying to gain admission. I've spoken to her myself numerous times. She's a sweet lady and she obviously loves you very much." She looked at the floor uncomfortably. "Maybe you should consider not making her worry so much whenever you get out."

CJ nodded.

"Well," said the nurse, avoiding eye contact as she gathered her Velcro blood pressure cuffs and thermometer, "I'll check on you again in an hour. Try to rest."

"Hey," he said to her back while peering beneath his sheet again, "who's gonna take this out?"

She turned around. "The same person who inserted it, I imagine."

"Oh. Who's that?"

"Me." She smiled and shut the door behind her.

He glanced back under the sheet at his shriveled manhood. Maybe it was the medication, maybe it was the tube running out of it, or maybe it was simply the temperature of the room, but it looked extremely small. Fifth grade small, swimming in February small, grub worm in a turtleneck small. He dropped the sheet and groaned with embarrassment at the thought of the pretty nurse working down there when he was so obviously unprepared for public viewing.

He looked up at the TV. A commercial was on.

"What am I charged with?" he asked the cop. "Do you know?"

The officer stretched and looked over at CJ. "Let's see . . . armed burglary, armed assault, carrying a concealed weapon, possession of a controlled substance, battery on a LEO . . . I think that's it."

"Battery on a LEO?" CJ blurted.

"Yeah, you attacked Detective Alvorado back at the station. You were pretty trashed, kid."

"*I* attacked *him?* He almost killed me!"

The cooking show was back on. "Yeah, yeah. Tell it to the judge."

CJ leaned carefully back in the bed. *No wonder they put me in that old office instead of an interview room,* he thought, *no video cameras.*

"When are you planning on moving me to juvie?" CJ asked the back of his head.

"Whenever the doc releases you. But you ain't going to juvie, kid. You've been direct filed. You're in the big leagues now."

~

It wasn't that Chris McCallister had snapped out of it all of a sudden. He still believed he was special, chosen, and quite possibly the messiah Peter Jennings claimed he was a year ago in the living room. But his wife had raised a valid point the other day: How could he possibly save the world when he couldn't even save his own family? That day was a genesis of sorts for him. He began by flushing the remainder of the weed CJ had given him down the toilet. Then he killed time by cleaning the entire apartment top to bottom while he waited for *World News Tonight* to come on. When the familiar theme music played and Jennings was introduced, Chris politely but firmly interrupted his monologue and told him in no uncertain terms that everything—even the fate of the world—would have to wait until he worked out a few personal things in his life. Petras ignored him, as he had been doing for months now, but there was nothing else Chris could do. His family needed him.

He walked determinedly up 164th Street toward the Harbor Oaks sign. He stopped at a crosswalk and pulled the Camels from the inside pocket of his jacket. The sun felt good on his face. He fired up a cigarette and walked on.

He was heartbroken when he received the call from that detective telling him that CJ was in bad shape as well as big trouble. He would never forget the way his hysterical wife pounded her small fists against his face, chest, and shoulders in a tearful fit of rage when he broke the news to her that night. He didn't budge nor did he turn away. He stood there and accepted every blow until she finally collapsed on the floor, sobbing loudly. He lowered his massive frame down next to her and began stroking her hair as she wept. At first, she angrily pushed his hand away. But watching her cry without attempting to comfort her was impossible, and eventually he reached out for her again, and again, until she finally relented.

He strode confidently through the parking lot of Harbor Oaks. He knew this place and his own destiny were intertwined. Even the first time he had seen the commercial on TV, it had resonated with something deep inside him. At the time he couldn't understand why. The ad itself was corny and low-tech with terrible acting, plus it wasn't like he needed the services they offered. Yet, he was still inexplicably drawn in each time the commercial ran. Now he knew why.

No, he hadn't magically snapped out of anything. There was nothing to snap out of. He was who he was. Unless he was crazy like his wife seemed to think. He shrugged. None of that mattered right now. His son was in serious trouble and Cheryl was falling apart. He had to do something.

His plan took shape quickly. There would be a court date at some point in the future. The last time CJ was in trouble he snuck tokes in the car and let Cheryl do the talking while he quietly fondled his rosary beads. Not this time. He would start by getting a respectable job. He'd attend N.A. meetings every night and even take public speaking courses if he had to so that when he was called on to speak on his son's behalf, he could make a solid impression and *maybe, just maybe,* save his life.

He glanced down at his suit as he approached the door. It was outdated and a little too big for him, but it was clean and pressed. The last time he wore it he was a 360-pound bank president in Alabama. Now, due mostly to the spiritual awakening he had last year, he was falling rapidly toward the Mendoza line at 295. Physically, he felt better than ever. His only complaint was a nagging respiratory problem that kept waking him at night, but that was more of a minor aggravation than a health concern. For a fifty-year-old overweight smoker, he felt surprisingly healthy.

He stepped into the air-conditioned lobby of the Harbor Oaks Assisted Living Facility and Retirement Village. A bell chimed and a smiling woman in her early sixties came out of her office and greeted him.

"Hello, can I help you?"

He extended a hand. "I'm Chris McCallister."

She accepted it readily. "Doris Harper. Do you have an appointment?"

"No ma'am, I—"

"Oh thank heavens. My secretary has the flu and I misplaced the appointment book. Yesterday I had to do two tours I was completely unprepared for, plus a Tony Orlando impersonator was apparently scheduled to do a concert in the banquet hall, which I knew nothing about, and on top of all that, I . . ." Her voice trailed off. "Forgive me. How may I help you, sir?"

"I'm here for a job."

"Oh," she frowned, "I wasn't aware we were hiring. Is there an ad in the paper?"

"No ma'am."

There was an awkward silence as they stood there in the lobby. A clock ticked loudly. She spent a few uncomfortable moments sizing him up before turning sharply on her heel.

"Follow me," she said over her shoulder.

She walked behind a desk in her spacious office and motioned for him to sit down. "Let's see," she began, "do you speak any Spanish?"

"No ma'am."

"Last grade completed?"

"Twelfth."

"Ever been arrested?"

"No ma'am."

"Married?"

"Yes ma'am."

"Enough with the ma'am," she scolded. "Kids?"

"One."

"Do you have a valid Florida driver's license?"

"Yes m—" he caught himself. "Yes."

She smiled without looking up. "Tickets?"

"Two."

"Speeding?"

"One speeding, sixty in a forty-five, and one parking."

She removed her glasses and studied him with penetrating blue eyes. "Are you a patient man, Mr. McCallister?"

He nodded sincerely.

"Tolerant?"

He nodded again.

"Kind?"

"I'd like to think so."

She smiled and reached in a desk drawer, producing a thick stapled packet of papers. "Do you like to drive?"

"Depends on the vehicle."

"We have four late-model Lincoln Continentals. You'll be expected to chauffer residents to doctors' appointments, church, the mall, restaurants, and wherever else they need to go. A schedule will be provided for you at the beginning of each week, but there are always additions and cancellations." She got up from her desk and reached in a plastic basket on the shelf. She extracted a small black Motorola beeper, glanced at the number taped to the side, then tossed it back and grabbed another before walking back to the desk. "That's why we give you these. The number's on the side. Never leave home without it. Okay?" she said, passing it across the desk.

He reached out to accept it. "Yes, ma'am," he said happily, before adding, "sorry."

She smiled. "If we beep you, we expect you to call in and be ready to roll regardless of the hour. That's why we allow you to take the car home. Keep in mind that the car is basically your office. We expect you to keep it clean. Many of our residents are senior women who are very sensitive to odor."

He nodded again. *Wow,* he thought, *I did it!*

"We pay a flat salary of five hundred dollars a week, but you'll get a lot of tip money as well, even though we try to discourage the residents from doing that. Of course, we cover all gas expenses, so save your receipts."

"Got it."

"So, Mr. McCallister," she concluded, handing him a pen, "if you'll just sign those papers," she nodded at the small stack on the desk, "and hand me your driver's license and social security card so I can make copies, we'll go ahead and get you on the road."

"Thank you so much, Ms. Harper," he beamed, "you won't regret this."

"It's Doris. And I know I won't. I'm a terrific judge of character." She looked out her office window and scanned the parking lot. "Did you drive here?"

"I took the bus. My wife uses the car to get to work."

"Oh, perfect. Well, your first customer should be waiting in the lobby now. I was going to beep our other driver before you showed up, but I think Mr. Frank may be the ideal resident to break you in with." Her voice dropped to a whisper. "He's got Alzheimer's."

Chris nodded empathetically as he signed the last paper. When he looked up she was holding out his license, social security card, and a set of keys.

"Welcome to our family." She smiled.

It was after midnight when April finally walked out of Peaches. Her manager shut the lights off and locked the door behind them. She dug in her purse for a cigarette. She glanced sadly at the pack before shaking one out and lighting it. They were Newports. CJ's brand. She had always been a Marlboro Lights girl, but the last few days she had been smoking Newports. They made her feel close to him.

"Come on, April," her boss said. "I'll give you a lift."

"That's okay," she declined. "It's nice out and anyway I'm gonna need a few of these after that shift." She smiled, holding up her cigarette. Her boss drove a brand new Mustang GT and would never allow anyone to smoke in his car, regardless of how bad he wanted to bed them.

"Are you sure? It's awfully late to be out walking."

"I'll be fine, Blaine," she said, already turning away. "See you tomorrow."

"Bye."

She was relieved when she could no longer feel his laser beam eyes burning holes in her back pockets. Blaine was a pretty cool boss and he was fine around other people, but when they were alone he gave her the creeps.

A car full of young people flew by her, heading in the direction of Coconut Grove. They honked and yelled something as they passed, but thankfully they didn't turn back. She was scared. She had grown so accustomed to CJ walking her home on late nights that she had forgotten how it felt to make the journey alone.

She walked fast. Just ahead was the worst part, a quarter-mile section of broken streetlights and eerie darkness. She had always squeezed his hand a little tighter during this leg of the journey. Now there was no hand to squeeze. The distinct sound of a bottle rolling on asphalt disturbed the otherwise quiet night. She glanced down a side street in the direction of the noise and saw a bum staggering toward a dumpster. She walked faster.

By the time she spotted the sign at the entrance to her apartment complex, she was sprinting. The keys and other items in her leather purse bounced rhythmically against her side as she rounded the corner and shot through the quiet parking lot of her apartment building. She imagined that the echoes of her own footsteps belonged to her pursuers. Her heart thumped rapidly in her chest as she cut through the deserted pool area and flew down the sidewalk of her building. She glanced frantically back into the night as she groped at the stairwell door, finally yanking it free and running straight into the outstretched arms of Mike Lozano.

She was momentarily torn between the warm safety of his strong arms and her anger at him for arresting CJ. She allowed her body to sag slightly in relief, feeling the fear and tension evaporate. She was home. She made it. *Next time I'll take Blaine up on the ride,* she promised herself.

Mike's hands had fallen dangerously close to the waistline of her jeans. She could feel his neatly clipped nails scratching lightly against her lower back while he held her tight against his body. His cologne was overpowering. She took a deep breath and wriggled free of his sensual embrace. She shot him a withering look before turning to walk up the four flights of steps to her apartment. He followed.

"We need to talk," he said from behind her.

"I have nothing to say to you," she shot back haughtily.

"April, I'm sorry."

"Fuck off, Mike," she replied as she emerged on her floor and turned down the hallway.

"Just please hear me out," he pleaded, grabbing her by the arm and pulling her back toward him.

He was unprepared for the slap. Actually, she was too. The acoustics of the narrow hall probably made it sound louder than it was, but she didn't waver or apologize for it. The last few days were the loneliest, most agonizingly stressful days of her life, and when he yanked her arm like that, her reaction was automatic.

"I deserved that," he said.

She curled her top lip in disgust before turning back down the hall.

"Listen," he said, "when your sister told me about him, I—"

"Kim?" April stopped in mid-step. "Kim put you on CJ?"

"It wasn't like that. She was worried to death about you and—"

"I'm fucking twenty-two years old!" She looked back at him, exasperated.

Now things were becoming crystal clear. Mike had his nose up Kim's ass ever since they moved in. April regretted not luring him to her bed a long time ago. She could have avoided this whole mess by doing so. She thought back to that first day by the pool. She had made up her mind back then that she was going to have him. His wedding ring didn't bother her at all. And his obvious interest in Kim only cemented her resolve. *What happened?* she wondered. *CJ happened,* she answered herself. The deeper she became involved with him, the less important everything else seemed. She had barely even noticed Mike anymore over the past year. Apparently that wasn't true regarding Kim. *That little slut,* she thought.

He was still talking when she reached her door.

"I only meant to hassle him," he was saying, "you know, scare him a little, but then things got out of control. April, I'm so sorry. Seriously."

She turned in her open doorway to face him. "Prove it."

~

Kim Curlac's ass was still sore as hell from her violent collision with April's little thug boyfriend. She tried shifting her weight to her right cheek to alleviate the throbbing pain in her left, but then the right started hurting. Driving to and from work was the worst. It was a long way from her apartment to the beach, and sitting for long periods of time was excruciating, especially with two football-sized bruises on her backside.

She looked at the clock on the dash. It was a little after one. Her boss had taken pity on her after seeing the way she hobbled around the bar and let her off early. It was a slow night anyway. She looked forward to a couple of extra-strength Tylenol and a glass of cold milk.

When she pulled into her apartment complex she smiled at her good fortune. There was an empty parking space right next to the stairwell entrance. Walking up four flights of steps was bad enough, but walking a mile before she even reached the steps was murder.

She took it slow and used the railing for support. She did it quicker than yesterday, but it still took her all of ten minutes to reach her floor. She fished in her purse for the key as she limped down the hall. She paused momentarily and sniffed the air. *Obsession,* she noted. *Mike.* She hurried to her front door, hoping to make it inside before he appeared.

She quickly unlocked it and slid inside, shutting it firmly behind her and breathing a sigh of relief. She set her purse on the table and took two steps toward the kitchen when a flicker of movement in the living room caught her eye.

She turned to see her naked sister straddling an equally naked Mike Lozano on the couch, their clothes strewn carelessly about the room. They were frozen in mid-act and looking back at her. Mike's expression was a mixture of shock and shame, while April smiled triumphantly.

"Nice," Kim muttered before limping to the kitchen for her Tylenol and milk.

~

By the end of his first week on the job, Chris McCallister was on a first-name basis with most of the residents. It was actually a perfect fit. He amused them by singing along with the oldies station as he drove. He listened to stories about their lives and shared his own stories as well. He didn't consider the residents of Harbor Oaks customers or clients. They were his friends.

Frank Dobbins was probably his favorite resident, though he'd never admit it to anyone. There was just something about him that Chris found fascinating. He'd spent most of his life as a pharmacist in Duluth, Minnesota, but he was also a decorated Korean War veteran, a former Golden Gloves boxing champ, a husband of thirty-five years, a father of two, and most recently, a victim of Alzheimer's.

It was amazing to Chris how one day Frank could fluently discuss molecular compounds and quote famous philosophers, then the next, show up in the lobby for a ride wearing his boxers over his pants. He was both riveted and profoundly saddened by Frank's condition. He wanted to heal him but was unsure how to channel the power. Many times he'd take him along on errands, even when he didn't have any appointments to be driven to. Chris enjoyed picking his brain, not only for the compelling stories of days gone by, which he told masterfully, but also for the slips and quirks related to his dementia.

One afternoon he pulled into the post office parking lot and handed Frank an envelope, a bill Ms. Harper had asked him to drop in the mail.

"Frank, drop this in the box over there, will ya?"

Frank looked at him uncertainly for a moment, then took the envelope and opened the car door. Chris watched him walk up the sidewalk toward the mailbox. He turned the A/C up a notch as Frank paused and looked hesitantly over his shoulder. Chris nodded at him and gave him the thumbs-up. Frank turned back toward the building and took a few more steps before stopping and looking back at him again.

He rolled down the window and stuck his head out. "It's okay, Frank, go ahead." He noticed a man walking back to his car and got his attention. "Sir, can you help him mail that?"

He looked over at Frank and smiled. "Sure. Come on, old timer."

By the time they made it to the box, Frank was looking extremely nervous. He gripped the envelope in his shaking hands and looked back at Chris again, who nodded encouragingly.

"Come on, buddy," the man coaxed.

There were now three hands on the envelope: both of Frank's and one of the man's, who used his free hand to pull the flap down while he tugged stubbornly with the other, guiding it toward the open slot in spite of Frank's obvious reservations.

Frank took a breath and released his grip, allowing the envelope to disappear down the throat of the mailbox. Then he turned and walked quickly back to the car.

"Do you know what you just did?" Chris asked curiously as they were driving away.

Frank nodded solemnly. "Voted for you."

Chapter 10

CJ turned eighteen in the infirmary of the Dade County Jail. He could have been released into population a month earlier, but the medical staff there were all longtime employees of the county and they happened to like him, so they conspired to find reasons to keep him in the infirmary until he was eighteen, thereby sparing him the experience of the tenth floor.

It wasn't that the rest of the jail was much better, but every nurse had volumes of horror stories regarding the tenth floor. As members of the medical team it was their responsibility to come running whenever someone was beaten or raped or killed, and nowhere else in the jail did those things happen as frequently or as brutally as they did on the tenth floor, the area reserved for juveniles who had been direct filed.

Unfortunately the infirmary needed to make bed space, and since CJ's wounds had completely healed and he was now eighteen years old, the medical staff cleared him for release.

He was herded into a freight elevator with fifteen other inmates by two hulking guards in tight uniforms. They paid little attention to the men they were responsible for transporting. The job was obviously second nature to them. Instead they traded comments about a new female employee who was training downstairs that morning.

"All right, fellas, when I call your name, hop off," said one guard.

The elevator dinged and the doors opened to the second floor.

"Vazquez, Harris, Evans."

The three men pushed through the crowd and stepped off. The elevator doors closed behind them.

"None on the third or fourth," the black guard told his Latino counterpart.

The doors slid open again.

"Byrd, Lopez, Baker, Andrews, Shiz . . . newsky?" the guard attempted.

"Shimkowski, sir," a voice said.

"Whatever. Get off."

The doors closed behind them and once again the elevator began to whirr as it ascended to the next floor.

"McCallister," the guard said as the doors opened.

CJ stepped past them out onto the floor. A female officer was talking on the phone in the booth. She made a come here motion through the glass with a bright red manicured fingernail.

"Hey kid," the Hispanic guard called from the elevator. "How old are you?"

"Eighteen," answered CJ.

"Damn," he said, shaking his head as the doors were closing, "don't drop the soap."

CJ could hear the other inmates on the elevator laughing. *Good one,* he thought, *I've only heard that fifty thousand times over the last two months.*

He walked over to the dimly lit bubble where the officer sat.

"Grab one of those bedrolls over there," she said, covering the mouthpiece of the phone with her hand. "Brown'll take you on the wing when he gets back. Just wait by the grill gate." She nodded at a large steel door with a "B" stenciled on it.

CJ assumed that was where he was going: B-wing. The Dade County Jail was composed of ten floors. Each floor had three wings—A, B, and C—and each wing had four pods. Beyond the grill gate where he stood waiting was a short hallway with two metal doors on each side that opened into the cage-like entrances of the dayrooms. The outer wall of each pod was made of steel bars and encompassed by a catwalk that allowed the occasional strolling guard an unobstructed view into the living quarters. *Thank God for that,* CJ thought as he looked up at the giant steel-reinforced door. *No wonder they call them death traps.* His legs began to tremble in growing anticipation of what was going to happen next. He fought back the fear by repeating a Geto Boys lyric in his head: "If it's going down, let's get this shit over with." It was off "Mind Playing Tricks on Me," Rick's favorite song.

"Did you get off on the wrong floor?" a voice asked.

CJ turned and saw a guard who was maybe an inch taller than he was and not much heavier. His hair was slicked back and he wore a pencil-thin mustache along with a diamond earring and a black t-shirt under his uniform. His name tag said "Brown."

CJ shook his head and nervously shifted the bedroll from under one arm to the other.

Brown pulled a folded sheet of paper from his back pocket and looked at it. "Paul McCallister?"

CJ nodded.

"You don't look like a Paul."

"Everybody calls me CJ."

"Okay, CJ, you're going to 6-B-2. It's fucked up in there, but it's less fucked up than anywhere else on the floor." He studied him a moment. "Can you fight?"

CJ shrugged. His mind involuntarily flicked to images of Duke balled up under the table and a howling Joey Barocela being dragged down the hall.

"Well, here's a piece of advice. Fight. It's easier."

Easier than what, CJ wondered.

"Kane runs a straight house. Nobody's gonna jump you in there, I don't think. When someone tries you—and believe me, they will—don't try to reason with them or talk your way out of it. Just swing. You might win, but even if you lose, the rest of them will understand that you're not a pushover." He smiled. "You're not a pushover, are you?"

CJ shook his head.

"Good." He opened the grill gate. "Oh, and CJ, we never had this conversation."

"Yes, sir," he replied, scared shitless now.

They walked down the hall and stopped at an orange door on the right. Officer Brown unlocked a metal box on the wall and began turning a wheel inside it. The door slowly creaked open to reveal a loading cage made of bars. Beyond the bars were tables where men were noisily slamming dominoes and peering secretively into poker hands. They all stopped what they were doing and half turned toward the creaking door.

"Step in," said Brown.

CJ walked into the cage.

"Fresh meat," a skinny middle-aged dude in a do rag announced loudly, causing the domino table where he was sitting to erupt in a chorus of snickers and catcalls.

The orange door behind him slid shut and moments later the barred door of the cage rolled open. He stepped into the pod. After a brief moment of silence, the card players dealt another hand. Dominoes began to rattle on the table again and the television was turned back up. CJ's presence was forgotten as quickly as it was acknowledged.

A large muscle-bound black man emerged from the bedding area. CJ tried not to stare at the network of hideous scars that slashed across his chest and stomach. In spite of all his fuck-ups, he was still Cheryl McCallister's son and a few of the values she tried to instill in him managed to stick. Staring was rude, especially at scars and physical deformities. So he sidestepped the approaching giant, set his bedroll on the floor, and walked purposefully to the domino table.

Do-rag was busy keeping score and never saw it coming. CJ reared back and slapped him so hard that he fell off the bench. Then he followed quickly with a torrential flurry of punches and kicks, causing him to ball up on the floor and yell for help.

CJ was ripped off of him by the scarred giant, and Do-rag immediately bounced to his feet as more inmates filed into the dayroom from the bedding area to see the fight.

"That's it," said the giant standing between them.

"Fuck that," spat Do-rag, "that cracker stole me, Kane! For nothing! I want a fade!"

Kane the giant looked at CJ questioningly.

He responded by pulling off his shirt and throwing it on his bedroll. "Let's go," he said, raising his fists and staring into the glowering eyes of his newest enemy. The crowd of onlookers buzzed with excitement as Kane smiled and backed out of his way.

They circled each other briefly, shooting a few jabs and measuring reach, waiting for an opening. At least one of them was; the other actually had no idea what he was doing. He was just hoping it would be over soon.

The crowd was getting antsy.

"Come on now," someone said, "it's a fight, somebody gotta get hit."

"Whachu waitin' fo', Greedy?" another said. "Light his little punk ass up!"

Apparently Do-rag's real name was Greedy. Suddenly he rushed. CJ luckily weaved his first blow and the second glanced off the side of his head, but the third, a left, caught him dead on the button, causing his knees to buckle. Then, a hard right sent him crashing to the floor.

Greedy dove on top of him and reached for his throat, but CJ landed a lucky knee to his balls and sent him tumbling over his head. CJ then attempted to scramble to his feet but was still drunk from the headshots and ended up tripping over them instead. He could hear the spinning crowd of men roar with laughter as he stumbled to the floor. Their faces went by in a slow-motion blur. The faces of strangers twisted and contorted in bloodlust. His rolling eyes caught glimpses of matted beards and missing teeth, dreadlocks and shitty tattoos. Suddenly he was driven to the floor by a foot in his back. His arms and legs splayed cartoonishly outward and his chin bounced off the concrete.

"That's enough," somebody said as the foot exploded into his back again.

By then CJ's mind had cleared enough to realize he was being stomped on. He rolled sideways and leapt unsteadily to his feet, scanning the swimming faces for Greedy's menacing bloodshot eyes.

When he spotted the do rag, he charged recklessly, only to be sent flying into the bars by Kane. He scowled up at the giant and rose slowly to his feet.

"I said that's enough, cracker!" Kane growled. He looked over at Greedy. "You straight, man? Is it dead now?"

Greedy stared at CJ and nodded once.

"How 'bout you?" Kane asked CJ. "You done?"

CJ stared back at Greedy with what he hoped was a hard look. "Yeah. I'm done."

He kept his back against the bars as the crowd returned to whatever they were doing before the fight. He maintained awareness of Greedy's location and proximity without actually watching him. He also noted how few whites there were in the pod. He spotted only two out of maybe thirty men and they both had a homeless look to them.

He realized Kane was still standing in the same spot. CJ once again struggled not to stare at the obvious stab wounds and possible bullet holes that littered his chest and stomach.

He smiled. "Damn, white boy," he drawled, "whatchu got against Greedy Greg? He sell you some bad dope or somethin'?"

CJ shook his head. "He called me fresh meat."

Kane laughed. "You probably ain't gotta worry 'bout that happening again."

CJ didn't know what to say, so he leaned over and snatched his t-shirt off the bedroll on the floor and slid it over his pale, thin torso. When his head popped through the collar, he caught sight of Brown looking at him through the grimy square of Plexiglas on the door. He nodded once before disappearing back down the hall.

"You goin' up the road?" Kane asked. *Up the road* was another way of saying *prison.*

CJ shrugged and tried to look unconcerned. "Probably."

Kane laughed again. "Well, you better start doing some push-ups then. My nephew's bigger than you and he's only eight."

CJ stiffened at the insult.

"But you got heart, white boy, I'll give you that. My name's Kane." He held out his huge hand.

CJ looked him in the eye and accepted it. "I'm CJ."

"This is my house," Kane explained. "I've been here over three years waitin' on trial. See the cat with the big forehead playin' poker over there?"

CJ glanced over at the card table and nodded.

"That's Ironhead. He's assistant houseman." Kane paused and scanned the dayroom. "The red nigga with the tattoos on his face watchin' TV is Yella, the phone man."

Yella, feeling eyes on him, looked over at them and raised his chin in acknowledgment before turning back to the TV.

"This is a 'down south' cell," Kane said. "Most everybody in here's from Richmond Heights, Goulds, Perrine, Homestead, shit like that. We got a few from Overtown and one from Carol City, but they stay in they lane and we all get along fine. Greedy, the cat you sparked, is from Broward. He ain't got no people in here, but he fucks with the Overtown niggas. Watch 'em," he cautioned.

The system of housemen and houses, as well as down-south and up-north cells, was an organic situation that evolved over time. Those like Kane who ran cells weren't nominated or assigned by guards. The power structure in the Dade County Jail was based on the most primitive of paradigms: the law of the jungle.

A cell was invariably run by the strongest man in the pod and his homeboys. There was a natural beef between South Miami 'hoods and North Miami 'hoods, but the guards never concerned themselves with where an inmate was from before they threw him in a cell. When someone from Liberty City was placed in a down-south cell, he kept a low profile until he could either move out or form enough alliances on the low to stage a coup. The same was true for someone from down south in a North Miami cell. The complexion of a cell could change drastically with the addition or subtraction of a few inmates in any given pod. Balances of power were tipped and houses were taken every day through force. This happened when a houseman and his clique were beaten down and made to bang on the Plexiglas with a scrub brush, alerting the guards that there was a problem and that they needed to be moved. Before these mutinies occurred there was always a palpable tension in the dorm. Any veteran houseman could sense and gauge friction, assess threat levels, and deal with potential insurgents before they gained any traction.

Kane glanced over at the domino table where the Overtown clique and Greedy Greg mumbled conspiratorially amongst themselves.

"So where you from?" he asked CJ.

It didn't really matter what part of town he was from in respect to the north/south blood feud. Whites made up a small, insignificant minority that was exploited by both sides.

"I'm from Perrine," CJ lied.

Kane laughed heartily. "Shut the fuck up!" he thundered. "Ain't no crackers in Perrine!"

"Nah," CJ smiled, "I'm from South Miami. I live close to the mall. But I do fuck around in Perrine a little. My homeboy lives over there."

"Who?"

"Rick."

"What Rick?"

CJ hesitated. "Why do you care?"

"Cuz I was born and raised in Perrine."

"Robinson," CJ finally answered.

"Aw shit." Kane laughed. "Red Rick? Car-stealin'-ass Rick? Ty and Mario's little brother?"

CJ nodded.

"I knew there was somethin' I liked about you," Kane roared. "Those are my cousins! I live right next door!"

"I know the house. Mike-Mike lives there. And Nino."

"Mike-Mike's my brother. And I bought Nino for a fifty rock when he was a puppy."

"Well, he's a monster now."

"Damn, I miss my dog . . ." Kane mumbled softly, a faraway look settling on his face before he snapped back to the present. "Come on, grab your bedroll. Normally you gotta ride the floor for a few days when you first move in. But since you damn near family, you goin' straight to the penthouse." He nodded at the open top bunk in the corner. "Hope you ain't scared of heights."

~

After two months of riding around in air-conditioned luxury, Chris McCallister was reminded of all the reasons he hated the rusty piece of shit his wife used for transportation. It was impossible to crank up, the brakes shrieked, it shook like hell when it was idling, and reeked like a wet fart in spite of the air-freshener that dangled from the rearview, which only produced the smell of someone taking a dump behind a pine tree. He felt guilty about the company Lincoln he drove around in every day. *We've got to get a new car,* he thought, but that decision was entirely up to Cheryl. She handled the finances. All he did was hand over his paycheck each week. It was something that was proposed by his N.A. sponsor, Jay, and he agreed readily and proudly, especially when she decided that the money would be used to pay for a good attorney for CJ. His motive for getting the job and going to 12-Step meetings in the first place was to make a good impression on the judge when he spoke on CJ's behalf, but as they say, the Lord works in mysterious ways. He smiled at the irony of himself making that statement as he pulled into the Texaco and got out to pump.

The only reason he was driving the raggedy Corolla to his meeting was so that he could fill it with gas on the way home. The needle on the gauge was broken and the only method of telling when it needed fuel was by the passage of time. It had been a week. One of his biggest fears was Cheryl running out of gas in a dangerous section of Miami at night.

He made sure he crammed every possible drop into the tank before screwing the cap back on and walking over to the bulletproof window to pay.

"Anything else, sir?" the attendant asked from behind the glass.

"No thanks," he answered, glancing nostalgically at the box of Zig-Zags on the shelf behind him.

"Fifteen-thirty then," the clerk said, sliding the metal tray forward for payment.

Chris extracted a ten, a five, and a one-dollar bill from his wallet. "Keep the change," he told him, dropping the money in the drawer and pushing it back.

As he pulled out onto Bird Road and headed toward home, he thought again of the packets of rolling paper on the shelf and began going over the 12 Steps in his mind. *One, we admitted we are powerless over our addiction and that our lives have become unmanageable. Absolutely,* he agreed. *Two, came to believe that a power greater than ourselves could restore us to sanity. Now see, this is where it gets a little confusing,* he thought, *because according to at least one news source, I AM that power.* He shook his head before moving on. *Three, made a decision to turn our will and our lives over to the care of . . .*

Oh my God! his mind screamed as the few remaining frayed ropes of his psychosis finally snapped and reality came crashing down. He was not the Messiah. Not the savior of the world. Not the fulfillment of prophecy in the books of Isaiah, Daniel, and Revelation. There would be no meeting of world leaders, no banquet, and the war of the end times was probably a long way off. He was just regular old Chris McCallister, sorry father, shitty husband, fat, lazy, stupid, worthless, same as it ever was.

He suddenly needed to get high. Now. *Fuck N.A., fuck Jay, fuck Peter Jennings, and fuck this piece of shit car!* he thought angrily as he ripped the wheel violently to the left, the tires loudly screeching their protest as he did so. He was on 67th Avenue heading toward the Wendy's where he used to work before his mind could even process his impulsive change of direction. *Good idea,* he thought, *Wendy's it is. Hopefully Tasha still works there.*

He was deep in conversation with himself when, a hundred feet ahead, a skateboarder ollied the thin swath of grass that separated the sidewalk from the curb and lost his balance on the landing attempt.

The skateboard squirted out from under him and shot across the street while he flailed his arms and landed on his back in the middle of 67th Avenue. Chris McCallister slammed on the brakes.

The Corolla closed the hundred feet quickly as Chris's white knuckles gripped the steering wheel and his eyes bulged in fear. The tires smoked and the car got sideways as it screamed toward the open-mouthed boy sitting helpless in the middle of the road awaiting his fate.

"Come on! Come on!" Chris pumped the stubborn brakes. Forty feet, thirty feet, twenty, ten . . . the car grabbed asphalt at last as he skidded to a stop just inches from the frozen teenager. The kid tentatively opened his eyes and, upon realizing that he was, in fact, not dead, bounced quickly to his feet. He located his board in the grass and, after glancing back at the fat dude in the car, skated serenely away.

Chris pulled shakily to the curb and cut the engine. He no longer wanted to get high. The range of emotions he'd been ripped through over the last five minutes was a high of its own. A bad trip. Humiliation suddenly hit him like an overhand right. Just like the boy skated off unconcerned down the sidewalk, forgetting his brush with death, Chris McCallister's mind also shook off the near-miss as images and memories from the past year flooded his thoughts. His shame and embarrassment were staggering. What did CJ think about him? What did his wife think? *What do you expect them to think?* he asked himself. *You've been acting like a psychopath.* He slammed his head into the steering wheel as the tears began to fall. How could he ever face them again?

He frowned and blinked when he noticed the orange pill bottle on the floorboard. It had rolled from under the seat when he slammed on the brakes. He reached between his legs and groped blindly around the area where he spotted it until his hand made contact with the small cylinder. The label said "Fluoxetine Hydrochloride" and had his wife's name and address listed below. This was perplexing because Cheryl hated pills. She wouldn't even take Tylenol when she had a headache. *Hmmm,* he thought while studying the bottle. *I wonder if they'll get me high.* He was abruptly aware of his own weakness, his "stinkin' thinkin'" as Jay called it. He had made some major inroads in recovery so far. Cheryl was beginning to trust him again and CJ now had an attorney. Getting fucked up at this stage would be the most counterproductive, self-destructive thing he could do.

He looked into the rearview and his own eyes stared back at him. He nodded slowly in recognition. Although the shame and embarrassment were still very real, there was a certain weight lifted from his shoulders as well. Saving the world was no longer his responsibility. He really wasn't the Messiah. He need only concern himself with saving the McCallisters. He was almost thankful for nearly running over the skateboarder. He was flying toward Wendy's and his old connection like a runaway train when that kid caused him to slam on the brakes. *Divine intervention?* he wondered, before starting up the Toyota and turning back toward home. He glanced suspiciously at the pill bottle once more before shoving it back under the seat. He had no idea what the medicine was for, but he knew exactly whom to ask.

~

April Curlac pouted her lips and stared appreciatively at her lovely reflection in the bedroom mirror. She wore only a small pair of lace panties and the bracelet CJ had given her as she stood there applying her mascara. Soundgarden's "Outshined" oozed from the speakers of her stereo.

She hummed to the music as she finished her left eye and re-dipped the brush in the thick black liquid to start on the right. A forgotten cigarette burned in the ashtray. The phone rang. She looked back at her messy bed. Somewhere in the swirling mass of sheets, blankets, and clothes was her phone. She considered ignoring it for a second but thought better of it when she remembered Omar, the cute guy at work who had asked for her number the other night.

She moved quickly to the bed, feeling around for the hard casing of the phone through the sheets and clothes, while discarding shirts, jeans, and bras on the floor as she searched. She kept expecting whoever was calling to finally give up, but somewhere around the twelfth ring she hit pay dirt and snatched the phone from between the mattress and the headboard where it was lodged.

"Hello?"

"April?" CJ asked.

"Oh my God! CJ! Where have you been?"

"I'm in the county jail."

"I *know* that," she said, rolling her eyes. "I mean, why haven't you called?"

"Well, I was in the hospital for a while—"

"Hospital?" She walked back to the mirror and admired herself as he spoke.

"Yeah. I got fucked up pretty bad, but I'm better now."

"Oh CJ," she cried, reaching again for the mascara to finish her lashes, "what's going to happen to you?"

"I don't know. My family hired me a lawyer and . . ."

Mike Lazano appeared behind her in the mirror. He cupped her ample breasts in his hands while kissing her neck. She covered the mouthpiece of the phone and whispered, "Stop it!"

". . . but my cell is pretty cool and I've got a few . . ."

Mike moved to kiss the other side of her neck while sliding his hands down her sides and hooking his thumbs in the elastic of her panties, gently pulling them down around her thighs while she reached back to caress his neck.

". . . so visitation is usually on Tuesday and Saturday nights and I was hoping that maybe if you don't have to work one night, you could . . ."

April giggled loudly. Mike was tickling her. She covered the mouthpiece again and spun to face him. "Wait!" she whispered.

"April? Hello?"

"Yeah, CJ, sorry about that. Can you call back later? This phone needs to be charged and I'm . . ." She did a terrible job of hiding her laughter as Mike tickled her again. "I have to work tonight."

"That's cool," CJ said. "I'll talk to you later."

"Bye." She laughed before the connection was severed.

Mike lifted her from her feet and carried her over to the bed, where he gently laid her on her back and sank to his knees before her. He began softly kissing the insides of her thighs.

There's no reason to feel guilty, she told herself as she stared up at the ceiling. She and CJ had a special relationship. They had made an agreement about this stuff a long time ago. He knew she dated other guys. It was no big deal. True, she had veered off course a little during those last few months with him, but she now realized how stupid she was acting. She had no idea what love was, but she was sure it was *not* the now faded emotional high she experienced concerning CJ McCallister. The sex was good, the drugs were great, but it was now time for her to move on. She banished all thoughts of CJ from her mind and shut her eyes as Mike pulled her wet panties to the side and began to pleasure her with his mouth.

~

CJ hung up and nodded at Yella, the phone man in 6-B-2.

"You done?" asked Yella.

"Yeah."

"But you only rode for three minutes," he said, looking at his watch.

"All I needed."

Yella shrugged and looked down at the phone list he drafted earlier. "Greedy! You up!"

CJ could still feel the undercurrent of Greedy's lingering animosity as they passed each other. The hierarchy of a cell corresponded directly with the use of the phone. Things like rank and status were clearly evident in a man's position on the phone list. CJ had the number seven slot. Greedy was number eight. The snub was intentional. The cell triumvirate of Kane, Ironhead, and Yella had for some reason decided that Greedy Greg was a cancer and needed to be removed. Apparently that would happen after they became bored with the psychological warfare.

His thoughts turned to April. She had a man over when he was talking to her. He felt like an idiot. *I hope they weren't fucking while I was begging her to come visit me.* He cringed at the thought. She had definitely moved on. That much was obvious. He had witnessed April dump others in the past. Her phony politeness and quick giggling dismissal were all the proof he needed. He was let down and humiliated and hurt, but the hurt was more like a slap than an uppercut. Maybe catching Rudy and Andrea clinging desperately to each other all those years ago had deadened the nerves in his heart, or maybe April's initial warning about falling for her had subliminally stuck, but for whatever reason, he wasn't crushed. Hurt? Yeah. Saddened? Definitely. Embarrassed by her casual rejection? Absolutely. But crushed? No way. That would never happen again.

All throughout his journey through the police station, the hospital, the infirmary, and the numerous van rides and holding cells, he had been nagged by the suspicion that her declaration of love on their final night together was just as baseless and chemically induced as his response. He suddenly regretted confessing to her that she was his only one that night. She didn't deserve that information. The scene of her pinning his hands to the bed and interrogating him about other girls flashed across his mind. The vivid memory of her naked body caused him to swallow hard. His attorney had told him the state was pushing for a thirty-year sentence. He assured CJ that he could get it knocked down substantially, but what did substantially constitute? Ten years? Twenty years? No matter what, CJ realized it might be decades before he experienced a woman again. *That* was crushing. April's inevitable departure was a minor annoyance in comparison.

~

"I forgot my suitcase," Frank said nervously as Chris nosed the Continental out into the heavy US 1 traffic.

"We're only going to the library," Chris reminded him, "you won't need your suitcase."

"Library?" Frank eyed him distrustfully. "I thought we were flying up to Duluth."

"Not today, buddy, but maybe someday."

Frank only stared out his window.

"Can I ask you a few health-related questions, Frank?"

"My health's fine," Frank bristled.

"I meant *my* health."

"Ask the doctor," Frank moodily replied.

Chris hid his smile and turned up the radio a notch. The Glenn Miller Orchestra was playing. He braked at a red light and hummed along with the song while they waited for it to turn green.

"All right. What is it?" Frank grumbled.

"What is what?" Chris asked, testing his memory. A valid question considering the off-and-on nature of Frank's dementia.

"What's your damn health question, Robert?" he snapped. He was staring at Chris intently with those steel gray eyes. Somewhere under all those wrinkles and liver spots was the face of a soldier and a warrior. Chris knew his son was named Robert. He considered it an honor when Frank accidentally confused him with his oldest boy. He never corrected him on it.

"I have two," Chris said. "The first is that I think something is going on with my ability to breathe when I'm asleep. It may be related to my snoring. I wake up over and over throughout the night in a panic because it's like I've stopped breathing or something."

"Sleep apnea," Frank said in the sanest version of himself so far that morning. "My bridge partner Sam's got the same thing. Old Chainsaw Sammy." He laughed. "Has something to do with your bronchial tubes closing up. He says he sleeps like a baby with the breathing machine, but the straps take some getting used to." He shrugged and glanced over at Chris. "I'm not making a diagnosis. I'm a pharmacist, not a doctor."

"I know. My other question is about medicine."

Frank shifted in his seat.

"Have you ever heard of . . . flux . . . itone or maybe . . . ?" He dug in his pocket for his wallet, where he'd written down the name of the pills he'd found on the floorboard.

"Fluoxetine Hydrochloride? Prozac?"

"That's it! The first one."

"One and the same. It's an SSRI—"

"A what?"

"An antidepressant. The new brand of wonder drugs for people who suffer from obsessive-compulsive disorder, panic attacks, or depression. A load of shit if you ask me. Where were all these *disorders* in my day? They didn't exist!" He pounded the dashboard for emphasis. "Folks were too busy fighting for the country or scraping to feed their families to worry about some pansy-assed excuse of a disorder!" He looked over at Chris suspiciously. "Oh, Robert, tell me you're not taking that shit!"

"No sir," Chris said, lost in thought.

What have I done? Chris lamented with a heavy heart. Sweet little Cheryl McCallister, who was once paranoid of Advil, had quickly graduated to popping big-time, cutting-edge pharmaceuticals to deal with her unbearable depression. *Well done, Jesus,* he smirked at himself in the mirror. *Just beautiful.*

Chris pulled into the library parking lot and found a vacant space near the entrance.

"Should I wait here with the luggage?" Frank asked.

Chapter 11

CJ kept his chin tucked against his left shoulder with both hands out in front of his face. He tried his best to remain a moving target while his opponent bounced lightly on his toes and smiled confidently back at him.

It was that time in the afternoon when shadows were longest. The opaque light from the catwalk window shone against the cell bars, causing their pattern to crisscross along the dank concrete floor of the bedding area. There were twenty-four bunks in the cell and easily double that number of inmates. The spillover, mostly crackheads and drunks, had to find vacant spaces to lay their mats. They slept in the dayroom, oblivious to the blaring TV, and along the aisles of the bedding area beneath the network of damp laundry that hung from makeshift clotheslines overhead. Some even made their home between the toilets. Such was life in an overcrowded jail. No place was off limits except the back of the cell, where CJ and his adversary continued to cautiously circle each other, awaiting an opening. Kane lived there.

Hound was a junkie from Coconut Grove, nicknamed for his eerie resemblance to a greyhound. He had a thin, bony face with a sharp, elongated chin and a lanky frame. Everything about him was a collection of right angles, all Ls and Vs, so that even when CJ was lucky enough to land a punch it was hard not to wince in pain. Hitting him was like hitting a butcher knife.

Hound's open hand flashed and caught CJ on the side of the head, knocking him off balance. As he recovered from the blow, his face reddened and he felt a surge of rage swell within him. He refused to yield to it. Unbridled rage would get him fucked up every time. *"You too little to fight mad,"* Kane had told him, *"you gotta fight smart . . . 'less you just dig gettin' your ass kicked or somethin'."*

CJ had been in the county jail almost nine months. On his last visit downstairs to medical for a routine follow-up, he weighed 142 pounds, almost twenty more than his initial weight at intake. He'd been eating like a savage and doing push-ups every day. But even so, Kane was right, at five-feet-eight and 142 pounds he was still the smallest in the cell, and an angry gnat was still just a gnat.

His opponent launched another flurry while moving in, attempting to back him into the cell bars, but CJ quickly ducked beneath the barrage and reversed their positions. Hound smiled briefly in acknowledgement of his slipperiness before feinting right, then slapping him hard in the ear. The smack echoed throughout the bedding area, eliciting the raised heads and craned necks of nearby inhabitants and lowly floor dwellers.

"What the fuck are y'all lookin' at?" Kane barked sharply from his seat overlooking the action.

The attention dissolved instantly.

CJ shook off the blow and again resisted the immediate tide of fury that ballooned within him. He focused instead on Hound's narrow face and shoulders, awaiting the next attack. He was aware of Kane and Yella sitting side by side on the top bunk watching quietly, legs swinging back and forth in his peripheral. He ignored them too as he searched for an opening. He had become adept at compartmentalizing things like ego, fear, and rage. Although if asked, he wouldn't be able to say what compartmentalizing meant. He just did it. He was evolving. Rapidly, like any other species in the wild developed defenses against its natural predators. The process wasn't limited to physical confrontation; he compartmentalized the gripping fear of his looming court date and the agonizing regret he felt concerning his worried mother. He even boxed up the dull ache in his heart as well as the sweeping lust that he felt whenever April crossed his mind. Each thought was placed in storage and only occasionally removed and dusted off like an old piece of jewelry or an antique weapon, usually late at night when the cell slept.

Hound's shoulder flinched, telegraphing the next volley. CJ didn't hesitate. He went low, slamming his own shoulder into Hound's stomach and poking his arm between his legs, lifting him off his feet. Before Hound could complete his swing, he was upside down in the air and rapidly approaching the concrete floor. He landed on his head. Drunk from impact, he awkwardly attempted to stagger to his feet, but CJ wasn't having it. In a blur he slid quickly behind him and yanked him back to the floor, locking his legs around his stomach and his arms around his neck in a vicious headlock. Checkmate.

He glanced up at Kane and Yella as Hound tapped his arm twice, signaling surrender.

"I see you, white boy," said Kane, acknowledging his victory, "but don't let it go to your head. Hound ain't no killa'. He just a baser from the Grove. And you still soft as cotton," he added with a smile.

Somewhere over the last eight months Kane had assumed the role of Mr. Miyagi to CJ's Daniel-san. Only Kane was no little old man from Okinawa, and the lessons were a lot harder than "wax on-wax off." In addition to giving CJ extra trays whenever possible and insisting that he do push-ups daily, Kane and his clique made CJ fight crackheads and winos, partly for practice but mostly for entertainment. Regardless of motive, it was working. He was toughening up. In spite of his two violent collisions with Duke and Joey Barocela prior to coming to the Dade County Jail, CJ was, at his core, a gentle-natured momma's boy whose natural inclination was to shy away from confrontation. Through repetition and regular combat, the dreadful aura that once surrounded physical violence had worn off and exposed the act of fighting for what it truly was: a sport. And like any other sport, you got better at it with practice.

"McCallister," called a voice from outside the cell.

CJ released Hound and bent backwards to look through the bars behind him. An upside-down Officer Brown was standing on the catwalk. CJ spun quickly to face him. "Yes sir?"

"Your attorney's here," Brown said, glancing over at Kane, who continued to swing his legs back and forth from the top bunk. "Get ready to come out."

"Yes sir," he said, jumping to his feet.

~

CJ slid in the booth across from his attorney and picked up the phone. On the other side of the Plexiglas, studying an open file, sat J. Richard Smith. At least that's what his business card said:

J. Richard Smith, P.A.2
Criminal Defense Lawyer
Trial Practice - Post Conviction – Appeals

CJ had a hard time believing he actually called himself "J. Richard Smith." He figured the first initial/middle name/last name moniker was simply a creative way of spicing up an otherwise bland name. "John Smith" just seemed to lack the professional oomph that was promised in a stuffy, old-money handle like J. Richard Smith, P.A. He looked the part too, in a business suit with a gold tie pin and a worn leather briefcase. He was tall, taller than Kane, with graying close-cropped hair and blue eyes surrounded by crow's feet. But the focal point of his face was definitely the nose. Before every visit with him, CJ silently vowed not to stare, but each time he failed miserably. He was riveted by its sheer grotesquerie: a knotted chunk of bright red lump-ridden flesh spider-webbed with tiny branching purple veins and the occasional rogue hair and sesame seed glob of pus. There was no telling how much crucial legal advice CJ had missed while staring transfixed at the bulbous nose of J. Richard Smith.

He smiled at CJ and reached for the phone on his side of the glass. "Good afternoon, Mr. McCallister."

CJ nodded and tried to concentrate on his eyebrows. He still couldn't get used to being called Mr. McCallister. He understood that

Smith was being paid by his parents to represent him and that he was supposed to be an advocate, but CJ still saw him as an authority figure just like any other attorney, cop, judge, teacher, or grown-up in the world. He knew in principle J. Richard Smith actually worked for him, but exercising his employer rights felt funny. And anyway, what could he demand? A Newport? A slice of pizza? Surely not anything regarding the law. Smith had been pacing in front of juries long before CJ was born. He'd leave the legal stuff to him; that's what he was paid for.

"Nothing's changed," he said. "They won't come down. They're practically daring me to take it to trial."

CJ's eyes fell to his nose. It was almost purple today. Violet.

"It's the victim," he continued, "that cop. Alvorado. If he wasn't pushing so hard I know I could at least get it down to around fifteen. Maybe even ten, but I can't gain an inch of ground with him barking in the prosecutor's ear."

"So what's going to happen?"

"Well, trial's out of the question, obviously. They've got us dead to rights with this Alvorado cop victim as their star witness. That stun gun sitting in the evidence room next to your dope isn't exactly helping either."

"Right."

"But the thirty years they're offering for a plea agreement is, in my opinion, extreme to say the least. Granted, your charges are serious, especially the armed assault and the armed burglary."

"Are you positive armed burglary is the right charge? They make it sound like I went in the house with a gun, ready to pop anybody who stuck their head around the corner."

"We've been over this," Smith said patiently, "the law is clear. If you arm yourself during a burglary, whether it's with a pistol, a shotgun, a buck knife, or even a stun gun, the charge is armed burglary and it's a PBL. We're really lucky they're not pushing for life."

They'd had this conversation before. CJ was just hoping for a different answer. "So what now?" he asked, dejected.

"Well, there's one more option. We could plea straight up to the judge."

"What's that mean?"

"It means we can't go to trial, but we also reject the plea offer from the State as too harsh. So we throw ourselves on the mercy of the court and pray that the judge is having a good day. With your age and lack of any significant priors we may catch a break."

"Let's do it," CJ said impulsively.

"Wait a sec," Smith lifted a cautionary finger, "he could also give you *more* time than the state's offering. It's a crapshoot."

CJ thought about it while staring absently at Smith's nose. It was really a no-brainer. He couldn't go to trial and there was no way he was copping out to thirty years. He was sick of county life and attorneys and holding cells and courtrooms. He just wanted to get to wherever he was going and know exactly how long he had to do. The waiting game was getting old. He had long accepted the fact that he was going to prison. He didn't even insult God's intelligence by praying for freedom. His only prayer was that his mom and dad stay healthy until he made it home. If no one else in the world loved him, they did. Not everyone had that. He lived in a cell full of people who were truly alone in the world. He was blessed. He just hoped like hell the judge would be lenient so that he could make it up to them before they were too old. Or dead.

"Let's do it," CJ finally repeated.

"You sure? I can probably squeeze another continuance out of them."

"Nah, let's get it over with."

"Okay," said Smith, closing his file. "I'll see you on Thursday then."

CJ hung up the phone and watched Smith gather his things. He shut his briefcase and nodded once more at him before exiting the booth.

After months upon months of waiting, things were starting to move.

Jose Ramos paused in mid-stride after swinging open the door of the executive offices. Cheryl McCallister was smiling. He tried to remember if he'd ever seen her smile before. He didn't think he had. At least not over the last year. Not since her son got arrested.

"Buenos dias," he greeted her.

"Good morning," she trilled.

"Some good news for CJ?"

"Not yet."

"But soon?" he asked, raising his eyebrows.

"I hope so."

Mr. Ramos studied his secretary of close to four years. Her diminutive size and frequent tears were misleading. Cheryl McCallister was a warrior and a lioness. He didn't know every detail of her life, but he knew enough. How she could perform at such a high level professionally while under the constant strain of stress and sadness at home was beyond him. Between her troubled son and her loco husband he knew she was being ripped apart, yet every day she showed up early and worked long into the night. He wanted to help her, but he'd already given her a fat raise and allowed her all the overtime she wanted. He also, somewhat uncomfortably, offered the expertise of his amigo Frankie Villanueva, free of charge, which she surprisingly accepted. Out of respect, he resisted the urge to give her any more assistance. She knew she could always turn to him for help. He left it there. *I wonder if she's still seeing him.* He almost asked Frank about it at the Dolphins game last Sunday, but he'd heard his spiel on doctor/client confidentiality too many times to even bother.

The rapid-fire staccato clacking of her typewriter filled the office, punctuated by the occasional roll-back ding. He had been trying to persuade her to upgrade to a newer, quieter model for months, but she was stubborn in her refusal. Apparently she was attached to the damn thing. Once, he had even caught her patting it lovingly and speaking to it like a small child. *A typewriter!* He shook his head in exasperation as he walked past her desk to his office. He frowned when he reached his door. *Was she humming?* He turned back toward her.

"What's that?" he asked.

She stopped typing. "What's what?"

"This song. I know it."

"Oh," she smiled shyly, "it's called 'We've Only Just Begun' by a group called—"

"I know. Karen Carpenter. Anorexia, no? So sad."

"Wow, I'm impressed."

"Before Mariel, back in the seventies, we used to pick up Miami radio stations in Cuba. This was the song of me and my girlfriend, Yanisbel." He was momentarily lost in memories of his native Pina Del Rio.

"It was mine and my husband's song too," she said with a sigh.

"How is he?"

"My husband?"

Jose nodded.

"Oh, Mr. Ramos," she gushed, "he's . . . he's wonderful."

He crossed his arms and raised a skeptical eyebrow. Wonderful? This was a new development. Brett Wagner seemed convinced that a divorce was imminent. He cursed himself for even listening to the decorator's gossip.

"Really?" he asked, studying her intently.

"Oh, yes," she said excitedly, spinning toward him in her chair. "He's been working for almost a year now. He was born for the job. Those old people adore him at that center and the extra money he's earning makes life so much easier. He's even paid for a private attorney for CJ."

"How about the . . . other things?" he asked uncomfortably.

"He's still clean. Almost a year now."

"Excellent," he said, "excellent."

Her phone rang. She picked up the receiver and pressed the blinking button. "Miami Airport Essex and Marina, this is Cheryl." She spun her chair back toward her desk. "I'm doing fine, Mr. Smith. What's going on?"

Jose Ramos watched her as she scribbled notes on a pad and listened intently, occasionally posing a question. She was a beautiful woman, both outside and in. He wondered if all women from Alabama were as lovely. She was the only person he knew from that state. The farthest north he had ever traveled since he arrived on the shores of Miami was West Palm Beach.

Her brow creased and she bit her lip as she processed the information the caller was relaying.

He had known only one woman as sweet and kind and as fiercely loyal as Cheryl McCallister in all his life: his mother. Although he would never admit it to another living soul, Jose Ramos, general manager of the Miami Airport Essex, married father of three, had fallen for his secretary.

She hung up the phone and looked at him. "I need Thursday off. CJ's pleading guilty."

~

CJ sat handcuffed in the jury box along with ten other defendants, awaiting his name to be called. He stared at an obvious prostitute in the front row of the audience who indifferently blew big pink bubbles while the woman next to her—another prostitute?—dozed off. A man in camo pants and a red mesh tank top staggered down the aisle in search of a seat. There appeared to be leaves in his hair. Circuit Court was a completely different experience than Juvenile Court. There were fewer worried mothers and crying babies since the bulk of the throng were street people out on bond. The courtroom itself was easily three times the size of Juvenile Court, with high ceilings, varnished wood, and movie theatre-type seats. But the most glaring difference was the absence of pretension. Circuit Court was not encumbered by the need to feign concern. Juvenile Court was about rehabilitation. Circuit Court was about punishment.

He scanned the crowd for the familiar faces of his mom and dad. He knew they were out there. They had never missed a court date. The thought of their unconditional love and support caused him to vow silently for the thousandth time never to put them through this again. He caught a glimpse of his attorney's nose toward the back of the room, then a flash of his father's gleaming head.

"All rise," called the bailiff, cuing the entrance of the judge. "The Honorable Judge Blevins presiding."

The crowd stood silently as a heavyset man in a black robe with a gray comb-over and a pinched facial expression made his way to the bench.

"Be seated," he said, pouring himself a glass of water and surveying the crowd.

Whether it was an unwritten rule, professional courtesy, or just a backhanded dig at the indigent, private counsel always went before the public defenders. Regardless of the reason why, the inferred message was: *If you're too broke to afford an attorney, get your ass to the back of the line.*

The crowd watched as a tall, regal man clad in an Armani suit and Italian loafers separated himself from the state attorney's desk and swaggered over to the podium. He left an adoring and blushing Sophia Lamont gazing at his broad back. Mrs. Lamont was the prosecutor in Judge Blevins's courtroom, and the impeccably dressed man was Edwin Santiago, hotshot defense lawyer. As CJ watched him turn back and aim a sparkling white smile at someone in the audience, probably his client, he noted for the first time that there was no trickery with him. He did not refer to himself as "E. whatever Santiago, the third" or any other such bullshit. He was simply Ed Santiago, the best lawyer in Miami. Not that CJ was complaining. Many of the guys in his cell had never even met their public defenders. At least J. Richard Smith came to visit, was well versed in CJ's case, and sober for his court dates.

As the judge and Santiago exchanged pleasantries, CJ looked back over to where he spotted his attorney and his father. Mr. Smith stood and shook hands with his parents, then quietly made his way down the aisle and across the courtroom floor to where CJ sat in the jury box. The inmate in the next seat slid over to give the attorney some room.

"Good morning," said Smith, extending a hand.

"Morning," replied CJ, accepting it.

"Listen, I've been talking to Lamont all morning trying to get her to come down. She won't."

CJ nodded grimly. This wasn't news.

"I did get her to at least agree to a cap. It's not much, but it's something."

"What is it?" CJ asked, half listening as Santiago held the rest of the courtroom captive behind him.

"It just means that she'll agree to a thirty-year cap on your sentence when you plea straight up to the judge. You can't get any more time than that, but the judge could give you less, or none. It's sort of like plea agreement but not really."

"Okay."

His mom stood in the back of the room and waved. He smiled back bravely. *Thirty years.*

"Mr. Smith, are you ready?" asked the judge.

Santiago had disappeared and the entire courtroom was looking in CJ's direction.

"Yes sir," the attorney said, rising to his feet and motioning for CJ to follow.

The clerk was still reading case numbers to the judge when CJ and Smith arrived at the podium. He was suddenly aware of the familiar smell of his father's Aqua Velva behind him and was comforted by his presence. His mother was standing there too. Across the carpet, State Attorney Sophia Lamont stood rigidly at the other podium making notes in an open file.

The judge looked sternly down at CJ. "Son, I understand you want to enter a plea today."

"Yes sir."

The judge studied him intently for a full thirty seconds before instructing CJ to raise his right hand. "State your name."

"Paul McCallister."

"Do you swear to tell the truth, the whole truth, and nothing but the truth so help you God?"

"Yes sir," CJ said quietly.

"Speak up."

"Yes, Your Honor."

"Are you certain you want to enter a plea today?" he said, repeating himself for the record.

"Yes sir."

"Has anyone forced or coerced you into making this plea?"

"No sir."

"Has your attorney promised you anything regarding the outcome?"

"No sir."

"And you're aware of the fact that I could potentially sentence you up to . . ." He glanced over at Mrs. Lamont questioningly.

"Thirty years, Your Honor," she interjected.

". . . thirty years in state prison for these charges?"

"Yes sir," CJ answered numbly.

"And knowing this possibility you still want to plead guilty?"

"Yes sir."

"Have you taken any drugs or alcohol within the last twenty-four hours?"

"No sir."

"Do you fully understand what you are being charged with?"

"Yes sir."

"Has it been explained to you that by pleading guilty you are giving up your right to a trial?"

"Yes sir."

"And you're okay with that?"

"Yes sir."

"And you're satisfied with the job that Mr. Smith here has done as your attorney?"

"Yes sir."

"Okay," he said, almost shaking his head as he flipped back a page in front of him and began to read. "As to Count One Armed Burglary, how do you plea?"

CJ hesitated a moment. "Guilty, Your Honor."

"As to Count Two, Aggravated Assault on a Law Enforcement Officer, how do you plea?"

"Guilty, Your Honor."

"As to Count Three, Possession of Cocaine, how do you plea?"

"Guilty, Your Honor."

"As to Count Four, Carrying a Concealed Weapon, how do you plea?"

"Guilty, Your Honor."

Judge Blevins again looked over at the prosecutor. "Counts Five and Six are being nolle prossed, correct?"

"Correct, Your Honor."

"Okay, Mr. McCallister, I'm going to accept your plea of guilty on Counts One through Four as being knowingly and voluntarily made, and I hereby adjudicate you guilty as charged on each count."

CJ's knees began to tremble.

"The State has elected to drop Counts Five and Six."

He looked over at the clerk. "When's the next sentencing date, the fourteenth?"

"The twelfth, sir."

"Okay," he said, "here's what we're going to do. I'm going to order a PSI in this case and on the twelfth of December, we'll have a sentencing hearing."

He paused and glanced at CJ's attorney.

"Mr. Smith, I assume you've already explained what a PSI is to your client."

He nodded curtly. "I have, Your Honor."

"Good," said the judge, lifting his gavel.

"Your Honor," a voice rang out from the foot of the gallery.

CJ turned to see his mom wringing her hands and looking up at the bench.

"Yes?" The judge frowned.

"Will his family be able to speak on his behalf?"

"At the sentencing hearing, ma'am," he said, brushing her off.

"And will you consider what we have to say?" she pressed.

Judge Blevins studied her a moment before responding, "I will give it great weight."

He banged his gavel and the clerk called the next case.

As they walked back to the jury box, CJ turned to his attorney and whispered, "What's a PSI?"

~

The calloused hand of Kane almost completely covered both of CJ's shoulder blades. "Let's go, man, I need at least five more outcha."

CJ's feet were propped on an upside-down mop bucket; his hands were flat on the floor. His arms trembled as he lowered his chest to the damp concrete and exploded back up against the oppressive weight of Kane's hand.

"Good. Four more."

Sweat dripped from CJ's face and formed a small puddle on the floor. He struggled to finish the set. Kane seemed to apply more pressure as he went, until the final rep felt like a refrigerator was lying on his back.

"Push, cracker," demanded Kane, "last one."

Veins burst from CJ's purple face as he strained upward, fighting for every inch. A guttural roar escaped his lungs as his arms locked in place, completing the set. "Eeraaghhh!" he bellowed.

"That's what I'm talkin' 'bout."

CJ collapsed on the dirty floor.

"Good one," Kane said, extending his hand to help CJ up.

"That's it, right?" asked CJ, exhausted.

Kane nodded, watching him.

CJ ignored the attention while gathering his towel, washrag, and soap. It had been a long day. Going to court was always a mission: waking up at four in the morning, getting cuffed and herded into packed elevators and holding cells, the inescapable stench of urine, rancid breath, and unwashed flesh, the fear, the hope, the noise, the waiting, only to get set off three or four months to repeat the process. *No wonder so many people plead guilty.*

He turned toward the shower. Kane's massive frame was blocking the aisle. His arms were folded across his chest.

"What?" said CJ, uncomfortable with the scrutiny.

"I think you ready," said Kane, nodding to himself.

"I've *been* ready."

Kane's face hardened into a menacing scowl. "Bullshit, cracker. Six months ago you wouldn't a made it. Believe that. They woulda raped and robbed your little ass 'til they got tired of weavin' them weak-ass punches you throw and then poked you full of holes and left you leakin' on a handball court somewhere."

CJ stiffened.

"Shit," Kane continued, "your scary ass caught hell with Greedy, and he was one good slap from being someone's bitch. You saw how he left up outta here."

"I'm not scared."

Kane abruptly stomped a foot in his direction, causing CJ to jump back and throw his set up. Kane laughed.

CJ dropped his hands. "Come on, Kane, I'm tired, I smell like shit, I've been sitting in holding cells all day . . ."

Although Kane was the closest thing CJ had to a friend, he was volatile as hell and impossible to read, even after almost a year. Living in a cell with him was akin to living in a home with an alcoholic father, where the rest of the family had to walk on eggshells for fear of an explosion. He was equally capable of extreme acts of kindness and brutal displays of violence. CJ had witnessed him giving his food to a hundred-pound AIDS-ridden crackhead, but he'd also seen him go ballistic. Seared into his brain was the vivid memory of him slamming Greedy's face into the bars over and over until it was a bloody, unrecognizable stump and tooth fragments were ricocheting off the floor like Tic Tacs.

"How much you weigh now?" Kane asked him.

"Hundred and sixty," CJ lied.

"That's a good weight for you. One seventy-five would be better, but you'd probably lose speed. You were like a cheetah goin' up under Hound the other day."

"Hound's just a baser," said CJ, repeating his words.

"Yeah," Kane smiled, "just a baser. So, did Blevins order a PSI?"

CJ nodded.

"When do you go for sentencing?"

"The twelfth."

"You'll be gone soon," he said, his voice trailing off.

Sensing the end of the conversation, CJ again attempted a step toward the shower.

Kane didn't budge. "You know, when you first came in the cell, claiming to know my family and my hood, I thought you was a snitch."

"You told me. That's fucked up. I've never snitched on anybody."

Kane shrugged. "Happens every day. Nigga'll come off in the cell, actin' down, claimin' to know who you know, tryin' to play up under you and pump you for info, then, when you go to trial, guess who's sittin' with the prosecutor."

"I wouldn't do that."

"I know that now. I see why Ricky fucks with you. You're all right. For a white boy."

CJ smiled. "You just like making me fight crackheads and bums."

Kane's face again knotted with hostility. "Is that really what you think?"

CJ's smile died slowly. *Another mood swing.*

"Do you know how long I been in this cell?"

CJ nodded. *Four years.*

"Four years!" Kane exploded. "And do you know why I'm here?"

"Murder." *Everybody knew.*

"Nah, not just murder. Capital muthafuckin' murder. Believe me, I got way more important shit to do than watch your dumb ass fight basers and winos all day."

CJ shifted his weight uncomfortably.

Kane stared at him. "You know Ty, right?"

CJ frowned. "Rick's brother?"

Kane nodded. "You know why he's in that wheelchair?"

"Yeah, he got shot in the back."

"Not just the back. The spine. Bullet still up in there too. Nigga named Sugarbear from Goulds caught him slippin'. Rolled up in a baser's Sentra and hit 'em while he was bent over shootin' dice." His jaw twitched as he recounted the tale, lost in the past. "Ty was a muthafucker out there. Takin' niggas' dope, runnin' 'em off the ave, fuckin' their old ladies, buckin' gamblin' debts. He was just wild. Know what I'm sayin'? Out of control. He was even hell on his own family, 'specially little Rick."

CJ remembered Rick's stories about Ty's cruelty from their days on Unit 8 in juvie.

"To this day Ty swears he ain't do shit, but nobody believes that." He looked hard at CJ. "I don't give a fuck either way. Somebody came on our block and shot one'a us. No way I was lettin' that go."

He lowered his voice and took a step toward CJ, towering over him like a statue chiseled from a slab of black granite. "I found out 'bout him from a chick I was messin' with in Homestead. She said he was drunk in the club, braggin' 'bout it." The lines in his forehead deepened and his nostrils flared. CJ looked away. "When I finally caught up with him, he was fuckin' some dirtyfoot in a trailer. The ho was hollerin' so loud, he never even heard the hammer cock. I only planned on slumpin' him, but a stray caught her in the face, so I went 'head and finished her off. Probably for the best. No witnesses."

An image of the grisly scene flashed through CJ's mind as he studied his feet.

"That's how serious I am 'bout my family," he said. "When I called home after you first came in the cell claimin' to know Rick, and my cousins asked me to look out for you, I gave them my word that I would." He poked a gigantic finger into CJ's chest. "*That's* why I've been feedin' your little narrow ass and makin' you do push-ups and givin' you game. *Because I promised my family.* Trust me, Cee," he smiled, "I've got a murder case to fight. There's a million other things I could be doing than sittin' around watchin' you throw hands with junkies." He looked down at CJ. "You do trust me, don't you?"

"Yeah," CJ said, tossing his towel over his shoulder, "I trust you."

"Good." Kane smiled. "Now I'm gonna get out your way so you can go bathe."

"Thanks."

Kane crossed his arms again, still blocking passage. "But first I gotta little test for you."

"Fuck! Come on, man!"

"It's easy."

For the last few months he'd been drilling CJ on prison survival tactics, how to spot game and common traps that newcocks always fall for.

CJ's shoulders sagged. "What is it?"

"Gimme three things you need to avoid in the joint."

"Borrowing," CJ said immediately.

Kane nodded.

"Dope."

"Uh huh. And?"

"Fags."

"That's it," said Kane, turning to the side like a turnstile, allowing him passage.

As CJ walked by, Kane suddenly released a savage right straight into his stomach, causing him to crumble to the floor. It was the first time he'd ever hit him. When his breath returned and his brain unscrambled, Kane's face swam into view, leaning over him.

"Last lesson. Never trust no one."

Chapter 12

The funny thing about sentencing hearings is that no matter how fucked you are, no matter how much evidence is stacked against you, no matter how many victims are lined up screaming for your balls, or how sturdy and fortified your walls of acceptance may be, hope still somehow trickles in.

Maybe Mr. Smith found a technicality . . . maybe Alvorado got arrested himself . . . maybe they lost the evidence and have to drop the charges . . . maybe the judge will give me probation . . .

The courtroom was only half full. CJ sat handcuffed in the jury box along with four other inmates. He smiled at his mom and dad, who were huddled with his attorney on the front row. J. Richard Smith looked over at him and stood. CJ watched his nose as he ambled across the carpet in his direction.

"Good morning," he said, sitting down next to him.

"Morning," said CJ.

"Your parents are going to speak on your behalf."

CJ nodded. "Will it help?"

Smith shrugged. "Won't hurt. How about you? Do you have anything to say?"

CJ glanced at his mom. "Yeah."

"Well, make sure you address the judge as either 'sir' or 'Your Honor.'"

"I will."

"And remember to show remorse."

"Okay."

His attorney shifted uncomfortably in his seat. "Alvorado's here," he mumbled.

"Where?" CJ asked, his newfound hope suddenly floating away like a balloon from a child's hand.

"Back row."

CJ scanned the audience. He spotted the detective immediately. He was hard to miss. He was the only person in the courtroom who was staring at CJ like a snarling rabid dog.

"All rise," the bailiff announced, "the Honorable Judge Kenneth Blevins presiding."

"Be seated," said the judge as he made his way to the bench.

Smith leaned close to CJ, his aftershave a strange mix of peppermint and rubbing alcohol. *Or was that his breath?*

"Everything's going to be fine," he said.

CJ glanced back at Alvorado. An overhead light gleamed off his tan, bald head and his white teeth glistened against the sculptured black hedges of his mustache and goatee. He pretended to scratch his ear, then brought his thumb across his throat as he smiled psychotically back at CJ.

The judge arranged some papers on his desk and slipped on his glasses. "Who's first?" he asked the clerk.

"State versus McCallister, Your Honor."

"We're up," said Smith, making his way to the podium. CJ followed.

"We're here today for sentencing," said the judge. "I have before me a sentencing guideline sheet, as well as the PSI performed by Mr. Mastrud. I understand his family would like to speak on his behalf."

"We would, Your Honor," said his mom, stepping forward.

"Raise your right hand, ma'am," the judge instructed.

She obliged.

"State your name for the record."

"Cheryl McCallister."

"Do you swear to tell the truth, the whole truth, and nothing but the truth?"

"Yes sir."

"Go ahead."

"Your Honor, I'm not that good at speaking, especially when so much is at stake. CJ—Paul—is our only child. I know you have probably read a lot of bad things about him in those papers up there."

Judge Blevins was turning a page in CJ's PSI as Cheryl spoke. He pushed the thick packet aside and looked at her.

"But those papers won't tell you how his Pop Warner football coach used to get mad at him for helping the other team up after he made a tackle, or how he used to give away his lunch money to the homeless people on the railroad tracks by the school, or read *Clifford the Big Red Dog* to his grandfather while he was dying in a nursing home." She lost it at that point, bursting into tears. "He's a good boy," she finished, sobbing loudly as her husband stepped forward and patted her back. "He deserves a chance," she managed to squeak out before completely breaking down.

CJ's heart was heavy as he watched his attorney hand his mother a Kleenex and pull her gently away from the podium. If someone else had made his mom cry like this, he'd want to kick their ass, but this was *his* doing. He was the reason she was so miserable. Him.

His father approached the podium. "May I be heard, Your Honor?"

The judge nodded. "Raise your right hand and state your name, sir."

"Chris McCallister."

"Do you swear to tell the truth, the whole truth, and nothing but the truth?"

"I do, Your Honor."

"Proceed," said Judge Blevins, pouring a glass of water and settling back in his chair to listen.

"First of all, I want to apologize for my wife. This has been a scary, emotional time for all of us."

As if on cue, his mom, still whimpering off to the side, blew her nose loudly. Everyone turned.

"No apologies are necessary," the judge said, waving him off. "Mothers cry when their children are in trouble."

"Our son *is* a good boy. He just had the misfortune of having me for his father."

The judge studied Chris McCallister as he leaned over the podium, measuring his next sentence.

"A child doesn't have any say in what family he's born into, just as he has no choice in the body he receives, his race, or his gender." He glanced over at CJ. "My son didn't ask for a drug-addict father. He absolutely didn't deserve one, but that's what he got. While other fathers were teaching their kids to fish or throw two-seam fastballs, I was stoned on the couch." A solitary tear swam quickly out of the corner of his eye and streamed down his face, followed by another. "He never had a chance, Judge. He's a smart kid, don't get me wrong, but some things have to be taught, and he was never shown how to . . . how to *be*." He paused to mop his sweaty brow with a handkerchief. "It's a father's responsibility to teach his son how to be a man. I wish I could go back to the beginning of his life and at least give him a fighting chance. It was on me to teach him about honor, discipline, and impulse control, and I failed him."

CJ felt his own eyes fill with tears as he listened. He wanted to tell his dad that he was being too hard on himself, that he was a good father, and that he loved him, but now obviously wasn't the time. He bowed his head and stared down at his cuffed hands while his father continued to speak.

"And it's not just that I *didn't* teach him those positive things, that's bad enough, but what I *did* teach him is probably the reason he's standing over there in handcuffs right now."

The courtroom was silent.

"My son was in his early teens the first time we got high together. It wasn't long after that, that I was sending him to the projects to score dope for me. It sounds terrible here in this courtroom. It *is* terrible. But at the time, it didn't seem wrong. Our relationship wasn't really father and son, we were get-high buddies. At least that's how my warped mind rationalized it." He dabbed his eyes with the handkerchief. "I'm clean now." He held up a bronze chip. "One year, last Tuesday, but that doesn't . . . help . . . my . . . boy." The tears were falling freely now. "If anybody in this room should go to prison," he choked out, "it's me. Please give him a chance. He's worth saving. There's gotta be a better option than warehousing him for the next thirty years. Have mercy on him, Your Honor . . . on us."

He backed away from the podium and went to stand by his wife, who was still sobbing quietly.

The judge looked over at CJ. "Do you want to say anything, young man?"

"Yes sir," said CJ, raising his right hand.

The judge quickly swore him in, then waited for him to speak.

"I just want to apologize, Your Honor, especially to Mr. Alvorado." He glanced over at the detective, who was staring straight ahead, stone-faced. "I feel terrible for the damage I did to his home and the items I stole."

"Bullshit," mumbled the detective.

"And I also want to apologize for hurting him."

"Hurt *me?*" he erupted. "You couldn't hurt me if you tried, you little—"

The judge slammed his gavel. "Order!" he demanded. "You'll get your chance to speak in a moment, Mr. Alvorado." He nodded for CJ to continue.

"And since this is all on record, I just want to say that my family didn't fail me. If anything, I failed them."

He looked at his mom and dad. "I'm sorry for making you worry and embarrassing you and letting you down. I won't again. I promise." He turned back to the judge. "I know I'm in a lot of trouble, sir, but if you give me a chance, I won't disappoint you. I've been in jail for a year now and I've grown up a lot. Being cool and being tough don't matter to me anymore. The people I was trying to impress disappeared the second I got arrested. The only people that matter to me now are standing over there crying." He nodded in the direction of his mom and dad. "I know you're gonna send me to prison. I only ask that you consider my parents' ages when you decide the amount of time. I just want the opportunity to show them that I *can* be a good man, Your Honor, and that I love them."

He felt Mr. Smith pat his back. His attorney then leaned over the podium and spoke into the small microphone. "The defense rests, sir," he said before mumbling something that sounded like "good job" to CJ under his breath.

"Okay, Mr. Alvorado," said the judge, "your turn."

After being sworn in, the burly detective addressed the court.

"To impress people? That's his excuse for defacing my property, stealing mine and my wife's jewelry, some of which was priceless in sentimental value, assaulting me in my own home with a stun gun, and making my entire family fear for their safety for years, wondering if this . . ." He sneered at CJ. ". . . this thug would return to harm them. *To impress his friends?* While he rode around with my grandfather's watch on his wrist bragging about how he robbed a Metro-Dade police officer and got away with it. NOT because he was poor or starving or psycho or dopesick, Your Honor, but simply because he wanted to impress his friends. Do you know what I think would make a bigger impression on his little friends and anyone else involved in violent crime?" He looked over at the McCallisters. "If you make an example out of him by showing that society will not tolerate this type of behavior and sentence him to the statutory maximum. That's what I'm asking, Your Honor. That's what my wife, my daughter, and the entire Metro-Dade police force are asking."

The judge turned to the prosecutor. "Anything else?"

"The state rests, sir."

Judge Blevins arranged some papers on his desk before removing his glasses and looking at the McCallisters.

"Your stories are heartbreaking," he said. "Young Mr. McCallister seems to be an intelligent, thoughtful young man who is obviously remorseful and cares for you both deeply." He locked eyes with Chris McCallister. "The idea of a young teenager being sent into dangerous high-crime areas to buy drugs at the insistence of his father is as unfathomable as it is unconscionable. There is very little doubt as to why he is in this position today, and you were right to accept responsibility because most of the blame does, in fact, fall squarely on your shoulders."

Chris McCallister nodded in agreement.

"It's a universal truth that bad families produce bad children, and this is a very sad situation but, nevertheless, Mr. Alvorado is correct. Society simply cannot tolerate this type of behavior."

He looked at CJ.

"As to Count One, armed burglary, I hereby sentence you to twenty-seven years in the Department of Corrections with credit for time served."

Alvorado smiled happily at the McCallisters as the judge handed down the sentence.

"As to Count Two, aggravated assault on a law enforcement officer, twenty-seven years in the Department of Corrections. As to Count Three, possession of cocaine, ten years in the Department of Corrections. As to Count Four, carrying a concealed weapon, ten years in the Department of Corrections. Counts One and Two are to run concurrent. Counts Three and Four are to run consecutive to each other but concurrent to Counts One and Two for a total of twenty-seven years, minus the jail credit. I have taken into account all the statements made today, as well as the recommendation on the PSI and the sentencing score sheet. You have thirty days to appeal this sentence. Good luck, young man."

He banged his gavel with an air of finality. The sound echoed in CJ's mind along with the distant wailing of his mother's protests. The bailiff's firm hand on his back guiding him out of the courtroom felt more like the icy claw of the reaper escorting him to the land of the dead.

~

On an uncharacteristically cool morning in Miami, Cheryl McCallister lay awake, staring up at the water-stained popcorn ceiling of her bedroom, replaying her last conversation with CJ's attorney over and over in her head.

"But he said we have thirty days to appeal."

"To appeal the legality of the sentence, Cheryl," he explained. "It's legal, I assure you, right down the middle of the guidelines."

"Well, it should be illegal to lock an eighteen-year-old boy away for that long."

"I agree," he said, "but keep in mind that CJ is NOT going to have to do the whole twenty-seven years. They'll take a third off as soon as he reaches the reception center and then for every month he does, he'll have twenty days extra subtracted from his sentence, assuming he stays out of trouble."

Cheryl did the math for the thousandth time as she swung her legs over the side of the bed. She walked into the living room expecting to find her husband drinking coffee and reading the Sunday paper. He wasn't there. She looked down the hall to CJ's room, where he'd been sleeping lately. The door was closed. She frowned. The green light on the VCR said it was 8:02 a.m. *Chris never slept past six anymore.*

She went into the kitchen and retrieved her coffee mug from the dishwasher. There was a full pot steaming on the counter. The Mr. Coffee was the most modern appliance in the McCallister kitchen, a gift from her last boss, Kevin Mizell. She poured a cup and padded down the hall to CJ's bedroom.

Chris liked to sleep naked, preferably with a pillow between his legs. She shook her head and rolled her eyes at the mental image as she passed the open door to the bathroom. He wasn't in there.

When she reached CJ's room, she knocked lightly on the door.

"Honey," she called.

Silence. She pushed it open and peeked inside. The bed was unmade, but he wasn't in it. Her brow knitted with concern.

Where was he?

She walked slowly back to the living room and sat down on the couch to wait, distractedly reaching for the remote and clicking on the TV. It was one of those Sunday morning political roundtable programs. She sipped her coffee and stared blankly at the television as her mind flipped through the list of potential reasons for Chris's absence. *Maybe he went for a walk or decided to go to mass at St. Lukes. Maybe he was just outside in the hall smoking. Wait! I know. He got an emergency call to drive this morning. Probably that sweet old man, what was his name? Frank?*

She impulsively stood and walked barefoot out into the corridor, leaving the door open behind her. The hallway was quiet and empty. She trotted quickly to the end and looked over the rail. Five stories below in the parking lot she spotted her rusty red Corolla sitting next to his company Lincoln. He hadn't driven anywhere. She bit her lip in consternation as she turned and walked back to their apartment.

Her coffee was still steaming on the table as the politicos on the TV continued their verbal jousting. She ignored both, concentrating instead on the hollow apprehension festering in the pit of her stomach. Something was wrong. After twenty years of marriage, she was an expert on Chris McCallister. He exemplified the term "creature of habit." She only hoped he wasn't off somewhere getting high again. He was just as crushed as she was regarding CJ's prison sentence.

It seemed unlikely that she could have missed him in their tiny apartment, but she looked for him anyway, beginning her search with a quick glance into the kitchen before moving through the living room to her bedroom. She knew he wasn't in there, but there was a small chance he was in the master bathroom. He wasn't. Again, she walked down the hall to CJ's room, checking the hallway bathroom on the way. There was still no sign of him. When she reached the bedroom, she half expected to see his pasty, naked body sleeping soundly. She pushed the door open and saw exactly what she had seen thirty minutes earlier, an empty, unmade bed.

Where could he be?

She walked into the room and halfheartedly checked the closet, knowing he wouldn't be in there. She glanced wistfully at CJ's clothes hanging limply in a row and noted sadly that none of them would fit by the time he made it home.

She quietly shut the closet door and turned to exit the room. Then she spotted his foot.

What is he doing on the floor?

"Honey," she called, almost tripping as she went to him.

His massive frame was lodged between the bed and the wall on the far side of the room. His face was almost blue.

"Oh Chris," she cried out, falling to her knees and reaching for him. His lifeless body was cold. He'd been dead for hours. Her head felt like it was splitting open as she got up and staggered toward the phone.

First CJ and now Chris, she thought as she shakily dialed 911.

"Emergency Services," chirped a young voice.

Cheryl heard her own voice as if someone else was talking.

"My husband's dead."

~

The old bus creaked and bounced its way down the two-lane highway heading west. Freedom pulsed on the other side of the mesh-plated windows. It raced by in passing cars and oncoming headlights, in distant sirens and hunched streetwalkers, in florescent white gas islands and flickering neon tavern signs. It was close enough to smell, but it might as well have been a movie screen to the passengers on the bus. A movie of which they were no longer a part.

Gradually, the traffic thinned. The storefronts gave way to industrial sites and warehouses before bowing out completely and surrendering all signs of civilization to the marshland. Dawn was still a ways off. The men rode in silence, each handcuffed to the next.

Earlier, just after midnight, CJ packed all his worldly belongings into a brown paper bag. It wasn't much, just a Bible, a toothbrush, and some letters from home. He bumped fists with Kane and stepped into the cage. The inner door rolled shut behind him and the outer door slid open. He looked back once at the overcrowded cell that had been his home for the last year. He then stood up straight and walked out into the narrow hallway, leaving 6-B-2 behind him for the last time.

CJ stared out into the passing darkness. Occasionally, a distant yellow light shone through the trees. He wondered why anyone would want to live in the swamp.

"Psst . . . Hey, Blue Eyes!" called a voice from across the aisle.

CJ ignored it.

A deranged cackle pierced the rumbling drone of the bus engine, causing heads to turn.

"Oh, you one'a dem lil' stuck-up bitches, huh? They gone luv your lil' pretty ass."

CJ leaned forward to see who was talking. The face across the aisle was ancient. His eyes glowed with insanity. CJ didn't bother to respond but he allowed his gaze to linger, memorizing the crazy old man's face. Seeing that no response was forthcoming, the man turned his attention elsewhere, rambling incoherently. CJ settled back in his seat.

They spotted the gun towers just as dawn was breaking, hovering over the tree line like modern-day turrets. A low murmur swept through the bus as the fences came into view. There were two of them, both twelve feet high, layered in spirals of flesh-ripping razor wire and wrapped securely around the sprawling gray buildings of the prison. As they drew closer CJ could see the silhouette of a guard holding a machine gun in the tower.

The bus finally rolled to a stop in front of a small building that jutted from the fence line. The engine continued to rumble as one of the transport officers hopped out and approached the bulletproof glass. When he returned, the outer fence slid open and the bus began to beep as it backed slowly into the sally port. Then the driver cut the motor and the fence rolled back in place. The men clutched their brown bags and peered nervously from the windows. Waiting.

There was a commotion at the rear as the locks clicked and turned. The shocks creaked. Someone was standing on the bumper. The back door swung open and daylight filled the bus. A group of brown-clad prison guards waited at the exit, talking among themselves while slipping on gloves.

"Damn, they smell like shit," said one.

"Hey, Espinosa," called another, "you got a handcuff key?"

All at once a humongous form filled the doorway, blocking the sunlight.

"All right, you dumb motherfuckers!" he shouted. "You've got two minutes to get the hell off this bus. Move it!"

The men stood and shuffled down the aisle. The chains that bound them rattled as they moved toward the door.

"Look at this little punk," one snarled as CJ staggered down the three metal steps to the asphalt. "Hey, kid! How old are you?"

"I'll be nineteen next month," CJ said softly.

"Speak up, goddamn it!"

"I'm eighteen."

The officer was quickly in his face, shouting. "When you address an officer at this institution you say 'sir,' you little fuckboy. Are we clear?"

"Yes sir!"

"Now how old are you, boy?"

"Eighteen, sir!"

"How much time you got?"

"Twenty-seven years, sir!"

The guard stared at him a moment longer, then shook his head and uncuffed him, moving methodically down the line of inmates.

"Men," he began, "you are here because you could not abide by the rules of society, but you *will* follow the rules of the Department of Corrections. Do you understand?"

Some mumbled, "Yeah," and some merely nodded.

"I swear to God the next motherfucker that doesn't address me as sir is getting the shit slapped out of him. Now do you understand me?"

"Sir, yes sir!" they responded.

"That's better. Now, I want all of you to strip down. Put all them dirty-ass clothes in your brown bags. Boxers too. I want you asshole-naked! You've got thirty seconds. Let's go!"

The men hurried out of their clothes and stuffed them in their bags as the guards paced back and forth, watching them.

"Now follow me," he instructed.

They walked through a metal detector into a long corridor with a wooden bench running the length of the wall.

"All right, I want you shoulder to shoulder," said the guard. "Set your shit on the floor in front of you."

CJ placed his bag on the floor and looked straight ahead, trying to ignore the unsettling feeling of another man's skin brushing against his.

Although one guard did most of the talking, five more spread out along the line, observing.

"All right, everybody get your hands in the air. I want your fingers wiggling. Keep doing it until I tell you to stop. Let's go!"

CJ felt like a fool standing there naked, wiggling his fingers above his head.

"Good. Now I want you to open your mouth. Take your right index finger and run it all around your gums."

The men complied as the pacing guards inspected their open mouths for contraband.

"Stop. Now I want you to bend at the waist and run your fingers through your hair. Keep doing it until I tell you to stop."

Again the men complied.

"All right, stand up straight," he instructed. "Now I want you to grab your dicks and lift them up. Not your balls, just your dicks. If you're uncircumcised, go ahead and skin it back. Let's go."

Each man's equipment was closely scrutinized.

"Now lift your balls," he commanded.

The men obeyed.

"Good. Now listen close. I want you to turn around and put your forehead on that wooden bench behind you. There should be forty-seven asses pointed skyward right now. Do it!"

CJ was a little off balance. He hoped like hell he didn't fall to the side and cause a domino pileup.

"Now I want you to reach back with both hands and pull your ass cheeks as far apart as you can. Come on now. Don't be shy. I want to see some intestines this morning. Let's go!"

Minutes ticked by as the guards smoked and laughed and made crude jokes. Mere words like degradation and humiliation could not begin to describe how CJ felt as he pressed his head to the bench and pulled himself apart. Somebody coughed. A phone rang. The old man on his left began to wobble against him.

"Who's McCallister?" a voice boomed.

CJ stood unsteadily. "Right here . . . sir."

~

With trembling hands, Cheryl twisted the cap from the pill bottle and extracted a small tablet. She hastily popped it in her mouth and downed it with a glass of water. Two years ago when she was first prescribed the antidepressants, no one could have convinced her that one day she'd actually be taking them. Now she doubted she could make it without them. Burying her husband and seeing her only child off to prison in the same week were daunting tasks by themselves, but handling the logistics and every minor detail on her own when she could barely summon the energy required to get out of bed in the morning was next to impossible. That's where the Prozac came in. It didn't cure the sadness; nothing could do that. It just assisted her with the strength to face the day.

Now, exactly one week after she found Chris on CJ's floor, there was nothing left to tackle. Even though doing things like finding a funeral home, selecting a casket, notifying distant relatives, breaking the news to CJ via the prison chaplain, and attending the burial were all heartbreaking, at least she had a mission to throw herself into. All those things had now been accomplished, leaving her to wander the quiet halls of the empty apartment while ghosts confronted her at every turn. She knew she should go back to work, that Mr. Ramos needed her, but she kept putting it off. She wasn't ready yet. The thought of tearful condolences and hushed whispers behind her back made her skin crawl. Maybe next week.

She flipped on the light in the hallway bathroom and walked in. The woman staring back from the mirror was a haggard stranger. She popped open the medicine cabinet and her reflection thankfully swung to the side. The shelves were lined with Chris's various medications: Vasotec, Cardizem, and nitroglycerin for his heart; Bumex to reduce water retention and make it easier to breathe. The bottom shelf held his anxiety and sleeping pills. She studied the bottle of Valium. *Do it,* said a voice in an urgent whisper. She shut the cabinet and left the bathroom.

She walked to the bedroom at the end of the hall and sat on the bed. Her husband and son were everywhere, in trophies and posters and records and toys and clothes. In cigarette burns on the carpet and holes in the drywall; even their distinct smells seemed to be woven into the air. She looked over at the dusty boom box on the dresser. A "C" and a "J" were grafitti'd on either speaker in white block letters. She thought back to the Christmas when she bought it for her little break dancer. He was so happy. One of Chris's tapes was in the cassette deck, paused in time. She reached over and pushed the power button, and the sounds of Motown exploded from the speakers.

She impulsively stood and opened the nightstand drawer. It was full of tapes, pennies, paperclips, Army men, baseball cards, and a picture of a pretty girl in a t-shirt that said "Peaches."

The opening notes of Jackie Wilson's "Lonely Teardrops" filled the room. The ghosts of her husband and young son were laughing and dancing to the music. She sat down hard on the bed and wept for her family.

Then something caught her eye, a purple velvet Crown Royal bag lodged in the back of the open drawer. She reached for it. The music seemed to swell as she undid the drawstring and dumped the contents on the bed. There was a small knot of twenties, a few gold rings, a bracelet, and a chrome snub-nosed pistol. She picked up the gun.

Do it, the voice whispered again. It was her husband, beckoning from beyond the veil.

Suddenly the dancing ghosts began to circle her, laughing. The speed of the music increased as the faces stretched demonically, slapping at her, clawing at her, pushing, pulling, howling.

She fell to the floor in the fetal position, crying and shaking uncontrollably.

Do it, the voice whispered.

"Oh God," she cried out. "Help me!"

She realized she was still gripping the pistol.

~

The voice echoed from the PA system, reverberating off the walls of the dormitories and handball courts, causing basketball players to pause mid-dribble and runners to slow their pace while looking up at the tower.

"Attention on the compound," the voice boomed. "Inmate McCallister, 271958. Report to the chaplain's office immediately."

The PA cut off with a loud click and all activity resumed. CJ dropped to the ground from the pull-up bar and grabbed his shirt. *Fuck the chaplain,* he thought as he headed toward the rec gate. His father was dead. What more was there to say?

Probably just a routine follow-up, or maybe he's gonna try to recruit me as a Christian. CJ wasn't interested. Not in the church, not in the chaplain, and not in the God he represented. His only prayer had been that his family would stay healthy until he made it back home. Nothing else mattered. He and God had a deal. A deal that was broken on his first day in prison.

He rattled the gate and looked up at the tower, shielding his eyes from the sun. The window slid open and a female guard with a feathered mullet scowled down at him.

"McCallister. Chapel."

She slammed the window back. He waited. The gate popped and he stepped through. It buzzed loudly until he shut it behind him. He looked across the compound toward the chapel. Most of the buildings mirrored each other: drab-colored, one-story, boxlike structures with no frills save for the occasional dying plant on a windowsill. The chapel was no exception. There was no steeple, no stained glass, no smiling priest out front welcoming the flock. The only feature that made the chapel distinguishable from dental, laundry, mental health, or classification was the massive wooden front door.

When he reached the building, he pulled the door open and stepped inside. The small lobby was quiet. The inmate clerks were already gone for the day.

"Hello," he called.

"End of the hall, McCallister," said the deep voice of the chaplain from down the corridor.

When he reached the room, he was surprised to see that the chaplain had company, a high-ranking officer in a starched white shirt and two men in suits. They sat at a long, wooden table, the kind with legs that fold in flat from either end. A single chair sat across from them.

CJ frowned.

"Have a seat," said the suit nearest the chaplain. His hair was slicked straight back and he had a painful-looking sunburn.

CJ sat down.

Sunburn smiled and flashed a badge. "My name is Detective Majesky, Metro-Dade Police, Homicide."

CJ looked at the chaplain in confusion. "Homicide? I thought you said my father died of congestive heart failure."

"It's not your father I'm here about," the detective said. "It's your mother. She was found in her apartment yesterday."

CJ's head began to pound.

"Gunshot wound to the heart. We believe it to have been self-inflicted. I'm sorry."

The room began to spin.

"She shot herself," said CJ.

"Son, your prints were all over the gun. Now we do realize that it would have been impossible for you to have been at that apartment, but it's procedure that we—"

"In the heart?" CJ cried in anguish.

Something inside of him snapped. He leaned slightly back, then slammed his head sharply down into the table, where his face exploded against the wood. The brilliant flash of pain lasted a second, but it was a welcome respite from the other pain that was twisting and whipping around inside him like a live electrical wire. So he did it again. And again. Until the splintered wood of the table was awash in blood and the legs collapsed inward. The men scrambled around the broken table to restrain him as he kicked it to the floor and jumped to his feet, shrieking like a wounded animal. He elbowed, punched, mule-kicked, and gouged as if driven by demons, destroying everything in his path, relishing the crunch of bone and the splash of blood. He *needed* it.

The men suddenly backed away, breathing heavily as a stampede of footsteps and jingling keys thundered down the hall. CJ turned and leapt into the crowd of officers pushing through the doorway. He was met in the air by a wall of liquid fire that sent him crashing to the carpet.

"Come on, you motherfuckers!" he roared. "Kill me!"

He was then stomped to unconsciousness.

PART THREE

1995

"We are all in the gutter,
but some of us are looking at the stars."

—Oscar Wilde

Chapter 13

The young man walked into the dormitory bathroom. He paused at the first stall and plugged one nostril while blowing forcefully through the other, sending a snot-rocket spiraling down toward the toilet, where it splatted against the seat then free fell down into the dirty water below like a bungee jump. He then kick-flushed the toilet and walked over to the long row of sinks to rinse off his hands.

He was suddenly aware of the repulsive stench of someone's bowels wafting toward him from the far end of the bathroom. He slowly turned his head and scowled in the general direction of the offensive odor. A chinless, baldheaded man in thick bifocals blinked curiously back at him from the last stall. His eyes were magnified to double their true size by the powerful lenses.

"Put some water on it, you fuckin' child molester!" he exploded.

The toilet instantly flushed as the glasses and bald head sank back behind the stall wall. The young man shook his head and mumbled something under his breath as he exited the foul-smelling latrine and walked past the officers' station into the living area of his dorm. He was met in the aisle by a smiling, middle-aged black man from Orlando nicknamed "Hustle," who was holding out a greeting card and a pen.

"You gonna gimme some play this week, Cee?" he asked, opening the card to reveal a square board for a preseason football game.

"Man, listen, Hustle . . ." CJ began, shaking his head.

"Aw shit," Hustle rolled his eyes. "Here we go."

"I can't afford to gamble right now," said CJ as he brushed past him. "I'm broke."

"Stop lyin'," he said, right on his trail. "I saw you in the canteen line today."

"Wow." CJ plopped down on his bunk. "You're watching me now, huh?"

Hustle lay back in the adjacent bed and laced his fingers behind his head. "A good businessman always monitors the shopping habits of his customers."

CJ glanced over at him. "Ali is gonna snap if he finds you lying in his bunk."

"Man, fuck Ali," said Hustle, quickly scanning the dorm for the gigantic Muslim. He sat up. "You got allergies, man? I got some allergy medication."

CJ shook his head.

"Hemorrhoids?"

"Hell no."

"Well, whatchu need then? Come on now. Spend a little of that bread with Hustleman. I got some triple-antibiotic ointment and some antifungal cream. Oh . . . wait a second . . . I know what you want."

He looked around conspiratorially as he dug in the pocket of his uniform pants and came away with a small piece of paper. He held it low and out of sight between the two bunks as he unfolded it carefully. In the center of the paper lay a tiny green bud about the size of a fingernail.

He looked up at CJ and smiled. "Ten bucks."

"Yeah, right."

"It's fire."

"That shit won't even go across the paper," CJ said, looking down at it.

"Yeah it will," said Hustle, folding it back and dropping it in CJ's pocket. "Gimme eight."

"Eight and two free squares on your board."

"Damn," said Hustle, holding out the board for him to sign, "you sure *your* name ain't Hustleman?"

"I just hope I feel this," CJ said, digging in his locker for eight dollars' worth of canteen items.

As he handed over five packets of tuna, Hustle was rifling through a stack of photos of naked women. "How 'bout some girls, you need some girls?"

"Nah," said CJ, "the last ones I bought are workin' fine."

"All right," Hustle stood, "I'll see you later on."

CJ watched him walk off. As he passed an area where a group of inmates was having a heated discussion, he turned and winked before throwing back his head and hollering, "Hey! I ain't got much!"

Everyone stopped what they were doing and looked at the crazy black man who smiled and produced his stack of photos.

". . . but I got a little pussy."

He was immediately engulfed by the crowd. CJ shook his head and fought off a smile. Hustleman was a trip. This was their second prison together.

~

After learning of his mother's suicide, he completely shut down, and the subsequent year was a Thorazine-induced blur of psych cells, crisis units, and solitary confinement. There were memory fragments of various shackled bus rides, but he had no idea how many times he'd been shipped or even the names of all the prisons he'd been to. He rarely made it through the front gate without getting gassed and thrown in the hole. His body was littered with scars that he couldn't remember collecting, especially his head and hands. That wasn't the case with the hideous gash running down the center of his left wrist and forearm. He knew exactly where that came from.

People are mistaken in their thinking that those who commit or attempt suicide are pain freaks. Nothing could be further from the truth. The whole point of suicide is pain relief. His mother was no pain freak. A paper cut could make her cry, but when his father died and he got sent to the joint in the same week, the pain became unbearable for her.

He blamed himself. The fact that the cops decided not to prosecute was no consolation. She would have never shot herself if he'd been there. She would have never shot herself if he hadn't made her so miserable with worry. And above all, she would have never shot herself if he hadn't left a pistol in that drawer.

He flinched as a scene flashed across his mind. The image of the wounded animal he had become after that: pale, thin, bloodshot, mangy, and completely vacant. He remembered swiping the disposable razor off the shelf while being escorted to the shower in administrative lockdown and gleefully concealing it like a small child with a new trinket. He remembered breaking off the handle and outer plastic to get to the blade. He remembered sinking to his knees in front of the toilet in his tiny cell and laying his outstretched arm across the cold steel toilet seat. He remembered watching his right hand slide the sharp blade into the sweet meat of his left forearm as if it belonged to someone else. He remembered ripping downward violently, exposing naked bone and tendon before the blood came gushing. He remembered how quickly the toilet water changed to bright red as he growled, "Die, motherfucker," while looking back at the Plexiglas window of his cell. He vaguely remembered the sounds of shouting, keys, and loud walkie-talkies above him as he drifted away. And of course he remembered waking up on the freezing floor of a psych cell with twenty-seven staples beneath the blood-soaked bandage on his arm. Alive.

He was written a disciplinary report for self-mutilation, given another thirty days in the hole, and sent back to confinement, but the Department of Corrections was clearly tired of his antics and within a month he was being shipped yet again. This time to a new close-management prison in the Florida Panhandle.

As a close-management inmate he was locked in a tiny cell twenty-four hours a day. His food was passed to him through a slot in the door, and three times a week he was handcuffed and escorted to the shower. Phone calls, visits, and tele-

vision were all privileges that could be earned, but since he had no one to call, no one to come visit, and didn't give a fuck about TV, he was instead content to lie in his bunk, zoned out on psych meds, watching the walls sweat. And sweat they did. It was August of '94 and the temperature was hitting triple digits regularly unless it rained. His cell was located on the west side of the wing, which meant that each day around one o'clock the sun crept over the roof of the dorm and started heating things up. By two his sweat-covered torso was stuck to his sheets, and by three you could grill burgers on the back wall of the cell. The window opened only four inches, and any draft that attempted to penetrate its two thick screens and mesh coverplate usually died on the journey. There were large rolling fans on the wing, but they didn't blow in the cells. The exhaust fans rumbled loudly but didn't pull, and the vents were only good for a line of communication between neighboring cells. This is how he met Hustleman.

"Hey, next door!" a voice called. "Hey, white boy next door! Man, you deaf or something, cracker? Hey!"

CJ ignored him.

He tried beating on the wall for a while, but CJ ignored that too. By that time he had mastered the art of withdrawing and turning inward. This was made especially easy by the heavy dosage of Thorazine the nurse was delivering to his flap each day.

"What are you, a racist or somethin'?" the voice asked the next morning, starting early. "You hate black folks? You one of them skinheads?"

CJ stared blankly at the vent. But Hustle was persistent. He talked to him nonstop throughout the day. On shower nights, he'd look in CJ's cell and frown as the guard escorted him past. CJ looked right through him.

"Man, what kinda dope they got you on?" he asked one day.

CJ rolled over.

"Look, I don't know you. Maybe you need that shit. Maybe you one of them sick-ass child molester types or maybe you just crazy as hell. I don't know. But that shit'll eat your soul, man, you hear me?"

His voice sounded as if it were coming from the top of a well, echoing down off the walls into the dark, dripping recesses where CJ lay motionless and trapped.

"Tomorrow, when that bitch come to your flap with that shit, cuff it under your tongue and spit it out when she leaves," he instructed. "See how you feel. Just try it."

The following morning when the nurse came, CJ impulsively took his advice. Once she left, he spat the pill into his palm. It was chalky and smeared from his saliva. He dropped it in the toilet.

Hustle talked all day. CJ slept. The next day when the nurse came, he noticed he was a little more present as he hid the pill in his mouth. More aware. He felt agitated and hungry and his cell light seemed harsh, but the fact that he was feeling at all made his heart leap. He was no longer stuck on pause. It was still early in the morning and he quickly drifted back to sleep, but it wasn't the comatose slumber of the dead. It was fitful and light. He even awoke with a boner. Of course Hustle was already on the vent.

". . . and so these two aliens are standing in front of a gas pump at the Texaco, right? Well, the other'n says to his friend, 'Man, leave that cat alone, that's a bad muthafucker!'"

CJ stared at the vent the way people in the 1940s stared at their living room radios.

"Well, the one alien, the stubborn one, don't wanna hear that, so he pulls out his laser gun and says to the pump, 'You got one mo' shot, take me to your leader, boy!' and his partner says, 'Man, leave him alone, I'm tellin' you, that's a bad muthafucker.'"

He paused for a second and CJ heard his toilet flush. He waited for it to go quiet, then he continued.

"So anyway the one with the laser gets mad when the pump don't answer and starts shootin' and course there's this big-ass explosion and they end up gettin' blasted back about three blocks down the road with they faces all burnt up and shit. The one with the laser gun says, 'What happened?' and his homeboy goes, 'Man, I told you not to fuck with that dude. Anybody that can wrap they dick around they waist twice and then stick it in they ear is a bad muthafucker!'"

CJ busted out laughing. He couldn't help it. It had been so long since he heard a joke. It felt good to laugh. He collapsed on his bunk in a guffawing fit.

"Well, amen," said Hustle. "What's your name, man?"

"CJ," he croaked. "CJ McCallister."

His own voice sounded odd to him. Familiar, yet different than he remembered. It had been awhile since he'd heard it out loud.

"They call me Hustleman," his neighbor said. "Welcome back."

They ended up talking late into the night.

"What type of dope were they feedin' you?" asked Hustleman.

"I don't know," said CJ, "Thorazine, I guess."

"That shit'll make you a real-live zombie. Why were you taking Thorazine?"

Something about the anonymity of the vent, the fact that he hadn't spoken in so long, and Hustle's friendly, good-natured voice compelled CJ to open up. He sat at the foot of his bunk and recounted his entire life story to the stranger in the next cell. He left nothing out. They both laughed at some parts, and CJ broke down when he got to his mom's suicide. "Damn . . ." was all Hustle could say. Throughout the story, as CJ spoke into the dusty holes of the vent, he kept thinking of the first time his father took him to confession at Saint Lukes. Was that only twelve years ago? Now, the child that once shyly admitted his sins to the varnished wooden church confessional was a grown man disclosing the inner workings of his life to the peeling paint of his cell wall and the complete stranger listening on the other side.

When he finished, he was met with total silence. He sat there in the dark, staring down at his hands in the sliver of light that was coming through his window.

"You there?" he finally asked.

"Yeah," said Hustle quietly, "I'm right here. Hey, you smoke?"

"Mm hmm," CJ mumbled.

"Go to your door."

CJ stood and stretched, then took the two steps to the steel door. A tiny ball of wet toilet paper rolled in his cell.

"See that?" Hustle called from the vent.

"Yeah," said CJ, bending to retrieve it.

"Don't touch it!"

CJ froze.

"Wait 'til I tell you."

He leaned against the wall and waited.

"Okay, pull!" said Hustle.

He grabbed the string that was attached to the ball and began to pull it into his cell. Soon, the orange cherry of a lit cigarette became visible. He untied it from the string and took a deep, satisfying drag. The smoke felt wonderful in his lungs. He walked to his window and blew it out, then hit it again. He was already lightheaded. He hadn't smoked in forever.

"You straight?" Hustle asked.

"Yeah," said CJ. "Thanks, man."

"That was on the house. Next one gonna cost you five stamps."

CJ heard the bed creak through the wall as his neighbor finally got off the vent to lie down.

"Hustleman still gotta hustle," he heard him say.

CJ took a final drag and flicked the short in the toilet. It had been forty-eight hours since he had taken any psych meds. He was still a little groggy, and the hurt from reliving his past was like a ripped scab, but just when his eyes filled with tears at the thought of being motherless, fatherless, and at the very beginning of a lengthy prison sentence, the punch line to the joke his neighbor told earlier leaped into his head: "Anybody that can wrap their dick around their waist twice and stick it in their ear is a bad motherfucker!"

His sudden explosion of uproarious laughter punctured the silence of the sleeping wing.

"Shut the fuck up!" boomed a patrolling guard a few doors down.

CJ dove in his bunk and feigned sleep. After the officer made his round and the beam of his flashlight disappeared down the hall, Hustle called through the vent.

"Psst . . . Hey! CJ?" he whispered. "On second thought, maybe you do need to get your crazy ass up and take your Thorazine in the morning!"

He smiled at the joke as he rolled over, but he knew in his heart that he would never take that shit again.

His Thorazine days were over.

~

CJ reached beneath the cuff of his bed and felt for his pouch of rolling tobacco. His eyes casually roamed over the other seventy-one beds in his dorm to see if anyone was watching him as he dug inside it for the packet of papers. He quickly extracted two and licked one, expertly sticking them together while digging in his pocket for the tiny sack he had just purchased from Hustle. He poured its contents on the paper and shook his head. It was super small. The first time he ever smoked weed in prison, he was astonished at how tiny the amount was, and even more astonished by the fact that he got so thoroughly wasted after burning it. And paranoid. There's nothing like being stoned in a room full of strangers, especially when the strangers all happen to be killers, rapists, and psych patients. He smiled at the memory.

He was fresh off the slab, white as a sheet from two years of no sunlight, and weighing in at his South Miami Junior High weight. He had talked his way off psych meds while on C.M., but his psych grade was still a two, which meant that every once in a while he'd pop up on the call-out for mental health.

When he got off the Bluebird at Lake Butler he assumed he'd be on another bus within a day or two, en route to his permanent camp, wherever that was. The prison at Lake Butler served mostly as a reception center for the northern part of Florida, as well as the Regional Medical Center for inmates with health problems. Very few people were classified as permanents.

Since the bulk of his time had been served on lockdown, he didn't expect to see a familiar face on the yard. He was wrong.

"What's up, Whitebread?" Hustle called to him from the bleachers. "I see you finally made it off the slab."

"The slab" was prison slang for C.M., the lockdown unit where they met. Hustle had gotten off four months before him.

"Man, you look like shit!" He laughed as he walked over to where CJ was standing. "You ain't back on that dope, are you?"

CJ shook his head. "You got a rip?" he asked, looking around.

Hustle reached in his back pocket and handed him an open pack of tobacco. "Keep it. What dorm they got you in?"

"C-two."

"I'll bring you some shit this afternoon."

"Hustle, you don't have to do that," CJ said, remembering the lessons that Kane had instilled in him regarding borrowing and trust.

"It's all good, Cee," Hustle said over his shoulder as he walked off. "You'd do the same for me."

Later that afternoon Hustle appeared in his dorm with a small canteen bag containing a bar of Ivory soap, a deodorant, two soups, and a lighter.

"Don't never say Hustleman ain't gave you nothin'," he said as he dumped the items on CJ's bunk.

CJ looked him in the eye. "I appreciate everything you've done for me."

Hustle waved him off. "Here's one mo' thing," he said, handing him a small folded piece of paper. "Don't get knocked off with it now."

CJ stared at it. "What is it?"

"Quit actin' green, cracker!" Hustle hissed. "You know what the hell it is. It's reefer."

"Oh."

"Ten dollars worth. You can smoke it or sell it and put some shit in your house. It's on you."

"Thanks."

"You'll probably be gone in the morning. If I don't see you, be easy, and keep your head up."

They shook hands.

"Why are you still here?" asked CJ as he was turning to leave.

"They made me a permanent," he said, pushing the door open.

CJ flipped the sack between his fingers and watched Hustle walk back across the compound to his own dorm.

Later that night he decided to smoke it, noting that the last time he smoked weed was with April the night he got arrested. He was expecting a minor buzz, if anything, considering the miniscule amount. Ten minutes later he was so blasted that he decided his best option was to get in his bunk and pull the covers over his head.

He didn't get transferred the next morning or the next, and after two weeks of waiting he was informed by the classification department that he, too, was being made a permanent. Just like Hustle. They ended up in the same dorm.

"Mail call!" thundered an officer's voice, causing CJ to rush one more hit from the pinner before flushing it down the toilet and blowing the smoke behind it.

He went straight to the sink, washed his hands, and swished some water around in his mouth in an effort to weaken the pungent odor, but he knew he was all right. He wouldn't get that close to him anyway. He never got mail, unless . . .

"McCallister!" yelled the officer.

Great, thought CJ as he warily approached the guard, averting his red eyes and extending his hand as far out from his body as possible. A white piece of paper was dismissively slapped in his outstretched palm as another name was called.

He glanced down at the paper, but he already knew what it said. It was a money receipt from somebody named J. Ramos, for fifty bucks. The third one he had received in the last six months. He had no idea who J. Ramos was or why he was sending him money. He figured it was probably a mistake. Hustle was convinced it was some rich distant relative, and Bones, the dormitory tattoo artist, was sure some sissy had spotted his mug shot on the computer and thought he was cute. It really didn't matter where it was coming from. He just hoped it kept coming.

Suddenly Bones appeared at the foot of his bunk. "Ahhh . . . I see the mysterious sugar daddy has decided to break bread yet again." He smiled.

"Fuck off, Bones." CJ smiled back. "You're just jealous."

"I am," he admitted. "Now, being that you've already excluded me from the joint you just snuck in the bathroom," he lowered his voice, "and, by the way, you look extremely trashed."

CJ's eyes darted to the mirror that was glued with toothpaste to the bottom of the bunk above him. He *did* look trashed.

"I was just wondering if you were going to share any of your newfound wealth with Uncle Bones."

"I might," said CJ.

"We could do that 'Cheryl' piece on your chest."

"I was thinking neck."

"I strongly advise against."

"It's my money," said CJ, whapping him on the back of the head with the rolled-up receipt.

Billy "Bones" Whitner looked exactly like his name: tall, pale, and skeletal. The letter E on his ID tag was misleading. Although it signified his sixth stint in prison, he was far from an idiot. He could recite the preamble of the Constitution, was fluent in world politics, and could fix, boost, or reconfigure any radio on the compound. He was also Michelangelo with a tattoo gun. His downfall was crack cocaine. He was well known in his hometown of Pensacola for riding his bike all over the city with a backpack slung over his shoulder containing sketch pads, ink, and his chain-gang tattoo gun. His customers were mostly dope dealers in trap houses, which was fine with him since he preferred being paid in crack.

Bones had run three different pieces on CJ since he became a permanent. When he first did the skull, CJ was so proud of it that people started picking on him for walking around with his sleeve rolled up. But the timepiece he did on CJ's other arm was even better than the skull, and the naked chick on his chest had them both beat. CJ was quickly becoming addicted to ink and Bones knew it.

"Well," said Bones, "we'll probably need to get started soon because once you go to the kitchen, they're gonna move you to B dorm."

"Kitchen? I work inside grounds."

"Not anymore. Go look at the job change sheet. I thought you knew, bro. It's been hanging in the dayroom all day."

"I'm not workin' in that hot-ass kitchen," CJ fumed. "They might as well take me back to confinement!"

"Easy now. There's gotta be somebody we can talk to with enough yank and enough connections to get you switched back."

"Who?" CJ asked, studying him intently. Bones was an old convict and CJ respected his counsel.

"Hey, CJ!" Hustle shouted across the dorm. "Where the hell'd you get this tuna from? The expiration date say June of '94. Last year! Oh *hell* nah! You gotta give me somethin' else or just give me my shit back."

He was mumbling to himself as he made his way toward them. "You already beat me outta two dollars and two squares, now you wanna gimme this old stank-ass tuna."

"Bingo," said Bones as he approached.

"What the fuck y'all smilin' at?" Hustle demanded.

~

Jose Ramos sat stoically in his leather chair watching Vasten Golic, the hotel detective, read aloud from the report he prepared concerning Gracia Nieves, a maid suspected of stealing from guests. He was already in a foul mood and the information did nothing to lift his spirits.

"So there's no doubt?" he asked when the detective finished.

"None, sir," said Golic. "We have her on camera."

"How old is she?"

"Twenty-two."

"Family?"

"None here in the States. At least none that I was able to locate. Except her kids."

Ramos tugged at an eyebrow. "How many?"

"Kids?" said Golic. "Two boys, ages five and three."

"Where's the father?"

Golic looked up from the report. "Dead. Botched robbery. Tried to hit a jewelry store off Flagler last year and the owner was uncooperative. It was all over the *Herald.*"

"Hmmmm," said Ramos, resting his elbows on his desk and placing his chin on the bridge formed by his interlocking fingers.

Vasten Golic waited.

"Have her arrested," Ramos finally said, "and fired of course."

His phone rang. The detective placed the paperwork back in a file and rose to leave as Ramos picked up the receiver.

"Executive offices."

"Jose, it's Frank."

"Oye, Frankie. *Como estas, hermanito?"* He held up a finger instructing Golic to wait.

"I'm doing well," said the doctor, "busy, but well."

"Good, good," said Ramos.

"Listen, I don't have a lot of time to talk right now, but I think I may have some info for you about . . . about Cheryl," he said quietly.

Ramos frowned. "My secretary, Cheryl?"

"Yes," said Dr. Villanueva. "I don't think I'd be violating confidentiality since she's deceased. Recently there've been a lot of reports about suicidal behavior exhibited by people taking antidepressants."

"Okay," said Ramos, staring through the waiting hotel detective as he listened.

"Jose, I know for a fact that she began taking Prozac the week her son went to prison and her husband died. She told me about it after the funeral. She had been prescribed the pills for almost two years but was adamant about not taking them until . . ."

"Until her world fell apart," Ramos finished.

"Exactly."

"Mierda," Ramos cursed, immediately thinking of her son in prison, the guilt he must feel. *Had he sent him any money lately?*

"Let's have lunch," Villanueva suggested.

"Okay," said Ramos.

"Thursday at La Carreta?"

"Sounds good."

"Twelve o'clock."

"All right, I'll be there."

"Adios."

"Adios." He hung up the phone and thought about his former secretary. If he had known that their last conversation would truly be their last, he might have bared his soul.

And when have you ever bared your soul, Jose Ramos? he thought with a tearful smile. He searched his memory until the sarcastic voice in his head sounded off again. *Exactamente.*

"Sir, did you need me?" asked Vasten Golic from the doorway. "Because if not, I'll go ahead and have Nieves taken to the station and booked."

Jose Ramos thought of CJ again and how tormented he must be, living under the oppressive notion that he was somehow responsible for Cheryl's suicide. He was overwhelmed by a surge of compassion.

"No," he said, "just have her come down here. I'll talk to her."

Golic was taken aback. "In cuffs?" he stammered, unsure of what to do.

"No," said Ramos, "no cuffs."

~

The main unit at Lake Butler is one of the oldest correctional institutions in the state. Most of the dorms as well as the chow hall and hospital are constructed from red brick, a long-abandoned material that fell out of favor prior to the prison building spike of the 1980s and '90s.

The inmates are confined within the sprawling compound by two towering fences draped with endless coiling layers of razor wire. Armed guards look down on the yard through mirrored sunglasses from mammoth rectangular structures that rise sporadically along the perimeter, like monoliths against the backdrop of the north Florida sky.

CJ wove his way down the sidewalk, stepping around slow-moving old-timers and cliques of reunited homeboys congregating on the pavement, blocking his passage. The inmate traffic was heavy this time in the afternoon. He could already hear the sounds of shouting and bouncing basketballs echoing off the backside of the chow hall as he approached the rec yard. When a familiar face crossed his path he nodded or, in some cases, extended his fist for a quick tap, but mostly he kept his facial features slack and expressionless. The delicate issue of eye contact is one of the nuances of prison life. CJ had already witnessed bloody battles erupt over two men locking eyes and refusing to look away. The stares would lead to cocky remarks and even cockier replies. Sensing the tension, a crowd would circle, horns would lock, punches would be thrown, and in one instance earlier that year, a knife was pulled, resulting in a life flight helicopter landing on the yard and ominous bloodstains on the concrete in front of D dorm.

CJ intuitively knew when to lock eyes, when to let them glaze over, and when to avoid eye contact altogether. It was part of the game.

He automatically checked the canteen line as he passed through the rec gate. It was a mile long. Hustlers and spot sellers worked the crowd as bored guards chain-smoked and pretended to patrol the area. At the entrance to the pavilion a quartet of older black inmates snapped their fingers and sang gospel in harmony. CJ acted like he was looking for someone as an excuse to stop and listen.

. . . Now pharaoh's army (Pharaoh's army)
Drowned in the red sea (Drowned in the red sea)
So I'm sayin', Mary (Oh Mary, don't you weep)
Whoa, Mary! (Oh Mary, don't you weep)
Tell Martha not to moan (Tell Martha not to moan)

The back and forth between the lead singer and the other three was pure magic. Gospel music had never sounded so cool. He knew who else would love it, his dad. He suddenly erupted in a burst of laughter. *His father would probably think they were singing about him. He'd probably join right in, snapping his fingers and attempting to sing in harmony.*

He shook his head, banishing the memory of his father back into the cellar of his heart. Thoughts of his father inevitably led to thoughts of his mother, and the rec yard wasn't the place to relive the torturous guilt and regret he felt concerning either of them.

He ducked under the shade of the pavilion and reached in his pocket for a rip. As he was cupping the flame to light it, he was almost bowled over by a fat, legless man in a wheelchair arguing heatedly with his pusher, who bore the molten stretched skin of a burn victim.

"Watch where you're goin'!" said CJ to their backs.

The burned man responded without even bothering to turn around.

Damn, thought CJ, studying the gnarled and twisted flesh of the man's middle finger. *Even his fingers are burned.*

The inmate population at the main unit was split among the sick, diseased, and crippled who were there for medical treatment, the new arrivals being dropped off daily from every county north of Hillsborough, the permanents who were assigned to the prison and performed the jobs that kept it up and running, such as food service and laundry, and the transients who were on their way from one camp to another.

Telling each group apart was easy: the sick looked sick; the new arrivals were sunburned, had shaved heads, and wore raggedy, ill-fitting blues; the transients wore jewelry, sneakers, and boasted the accumulated property of those who'd been down awhile; and the permanents at Lake Butler wore white uniforms.

CJ walked between the steel tables where jitterbugs slapped cards at spades, older men bid their pinochle hands, and Cubans pushed dominoes. Every table was full. He came to the edge of the concrete and surveyed the yard. The basketball court was lined with spectators as some of the best athletes from Florida's inner city blacktops showed their skills. The white boys bumped and spiked in the brown sand beneath the volleyball net, while shirtless giants hung from the pull-up and dip bars with shuffling lines behind them awaiting their turn for a set.

He stepped out onto the huge track and walked the stretch that led to the orange clay diamond. A game was going full swing as he crossed the grass to the bleachers where spectators lounged and heckled the players.

The bat cracked just as he was sitting down. He looked up to see the ball flying to deep center field. Gone. It cleared both fences and landed out on the perimeter road.

Cody, the kid who hit it, jogged around the bases with a big shit-eating grin on his face, clenching his package through his pants and shaking it at the hecklers in the stands as he rounded third. He and CJ had arrived on the same day. He was loud, brash, and country as hell. The exact opposite of CJ in every way, yet they got along well.

"You see that, CJ?" he shouted as he trotted by.

CJ nodded and suppressed a smile.

"Whooo!" he yelled as he crossed home plate and headed back to the dugout.

A voice suddenly cut through the murmuring crowd. "What a dumb fuck."

CJ waited a few minutes before looking back to see who spoke. After the next batter lined out to short, he glanced over his shoulder. There, at the top right corner of the bleachers, sat Dane Baker holding court.

The Great Dane, as he called himself, was notorious throughout the Florida prison system: Aryan blond, with dead gray eyes and every bit of six-feet-five, 260 pounds. Raised by a group of white supremacists in Crystal River, he was beaten mercilessly by his father from the age of five in preparation for one day ascending to a leadership role in the organization. He ended up coming to prison for murder instead.

In an act of defiance toward his father, he established a splinter chapter of the same group and declared war on everyone outside his circle. Almost twenty-five years later, the seed he planted had spread into every camp in Florida and was beginning to appear in Georgia and Alabama as well.

His skin was covered with crackerbolts, swastikas, and iron crosses. The word "unkillable" was inscribed across his stomach in three-inch letters. Many believed the tat was an apt description. He'd been jumped, stabbed, beaten with steel, and left for dead in some of the bloodiest riots in the history of the state prison system, yet he was still around. And the years did nothing to soften him. He was as full of hatred as ever.

His comrades and minions were much less remarkable, with greasy, stringy hair, scrawny builds, and more than a few cases of meth mouth. They sat around him in thinly veiled admiration, passing around cups of buck and what smelled like pretty good weed, laughing boisterously at everything he said.

CJ listened as the Great Dane drunkenly toyed with his loyal subjects, boldly espousing a belief which they vehemently seconded and nodded in agreement. Then, reversing course and declaring the exact opposite, forcing them to backtrack as well. CJ rolled his eyes. *Spineless fuckin' jellyfish.*

As some of the comments from the top of the bleachers grew louder and more incendiary, a few of the older men, both black and white, got up to leave, glancing uncomfortably in the direction of the oncoming slurs before walking off. CJ was grateful that he had, so far, escaped the attention of Dane Baker as well as some of the other bullies and sadistic guards who roamed the compound like predatory, carnivorous animals. He tried his best to remain a blurred face in the crowd.

"Heyyy! I ain't got much!" a familiar voice boomed from the front of the adjacent bleachers.

CJ pinched the bridge of his nose and smiled. *Hustle.*

"But I got a little . . ." He noticed CJ. "CJ! My man! You owe me ten dollars, cracker."

CJ stood. "For what?"

"For bonding your ass up out that kitchen." Hustleman smiled broadly. "I got you a sweet job!"

"Where?" he asked, acutely aware of Dane's clique, who had frozen and were coldly observing their exchange from the stands.

"The hospital," said Hustle with a twinkle in his eye.

"Really?" CJ headed for the track.

Hustle nodded. Then, noticing Dane and his boys for the first time, he raised a clenched fist and said, "White power!" before falling in step with CJ.

Dane spat over the side of the bleachers as they walked by. "Sympathizer."

CJ turned and for the first time, he made eye contact with the ruthless, murderous Great Dane, who was glowering down at him from the stands. An icy smile crept across the cruel features of his face and he nodded slowly. CJ resisted the urge to shiver.

To Dane Baker, he was no longer a face in the crowd.

Chapter 14

CJ walked the waxed hallways of the hospital as doctors, nurses, inmates, and guards impatiently brushed by him in either direction. He had no idea where he was going. Not helping at all was the fact that at every turn another beautiful woman would materialize, holding three of his five senses hostage and leaving him painfully aware of the two left unfulfilled. They all looked like April. When he steeled himself and compartmentalized his raging twenty-year-old hormones, it was her voice in his head admonishing him. *C'mon, perv, don't get fired on your first day.*

April never wrote. Nor did Rick or anyone else from his former life. During that hazy psychotropic first year he remembered being handed an envelope through his flap once in a while, but he never opened or read any of them. He just left the letters lying under his mattress, unopened and unread, when he was relocated to another psych cell or a different prison. Eventually they stopped coming.

The hospital was a confusing maze of dead-end corridors, breezeways, offices, stairwells, examination rooms, elevators, and the ever-present cameras charting his every move.

A tall blonde with sparkling green eyes, tight jeans, and high heels clicked noisily down the hall in his direction, smiling broadly as she passed. He glanced up at the camera mounted on the ceiling, silent, sinister, and daring him to look back. *Fuck that,* he thought, turning his head to check out her ass. It was well worth the rebellion, round and juicy as it bounced and swayed down the hall. His tongue curled and whipped against the roof of his mouth involuntarily, and his muscles tightened. It almost hurt to look.

When she finally disappeared around a corner, he gathered himself and turned back in the direction he was heading. The remaining fragments of his lust quickly evaporated at the sight of the woman blocking his path. She was close to his height and probably double his weight, with a gray military buzz cut and cold, beady eyes measuring him through black-framed glasses. Her pale arms were short, fat, and sectioned off in rubber band-like creases, morphing into doughy, unmanicured hands that clenched and unclenched in gunfighter fashion. The only evidence of her womanhood were the massive boobs resting atop her ample gut.

"McCallister?" she rasped.

"Yes ma'am."

"You're late. Where the hell have you been?" Her fleshy neck waggled when she spoke.

"I—"

"Never mind. Follow me."

Wow, CJ thought as she led him down the busy hall, *out of all these pretty women, this is my supervisor.* He shook his head in disbelief.

She stopped at a nondescript wooden door and pulled it open, exposing a narrow flight of stairs. He was blasted by the smell of wet paint.

"Don't touch the walls," she warned before bounding up the stairs two at a time.

She was holding the door open, studying him when he reached the top.

"You ain't a gunner, are you?" she asked.

He hid his smile. "No ma'am."

He wasn't lying. He only smiled because of the blunt, direct manner in which she asked the question. *A gunner* was prison slang for someone who exposed himself and masturbated to female employees. It was becoming an epidemic in the system. Every dorm in every prison had gunners. It was almost cool in some circles. Not to him. He saw it as weak and disrespectful. He ached for a woman just as bad as the next man and if a female employee specifically asked him to show her his dick, he would. Proudly. But hiding behind a sink, whacking off while some unaware guard did her paperwork was just weird. He was raised better.

"Well, this is where you'll be working." She squinted at him. "If you last."

"Yes ma'am," he said, looking up and down the empty corridor. *The Price Is Right* theme song blared from a TV somewhere.

"Yes ma'am, yes ma'am," she mimicked. "Stop that! You're makin' me nauseous."

Whoa. "Sorry."

She exhaled deeply. "You're probably too young for this job, but whatever, we'll see how it goes. My name is Mrs. Carroll. I'm the charge nurse."

"Yes m—"

She pointed at him and cocked her head. "Mrs. Carroll," she enunciated slowly. "Got it?"

He nodded.

"Good boy," she said, while turning and extending a puffy, upturned arm. "This is Two East. You sweep, you mop, and you make sure the trash is emptied."

"I got it," he said, hating it already.

"Once that's done," she nodded in the direction of a large open door, "you'll clean the shower and toilets, change any dirty linen, make sure water pitchers are full, adjust pillows, help feed, and basically assist them in whatever it is they ask for . . ."

Someone won a new car on *The Price Is Right.*

". . . within reason," she finished.

"They?"

"Come on, I'll introduce you."

He followed her through the double doors where Bob Barker's voice thundered loudly off the walls. There were twelve single bunks with wooden nightstands in the living area, six on either side of a wide aisle that allowed nurses to navigate their carts freely throughout the room. Eleven of the beds were currently occupied, and the twelfth was neatly made with a Bible and a few other books stacked on the pillow. Most of the men had their blankets pulled over their heads in a futile attempt to escape Bob Barker, but a few stared listlessly at the TV, the ceiling, or through the window, which offered a drab view of the dental building.

Mrs. Carroll scowled at a shirtless, sideburned man in his sixties with his back propped against the wall behind his bed. A prosthetic leg and dusty boot stood on his nightstand.

"Ryker, turn that down, now," she ordered.

The green volume bars appeared on the bottom of the screen and incrementally diminished until the only sound in the room was a dripping sink.

"That's better. Now, men, I have someone here I want to introduce to you."

A few heads peeked out from under blankets, and beds creaked.

"This is Inmate McCallister, the new orderly."

The sink dripped. The silence swelled. Somebody farted.

His new career had begun.

~

It was close to sunset by the time he got off. He slunk back to his dorm defeated and exhausted. His shirt was untucked, his pants sagged, and his untied brogans clopped loudly against the crosswalk. The kitchen employees were filing out of the chow hall as he walked by, laughing and high-fiving each other in their aprons and hairnets. The irony of their exuberance was not lost on him. *They were probably happy because their job was so awesome. The same job he was paying to get out of so he could go change shitty sheets and put bloody boxers in biohazard bags.*

Lake Butler has a network of thick metal pipes that diverge and intersect twenty feet overhead all throughout the property, carrying steam from the boiler room to the rest of the prison. The way they encircled the compound and ran high above the sidewalk made him think of the monorail at Disney, and stopping there when his family moved from Alabama to Miami. He immediately fought off the random memory of his mom and dad and the rusty family Toyota. The pain flickered and died.

He rattled the door to his dorm and it buzzed loudly, allowing him entrance. He let it bang shut behind him and staggered into the living area.

Hustle and Bones were waiting on him with expectant smiles. Bones cupped his hands over his mouth and mimicked the sound of a PA system. "Paging Dr. McCallister, Dr. CJ McCallister, please report to Gynecology ASAP."

Hustle laughed. "You look tired, man. How was it?"

"It sucked," said CJ. "I want my ten bucks back."

"Shit, you never *gave* me the ten bucks!"

"Oh." CJ smiled tiredly at his friend. "Well, that makes it easy then."

Hustle swore under his breath, "Muthafucker."

"So where'd they assign you?" asked Bones.

"Two East."

Hustle and Bones glanced at each other. "Really? Two East?"

"Yeah," said CJ as he snatched off his shirt and dug in his box for soap and shampoo.

"And you don't dig it, huh?"

CJ looked back at them. "Fuck no, I don't *dig* it. They shit and piss and bleed all over the sheets and complain about everything. They're a bunch of snoring, farting, whiny old men. And that evil butch drill sergeant nurse—"

Bones cut him off. "CJ, Two East is the terminal unit. Those dudes up there are dying, man."

~

He didn't notice the blisters until the following morning. He was putting on his socks when he saw the bubbled liquidy sacks that had formed on his heels the day before. *Fuckin' job.* He slid his feet into his black brogans and stood slowly, anticipating pain. There was none.

He exited the dorm amid a slow-moving crowd of traffic that merged into already flooded sidewalks like commuters on their way to work. The steam from their coffee and smoke from their cigarettes rose above their heads like rush hour exhaust fumes.

With slumped shoulders he plodded ahead toward the hospital, dreading the smell, dreading Mrs. Carroll, dreading another day with the occupants of Two East.

As he passed the mental health clinic under I-Block, he spotted a familiar face leaning against the bricks and watching him. Had he seen Dane Baker first, he would have avoided eye contact altogether, but that wasn't an option now. Without any spoken words or even so much as a hand gesture he realized he was being challenged, probed, examined for potential weakness. And it all started with the eyes. While there were times to look away and times to not look at all, there were also times when you set your jaw and stared coldly back into the face of your enemy. CJ recognized this as one of those times. He squared his shoulders and raised his chin as he continued toward the crumbling prison's medical unit while reciprocating the bully's glare every step of the way.

A group of birds waddling around the double doors of the hospital burst into flight upon his arrival, momentarily distracting him. When he glanced back across the compound to the mental health building, Dane was gone. He exhaled heavily. He did not want this guy for an enemy. He was a whole other level of bully. Lunch money and black eyes were one thing. Dane Baker raped, stabbed, extorted, and murdered, and if that wasn't enough by itself, he was also the supreme leader of his own hate group, with brothers and chapters all over the state. CJ had hoped Dane had forgotten their minor exchange by the softball field. It was really nothing anyway. But like the birds that were now barely visible specks over the distant tree line to the south, his hope was fading too.

He swung open the glass door and walked purposefully through the busy lobby, down the series of corridors where big-haired women sat typing in windowless offices and hungover Vietnamese doctors slept at their desks, past break rooms, nurses' stations, and janitorial closets, through the small wooden door and up the narrow steps that led to Two East.

"You're late," announced a raspy voice as he shut the door.

"Good morning, Mrs. Carroll," he said, glancing up at the clock. It was 8:04. *Four fuckin' minutes? Really?*

"I expect you to be punctual, McCallister."

"But I'm only a few min—"

"No buts!" she snapped, pointing a nicotine-stained finger in his face. "Refusing to work carries sixty days in the box and ninety days loss-of-gain-time. Don't fuck with me, McCallister."

I'm going to kill Hustle. "I apologize, Mrs. Carroll," he said, glancing at the clock again. "I'll be on time tomorrow."

"Hmmph," she replied, crossing her short penguin-esque arms over her colossal breasts and walking away.

He imagined tufts of gray hair sprouting around her nipples and shoulder blades. The random visual almost made him laugh out loud.

"Get to work," she said, over her shoulder.

He opened the mop closet and retrieved a push broom and the bucket of bathroom cleaning supplies, then walked quietly across the hall to the bedding area, cursing her out in his mind every step of the way. *No, you get to work, you ugly, miserable bitch.*

He looked up as he entered the doorway. A few of the men in Two East were smiling at him.

"Welcome to death row, man," said a gangly fiftyish man in John Lennon specs and wooden rosary beads. "Gotta cigarette?"

"Oh shut up, Hippie!" said the one with the prosthetic leg on his nightstand, rolling his eyes impatiently. "I'm Sergeant Ben Ryker, son, ninth infantry. I don't believe we were properly introduced. I've got bladder cancer and diabetes. That's how I lost my leg. People always assume I got it blown off in 'Nam. Not so."

CJ nodded at him. *Okay.*

"This draft-dodgin', dope-smokin', America-hatin' liberal over here is named Hippie—"

"Hey, I don't hate America, man," Hippie interjected indignantly.

"He's got hepatitis C and dead kidneys," Ryker continued, "and for some reason, convicts don't rank too high on organ transplant waiting lists."

"Bastards," Hippie whispered.

"Y'all, PLEASE let me sleep!" bellowed an old black man in the corner, kicking violently in his sheets as he rolled over. He was completely bald on the top of his head, with a thick Afro along the sides and back.

"That's Baby Jesus," explained Ryker. "You'll understand the name after a while. Nobody knows what he's dying of—"

"I ain't dying, honky!"

"—but he's crazier than shit."

"You the one crazy," the old man protested loudly.

"Hold it down in there!" boomed Mrs. Carroll from down the hall.

CJ stiffened at the sound of her voice.

Ryker ignored her and motioned to the bed directly across the aisle. "That's Gene. Full-blown AIDS."

"Gina," corrected an emaciated, blanket-covered black homosexual with lesions marring the stretched skin of his feminine face. "My name is Gina."

CJ shivered involuntarily.

"Exactly," Ryker agreed, studying him intently. "And so that's about it for introductions, except for Smoke." He jerked his thumb toward the empty bunk with books stacked neatly on the pillow. "But he's dying too. We all are except Mrs. Carroll." He smiled crookedly. "I don't think she'll ever die."

CJ looked at the other bunks in the dorm questioningly. Ryker didn't introduce any of them or disclose their fatal illnesses like he did everyone else.

"I don't know them," Ryker said. "They come and go every day. This is really just a pit stop on the way to Boot Hill. For all of us."

"What's Boot Hill?" CJ asked uncomfortably.

"The prison graveyard," Ryker said, nodding toward the window, "back behind them trees out there by the shit plant. But me, Hippie over here, Baby Jesus—"

"I ain't dyin'!"

"... Gene ..."

"My name's Gina!"

"And ol' Smoke, we've been hangin' in there for a while." He smiled sadly. "Just don't get too used to us."

CJ glanced at a spreading stain on Gina's pillow formed by the drainage of a weeping sore on his face. "Don't worry," he muttered.

~

Dr. Garvin Ponder was over the Mental Health Department at Lake Butler. During his fifteen-year tenure in the Department of Corrections, he'd met serial killers, pedophiles, rapists, and all other manner of violent criminal, yet he was still baffled by Dane Baker.

The imposing, tattooed giant was an enigma. His court records and prison jacket told the story of a cold-blooded killer, a street fighter, a predator, a thug, and the brutal leader of a hate group. He was fairly sure that many of the department's unsolved murders and assaults over the last twenty-four years were either ordered or handled personally by this man.

Prior to meeting him, he reviewed his case file extensively and even contacted long retired colleagues whose names appeared on the pages in an effort to form a workable profile. That got him exactly nowhere. It was equally impossible to glean any reliable data from his numerous MMPI tests over the years because Dane admittedly and repeatedly Christmas tree'd them until he finally became tired of taking them at all and had since vowed to never bubble in another tedious answer sheet again. His entire jacket was a collection of contradictory reports and diagnoses ranging from malingering to manic depression to paranoid schizophrenia.

In the end, Dr. Ponder decided to throw out the book concerning the dangerous inmate and make his own evaluation based on what he learned in their sessions. It appeared destined to fail from the outset. The initial meetings were awkward and one-sided. It took a month for Dane to even look at him, and when he did his eyes were cold fire. Hatred smoldered from his pores.

In his experience Dr. Ponder had never met an inmate who was one hundred percent devoid of humanity. Never. Even the most vicious child killer on death row had at least one redeeming quality somewhere deep down in his tortured, festering soul. He was beginning to think he had found an anomaly in Dane Baker. Then, a month ago, a crack appeared on the surface of his hardened exterior, and before long he was sharing so much that their sessions were running overtime.

He studied the killer from across his shabby, state-issued desk. He looked enormous in the small blue chair that was probably built with a fifth grader in mind. Dane gazed searchingly out the window in the direction of the dorms as if the memory he sought might walk by at any moment.

"I think I was eight years old at the time, might've been seven though. I'm not real sure."

"Here?" Dr. Ponder asked, more as a prompt to continue than an actual question.

"Crystal River," said Dane. "We moved down from Indiana maybe a year before. The trailer park was just a dead-end street in the middle of nowhere, abandoned mostly. The few families that were living there hauled ass quick when they realized their neighborhood had become a commune."

"A commune? Really?" Ponder shifted uncomfortably in his chair.

"Basically. I mean nine other families moved down with us, following my father, and we were always looking to grow. That old rundown trailer park—Whispering Pines it was called—became our headquarters."

His brow furrowed and his jaw twitched as he looked down at the carpet. "I was terrified of the neighbor's dog," he said quietly. "A black chow and pit mix that was meaner than hell. I ain't sure if her name was Gunpowder or if I just heard folks sayin' that's what ol' man Eddins used to feed her and got confused." He looked up. "You know how kids are."

Ponder nodded and smiled reassuringly.

"He kept her chained to a tree out front of his trailer. Whenever somebody'd walk by she's go ape-shit, snarlin' and barkin' and turnin' in circles. The scariest part was the way she'd run right at you, full speed, launchin' her body off the ground, with those sharp teeth ready to snatch your throat out. But then she'd run out of chain and get yanked hard back to the ground. Course that only pissed her off worse."

"Naturally," Ponder agreed.

"So one morning I guess my father got sick of seein' me jump every time she barked and decided it was time for me to face my fears. 'Go on out there and pet her,' he told me."

"Was he drunk?"

"Nah," said Dane, lost in his past. "He didn't start drinking 'til Mom died. He just didn't tolerate weakness, 'specially in his own blood."

"So what'd you do?"

"Cry. All the way out the door. I'll never forget the way he looked that morning, standin' there in the doorway, barefoot, no shirt, thumbs hooked in the front of his jeans, smoke pourin' off the cigar hangin' out of his mouth, watchin' me. I kept hopin' he'd call me back."

"Wait a minute," Ponder said, "you went out there with that dog?"

Dane nodded. "By that age I had learned never to disobey my father, or disappoint him."

"Shit," said the doctor, riveted.

"I had to shut my eyes on the way to the tree where she was chained. Every time I peeked I could see her bloodshot eyes rollin' around in her head and slobber drippin' off her fangs. Her barking got louder and louder, demandin' I get the fuck away as I moved into her territory."

As Ponder listened he tried to imagine this prison-hardened Aryan behemoth as a terrified child with a quivering chin and eyes closed, walking slowly across the sun-baked dirt lawn of a dilapidated trailer park while a rabid, salivating dog growled and snarled at his reluctant approach.

"I didn't have to see to know she was comin'. I just shut my eyes harder at the sound of her jinglin' chain. And prayed. I was really in a lose-lose situation. In front of me was a vicious fuckin' psycho dog and behind me was my vicious psycho father."

"How'd you survive it?"

"Stuck my hand out. Her barkin' trailed off and I could hear her shufflin' around in the dirt, tryin' to figure what to make of me. I opened one eye, barely, just as she started sniffin' my palm. Then, if you can believe it, she gave me a good long lick."

"Ha!" Ponder smiled, relieved for the young Dane Baker in the story.

"I reached out slowly with my other hand and ran it over the dirty matted fur of her massive head and glanced back at my father with pride. I might've did it with my eyes shut. Might've cried a little, hell, I might've even shit in my underwear some, but I remember feelin' like a man as I walked back to our trailer."

"Was your father proud?"

"Proud?" Dane asked, staring at a poster of a man scaling a steep, rocky cliff that ironically said *Courage* in bold letters across the bottom. "Yeah, he was proud all right. So proud he gave me a medal of honor. Wanna see?" He lifted his shirt over his chest and pointed to his sternum. There, among the blown lines and faded blue ink of his many tattoos, was a ring of eight nickel-sized circles of gnarled white scar tissue with one more in the center, directly over his solar plexus.

Dr. Ponder leaned in for a better view and looked up at him questioningly.

"I think he was pissed that the dog didn't chew me up. He stood in that doorway, poker-faced as always, suckin' on his Tampa Jewel, watchin' me bop up those rickety steps to the front door with all the swagger of a soldier comin' home from war." He paused and stared down at the old scars himself. "The dog, Gunpowder, must'a sensed it first cuz I could hear her growlin' behind me. Too late. When I got to the top step he reached out and grabbed a fistful of my hair and slung me through the door. I remember the loud barking outside as he punched me in the head over and over while I balled up and tried to wait out the storm. Years later, as a teenager on a trip to Daytona Beach, I got sucked up in an undertow and it was the same thing. Bein' trapped underneath the force of something way more powerful than you and gettin' rolled around and beat on until it finally shoots its wad and everything is calm again. That was my dad."

Ponder noted that the undertow analogy was a relatively deep thought for someone who was widely regarded as bullheaded and oafish.

"He knocked me out. When I came to, he was sitting on my stomach and had both my hands pinned over my head with one of his. The ashes from his cigar fell on my face as he puffed and puffed to get the cherry good and hot. I remember screamin' my head off that first time, but even with all the hollerin' and all the extra noise from the dog outside, I could still hear my skin cookin' as he twisted the business end of his Tampa Jewel into my chest. I'm sure he had to relight it a few times to finish the job. I didn't see the whole thing cuz I kept passin' out. I'd pass out from the pain, then get woke back up from the pain. It was a nightmare." He looked up at Ponder and his voice dropped to a mumble. "It still is."

Outside, the boiler room whistle blew and the sidewalks that were moments ago empty, quickly filled with a sea of inmates headed back to their dorms for the lunch count.

"Well," Dane said, standing, "it's been a blast, Doc."

Ponder rose with him and opened the door. "Keep up the good work, Dane. A lot of people around here are impressed with your progress. I'll see you in a few weeks. Watch for your name on the callout."

Dane nodded and walked regally down the hall to the exit door, instantly reverting back to his hard-core convict persona. When he reached it, he looked back at Ponder and nodded once before stepping out into the crowded lobby of waiting inmates.

Ponder ducked back into his office and sat down heavily in his leather chair. He stared out of the murky row of windows on the far wall and immediately spotted the hulking frame of his last appointment strutting imperiously down the sidewalk. As he watched him pass, he thought back over the horrible tale that was just recounted to him. A picture of Stephen, his son, smiled up at him from his cluttered desk. *How could anyone torture their own child? Or any child for that matter?*

The fact that Dane Baker trusted him enough to reveal such a personal piece of his life was a major milestone in their patient/doctor relationship. It was hard for him to not feel a little professional pride. He laced his fingers behind his head and rocked back in his chair.

How many of his colleagues had session after session with Baker over the last twenty years only to be stonewalled? How many tests had he blown off or bullshitted his way through?

This murderous white supremacist would never be regarded as open or a "feeling sharer." That was the astonishing part, that he would drop his guard and open up to him, Garvin Ponder, the son of a black political science professor from Howard University and a Brooklyn Jew.

Remarkable, he thought as he studied Dane's thirty-pound case file lying unopened on his messy desk. *Truly remarkable.*

~

It was close to dusk when CJ exited the double doors of the medical unit. He looked up at the windows of Two East as he crossed the compound and imagined Mrs. Carroll glaring down at him. *Bitch,* he thought, deliberately adjusting his nuts and hoping she was watching. After his second full day on the job, it had become crystal clear to him that he simply was not cut out to be a medical orderly. Mrs. Carroll was unbearable. The bedpans and soiled linen and colostomy bags were a minor inconvenience compared to cleaning the nurses' station, where she berated and nitpicked and threatened him with lockup the entire time.

The old men up there were actually not nearly as bad as he initially thought. Their constant bickering with each other was entertaining. The one named Hippie was especially funny. Every time CJ refilled his water pitcher, he tried to talk him into bringing him some weed. *"C'mon man, how about just a half-doobie, please."* CJ smiled. Mrs. Carroll would love that.

There was very little inmate traffic on the sidewalks and no guards in sight. The rec yard and gym were already shut down for the night and the compound was relatively quiet save for the occasional fly-by cawing of the local crows. The sprawling green manicured grounds of the prison could easily be mistaken for a college campus were it not for the gleaming rolls of razor wire and shit-splattered gun towers in the background.

A splash of motion under the I-Block stairwell piqued his interest. He wasn't exactly sure what he saw. *A smoking guard? An inmate headed upstairs to the wing? Dane Baker crouching and sharpening his shank?* He shivered as a shadow swam through him. A voice from the past bubbled to the surface of his racing thoughts: *"Never go against your gut."* Kane.

CJ slowed his steps and silenced his babbling mind, which had defaulted to its time-chiseled pattern of ticking off every catastrophic eventuality imaginable. *You're gonna get stabbed you're gonna get jumped you're gonna get raped they're gonna snap your neck.*

A head appeared across the building from the stairwell and popped quickly back behind the brick column at the sight of CJ. *That makes two.*

He nonchalantly looked up and down the crosswalk. To his right, a few stragglers were returning to their dorms from the med-pickup window. To his far left, an officer was escorting a heavily chained and shackled old man through the confinement gate toward medical. Otherwise, the compound was quiet.

He knew that if he fell on the sidewalk and starting flopping and screaming, officers would come running from every direction, but that was a check-in move and a coward's way out. His only other options were to either reverse course and head back to the medical unit, which would most likely earn him a disciplinary report and thirty days in the hole for violating count procedures, or continue walking toward the I-Block breezeway and face whatever trouble awaited him there. He decided to walk on.

I-Dormitory was a massive, crumbling brick structure that was the center point of the prison. To its north was the receiving area and the medical unit, to its east and west were the chow hall and gym respectively, and to its south was the row of open bay dorms where CJ lived. He knew he could probably circumvent whoever was lying in wait behind the columns by turning right on the last intersecting sidewalk and making a broad loop around the compound, taking the long way to his dorm, but night was gathering and *recall* had already been announced over the PA system, instructing all inmates to return to their dormitories. He bypassed the final turnoff and forged cautiously ahead.

The living quarters of I-Block were on the second story of the ancient building. CJ could hear the random bursts of conversation above him through the broken glass of the catwalk windows. The bottom floor was comprised of stairwell entrances that led up to the cell blocks, the mental health department, the chaplain's office, the barber shop, a canteen window, and two breezeways that served as thoroughfares for inmate traffic. CJ paused just below the overhang of the building and lit a cigarette before stepping into the shadowy underpass.

Four figures emerged from the walls, blocking his path. All white, heavily tattooed, and stone-faced, with forearms folded, waiting.

"Look who it is, y'all. Vanilla Ice."

"Where's your mooncricket wardaddy, fuckboy?"

"We got a message for ya. From Dane."

"You know who that is? Huh, faggot?"

CJ recognized them from the softball game. Surrounding Dane Baker on the bleachers, hanging on his every word, laughing at his jokes, nodding in agreement whenever he spoke, they'd now apparently been sent on a mission to threaten him. Or jump him. Or worse.

Suddenly he was back in the county jail, in 6-B-2, listening to Kane's instruction on the art of the sucker punch. *"When you wanna steal a muthafucker, don't ball your face up and look crazy. They'll know it's comin'. Whatchu do is walk up smilin', then, when you close enough, BLAM! You unload on they ass. They'll never expect it." He launched a killer hook that grazed CJ's shoulder and smiled. "Like that. Jus' make sure you swing all the way through they face, 'stead of pullin' back like you do on Hound."*

CJ forced his face to smile as he closed the distance between them.

"What the fuck are you smiling at, dude? You stupid or something?" asked the one on the end with the black stringy hair and rotten teeth.

CJ ignored him and approached the biggest one in the middle. He willed his face to smile even harder just as he unleashed a savage right into and through the jutting chin of his target. Sparks from CJ's lit cigarette exploded against his face on impact as he staggered and fell from the unsuspected and powerful shot. CJ wasted no time going to work with his fists and his knees, beating him down into the pavement with blow after blow.

"Always make your first fight count, Cee. Don't fuck around with 'em. Muthafuckas in the joint love to gossip, 'specially 'bout fights. The rep you build off one serious ass-whuppin' could last for years, even follow you from prison to prison. So when that first one tries you, make sure you make an example out his ass."

After a few beats of shocked silence, his brothers came to his aid, tackling CJ and driving him to the ground in a barrage of raining fists and boots. The loud rumbling and muted grunts and curses echoed off the walls and resonated throughout the bowels of the old building.

The stairwell door sprung open. "Cut it the fuck out," growled a low, deadly voice. "Now!"

The kicks and punches immediately stopped and everyone looked in the direction of the gravelly voice. CJ struggled to his feet and ran his hand across his mouth, checking for blood.

The guard in the doorway stuck a cigarette in his mouth and cupped the flame from his lighter even though there was no wind. The orange flame illuminated the hard weather-cracked face beneath the bill of his faded brown D.O.C. cap. Although he was probably close to sixty, rail thin, and alone under the breezeway with five convicts, there wasn't a trace of fear or uncertainty in his eyes. His loose, lanky stance made CJ think of the cowboys in Louis L'Amour novels.

"I don't know what's going on down here," he said in a low, measured southern accent, "and I don't really give a rat's ass." He frowned at the inmate still lying sprawled on the concrete. "Hey, somebody wake his ass up. He ain't dead, is he?"

Two of his homeboys knelt beside him and slapped him a few times. Finally, he groggily came to and blinked repeatedly as he sat up, tentatively testing the movement of his jaw. CJ felt a rush of adrenaline as he studied him. His first legitimate K.O.

"Fellers, this is how it's gonna go," said the cowboy guard. "I'm gonna pretend like I never saw this little party you all had goin' down here and you're gonna haul ass back to your dorms for count. You caught yourselves a break this evenin' cuz I'm hungover and don't feel like fuckin' with the paperwork." He paused to scan their faces, and his glowing yellow eyes bored malevolently into each of them from under the bill of his cap.

The radio hanging from his low-slung belt began to squawk. He reached down without looking and silenced it.

"I been workin' here close to thirty years. Ask some of your dawgs about K-Wing Slim. They'll tell ya."

"We know who you are, sir," said one of Dane's boys.

"Shut up!" he bellowed, staring hard at the speaker until he looked away, then allowing a yellow-toothed smile to spread across his leathery face. "Pussy," he mumbled, taking a drag from his cigarette. "I've seen thousands of inmates come and go. Thousands. I ain't never forgot a face." Smoke billowed from his mouth as he spoke. "If I catch any of y'all fuckin' up again, your feet ain't gonna touch the ground all the way to confinement, you understand?"

CJ nodded along with the rest of them.

He flicked his cigarette out in the grass. "Now git."

They dispersed immediately, each heading to his own dorm. The one with the rotten teeth hurried to catch up with CJ as he strode quickly down the sidewalk. He slid beside him just as he reached his dorm.

"You're just makin' it worse."

"Fuck you," said CJ.

"Dane always gets what he wants, man."

CJ rattled the door to his dorm and looked through the window.

"It's not that bad."

"*What's* not that bad?" CJ asked without looking back.

"Being a brother. It's better than being our bitch. Those are your choices."

The door buzzed and CJ pushed it open. He glanced over his shoulder before he stepped in. Rotten Teeth was smiling. "You'd look funny with shaved legs and arched eyebrows." He giggled as he walked away.

CJ slammed the door behind him and walked past the officers' station into the noisy living area of Delta Dorm. There were card games going on empty bunks and dice being shot in the corner. There were cliques doing push-ups in the aisle, while across the room a heated argument about Roy Jones, Jr. and James Toney threatened to escalate into its own boxing match. The hum of Bones's tattoo gun zzz'd in the background as Muslims knelt to the east on colorful prayer rugs. Christians held hands and prayed, and law clerks debated the legality of the new eighty-five percent gain time law. CJ was oblivious to it all as he crisscrossed his way to the bunk where Hustle lay reading the sports page in his pajamas.

"I need your knife."

Hustle slowly rested the paper on his chest and studied CJ through a pair of reading glasses that were held together by twined string, melted plastic, and paperclips.

"You bullshittin'?"

CJ shook his head.

"Who's fuckin' with you?"

CJ shrugged. "You don't know him."

Hustle sat up. *"I don't know him?* CJ, you know damn well I know every bitch on this compound. Now who is it?"

"It doesn't matter. Just let me use it. I'll get it back to you."

"Wait a minute. You wanna use my shit to go poke somebody and won't even tell me who the fuck it is? What if I'm cool with whoever you plan on stickin'?"

"You're not."

"I'll tell you what," said Hustle, "fuck the knife. Tomorrow we'll strap up and go straighten whoever's tryin' you. Together. If it's more than we can handle, I'll stop by A-Dorm and get some backup. All my homeboys are in there."

"I don't need all that. I just need to borrow your knife."

"Quit bein' so goddamn stubborn, cracker!" he erupted before fixing CJ with a tired look. "Have I ever steered you wrong? I'm the same Hustleman that was down with you back when you were poppin' pills on lockdown. Just trust me, Cee, I've been doin' this a long time. You don't want no stabbin' case on your jacket 'less you absolutely can't help it."

"Who do you think you are? My fuckin' wardaddy?" CJ exploded, repeating the term that Dane's boys used earlier. Heads turned at the outburst.

Hustle removed his reading glasses and got in CJ's face. "Nah," he growled, "I ain't your wardaddy, I'm your nigga, and don't you ever forget it."

His words hung in the air between them like icicles.

"Count time!" boomed a voice from the front of the dorm, forcing them to break eye contact. "Everybody on their racks!"

CJ turned on his heel and headed toward his bunk. He glanced up at the light fixture in the bathroom on the way. Hustle's secret hiding spot, which was not much of a secret. He nodded to himself. *One way or another.*

A clipboard-wielding guard was standing at the foot of his bunk with an eyebrow raised.

"McCallister," CJ said, displaying his inmate ID card. "271958."

Chapter 15

CJ walked haltingly among the morning traffic to the medical building. His slow pace had nothing to do with his fear of being attacked, although he was hyperaware of his surroundings. His tentative gait was due mostly to the twelve-inch knife jammed discreetly in the waistline of his pants, rendering his natural stride impossible.

When he neared the hospital an officer hurried across the grass and began herding the inmates into a single-file line on the left side of the sidewalk. Although his progress slowed significantly, at least CJ didn't have to sweat someone attacking him in the anonymity of the crowd. His biggest worry now was Mrs. Carroll.

He turned to the guy behind him. "What time is it?"

"Seven forty-two," he said.

Okay, plenty of time, he thought, leaning to the side and trying to see what the hold-up was.

The line continued moving ahead two or three steps at a time and stopping every minute or so. After five minutes, he started getting antsy again, standing on his tiptoes and attempting to see the front of the line. Then he saw the reason for the delay, and began to panic. He quickly stepped out of line and turned back toward the dormitories.

"Back in line, jackass," drawled a nearby guard.

His shoulders slumped as he turned and walked back to his spot. Forcing the issue would only draw unnecessary attention. He was trapped. He couldn't turn back and fifteen people ahead of him, just inside the entrance to the medical unit, stood a guard scanning each inmate with a metal detector wand.

The once slow-moving line began moving faster. He could feel the tip of the shank biting his inner thigh as he shuffled forward. There were only five people in front of him, then three, then two, then one, then . . .

"Come on," said the guard, gesturing with the yellow wand. It beeped and chirped spasmodically as CJ stepped through the doorway. "Arms out."

CJ obeyed, resigned to his fate. He tried to appear aloof as the metal detector was run over his shoulders and shirt sleeves. The officer was obviously bored and going through the motions as he scanned his chest and stomach. CJ tensed as the wand approached his waistline, cringing as it sputtered and shrilled to life. Its high-pitched wail screamed in alarm. *Busted!* The guard quickly drew it back, momentarily jolted awake. Then his eyes fell flat again as he glanced at CJ's waist.

"Belt buckle," he said, looking out the door at the waiting line before muttering, "Idiot."

CJ removed the metal buckle, careful not to disturb the position of the knife. He slowly raised his hands again, willing the batteries to die. The guard waved the wand back over his waist, then scanned his crotch before moving it up and down his legs.

"Next," he called, waving CJ off.

There was no time for exultation. He moved as fast as possible through the bustling hallways. He held the shank in place, sprinting when he could and ignoring the overhead cameras. He slid around corners and weaved his way between nurses' carts and gurneys, arriving at the door to Two East and flinging it open. The echoes of his footsteps flying up the narrow staircase pounded in his eardrums and matched the pace of his hammering heart. When he reached the top, he ripped open the door and almost tripped out into the quiet hall. Even as his arms flailed to regain his balance, his neck stretched upward to see the clock. The second hand ticked loudly as it struck eight.

He glanced toward the nurses' station and the sour-faced Mrs. Carroll.

"Hmmph," she muttered, returning to her paperwork.

~

He was kicking himself in the ass for the knife. He should have never stolen it in the first place and he absolutely should have never risked bringing it to work.

He pushed the broom into the bedding area of Two East. The TV was off and the unit was wrapped in silence. He began sweeping under the beds, taking care not to disconnect random wires tangled beneath or clash the broomstick against the bed frames. The amount of dust that seemed to grow from the floor overnight was one of the mysteries of the job. He swept it out into the aisle and moved down the row.

That's when he noticed that not everyone in the unit was still sleeping. Two beds down from Gina the AIDS patient, an old skinny, baldheaded man sat Indian style. He was wrapped in a standard prison-issued wool blanket. His back was ramrod straight, eyes closed, with a slight smile touching his gray stubbled face. Although CJ had never met him, he knew who he was. His bed had been empty the last two days, but the veteran with the fake leg and bladder cancer had referred to him as *Smoke.*

CJ swept in silence while continuing to eye the old man curiously, the rhythmic *shhhk* of the broom declaring his presence in the unit. No one stirred. As CJ entered the space beside his bed, extending the broom beneath it, he noticed the deep ebb and flow of the man's breathing. He glanced over at the books on the nightstand: a Holy Bible, a Quran, a Bhagavad Gita, and a book by someone named Bo Lozoff. CJ leaned in closer to read the title.

Suddenly, the knife broke free of his waistline and bob-slid down the inside of his thigh, diving from his pants leg to the cold, quiet floor, where it bounced and spun. Although it wasn't very loud, it may as well have been a car crash. A jackhammer. In prison there is no sound more distinct than a shank hitting the floor.

He bent quickly to retrieve it, listening for Mrs. Carroll's footfalls in the hallway. When he stood, his wrist was seized in a grip of iron, and before he could react, he was yanked violently across the old man's bed.

What the fuck?

Two wiry legs wrapped around his pelvis and locked, immobilizing him, while his neck was stretched incongruently from his body by an unyielding elbow. He still held the knife in a white-knuckle grip, but he couldn't see it because that arm was being pulled in the opposite direction of his neck.

The pace of the old man's breathing remained unchanged. A steel thumb dug into his wrist, causing his hand to tingle, numb, and release. The knife fell to the bed with a soft thud. The old man scooped it up, and in a flash, it was pressed against CJ's Adam's apple. He swallowed.

"Fiberglass," the old man remarked, "nice. Metal detectors be damned, eh?"

CJ struggled.

"Stop that!" he hissed, tightening his hold. "Who sent you, boy?"

"No one," CJ croaked, the knife twisting in his flesh like a Phillips head.

"Liar!" snapped the old man.

"Let me go!"

"Don't they know that I'm already dying?"

CJ again tried to break free.

"Can't they let me go quietly?"

"I just work here," CJ said.

"Isn't it enough that I . . ." He paused and glanced down at the broom on the floor. "Wait a minute, you're the new orderly?"

CJ looked coldly up at him, indignant at being manhandled and disarmed so easily by a dying old man. He finally broke free and stumbled away from the bed as the old man threw back his head and laughed heartily.

"I guess I owe you an apology," he said, wiping the tears from his eyes, "and a big thank you as well. It's been a while since I've laughed like that." He rolled the shank in his palm. "My government name is

Ulysses Griffith, but only my mother calls me that. Everyone else calls me Smoke."

There was a pregnant silence as he waited for CJ to introduce himself. *Fuck that,* CJ thought, still stinging from being rag-dolled so handily. *I'm not here to make friends.* But the patient, grandfatherly twinkle in the old man's eye eventually won the war and forced him to mutter, "CJ," as he took up the broom again.

"So," he said, holding up the knife, "if not for me, who then?"

CJ stopped sweeping. "It's not mine. I really need it back."

"Oh, I don't want it," said Smoke, "but I'm going to have to insist on holding it for you, at least until you get off. If it slid down your pants in front of Mrs. Carroll, she'd probably do a lot more than just put you in an arm-bar."

His smile was infectious, and CJ found himself smiling too.

"Where'd you learn that stuff?" he asked.

"What? The grappling?" said Smoke. "I had a buddy in the Mossad."

"What's that?"

"Israel's answer to the CIA."

"Oh," said CJ, watching him tuck the knife under his mattress.

"For a time in my life, I assumed the role of fighter, learning every style I could, even making up my own, but I gave up violence when I became a seeker."

"I see that," joked CJ, rubbing his neck.

Smoke smiled. "Self-defense is actually a form of non-violence. By keeping you from harming me, I was, in essence, protecting you from creating negative karma for yourself."

"If you say so."

"I do," he said, "but the role of seeker is just that: another role. Now it seems that central casting wants me to try out the role of cancer patient."

A voice from across the aisle interrupted their conversation. CJ instantly recognized the burnt drawl of Hippie. "Hey, Smoke? What time is it, man?"

"Now," Smoke automatically answered, looking at CJ. "The time is right now."

"Whoa," said Hippie, chuckling.

"You seem pretty strong for someone with cancer," CJ said.

"Yeah, well, they just found it not too long ago. We'll see how strong I am after a round of chemo and maybe some radiation therapy. The doc says only about twenty percent of people with pancreatic cancer are still living a year after being diagnosed. At least he's honest."

"Damn," said CJ.

"So what about you? What role are you playing?"

"What *role?"* CJ frowned.

He affected a Shakespearean accent. "All the world is indeed a stage and we are merely players."

"Damn! Shut up, honky!" said Baby Jesus from the corner bed, pulling the blanket over his head and rolling over.

Smoke acknowledged the interruption with a smile but otherwise ignored it.

"You're obviously an intelligent young man. How'd you get to the point where you were running around prison with a shank in your boxers?"

"Long story," said CJ.

"Well, you better get started then," he said, "the credits could be rolling soon."

"Maybe tomorrow," said CJ, sweeping the dust into the aisle and moving on.

"Hey," Smoke said to his back, "did the Braves win last night?"

"Who?"

"The Atlanta Braves. You know, Tom Glavine, John Smoltz, the kid from Daytona, Chipper Jones. Did they win?"

"I don't know," CJ said.

"Oh," said Smoke, adjusting his blanket and refolding his legs in the Lotus, "okay."

The sound of his deep, rhythmic breathing again filled the unit.

~

Marcus "Forty" Reed was running out of time. He was down two hundred dollars on the books and the yard would be closing any minute. Normally he'd just buck payment. He knew how to fight, but this wasn't just any poker game. Dane Baker was housing today. Forty knew the stories. Everyone did. The big cracker had killed for less. A whole lot less.

"Airborne," said Forty, calling his game as he slid cards to the five other players around the table. "Five dollars for the first draw. Ten dollars for the second, thirty-five for fifty on the end."

When he finished dealing, each player had four cards. He placed the deck on top of the hand he dealt himself, then nonchalantly reached beneath his shirt for the four cards he cuffed after folding a previous hand. Cheating was always a last resort to Forty. He didn't need to. He grew up around the poker and skin houses in the Pakistan area of Jacksonville. Gambling was in his blood.

Airborne is played on every prison yard across the U.S., though under different names and variations. The best possible hand is "the wheel"—ace, two, three, four/heart, diamond, spade, club—but the odds of drawing a wheel are about the equivalent of pulling a straight flush in five-card stud. Maybe a little better than that, but not much.

"Five to draw," said Forty.

The old man to his left set down his cards and pushed five one-dollar chips into the middle of the table. The rest of the players followed suit.

When the bet reached Forty, he raised. "With five more."

Despite much grumbling and muttered curses, nobody folded. Sixty dollars worth of chips lay piled in the middle of the table.

"Get loose," said Forty.

Everybody drew. Except him.

"You ain't drawin' none?" asked Bones, the tattoo man from D-Dorm.

"Nah, I'm straight," Forty said with a smile, revealing four silver front teeth. "It's ten dollars for this last draw."

The old man on his left glanced at his cards and shook his head in disgust, throwing them in the dead. Bones folded behind him. The next two players quickly threw their chips in the pot, both calling.

Forty waited to see what Dane would do. It was always good to have the houseman in on the hand since he couldn't claim "all in."

"I call," said Dane, pushing ten dollars worth of chips into the middle.

"I raise," said Forty, "with twenty more."

"You're full of shit," said one of the remaining players before tossing his hand into the dead, "but I can't afford to prove it."

The next one studied his cards through a cloud of cigarette smoke. "Me neither," he finally said.

That left only Dane and Forty.

Come on, you big ugly cracker, Forty urged, *call!*

"I call," said Dane.

Got him! "Cards," said Forty.

"I'm good," Dane said.

"Me too." Forty smiled as he pushed the deck to the side. "It's thirty-five to get back."

Dane counted out thirty-five dollars worth of chips and glared at him. "You got the whole thirty-five over there?"

"To the hotball," said Forty.

"I wish you had some more," said Dane, dropping his chips in the pot.

"Trust me," Forty smiled, "you don't wish that."

Dane's face hardened and his eyes narrowed. "Tell you what, you're already down two hundred bucks on the books. You got anything else in your locker?"

Forty looked at the pot. With his thirty-five dollars, there would be exactly two hundred in there. After Dane subtracted his ten percent cut as houseman, he'd win one-eighty. That would damn near clean his face. But now, he had the opportunity to do better than just break even. He had a five-nothing: ace, deuce, trey, five. The only thing that could beat him was the wheel.

"Yeah," Forty said. "I gotta little more. What's up?"

"Bet two hundred more . . . *homie,*" Dane challenged, making the word *homie* sound like a racial slur.

"I call that," Forty said, laying out his hand. "I gotta big five."

He reached for the pot, exhilarated by the thrill of victory. The humongous fist of Dane Baker immediately clamped down on his wrist, stopping him short.

"I've got a big four," he said. "You lose."

Forty's shoulders sagged as he stared at Dane's upturned cards. He had the wheel, and the yard was closing. Game over.

He rose weakly to his feet, feeling as if someone had just punched him in the stomach. He owed the Great Dane four hundred. That was four hundred more than he had.

~

CJ rolled the squeaky cart down the aisle, alerting the occupants of Two East that lunch was on the wing. Most of the men pushed off their blankets and struggled to sit up. The TV came on. Hippie staggered past him toward the bathroom. Smoke set his Bible on the nightstand.

"Chow time, boys," announced Ryker the one-legged vet. "Up and at 'em!"

CJ looked around at the ancient bedridden convicts. Their skin was prison gray and bore the scars of long forgotten battles and pick-n-poke tattoos from another era. He saw missing limbs and eye patches everywhere, while a constant soundtrack of phlegm-racked coughing and painful moans filled the unit.

"Hey, Smoke," called Ryker, "time check."

"Now," Smoke answered, "the time is right now."

"Beautiful," said Ryker, "just beautiful."

Lunch consisted of spaghetti, salad, garlic bread, and applesauce. CJ removed the first tray from the cart and set it down on the bedside table of the man they called Baby Jesus, who had already tucked a napkin in the collar of his shirt in anticipation. He was a short, feisty man who moved in quick bursts and sported the lean frame of someone who had spent a lifetime on pull-up and dip bars. He wore his Afro proudly and spent much of the day meticulously combing it out despite the fact that he was completely bald up top.

When CJ filled a cup of murky, lukewarm, grape-flavored juice and set it by his tray, the old man's eyes were shut and his hands were raised in prayer.

"Thank you, Baby Jesus," he called, his loud voice causing the few remaining sleepers to stir. "Thank you for blessing me with this food and drink!"

CJ looked at Ryker, who was smiling broadly at him. *So that's why they call him Baby Jesus.*

"Baby Jesus!" he cried, squeezing his eyes shut even tighter and waving his arms at the ceiling. "We're not worthy, Lord!"

As Hippie returned from the bathroom, he smiled slyly before reaching over and snatching the garlic bread from the praying man's tray. He hurried back to his bed, eating it on the way.

CJ placed a tray on Gina's nightstand and went to get his juice. When he came back, the old sissy was staring up at him through sunken, jaundiced eyes. His dry, cracked skin was pulled taut against his skull and he looked more like a rotting corpse than a living person. But it was the oozing and weeping purple sores on his face that caused CJ to cringe.

"Can you help me up, honey?" he asked, his voice a thin whisper.

CJ ignored him and pushed the cart forward, pretending not to hear. He wasn't intentionally being cold, but he did not associate with faggots and anyway, those sores looked contagious.

When he looked back he was surprised to see Smoke sitting on the bed with Gina, gently helping him to sit up and eat, smiling tenderly and speaking with a kindness that sounded alien in the harsh world of prison.

CJ turned away and acted as if he didn't see them, overwhelmed with shame. He felt . . . *small.*

"And so we thank you, Baby Jesus!" the man continued to shout. "Thank you, most high. We exalt you, Lord, and praise your name. Now and forever. Amen." He opened his eyes and looked down at his tray. "Goddamn it!" he exploded. "Which one of you punk motherfuckers stole my garlic bread?"

~

Forty Reed was having a hard time eating. Any other day he would've attacked his tray like a starving dog and been out of the chow hall before the rest of his dorm even sat down. Not today. Fear and nervousness had shut down his taste buds to the point where each unswallowable bite tasted like wet cardboard and only seemed to multiply into more when he chewed. His eyes darted anxiously from table to table as he forced another flavorless sporkful into his mouth.

He replayed that last hand over and over in his mind. *Cheatin'-ass cracker,* he thought. Never mind the fact that *he* was cheating too. Everybody at the table had to know. A wheel beating a five nothin' in double-draw airborne was like a royal beating out poker aces in cowboy poker. It just didn't happen. When he first sat down to play, his intention was only to touch 'em for a few packs of rip, maybe a bag of coffee, then just play "lock" until the yard closed and leave a winner. Basic chain-gang stick and move poker, get in the game with no money, hit a few good hands, and get out. The problem was he never hit that good hand. Even when he cheated, the best he could do was second best.

If it was anybody else, he'd just tell 'em they couldn't get paid and handle it from there. *He didn't have it. You can't squeeze blood from a turnip. It was the houseman's fault for letting him fall so deep on the books anyway.* The problem was that the houseman was Dane Baker. And that racist-ass cracker was not about just fightin' in the bathroom and lettin' shit go. Somebody was gonna die, and Forty understood that there was a good chance of that *somebody* being him, especially if he didn't think fast.

He grabbed his tray and headed for the exit. For the first time ever, he considered checking in. "Checking in" meant going to the guards and claiming he was in fear for his life and seeking to be placed in protective custody until he could be shipped somewhere else.

Fuck that, he thought. *I don't check in. I'm Forty Reed. I make other motherfuckers check in.*

In the back of his mind a cold, rational voice pointed out that Dane had people on every compound in the state. There was nowhere to run anyway.

Forty was not a coward. He grew up fighting. He would never run from a callout. From anyone. But it was hard to fight a knife in your sleep.

He dumped the remaining food in the trash can and slid his tray in the dish room window. Dane was leaning against the wall smoking a rip when he stepped outside.

"Forty," he said, "just the man I wanted to see. You got my money?"

"Yeah," Forty lied, "it's just spread out. You ain't gotta sweat me, man. I'll pay you."

"Right," said Dane, staring at him. "Tell you what, you live in A Dorm, right? Low side?"

Forty nodded. *Motherfucker probably knows my bunk number too.*

"I'll send somebody over there in the morning to pick it up."

"I might not have it all by then."

"Well, just shoot whatever you've got."

Forty looked away. "All right."

Dane flicked his cigarette out in the grass and pushed off the wall. Waiting pigeons swept down from the fence, confusing it with a piece of bread, only to waddle off unfulfilled.

"I saw you, you know," said Dane, a cold smile creeping across his face.

Forty slowly turned back to face him. "Saw me, where?"

Dane smirked. "Don't act stupid, man. I was playin' poker on prison yards before you even hit junior high, and I ain't talkin' about no soft-ass reception center. I'm talkin' about the Rock . . . Martin . . .

Charlotte. Spots where they would've been life-flightin' your black ass off the yard for stickin' them cards up your shirt."

Forty had heard enough.

"Fuck you, cracker," he said, attempting to push by him.

Dane slung him against the wall. "Fuckin' me will make your asshole bleed, boy."

Forty pushed back hard, causing him to stagger into the grass. The remaining pigeons scattered. They both automatically raised their fists, ready.

"You're gonna get what you lookin' for, cracker," said Forty.

Dane dropped his hands and began to chuckle quietly.

"All I'm lookin' for," he said, "is my four hundred bucks, which I suspect is a lot more money than you can put your hands on."

"You don't know what the fuck I got," said Forty, watching him like a coiled rattler.

"You're right. I don't. But I've got a proposition for you anyway."

"Save it," Forty bristled, "I ain't no faggot."

Dane laughed. "Not *that* kind of proposition. You're a little too dark for my taste, plus I prefer my boys to be toothless and you've got all that silver in your mouth." He felt in his pocket for another cigarette. "Want one?" he offered, lighting up.

Forty didn't respond.

"Listen," said Dane, "I know you're broke and I know you were cheating. Why you would try *me* of all people is what I can't figure."

Forty sputtered and wound up for another denial.

Dane raised his hand. "But it doesn't matter. Honestly, I respect your balls. That's why you're not dead."

Forty sucked his teeth.

Dane ignored him. "I'm willing to overlook the cheating, clear your face for the four hundred you owe me, and give you a shot at makin' a whole lot more. If you're interested."

Forty eyed him suspiciously. "How?"

Dane smiled coldly. "You ever stick anybody?"

Forty lifted his chin. "A couple of times."

It was actually just once, years ago at a youthful offender camp. But he had just got off the slab for beating a nigga from St. Pete with a combination lock at A.C.I. and he was in prison for shooting into an occupied dwelling. Violence didn't faze him.

"I figured you had," said Dane. "I got somebody who I need fucked up. Bad."

"Ain't you 'posed to be the Great Dane?" Forty asked sarcastically. "The famous killer Klansman? What you need my help for?"

"I've got my reasons," Dane said quietly. "I'll give you five hundred bucks for stabbin' him and another five hundred if you manage to kill him. You can get paid however you want. Dope, cash, canteen, or money on your books, and as soon as you give me your word, I'll shoot you an advance just to show you I'm serious."

Forty stared at the lightning bolts tatted on his throat.

"Or I could just pay you the four hundred that I owe," said Forty.

"Right."

"I'll think about it."

The beginnings of a scowl moved across Dane's face before his features went slack. Only his eyes continued to burn. "You do that," he said, turning to walk away.

Forty watched him go. He didn't really need time to think. This was the lick he'd been waiting on. With that kind of bread he could open up a loan shark operation, start a parlay ticket, or get a plug in the dope game. He knew how to hustle; he just needed a toehold. When he broke into a smile the sun glimmered off his silver teeth. That morning he woke up wondering if he was going to die. Now it appeared that his run of bad luck was over.

All right, Great Dane, he thought, *I'll take that grand off you. Just point his ass out. Forty got this.*

Bones and Hustle were playing chess on his bunk when he got back from work. CJ maneuvered his way around their outstretched legs en route to his footlocker.

"Don't let me distract you," said CJ. "I've only been on my feet since eight this morning."

"Hey," said Hustle. "Look who it is. The white Mike Tyson." He jabbed and hooked at the air in front of Bones's face, bobbing and weaving like a boxer.

"We heard about you, dude," said Bones. "You're the talk of the pound."

"What?" said CJ, sitting down slowly on his locker.

"Dane's right-hand man checked in this mornin'," said Hustle. "He was all fucked up too. Both eyes black, broke nose, fat lip, head all knotted up and shit. Looked like he got hit in the face with a shovel."

"You shoulda seen Dane at the poker table today," said Bones. "I thought he was fixin' to cry for a minute. Big John was his best friend."

"Now I see why you wanted my knife," said Hustle, studying the chessboard.

"Oh," CJ began, "about that . . ."

Hustle looked over at him.

"I'm gonna put it back."

"Wait a minute," said Hustle, "you took my knife to work with you?"

CJ nodded.

"Are you outta your goddamn mind?" he exploded. "Do you just *want* to go back to the slab? You don't carry a knife around Butler like you got a license, cracker! Don't you know where the hell you are?"

Bones slid his rook across the board. "Check."

Hustle ignored him. "How the fuck you know about my secret stash spot anyway?"

CJ rolled his eyes. "It's not exactly the world's best kept secret."

"Nosy muthafucka," Hustle grumbled, moving his king out of check.

"What happened?" Bones asked.

"They caught me on the way back last night," CJ said. "In the blind spot under I-Block. There were four of them. All Dane's boys. I just picked the biggest one and swung."

Bones laughed. "You got some brass danglers down there, don't ya?"

"Not really," said CJ, "I was scared shitless. They all jumped me after that, but a guard broke it up before they could really do much. I got lucky."

"I'm surprised you didn't go to the box," said Bones.

"I'm not," Hustle muttered, "cuz it was all crackers."

"The guard said he was hungover and didn't feel like doing the paperwork."

"Whatever," said Hustle, holding out his hand, "just gimme my knife."

Bones brought down his queen. "Check," he said.

"I see it," Hustle grumbled.

"I left it at work," said CJ.

"What?" Hustle looked at him sharply.

"I had to," CJ rushed to explain, "this morning they were scannin' us with the metal detector and I barely made it through. I didn't want to risk the—"

"Goddamn!" said Hustle. "A metal detector?!? You a real live crash dummy, ain't you?"

"Check," said Bones.

"You ain't gotta keep sayin' check, cracker," said Hustle. "I can see."

Bones winked at CJ.

"I'll bring it back tomorrow," CJ said.

"Nah," said Hustle as he exhaled, "just chill until all this bullshit dies down."

"Are you sure?"

Hustle ignored him and studied the board.

Bones made his final move with an ostentatious flourish.

"Checkmate," he said.

~

Dane Baker lay in his bunk staring at a page from a Robert Ludlum novel without reading it. His thoughts were elsewhere. Just over the top of the book, three feet from where he lay, was the empty bunk of his best friend and comrade, Big John Caldwell.

For the last two and a half years they lived side by side. They ate together, did push-ups together, got high together, and if anything popped off in the dorm, they fought together.

The sight of his empty locker and folded mattress leered tauntingly back at Dane. He rolled over. The fact that Big John got his ass beat by that little fuckboy McCallister was embarrassing enough, but his checking into protective custody was an act of cowardice that could not be tolerated. He had tarnished the reputation of every brother in the circle by walking head down across the compound with a police escort. He would have to be dealt with wherever he landed once released from PC. There was nowhere to hide. Big John of all people knew that.

An old tattooed con named Popcorn pushed a mop bucket down the aisle and casually dropped a folded piece of paper on his bunk. He looked around as he sat up to open it. The words on the paper were cryptic, written in poker terminology, but Dane understood exactly what they meant.

I call.
40

A smile broke over the cruel features of his face as he crumpled the paper and lay back in his bunk.

Excellent, he thought, *and I raise.*

Chapter 16

Smoke was meditating again. CJ carefully set the broom against the wall and moved stealthily down the aisle like a ninja. As he drew near, he could see the rise and fall of the old man's shoulders through his blanket, and he became aware of a low hum emanating from his wiry body. It sounded like a motor or maybe a heater. One of those quiet, constant drones in the background that is barely noticeable. Until they suddenly click off.

"Did the Braves win last night?" he asked.

CJ jumped. "Shit," he said, startled, "how could you hear me?"

"I didn't hear you," said Smoke. "I felt your energy."

"Whoa," said Hippie from across the aisle, "energy, man."

"Oh shut up, Hippie," said Ryker, from under his blanket.

Smoke smiled and opened his eyes. "Well? Did they?"

"Yeah," said CJ, "Chipper hit a two-run walk-off in the tenth. They won seven to five."

He had begun listening to ESPN radio at night before he fell asleep to get the Atlanta score for Smoke.

The old man opened his eyes and smiled. "All right! Now, where were we?"

"Come on, man. I don't feel like talkin' about that shit this morning."

"I believe you just received twenty-seven years, correct?"

CJ studied the rust marks on the linoleum floor.

"Twenty-seven years isn't so bad," said Smoke. "Not after they take off the third. You'll probably only end up doing eleven or twelve if you stay out of trouble. You're lucky you fell in '91. You'd probably have to do double that under these new eighty-five percent laws. This next generation is in for a ride."

"I'll probably have to do a little more than twelve," said CJ.

"How come?"

"I lost a lot of gain time during my first year in."

"Really," Smoke frowned. "You don't strike me as a troublemaker. What were you doing?"

CJ sat down at the foot of his bed. "I can't remember all of it. I know I had a few assaults and a self-mutilation case. A lot of it's a blur though. They put me on Thorazine."

Smoke glanced at the ugly scar running down the middle of his left arm. CJ self-consciously dropped it to his side.

"Why?" Smoke asked.

"Why was I on Thorazine?"

"That too," said Smoke, "but why did you do that to your arm?"

CJ was silent.

"Don't you know that God loves you—"

"Please don't start talkin' that 'God' shit to me."

Smoke glanced at him sideways. "You got a problem with God?"

"Nah. I ain't got a problem with God or Santa or the Easter Bunny or the Tooth Fairy . . ."

"Oh, I get it," said Smoke, "you don't believe. Well, I guess I didn't either when I was a young man. I spent a lot of years entangling myself in hate and violence and fear and excess before I finally surrendered."

"When I was in the county jail," CJ said softly, "I never prayed for freedom, or safety, or my girl to come back. All I asked was that my family stay healthy until I made it back home."

"A very honorable and selfless prayer," said Smoke.

"My dad died a week after I was sentenced. Congestive heart failure."

"I'm sorry."

"A week after that my mom found a gun I stashed in my room and used it on herself."

"Oh man . . ."

Tears spilled from CJ's eyes. "She shot herself in the heart. Because of me."

Smoke reached over and gently patted his back as CJ's body convulsed in sobs. The human contact was comforting. He tried to recall the last time someone patted his back. *Not punched, not elbowed, not kicked.* It had been years.

He was struck by the irony of it all. Here he was, young and strong with his whole life ahead of him, crying and feeling sorry for himself while a man who was dying of cancer in a prison hospital ward attempted to console him.

He began to laugh, first softly and to himself, but then louder. Smoke stopped patting his back and raised an eyebrow. Two beds down, Gina struggled to lift his head. When he saw CJ laughing, his skeletal face slowly stretched into a smile. Then he began laughing too.

"Heh, heh, heh," he croak-whispered, pointing a long, slender E.T.-like finger at CJ.

"Whoa . . ." said Hippie, mystified. "Phone home, man . . . heavy."

Suddenly the entire wing was laughing, from the little Mexican in the first bed with the hole in his throat, to the normally bitchy Ryker. Even Baby Jesus, the grumpiest old man in the unit, was cracking up, and for one fleeting moment, the black cloud of death that lingered above Two East broke open and sunshine poured into the dorm.

A voice from the doorway cut through the laughter.

"Hey, man, where you want these at?"

A short, stocky black man was peering at him from over a stack of blankets.

CJ stood. "I'll take them."

"What's so funny?" asked the man, looking around as he handed over the delivery.

CJ considered the question. "You know, I'm not really sure."

"Man, y'all worse than the psych wing up here," he said, shaking his head. When he smiled his top lip rolled back, exposing his teeth. CJ noticed that the front four were polished silver.

~

Dane Baker was irritated. Ponder knew him well enough by now to recognize the signs. The twitching jaw, the deep lines etched into his Neanderthal forehead, the muscles of his tatted forearms tensing and relaxing as he stared down at the carpet.

Ponder finally broke the silence. "Rough week?"

Dane looked up. "Rough life."

"You know if you don't feel like talking today, I can always reschedule you."

Dane smiled. "One day is no different than the next in here, Doc. They all run together."

"Well, how have you been?"

"I'm makin' it."

"Anything noteworthy happen since our last session?"

"Not really. Well, kinda. I lost my dawg, my best friend."

"That's pretty big. Did he go home?"

Dane shook his head.

"The box?"

"Nah."

"Transfer? Infirmary? Wait a minute, he didn't die, did he?"

Dane smiled. "Not yet. He checked in."

"Oh. Was he a . . ."

An uncomfortable silence hung between them.

"A brother?" said Dane. "Yeah, handpicked and initiated by me. That's what's so hard to swallow."

"What happened?"

"I don't really know," Dane lied. "From what I hear some little punk got off a few lucky shots on him. Probably hurt his pride."

"How about yours?"

"What . . . *my* pride?"

Ponder nodded.

Dane cracked his knuckles and smiled. After a long pause he looked up at the ceiling and began to speak. "Back when I was seventeen or so, I took to hangin' out at the river, smokin' dope and drinkin' beer with some of the kids from town. We had a rope swing out there. That's where I met Flip."

"The same guy? You were here together after all these years?"

Dane shook his head. "Nah, Doc, different guy."

Ponder waited for him to continue.

"At first I thought that was just his nickname, cuz the way he came off the rope swing, spinnin' and twistin' in the air before he hit the water. But it turned out to be his real name. Flip Atkins."

A pigeon landed on the windowsill behind him. Ponder tracked its movement across the ledge in his periphery.

"Momma was gone by then and my father was even worse with Jack Daniel's runnin' through his veins. Some nights I just slept in the grass by the river. It was a lot more peaceful than our trailer, that's for sure."

Ponder nodded.

"So anyway, this one night I was crashed on the riverbank when I woke up to the sound of music. I thought I was dreamin' at first, but when I sat up and looked around, I heard it again. It was comin' from above me." A flicker of a smile played on Dane's mouth like a florescent bulb sputtering to life. "I caught sight of him up in the tree. The light of the moon was reflectin' off his harmonica. It was silver. When he come down, we smoked a joint and talked until the sun came up. We hung out every day after that, me and Flip."

Another pigeon popped up on the window ledge and stared at them a moment before moving on.

"From the beginning, there was a natural competition between us. I was a little taller but he was probably smarter. We were always racin' each other, wrestlin', having drinkin' contests, stuff like that."

Ponder continued to study him as he leaned back in the small chair and crossed his legs.

"It went on like that for months, 'til Halloween of '71. We had some girls out there with us that day, foolin' around and stuff, you know. The river was cold but we dove in anyway, racin' to the other bank. I could hear the girls whoopin' and gigglin' as we swam back 'cross. He had me beat by at least three or four feet. I reached out and grabbed his ankle when the water got shallow."

Suddenly Ponder's collar felt a little tight and he moved to loosen his tie.

"He was laughing and splashing around when I grabbed his throat and forced him under, but he started to struggle after a few seconds, and the girls started to scream."

Dr. Ponder swallowed hard.

"When he finally stopped moving and the last few bubbles come to the surface, I turned him loose. The girls had run off. I probably should've chased them down, but I didn't have the energy." He looked up at Ponder. "Earlier, you mentioned pride. That was the motive they used at my trial. They said I was mad 'cause I lost that race in front of them girls like that. They said my pride was hurt. But between me and you, Doc, that ain't why I did what I did."

The ticking clock on his desk grew louder as the silence swelled.

"Why did you?"

Dane's features hardened and froze. "I wanted to know what it felt like to kill."

~

The rain came sideways, battering the windows like shrapnel fragments from thunderclap bombs while tracer-fire lightning streaked across the blackened afternoon sky.

CJ watched an empty bag skip and tumble down the sidewalk until a stronger gust sent it airborne, impaling it on a blade of razor wire. The muted TV flickered black-and-white images across the screen, creating a strobe light effect throughout the unit. He set a fresh pitcher of ice water on Hippie's nightstand.

"Thanks, man," said Hippie, staring transfixed at the television.

"Where's mine?" said Ryker.

"Gimme a minute," said CJ. "I've only got two hands."

Thunder cracked as he returned with the pitcher and set it next to the prosthetic leg. He noticed Smoke smiling at him from across the aisle.

"What's so funny?" asked CJ.

"Oh, I was just imagining you fighting those homeless fellas in the county jail. Old Ryker over there wouldn't have stood a chance. Especially with that fake leg. You might've snatched it off and beat him with it."

"It wasn't like that," said CJ. "It was just practice."

"I know," said Smoke. "I'm just playing with you, but tell me something. Is prison the treacherous battleground you imagined?"

CJ thought of Dane. "In some ways, I guess."

Gina raised his head and mumbled something unintelligible, pointing at Smoke's nightstand. Lightning blasted outside the windows. The old building shook.

"Lord, help us, Baby Jesus!" cried a voice from the back.

Smoke reached for a book and held it out to CJ. The cover showed chains breaking and birds flying out of them. He read the title. *We're All Doing Time: A Guide to Getting Free,* by Bo Lozoff.

"Take this over to Gina, please," said Smoke.

CJ hesitated. "Listen, Smoke, I don't really associate with faggots. I mean, I'll give him a tray and fill his water and change his sheets when I have to, that's my job, but I'm not doing him any personal favors."

Smoke studied him. "What's your problem with Gina? Did you know him before he was bedridden?"

CJ shook his head.

"Do you think his way of life is contagious?"

"No. But AIDS is."

"And you think you might catch it from handing him a book? Come on, CJ, I thought you were smarter than that."

CJ shrugged.

"Are you worried that he might snatch you in the bed with him?"

"Yeah, right."

"Are you scared he might beat you up?"

CJ rolled his eyes. "Whatever, man . . ."

"So why do you feel threatened, then?"

"I don't."

"What are you so afraid of?"

"I'm not afraid of anything."

Smoke smiled and adjusted his pillow. "Hate is like poison, CJ, it's toxic."

The rain settled into a downpour, drumming against the roof and hammering the windows, filling the unit with the soft sound of white noise.

"Long ago, in another role, I was consumed by it. I allowed it to spread into every aspect of my life until I no longer even recognized myself. Years later, about ten into this life sentence, I was doing sixty days in the hole at Raiford. I was miserable, beaten, and broken when a thought hit me like that lightning out there. I was looking back at the wreckage of my life. The family I destroyed, the people I hurt, the fragile spirits I crushed. It was all rooted in hate. All of it." He stared at CJ. "And hate is really just violent fear." A tear slid from the old man's eye. CJ was suddenly uncomfortable. "People sometimes fear what they don't understand, CJ."

He glanced over at Gina. His lips were cracked. His eyes were shrunken and crusty in the corners. Lesions covered his head and body.

"Consider the dragonfly," said Smoke. "That syringe-like body and those horrible-looking eyes. For centuries people were terrified of it. Myths were born, each one more terrible than the last. They were agents of Satan and weighed people's souls as they flew around their heads. They were in cahoots with snakes. They sewed the eyes and mouths of children shut as they slept. They could pluck people's eyeballs out."

CJ was struck by the visual of a dragonfly fluttering around someone's head, landing on their cheek, rearing back, and plunging its needle body down into the eyeball, quickly plucking it out and discarding it, then stitching the empty socket shut with the rapid-fire precision of a pedal-driven sewing machine.

"Well, it turns out that dragonflies can't even sting or bite, except for maybe a slight pinch. This beautiful insect that predates the dinosaur is actually helpful by eating mosquitoes and serving as a water quality indicator. Don't get too caught up in appearances, CJ. They're bullshit." He paused and glanced over at Gina. "And never let fear dictate your life."

CJ sighed and held out his hand.

"Gimme the damn book."

~

Forty strolled casually down the espionage/thriller section pretending to read the dust jackets of various books. He never came to the library. Ever. It was full of child molesters. The only place on the 'pound that was worse was the chapel. *It's like they are breedin' up there.* He shook his head and picked up a Ken Follett novel.

As if on cue, a timid voice from behind him offered, "Is there anything I can help you find?"

Forty turned slowly.

He was young and pale with a tight-fitting uniform and Coke-bottle glasses.

Forty tilted his head to the side and scowled. "Yeah, I'm lookin' for some ass, bitch. You got any stuffed in them tight-ass pants? Let me see."

He laughed as the library clerk hurried away. He slid the Follett book back on the shelf and grabbed a Forsythe.

"Nice," said a voice behind him.

He didn't bother to turn. He knew who it was.

"Did you see him?" asked Dane.

"Yeah," Forty said, "I saw him."

"And?"

"It's not gonna be a problem. I got this."

"Good," said Dane. "When?"

Forty looked over at him. "When the time is right. Don't sweat it."

Dane nodded.

"I didn't know he was gonna be so small," said Forty. "It might be easier to just snap his neck. Cleaner. Know what I'm sayin'?"

"Nah, too quick and painless. I want him to bleed."

"All right," said Forty. "I got somethin' for him. You got somethin' for me?"

"I might," said Dane, looking down at him with cold, reptilian eyes. "You know that once you take my money, you're locked in, right?"

Forty looked hard back at him. "I was locked in when I gave you my word."

"Good," said Dane, walking away. "Have you ever read *Master of the Game* by Sidney Sheldon?" He turned once more and smiled at Forty. "Find it. It's a mandatory read."

Forty watched him duck through the door and tracked his hulking frame all the way down the sidewalk. He looked down at the section he was in and walked quickly down the aisle, scanning the names of authors until he reached Sheldon. Forty had never heard of Sidney Sheldon, but apparently he was a bad motherfucker because his books took up three shelves.

Master of the Game, *huh?* he thought, searching for the book. *Cocky-ass cracker.*

It only took a second to find. It was thicker than most of the others. He lifted it from the shelf and looked at the cover. There was a huge diamond on the front. He opened it and thumbed through the pages, looking for cash. There was none. When he reached the end, he noticed a small pocket glued to the back of the book. It held a stamped library card. He stuck his finger behind it and fished out a folded piece of paper. It had been flattened, maybe stomped on, but it was still relatively chunky. He looked around before opening it and sneaking a peek. Buds. Green compressed buds crawling with red hair. Easily a hundred dollars' worth. Maybe two. Forty smiled. He had his advance.

CJ was bleeding. His fists were balled, his muscles tensed, his eyes shut tight, his teeth clenched. The popping sound of his flesh being punctured at a thousand beats per minute was magnified in his head. The buzz of the gun was a relentless swarm of bees.

Bones paused to wipe the blood and ink from his chest. CJ opened one eye.

"You're fighting it," said Bones. "You've got to welcome it, bro, become one with it."

CJ leaned back as the motor began to hum again. He willed his body to relax. Bones was shading now. Shading was always less painful than the outline.

"That's it," said Bones, "just chill. Almost done now."

He sensed someone standing over him.

"Aw shit," said a voice, "is he cryin' again, Bones?"

CJ didn't have to open his eyes to know who it was. *Hustle.*

"I'm not crying," said CJ.

Bones stopped to wipe his chest again. CJ craned his neck to inspect his progress.

"They're changin' shifts," said Hustle. "It looks like we got Loosebooty tonight."

"Who's with him?" asked Bones, restarting his gun.

"Rick Flair, I think."

Every guard in the Department of Corrections had a nickname bestowed upon them by the inmates in their charge. Some were self-explanatory like *Grandma Baywatch,* a woman in her late sixties with an hourglass figure; or *Def Jam,* who wore twin hearing aids. Others were more obscure like *Tommyknocker,* a woman named after a Stephen King novel; and *Lion King,* so named for the way her thick red hair framed her face. There was *Mighty Mouse* and *Grape Ape, Shorty Dumptruck* and *Three Teeth, Big Bird, Big Red, Big Dummy,* and *Big Momma.* Sometimes even the guards themselves referred to their counterparts by the nicknames inmates had given them.

Sergeant Loosebooty surveyed the dorm from inside the officers' station. Legend had it that he earned his name during a riot at the Rock when he shit in his pants at the sight of the widespread violence that filled the yard. His coworker, Rick Flair, was actually a woman, but her white flowing hair and manly facial features bore an eerie resemblance to the wrestler she was named after.

"All right," said Bones while disconnecting his gun and wiping CJ's chest a final time. "Make sure you keep it clean. Put Chapstick on it after you wash it, 'til the first peel, then you can switch to lotion."

"I know," said CJ, "you tell me every time."

He sat up and looked at his new tattoo. It was awesome. Bold, sweeping lines covered the entire left side of his chest. The letters were black and swirling around each other in Bones's own unique style of chain-gang calligraphy, with twinkling stars, soaring birds, and angels woven into the tat. CJ smiled. It was a masterpiece.

"One time!" someone shouted from the front of the dorm, signaling that a guard was coming in.

"Put your shirt on," said Bones, snatching off his gloves and sticking his ink and gun in a boot.

"Mail call!" shouted the sergeant. "Reddick, Valdez, McCallister, Ingram."

"Shit," said CJ, glancing down at his shirt to see if any blood had soaked through yet. A fresh tattoo was a violation, punishable by up to thirty days in the hole. Loosebooty would not hesitate to lock his ass up if he spotted it.

"McCallister, sir," said CJ, as he approached him, turning slightly to shield his left side.

The sergeant dug through the stack of mail in search of his name. CJ figured it was either a response to a request or another money receipt from J. Ramos. He hoped it was the latter.

He frowned when he was handed a letter. There was no mistake. It was addressed to him. The return address was the Essex, the hotel where his mom had worked. He sat down on the bunk and opened it.

The letterhead said *Jose Ramos, General Manager.*

"So that's who he is," said CJ.

He read the letter quickly the first time. When he reached the end, he started over and read slower, taking in every word, letting it sink in.

All around him the bustle of life in a prison dorm persisted. People gambled and argued, wrestled and sang, prayed and plotted. CJ sat motionless in the center of it all. Numb. He slid the letter under his pillow as a tear broke free from his eye and dove down the side of his face. He quickly wiped it away.

Blood had soaked through his shirt. *Like a gunshot,* he thought. He pulled the sticky material away from his chest and glanced down at the fresh ink that covered the skin that covered the bone that covered his heart. It said Cheryl.

~

Mrs. Carroll was waiting on him when he walked through the door. His eyes darted to the clock. He was five minutes early.

"You're not in trouble," she said.

He relaxed.

Her fat white arms reminded him of the floaties he had to wear in the pool when he was little. She clasped her hands together, faint nicotine stains intermingled with gnawed fingernails. Her steel gray flat-top matched her drill sergeant personality. She glared at him through black horn-rimmed glasses.

"I need less talk and more work out of you today. There's dust on the baseboards, the windows are filthy, and there's a puddle of urine in the bathroom. Keep an eye on Ryker. He's been throwing up all night, and for godsakes do something about that shower! The mildew—"

The phone rang. She continued rambling orders as she turned and walked back to the nurses' station to answer it.

"Okay, okay," she said to the loud ringing.

CJ shot a quick bird at her back before scrambling to grab his cleaning supplies and setting them inside the double doors of the unit.

Everyone was asleep. Even Smoke, who was normally up and meditating by now.

CJ paused and studied his face. The bushy white eyebrows were gone, along with the beard stubble and thick gray sideburns. CJ looked closer. Even his eyelashes had fallen out. The chemo had already begun to work its tragic magic. A small puddle of drool had formed on his pillowcase. CJ smiled. He liked the old man. It was hard not to. He was a different breed. He was the only person CJ knew who meditated. *Who the hell meditated in prison?* He was kind to people who were of no benefit to him. One minute he was quoting Shakespeare and the next, he was breaking down the dragonfly. He read the Bible, the Quran, and any other spiritual text he could find. He even knew martial arts. He was just different than anyone else CJ had met during his journey through the system. He was real. And he was dying.

CJ glanced over at Gina. His blanket had fallen to the floor beside his bed during the night. The bones from his emaciated back protruded from his dingy yellow t-shirt as he lay there shivering. Smoke's Bo Lozoff book peeked from under his soiled pillow. CJ grabbed the blanket from the floor and gently covered him with it, taking care to tuck it around him so it wouldn't fall again.

"Caught ya," Smoke whispered.

CJ looked sharply in his direction. The old man's eyes were twinkling. He reached in his pocket for the letter and went to his bed.

"Read it," said CJ, handing it to him.

"Who's it from?"

"My mom's old boss."

Smoke sat up and grabbed his glasses from off the nightstand. He read it out loud.

Dear CJ,

I hope this letter finds you healthy and in good spirits. I know it must be hard in there. Just keep your faith in God. He will protect and guide you.

I'm writing this letter for your mother. She was my secretary. I realize this may be a sensitive issue but there are certain things I've discovered concerning her death that I feel you must know.

I have a good friend in the field of psychology. Your mother visited him regularly during the last years of her life. We recently had a conversation about a drug she was prescribed for depression. There's a new study out regarding its side effects. Apparently a spike in suicidal thoughts and behavior was detected among its users. Cheryl began taking it the day your father died.

No one can say for sure that this is what happened to your mother but I believe it to be true. Her doctor does too. Cheryl would have never done this. It just doesn't fit.

I hope that somehow this letter gives you some peace. Your mother loved you with all her heart. My guess is that you've spent the last few years blaming yourself. I can't even begin to imagine the incredible burden you've been carrying around. It wasn't your fault.

Please know that you're not alone. There are many people praying for you. I trust that you've received the money I've been sending. You can repay me when you get out. As long as I'm General Manager, there will be a job waiting for you at the Essex.

Until then, don't give up hope. Think about what I've said regarding your mom. It's the only logical explanation.

Sincerely,
Jose Ramos

Smoke folded the letter and handed it back to him.

"Interesting," he said. "How does it feel to not have to carry around that weight anymore?"

"I'm not sure," said CJ, watching him closely. "Do you believe it?"

Smoke settled back in his bed. "You know, when you first told me about your mom, I remember thinking that something didn't jibe. The woman you described seemed to love you so much. The idea that she would willfully abandon you in your darkest hour, that she would *choose* to have you walk this road alone with this insane amount of guilt hanging from your neck like a hundred-pound chain. It just didn't add up, you know?"

CJ nodded, his eyes brimming with tears.

"And now we know why," said Smoke.

Mr. Ramos's words meant a lot and the psychologist's professional opinion was persuasive, but having Smoke, the smartest man he knew, agree with them was what did it for CJ. He rushed the old man without thinking, hugging him fiercely as the tears broke free.

"Hey, Smoke," someone asked, "what time is it, man?"

"Now," he said, patting CJ on the back. "It's right now."

Neither noticed Mrs. Carroll in the doorway. She watched a moment before turning and walking back down the hall.

~

"What's up, CJ?" called a passing voice.

He turned to see who it was but didn't recognize the face. He nodded and kept walking.

Someone else slapped him on the back. "CJ, my man."

Another stranger.

"That's the dude who fucked up Big John."

"He doesn't look like much."

"They say he's a black belt."

"Ahh . . ."

The voices trailed off. CJ stifled a smile. Kane was right.

He took the long way back to his dorm, smoking a couple of cigarettes and enjoying the crisp fall air. His mind kept returning to something Smoke said. A quote. "To live in the hearts of others is to not die."

Even if it was the medication that caused his mom to be suicidal, he still felt responsible. *He was the reason she was on the medication in the first place,* yet he couldn't deny feeling different. Changed. Maybe it was the letter and its subtle shifting of weight from his shoulders to his heart.

Maybe it was simply time doing its thing, or maybe it was the friendship he had formed with the old man on Two East. He knew it was something, whatever it was.

To live in the hearts of others is to not die.

Maybe it was time to let the memory of his family breathe within him instead of stuffing it each time it bubbled to the surface of his consciousness.

"Well, well, well," said a voice dripping with sarcasm, pulling him from his reverie. "Look who it is. Wonderboy."

He almost walked right into the massive chest of Dane Baker. His instincts took over as he spun around to run. Too late. Dane laughed as he snatched him by the collar and flung him easily into the grass. When CJ rolled to his feet, Dane was right in his face. There was nowhere to run. He was caught in a blind spot, crippled by panic and fear. A voice from the past shouted through the gusting winds of blood and adrenaline shooting through his veins and pounding in his head.

Always, always, always get off first. You too damn little to take punches.

CJ crouched and shot a cannon hook straight into the chin of the bully, throwing everything he had into the blow and even leaving his feet to land it. Dane's head rocked back and he staggered as CJ cocked his fist to deliver another.

A few stragglers stopped on the sidewalk to watch the action.

Dane backed up a step and looked around before smiling at CJ.

"You're dead, bitch," he growled, moving toward him.

CJ then threw another punch and Dane easily slapped it away. He ventured a kick to the balls that somehow missed the mark and glanced harmlessly off Dane's thigh. He began frantically throwing combinations as he moved backwards. Dane walked purposefully through the blows and reached for his throat. CJ's retreat was halted by the brick wall of the dormitory at his back.

Dane's immense hand shot under his chin, clutching his throat. CJ's face throbbed red, then purple, as the life was choked out of him. His legs flailed as he was lifted from the ground. Dane laughed at the frantic helplessness in his rolling eyes.

The group of inmates watching from the sidewalk began to murmur excitedly.

While holding CJ pinned to the wall with one hand, Dane went to work with the other, knocking the air from his lungs with crushing rights to his sternum, ribs, and even his nuts.

CJ's eyes bulged from his face as blackness seeped across his vision like liquid on a paper towel. He gave up fighting and went limp as a fist exploded against his temple, turning his head and driving it into the bricks.

"One time!" shouted his mom, *or was it Rick?* Someone was warning them that the guards were coming.

He fell to the ground. The sound of feet crunching through the grass passed loudly by his face before fading to silence. He recognized the spinning sky. White clouds swam over the sun. He tracked their movement as they separated and rejoined high above him. Then his view was obscured by a familiar black face.

"Are you all right, young man?"

CJ sat up and worked his jaw.

"I'm good," he said, looking around.

"I know you," said Dr. Ponder. "You're on my caseload. Is it McKinney, McNally? I know it's something like that."

"McCallister."

"Yeah, that's right," Ponder said, kneeling in the grass, "McCallister. I remember now. So what are you doing lying out here in the grass? And don't tell me you're tanning."

CJ wiped the dirt from the side of his face and rose unsteadily to his feet.

"I just . . . got dizzy."

"Dizzy, huh? Maybe I need to call medical, get you a wheelchair down here."

"I'm really all right."

"Or maybe I need to call security."

"NO! Please. Really. I'm okay now."

Ponder eyed him skeptically. "Was that Dane Baker I saw running off when I came around the corner?"

"Who?" said CJ, testing a step. "I don't know who that is, sir, but I'm okay now. Honest."

He was still a little woozy as he walked away, leaving Ponder clutching his briefcase in the grass. He could feel eyes boring holes into his back, assessing, processing, diagnosing. He tried not to stagger on the wobbly ground as he made his way to the sidewalk. CJ was lucky that it was Ponder who found him and not inside security. He could have easily been in handcuffs and on his way to confinement.

"McCallister," called the doctor as he walked away. "I believe we have a session coming up. Keep an eye on the callout."

Chapter 17

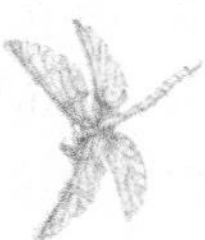

April was in his bed with him. She smelled of apricot scrub and TRESemmé. Her silky legs intertwined with his beneath the blanket as he cradled her face and kissed her candy lips. Her hand brushed playfully against his throbbing erection before finally seizing it in her warm fist. She sighed in his ear as he kissed his way down the soft skin of her throat and found her perfect breasts. She ran her fingers through his hair as he sucked her hard, pink nipples and licked her areola. He was drunk with passion. Every inch of her warm body was exquisite and begging to be explored. Ravished. Devoured. After sucking and caressing her breasts for a time he reluctantly moved on. *Where is the agony coming from?* he wondered. *This is Heaven. Why does it hurt?* She laughed and pushed him away when he darted his tongue in her belly button. He then discovered the delicate curvature of her slow-grinding hips and licked his way along the elastic of her panty line. She arched her back as he teasingly kissed her pretty thighs, occasionally raking his tongue across the thin material of her panties, causing her to cry out softly in the dark.

"Shh. Don't let the guards hear you," he said as he pulled her panties to the side and began making love to her with his mouth. He couldn't get enough of her. He slid his hands under her ass and pulled her to him. She cried out his name as her lovely body began to tremble and spasm in his arms.

"Shh!" he whispered again, tasting her on his lips. "Don't let the guards hear you."

"Man, ain't no muthafuckin guards in here!" said Hustleman. "Now wake your scary ass up and listen!"

April turned to sand in his fingertips and was gone in seconds, leaving him with only the agony part of the dream, the only part that was real. It *hurt* to want, to need, to crave.

Hustle was sitting on his locker, smoking in the dark. "Did you hear anything I just said?"

"Not really," said CJ. "I was too busy having a wet dream. Until I woke up and saw your ugly face."

Hustle laughed.

"You little freaky-ass cracker!" he said, lowering his voice. "You know I got some new pictures for the low-low, right?"

CJ stretched. "No thanks, man. I just want some sleep."

"All right," Hustle said. "Well, listen, I need my knife."

"For what?" asked CJ, sitting up in his bunk.

Hustle waved him off with a flick of the wrist. The orange cherry of his cigarette made a zee in the dark. "Nothing like that. My locker's just low and I know I can sell it for a quick twenty. You still got it, don't you?"

CJ nodded. "Yeah, it's put up." He hadn't thought about the knife in months.

"Well, get it. Tomorrow if you can."

CJ fell back against his pillow as Hustle walked off. He rolled on his side and pulled the cover over his head, hoping April would return before morning came.

~

He snuck a joint during his lunch break. He had never been high at work before, but he wasn't worried about anyone finding him out. He had a Jolly Rancher for his breath and some Visine he snagged off the nurses' cart for his red eyes. He nodded politely as he passed guards and hospital staff in the hall.

On the outside he was a model inmate. Submissive. Quiet. Respectful. "Good afternoon, Officer Powell. Hello, Mrs. Daniels. How are you, Dr. Nichols?"

Inside his head the conversation was a little different: *Nice wig, asshole. Mrs. Daniels, you have the nicest breasts. Doc, people are talking, man, no inmate should have to drop his pants for a sore throat or an earache, you sick, twisted freak!*

CJ laughed as he walked up the stairs to Two East. The hospital was way more interesting with a buzz.

Mrs. Carroll was standing in the hall when he opened the door. "What the hell are you laughing at?"

He froze. "Oh. I . . . was just thinking about something."

"Yeah?" she said, turning to walk away. "You need to be *thinking* about getting to work. This place is a pigsty."

I'm thinking about throwing you down the stairs, he thought as he watched her go. For some reason his eyes were drawn to her ass. He had no idea why. It was flat, wide, and dimpled with no redeeming qualities, yet he could not tear his eyes away. It was like his attorney's nose; he was mesmerized.

Suddenly the worst thing that could have happened, happened. She turned and caught him staring. In the following seconds as she stood there glaring at him, he considered his next move. The problem with trying to explain himself when he was stoned was that his foot inevitably flew straight into his mouth. Many times, the other person was not even aware of what the hell he was talking about, and his fumbling attempt at an explanation only made the situation more awkward. But he couldn't let Mrs. Carroll think he was looking at her ass.

She removed her glasses and cleaned them on the hem of her shirt. "Well? Are you going to stand there all day with your thumb in your butt?"

He opened his mouth, then shut it. Sometimes the best course of action was no course of action. No explanation. No apology. No denial. The truth needs no defense. And the truth was that he was really wasted and in no shape to talk with Mrs. Carroll. He grabbed the broom and dustpan and walked across the hall to the living quarters.

"Hmmph," said Mrs. Carroll behind him.

As he entered the bedding area, he silently applauded his own wisdom. A weaker, less experienced man would have lost it back there. Not him. If there was anything in this world he was skilled at, it was concealing a buzz. He'd been doing it his whole life. It was genetically encoded in his DNA. After all, he was the son of Christopher McCallister.

He began sweeping at the far end of the aisle by the entrance to the bathroom. Most of the men were either napping or watching TV. Out of the corner of his eye he saw Smoke lay his book on his chest and watch him. CJ pretended not to notice as he swept by his bed.

"You're high," said the old man.

CJ almost dropped the broom. He quickly scanned the other beds to see if anyone had heard. When he looked back at Smoke, he was smiling. His hairless face, a thousand lines; his eyes, a twinkling challenge.

"How could you tell?" asked CJ, sitting on his bed.

Smoke scooted over to make room. "Slumped shoulders, slack facial expression, no eye contact, different energy. I don't really know." He shrugged. "My son was a pothead."

CJ looked at him sharply. "You have a son?"

"Had."

"I didn't know that."

"He wasn't my biological son. I married his momma in '56. He was three years old at the time. When she died a few years later in a car accident, I raised him like he was my own."

"What happened to him?"

Smoke's eyes glazed over. "He's gone."

They sat in silence for a while, each lost in his own thoughts. CJ had cottonmouth. He reached over and dug a cube of ice out of the water pitcher on Smoke's nightstand.

"Help yourself," said Smoke, shaking his head.

CJ swung his legs back and forth over the side of the hospital bed. "Smoke, what are you in prison for?"

"Murder," said the old man.

CJ's legs went still.

"I've actually got two counts, but one of them is an out-of-state detainer and I'll probably be dead before they ever get me in a courtroom on it."

"Why?" asked CJ, too stoned to care about prison etiquette.

"I saw a man with a gun on my back porch peeping through the windows. I thought he was trying to kill me, so I killed him first. Turned out to be a cop investigating me for the other murder charge up north. The only thing that saved me from the chair was the fact that my crime occurred during a small window of time when the Supreme Court ruled that the death penalty was unconstitutional."

CJ had a hard time imagining Smoke as a ruthless killer. Kane fit the part. There was a strong undercurrent of violence in everything he did. Smoke was a pacifist. CJ had never met a kinder human being, inside or out. Except maybe his mom. "What about the other one?"

"The other murder?"

CJ nodded.

"That," said Smoke, "was pure revenge."

CJ decided not to ask any more personal questions.

"Sorry," said Smoke after a few minutes of contemplative silence.

"For what?" asked CJ, still trying to picture him with a gun in his hand.

"For blowing your high," he said, smiling. "I'm assuming you smoke pot to escape the reality of prison, not to wallow in its sewer of odious truths."

CJ frowned as he turned over those words in his head. "I'm not exactly sure what you just said, but there's no reason to apologize. You didn't blow my high."

Smoke laughed. "Apparently not. Why do you do it, CJ?"

"Why do I do what?"

"Why do you smoke pot? Do you even know?"

CJ shot him a sidelong glance. "Yeah, I know. I smoke it cuz . . . it's fun."

"Fun."

CJ nodded.

"Doesn't it affect your confidence?"

Yeah, CJ thought. "No," he said.

"Doesn't it make you overthink everything?"

Yeah, CJ thought. "No," he said.

"Didn't you tell me you swore off drugs when you got arrested? I thought you made a promise to God."

"I don't believe in God!" said CJ, way too loud. His own words echoed in his head. An image flashed through his mind of a petulant little boy, pouting in his room because he couldn't have his way.

"Doesn't it make you self-conscious?" Smoke asked softly.

CJ didn't answer his question, but a surge of suspicion burst forth within him, causing him to squint at the old man. "Smoke, can you hear my thoughts?"

"What?" Smoke laughed.

CJ realized how ridiculous he sounded. "Nothing."

"Grab that Bible off the nightstand."

"Okay, *now* you're blowing my high."

"Don't worry, we're not going to have a Bible study. I just want you to see something."

CJ rolled his eyes as he reached for the black leather-bound book.

"Open it."

CJ flipped back the cover. In small printed letters in the top left corner it said:

To Ulysses Griffith
From Megan Snow

CJ looked at Smoke. "Who is Megan Snow?"

"Megan Snow is a Christian missionary in El Salvador. She sent me that Bible."

CJ thumbed through the pages of highlighted verses. "Cool."

"She's also the daughter of the police officer that I shot and killed."

"Whoa," said CJ, flipping back to the front to see her handwriting again.

"Fifteen years ago on the chaplain's phone, she told me something that changed my life forever."

CJ set the Bible back on the nightstand.

"She told me that non-forgiveness is like swallowing poison and expecting someone else to get sick." Smoke's lashless eyes blinked as he stared up at the ceiling. "And she told me that God loves me and has a plan for me."

CJ shifted uncomfortably.

"So if God can forgive me for taking away that little girl's father, if she can forgive me, then surely you can forgive. God loves you and has a plan for you too."

They locked eyes across the bed. Neither blinked. He considered Smoke's words beneath the blank mask of his face. Then he leaned forward and hardened his expression.

"Do you feel like playing baseball?" CJ asked.

Smoke frowned. "Huh?"

"Baseball. Do you feel like playing?"

"How? I can't leave the unit and I doubt I could make it to the rec yard anyway."

"Come on," CJ said, smiling. "I'll help you up."

~

"Come on guys. Give it back!" Ryker demanded.

"Shut up, honky!" said Baby Jesus, smiling as he wound up and pitched the sock to Gina, who sat in a chair at the end of the aisle.

"Ball one," called CJ.

"Bullshit!" cried Baby Jesus. "That was a strike, all day!"

"It *was* a strike, honey," Gina weakly agreed as he handed the balled-up sock to CJ to toss back to the pitcher.

“That’s all right, that’s all right,” said Baby Jesus, gathering his composure while circling the linoleum tile that was the pitcher’s mound.

“Hey, batter batter batter,” called Hippie from the outfield, which was actually the far end of the aisle by the bathroom.

Smoke held Ryker’s prosthetic leg over one shoulder and awaited the next pitch.

“Goddamn it!” said Ryker. “Gimme my leg!”

Smoke attempted a lazy swing as the sock came whizzing by.

“Stee—rike!” said CJ.

“That’s what I’m talking ’bout!” said Baby Jesus.

“Yes!” said Gina.

“One and one,” said CJ as he watched Smoke feebly heft the bat back over his shoulder. He looked tired and weak, but he also looked determined.

“Smoke, please give me my leg. Come on, man. Where’s that kindness you’re always preaching about, huh? Hey, Smoke, what time is it? Damn it. *What time is it?”*

“Right now,” Smoke answered through clenched teeth, eyeing the pitcher grimly as he twirled the prosthetic leg in slow circles just above his shoulder. “The time is right now.”

Baby Jesus went into his jerky windup and side-armed the sock down the center of the aisle. It was chest high and hanging over the outer third of the tile that represented home plate.

Smoke’s eyes widened and his nostrils flared as he extended the bat and made contact.

Thunk.

He followed through and dropped the faux leg on the floor.

“Goddamn it!” Ryker protested.

The sock soared through the unit, almost grazing the ceiling as it passed.

“I got it, man,” said Hippie, “I got it.”

He mistimed his jump and it flew over his outstretched hand into the bathroom, where it fell to the tiles and rolled under the sink.

"Home run!" CJ pronounced.

Many of the men who were watching from their beds applauded. Even Gina, who was technically on the other team, clapped and beamed proudly at Smoke.

"What the hell you clappin' for, sissy?" groused Baby Jesus. "Somebody flash they dick at you or somethin'?"

Gina stopped clapping. "Fuck you," he whispered.

CJ grabbed Ryker's prosthetic leg from off the floor and set it on his nightstand. Ryker snatched it up immediately and inspected it for damage.

"Assholes," he grumbled. "Do you know how expensive this is?"

"A thousand dollars?" Hippie guessed as he sat down next to him.

"Oh shut up, Hippie," said Ryker.

Suddenly Mrs. Carroll rounded the corner, causing everyone to freeze. "What the hell's going on in here?" Her eyes narrowed as she looked around the room.

"Nothing," said CJ.

She studied him coldly for a moment before allowing her gaze to flash over to Ryker, who was embracing his prosthetic leg like it was a woman in his bed.

"Hmmph," she said, turning to leave.

The men looked at each other, smiling.

"Adams," she called from the doorway.

Hippie stiffened. "Yes ma'am? I mean . . . Mrs. Carroll."

She shot him a withering glance over her shoulder. "Dialysis. Get ready."

CJ sat on the corner of Smoke's bed and nodded at him. "Nice shot, old man. I didn't know you had it in you."

Smoke leaned back against the headboard. His breathing was labored, and his hairless face was red. "I was knocking softballs over razor wire before you were even thought about." A trickle of sweat shot down his temple.

"Want some water?" CJ offered.

Smoke shook his head.

"Mrs. Carroll looked pissed, didn't she? She's such an old bitch."

Smoke pointed a tired finger at him and smiled. "Appearances are bullshit, son. Remember the dragonfly."

"Not always," said CJ, thinking of Dane. "Sometimes a turd is just a turd."

Smoke laughed.

CJ glanced around the unit before leaning close and whispering, "I need that knife back."

The old man's face clouded with concern. "Why?"

"Because it's not mine and I need to give it back. You still have it, don't you?"

Smoke nodded and patted the side of his bed. "It's been there so long, it's going to feel strange sleeping without it. I hope none of these crazy old farts try to attack me in my sleep."

CJ recalled their first meeting. "I think you could take them," he said with a smile.

"You're not in any trouble, are you? Is that bully still hassling you?"

"Nah," CJ lied, "not really and anyway I've taken his best shot. I don't need a knife for him."

Smoke reached under the blanket. "Be careful, son," he said, sliding him the knife.

"I will," said CJ, slipping it in his waistband.

"And for godsakes stick it in your sock or something," said Smoke. "If that thing falls out of your pants in the hallway and one of those free world doctors or nurses sees it, I doubt we'll be playing prosthetic leg baseball again anytime soon."

CJ laughed and quickly transferred it to his sock, rising to his feet and taking a few test steps in the space next to the bed.

Smoke's eyelids were becoming heavy. "Promise me that after you return that to your buddy, you'll never touch another one," he mumbled.

"I promise."

Smoke was already snoring as he turned to leave.

~

CJ took a last drag from his rip and dropped it in the butt can outside of mental health. The cigarette had barely landed when a scraggly-looking man who was leaning against the wall sprang into action, plunging his hand down into the can and snagging the short. As CJ reached for the door, he glanced back at the man. He was puffing wildly on the small cigarette butt while loose ash and smoke swirled around his face. CJ flinched. The eyes staring back at him were milky gray and iris-less.

The blind man smiled. "What the fuck you starin' at, punk?"

CJ yanked the door open and stepped inside. The benches were packed. The lobby was the worst thing about the mental health clinic. Most of the inmates waiting to be seen were either already on psych meds or needed to be on them. He looked around the crowded room for a seat. Some people slept, while others held angry debates with invisible counterparts. There were nervous tics and violent tremors, senseless laughter and quiet whimpering, cackling, muttering, cursing, and chanting. All under the watchful eye of the guard sipping coffee in the booth.

"Sit down!" the guard ordered.

"Where, sir?" asked CJ.

There was a commotion to his far right. The guard looked and pointed. "Right there."

CJ followed his finger to the bench against the wall where a space had been cleared. Dane Baker smiled and waved him over.

He hesitated and glanced back at the guard, who was scowling from the booth. "Move it, numbnuts!"

CJ forced a step, then another, locking eyes with Dane as he approached the small space next to him on the metal bench.

"Morning, fuckstick," said Dane as he sat down.

CJ leaned forward, resting his elbows on his legs and ignoring the gigantic bully beside him.

Dane leaned forward too. "It ain't over," he whispered.

CJ stared at the floor.

"I bet you're cursin' yourself right now," said Dane. "You've managed to dig yourself one helluva hole. You know when I first saw you backslappin' and carryin' on with that crow by the softball field, I figured you were just green and needed a little orientation into how things are in here."

A sallow-faced man with mustard stains on his jacket and cornflake dandruff was sitting on the other side of CJ, digging furiously in his ear.

"Then," said Dane, "I started thinkin' that maybe I'll just fuck you for a while. It's been a minute since I've had any young ass."

"You'd have to kill me first," said CJ.

"Oh, I plan on it," said Dane. "Just be patient."

CJ watched the man remove his finger from his ear and inspect it. After checking it thoroughly, he brought it to his nose and gave it a whiff before casually sticking it in his mouth. When he noticed he was being watched, he shrugged and flashed an innocent smile. CJ looked away and swallowed a small surge of vomit back down.

"But in the meantime," said Dane, "I'm gonna make your life miserable. I was hoping I broke your jaw last month or at least a rib. Next time you won't be so lucky."

CJ had heard enough. "Yeah, well, maybe next time you'll fight me like a man instead of sneaking up behind me like a coward."

Dane shook with laughter. "You've got balls, I'll give you that. Which is more than I can say for most of these pussies 'round here."

CJ couldn't resist saying, "Like your buddy Big John?"

Dane went still beside him. Even the ear digger to his right sensed the tension and after smelling his finger once more, he clasped his hands in his lap and watched from the corner of his eye.

"You're lucky I'm dealing with this parole shit," said Dane. "You shoulda been dead months ago. You have no idea who you're fucking with."

CJ forced his head to turn. Dane was staring at him with a look of utter disgust. He stared back without blinking. Their faces were so close that their noses almost touched. CJ could smell the chow hall tuna on his breath.

A door opened on the other side of the room and Dr. Ponder scanned the crowded lobby.

"McCallister?" he called. "Is McCallister in here?"

CJ allowed his eyes to remain locked with Dane's for a moment longer before he finally stood and turned.

"There you are," said Ponder, smiling from the doorway.

"Hey, CJ," said Dane from behind him, "I'll see you around."

~

Forty stepped under the giant pavilion, looking for his hook-up.

"Hey, two-forty shorty!" someone called from the domino table. "What's up, dirty?"

Forty recognized a couple of his homeboys. He nodded to them but didn't bother stopping.

Funny how everybody knows you when you got a little bread, he thought.

Dane's small advance on the hit was all he needed to come up. He broke down the package into twenty-one compound dime sacks and boomed twenty of them within a week, smoking the last one. He flipped that money by storing it all out, mostly to white boys and gamblers. He would gladly go to sleep hungry if he could loan out his last five soups for eight back. He was trying to build an empire. His initial two hundred quickly turned to three hundred, then that became five hundred, then that became eight hundred. Now between everything he had in his lockers and everything he had out, he was sitting on about $1,300. Not bad when you considered that every penny of it was off the land. But he was still in debt and Dane was getting impatient. He wished he could just give him six or seven hundred dollars' worth of canteen to clear his face. He could easily make that back in a couple of weeks. Problem was the Great Dane didn't want money. He wanted blood.

The familiar faces around the poker tables watched him as he passed.

"Hey, Forty!" someone called. "We got a seat open over here."

He kept walking. Forty never gambled for fun. When he sat down at a game it was strictly business. Prison poker was an opportunity for those who had little or nothing to come up off the wealthier players at the table who were just passing the time. His strategy never changed. *Find the richest motherfucker at the table and circle his ass.* But now *he* was the richest and he hustled way too hard for his money to donate it all back on the poker table. He popped the collar on his jacket and stepped off the concrete onto the grass.

The wind cut through him as he walked across the track. He removed the hat from his back pocket and put it on, pulling it down over his ears. To his left, a backboard shook and the chain metal net that hung from the rim rattled as a basketball was flushed. The cat who dunked it pounded his chest as he ran back down the court. In spite of the wind, a full court game was in progress. The pounding dribble of the ball quickly faded behind him as he approached the swath of dead grass and dirt that was used as a football field.

Spectators stood along the boundaries, smoking and cheering on their homeboys, who wore either red or yellow flags and lined up in formation across from each other. The ball was snapped and a tall kid from Tampa threw a quick slant to the slot receiver, who was immediately popped by a linebacker patrolling the area. The flags were only there for decoration.

The crowd celebrated the hard hit, then roared even louder when the receiver bounced to his feet and sent a quick right into the jaw of the defender. A few more punches were thrown before the two were separated by their teammates and escorted back to their huddles, talking shit over their shoulders as they were pulled away.

Forty smiled his silver-toothed smile. *Nothin' like a peaceful game of chain-gang flag football.*

"Your name Forty, playa?" asked a high-pitched voice from beside him.

He turned to see who was asking. The man was about his height, darker than he was, with waves in his hair and a creased white uniform.

"Who wants to know?" asked Forty, turning his attention back to the game.

The ball was snapped and the QB dropped back five steps and launched an arching spiral down the far sideline. It fell to the ground just inches beyond the outstretched hands of the receiver.

"Listen, youngblood," said the man, "it's too goddamn windy out here to play games. Now my name is Hustleman. I heard that you was lookin' for some steel. I got it. What's up?"

Forty looked back over at him. "You got it on you?"

The man nodded.

"Let me check it out."

He slid closer and reached inside his jacket. They both glanced up at the tower and over at the pavilion where the guards were gathered drinking coffee and smoking. No one was paying them any attention. Hustleman smoothly passed him the knife. It was long and sharp with a handle wound in boot string.

"This ain't steel," said Forty.

"Nah," Hustle said. "It's better than steel. It's fiberglass."

"Why's that better?"

Hustle smiled. "Metal detector won't pick it up. My homeboy had it on him a few months back and got pulled over with the wand. Never even beeped. Walked right through."

Forty tested its rigidity. "Will it break?"

"No way."

"How much you want for it?"

"Gimme thirty."

"You're crazy." Forty laughed. "I'll give you twenty."

"Gimme twenty-five."

Forty studied him for a few seconds. "All right, that's a deal. But all I got is rip and coffee."

"Shit," Hustle smiled, "that's all I want."

"I'll bring it out next yard."

"I'll be here," said Hustle, turning to walk off.

As Forty watched him go, a thought struck him. "Hey, Hustleman," he called, "we never had this conversation, right?"

Hustle turned and squinted at him. "Man, who the fuck is you?"

~

The mop water sloshed around in the bucket as CJ rolled it across the hall, careful not to spill any. He paused at the entrance of the bedding area and reached down to lift the front wheels over a treacherous lip in the flooring. A pang of tension ripped through him and his head snapped upright. He surveyed the dorm.

Normally the men of Two East would be sleeping soundly this early in the morning, except maybe for Smoke, who liked the silence for meditative purposes, but even that was a rarity lately because of the chemo. Few were sleeping now.

Ryker was staring blankly at the ceiling, while Hippie gazed through the dirty window at the shuffling parade of inmate traffic below. Some of the newer patients on the wing looked questioningly at CJ as Baby Jesus rocked back and forth and mumbled a prayer. Almost immediately CJ noticed that Gina's bed was vacant and stripped of all linen. Smoke looked over at him through the black reading glasses that were perched on his nose. He set his book on the nightstand and motioned CJ over to his bed.

"Where'd he go?" asked CJ.

"He's gone," said Smoke.

"Gone as in transferred to an outside hospital," asked CJ, "or gone as in gone?"

"He's dead, man," Hippie interrupted, his voice thick with emotion.

Baby Jesus's bed squeaked from behind them as his rocking suddenly intensified. "Sissy-ass bitch," he muttered, angrily swatting a loose tear from his face.

CJ stared at the empty bunk while scenes of Gina roared through his memory, one after the other, like passing headlights on a lonesome highway. After the convoy of still frames and flickering images rounded a final curve in his mind, trailing off into darkness, a single thought settled over him like a blanket of dense fog.

Gina was tough.

He almost laughed out loud at the notion. *Gina was not tough. Kane was tough. Rick and Ty were tough. Rudy was tough. Smoke was tough. The Barocela twins, Duke, Dane Baker, all tough. But Gina? Tough? No way.*

Still, the thought persisted, stubborn and fixed like a thick wooden stake driven deep into the frontal lobe of his brain.

"Was Gina tough?" he asked aloud.

Smoke frowned. "Now that's an odd question."

CJ waited.

"Tough?" said Smoke. "I don't know, but I will say this—the path he walked was certainly not the easiest. Who catches more hell than gays in prison? Maybe child molesters and snitches. Maybe."

"Yeah, man, but those dudes deserve it," Hippie interjected.

"Gina was true to the integrity of his own spirit," said Smoke. "He never tried to hide who he was."

"Never," echoed Hippie, shaking his head.

"We've been at a few prisons together over the last twenty years. The east unit, Martin, the Muck, and now here," said Smoke. "He was always the same old gentle, soft-spoken Gina in spite of the beatings and the rapings and the brutality that was heaped upon his plate. The same old Gina."

"And that took *balls,* man," said Hippie.

Ryker rolled his eyes. "Oh come on, Hippie, what are you, a gay rights activist now?"

Smoke smiled at CJ. "So was he tough? I guess that all depends on your definition of the word. But he sure did have a high tolerance for pain. I was beginning to think that not even full-blown AIDS would break him."

"McCallister?" called Mrs. Carroll from the hall. "That mattress needs to be wiped down with bleach. These baseboards are covered in dust. This gurney needs to be taken back downstairs, and there's *still* mildew all over the showers. You're starting to stretch my patience, bucko. I've been cutting you a lot of slack here lately. Don't make me have to do my job."

Smoke smiled at CJ and raised a chemo-deleted eyebrow. *"Bucko?"* he mouthed.

CJ shrugged and stood. "I'm sorry about Gina. I know he was your friend."

"To live in the hearts of others is to not die," Smoke quoted, reaching for a book on his nightstand.

CJ walked back down the aisle, past Gina's empty bed. *Maybe he was tough.*

"Hey, Smoke," called Hippie from behind him, "what time is it, man?"

"Now," Smoke answered, "it's right now."

~

"So what's the deal with you and McCallister?" the doctor asked.

"McCallister?" Dane frowned. "I'm not sure I know him, Doc." *That little snitching fuckboy.*

"Sure you do," said Ponder. "Young white kid, about half your size. Been a permanent here for close to a year."

Dane furrowed his brow and his eyes shot right and left, affecting a memory search. *I'm gonna kill him.*

"Maybe this will jar your memory," said Ponder. "He's the one you were beating up on the side of I-Dorm a few weeks ago. You were just sitting next to him in the waiting room on Tuesday."

"Oh," said Dane, "him." He felt like a fifth grader in the principal's office after a schoolyard fight. He shifted uncomfortably in the tiny blue chair as Ponder twirled a pen between his fingers.

"Why are you bullying him?" the doctor asked.

Dane bristled. "I'm not bullying him. Did he tell you that?"

Ponder exhaled. "No, he didn't tell me anything. He never does. Getting more than two or three sentences out of him in a session is like pulling teeth. That's why I'm talking to you about it."

Fuck this, thought Dane. "Yeah, well, I'm not here to talk about him. So if that's what this session is gonna be about, you can go ahead and get a refusal form ready."

Ponder didn't move. "How long has it been since you've had a disciplinary report?"

Dane squirmed. "Two and a half years."

"And when do you go before the board?"

"March."

Ponder sat up and began organizing the files that were spread over his desk. "I probably should have reported the incident when I saw you two on the side of I-Dorm, but since you're both on my caseload, I wanted to give you the benefit of the doubt. I hope I didn't make a mistake."

Dane stared down at the carpet.

"I want your word right now that whatever beef you've got with McCallister is squashed."

Dane nodded. The doc had him bent over a rock, hands tied and cheeks spread.

"You've made so much progress," said Ponder. "It'd be a shame if you lost focus now."

Spare me, thought Dane.

"So is it dead?" asked the doctor.

Dane fought to suppress a smile at the irony of his choice of words. *Sure is, Doc. Dead fucking meat.* "Yes sir."

"I have your word on this?"

Dane lifted his head and looked into the doctor's eyes. For a moment he imagined himself going ballistic, flipping the desk, tossing chairs, and trashing the tiny office. Maybe even choking the doc with his own tie and slamming him into the floor, stomping the life from his body. It would be so easy, like sliding a foot off the brake pedal or removing a finger from a hole where water gushed. The rage was always there. It took neither summoning nor effort to bring it forth. Constraining it was the hard part. *That's* what took effort.

But Ponder was right. He was too close to fuck it up now. He could smell the finish line.

"You've got my word, Doc," said Dane, "and I apologize for letting you down. It was nothing serious in the first place."

The doctor studied him a moment before finally nodding. Dane noticed how the hard lines in his face softened as the tension went out of the room. He needed Ponder. Without him there would be no sense in even going in front of the parole board. He'd be laughed right out of the room. *A known white supremacist doing life with a mandatory quarter for murder? Good luck with that.* But with a black psychologist testifying that he was a changed man, a rehabilitated man, anything was possible. Even freedom.

~

Some young men spend their twenty-first birthdays in bars ordering alcohol for the first time. Some have parties or quiet family get-togethers. Some are too busy fighting wars overseas to celebrate at all. CJ began his first day as a twenty-one-year-old with a bottle of bleach and a scrub brush.

As he crossed the hall to the bedding area, he glanced over at the nurses' station. The orange chair that normally squeaked and groaned in protest beneath the oppressive weight of Mrs. Carroll's wide ass was empty. The absence of her scowling face was all the birthday present he needed. But he knew it wouldn't last. She was probably downstairs smoking and would be back any minute. *Mean old bitch.*

He walked quietly down the aisle of the snoring unit toward the mildewed showers in the back. There were no curtains to hide the black fungus that crept along the grout between the small tiles. The showers *were* filthy. He doused them with pure bleach and started on the floors.

~

Forty carried a stack of blankets across the hallway of Two East. The crazy bull-dagger that worked the desk was on the back patio gossiping with the rest of the nurses. He spotted her on the way in. He had five minutes, maybe. There was no time to fuck around.

He stepped through the doorway of the wing and set the folded blankets on the first nightstand he came to. Then, he reached down the front of his pants and withdrew the knife. He had sharpened it the night before and added an extra boot string to the handle for grip.

The rhythmic, abrasive sound of a scrub brush grated from the bathroom in the back of the unit.

Forty stretched his neck left, then right, loosening the tension as he walked down the aisle with the knife clenched in his fist.

~

CJ's face was already pouring sweat, the muscles in his shoulders burned, and the surface of the floor felt like nails in his kneecaps. He raked the scrub brush back and forth across the dirty tiles, chipping away at the caked mildew.

The acoustics in the shower were incredible. The sound of the bristles scratching the floor enveloped him. Slowly a pattern emerged from the random noise, a familiar beat. Suddenly he was no longer in a prison shower. He was in the studio. He began bobbing his head to the rhythm of the scrub brush. The pain in his shoulders and knees disappeared. An imaginary crowd roared before him. A spotlight fell over him. He stared down at his hands and began to freestyle.

These hands have smacked so many asses
Held a few glasses, caught a few passes
They're some of the fastest
They're quick when they're working on shatterin' jaws
Quicker when they're workin' on unfastenin' bras
Broke a few laws but I—

Movement in his peripheral caused him to go still. Out of the corner of his eye he noticed a reflection slip across the steel-plated mirror over the sink. He knew he was probably imagining shit. The mirror was so scratched up and worn that he couldn't recognize himself in it, much less another person. Still he watched it for a moment longer. Just to be sure. He was gonna be embarrassed as hell if Mrs. Carroll was out there listening. He stood to give his knees a break.

~

Forty froze halfway down the aisle. The scrubbing had stopped. The unit was silent. A sink dripped. He dropped to the floor and knelt between two bunks, watching the entrance to the bathroom from beneath the bed frames. Above him on either side, two old men slept peacefully, oblivious to the fact that a killer crouched below them. Their snoring reminded him of the call and response of animals communicating in the night. He shook his head and smiled. *Goddamn, Forty, you been watchin' way too much* National Geographic. He glanced up at the nightstand and noticed a fake leg rising from a dusty boot behind the lamp.

Suddenly there was movement at the end of the aisle. His neck swiveled back in the direction of the bathroom. He could see the bottom half of a figure standing in the entrance, bathed in yellow light. He clutched the handle of the knife and held his breath.

~

CJ looked out over the sleeping unit. No Mrs. Carroll. *Good,* he thought, mopping the sweat from his brow with a shirt sleeve. His eyes darted from bed to bed. He paused on the empty gray mattress where Gina used to sleep. He was gonna miss the old sissy. He started off wanting to hate him, but in the end he just couldn't. There was no reason to. He wondered if anyone on the street cared that he was dead.

He looked over at Smoke bundled in his blankets and sleeping soundly. His pale bald head rose slightly, then plummeted back into the pillow with every ragged breath. He was growing weaker by the minute. He almost seemed to be shriveling even as CJ watched. Fading. But that was on the outside. *Appearances are bullshit, CJ, consider the dragonfly.* Inside he was as sturdy as ever.

All his life CJ had envied toughness, yet here in the crippled, cancer-ridden body of a dying old man in prison was the real deal. Not the manufactured hardness and loudmouth posturing that was actually rooted in fear. Smoke feared nothing. Not even death.

How long until he's gone too?

CJ slammed the door on that thought, not allowing it to breathe. It flew right back open.

"Only twenty percent of patients diagnosed with pancreatic cancer are still living after one year."

He couldn't bear the thought of the old man dying. Smoke was more than just a friend. He was a grandfather, a teacher, a way-shower. He was the smartest person CJ knew and the most honest. There was never a hidden agenda with Smoke or even an unkind word. He was family. And he was dying.

CJ turned and walked back to the shower. The floor was covered with grimy, dirty water. He pressed a button on the wall, and water rained down, washing away the filth and giving him a clear view of his progress.

Not bad, he thought as he poured more bleach on the floor and sank to his knees. The sound of wet bristle on the tile echoed off the walls. There was no beat this time. No rhythm, no pattern, no rap. He just wanted to work until his shoulders screamed and his knees bled and the steady reverberation of the scrub bush drowned out the fearful voice in his head.

~

Forty stood and looked around. The entire unit remained asleep. He glanced back at the entrance to ensure no one was there before stepping out into the aisle. A loud fart trumpeted from a nearby bed, causing him to jump. He spun and pointed the knife in the direction of the noise.

Nasty old muthafuckers.

He turned and walked up the aisle. The sound of scrubbing grew louder with his every step. A droplet of sweat trickled down the blade of the knife. Just beyond the yellow light of the bathroom, superimposed over the back wall, a hunched shadow was cast. Forty watched the repetitive movement of the profile as the scouring continued.

Good job, white boy, he thought, squeezing the knife handle. *Just keep it up for a few more minutes.*

He stopped at a bed with the number 209 stenciled on the headboard. The old man who lay in it looked different than he did a few months ago. *Like a hairless cat,* thought Forty as he stepped between the beds.

The relentless scrubbing in the bathroom paused. Forty glanced over at the shadow. It resumed almost instantly. Louder. He quickly surveyed the rest of the unit before turning his attention back to the pitiful old man in front of him.

He's damn near dead already. Why the hell would Dane spend a grand on killing somebody with one foot in the grave?

Forty shook his head, then shrugged. He slammed his left hand over the old man's mouth. His eyes popped open and widened at the sight of the raised knife. He tensed. Stiffened. Almost struggled. Then, strangely, he relaxed and shut his eyes, tilting his head back, submitting to destiny.

Forty frowned, hesitating a second before driving the knife deep into the exposed throat of the old man. Upon working it free, he brought it down again and again, shutting his eyes and plunging randomly until he was certain it was over.

Finished, he stepped away from the punctured, blood-soaked body and examined himself. He was relatively clean, except for his hands. He reached down and wiped them on the foot of the bed, then hurried back down the aisle.

He stashed the knife within the folds of the stack of blankets he brought with him, then hefted the load and walked quickly out into the hall.

He could still hear scrubbing as he escaped down the stairs.

~

CJ was pouring sweat. He dropped the scrub brush on the floor and stood to stretch. His kneecaps were numb and his neck was cramping. He needed a cigarette. *It's gotta be getting close to lunchtime,* he thought. He washed his hands and walked out into the unit, squinting up at the clock on the far wall. It wasn't even nine o'clock. *Damn.*

He was surprised Smoke wasn't up reading or meditating yet. Even though the radiation and chemo were taking their toll, he was still usually the first one awake. He looked over at his friend's bed. He was turned on his side, facing the other direction with the wool blanket covering his back. CJ could barely make out the top of his head in the dim lighting. Two East was cool and bathed in shadows in the mornings. The windows faced west, so the sunshine never came before *Days of Our Lives* was on, Hippie's favorite show.

CJ stared at Smoke's back. *Was he breathing?* He shook his head and berated himself for being so paranoid. *Of course he's breathing, dumbass, but he won't be for long if you keep smothering him.*

He turned to walk back to the bathroom but hesitated. He glanced back over his shoulder. Something was wrong. He wasn't moving at all. No labored breathing, no wheezing, no snoring. He was never so still. CJ reversed course and walked down the aisle to his bed.

There was blood on the floor. The room tilted. A minor chord sounded in his head. He looked up at Smoke. There were gashes in his face, throat, and chest. Holes were ripped in his flesh. Some still managed to pump blood, however weakly, over his soaked sheets.

CJ leaped onto the bed.

"Smoke?" he called, patting his torn face. "No . . . God . . . please." He laid his head against Smoke's bony chest, listening for a heartbeat, praying for a heartbeat, but his body was cold and quiet. When CJ pulled away, half of his own face was smeared with blood.

"Who did this?" he cried before screaming over his shoulder. "Mrs. Carroll! Help!" He cradled Smoke's head in his hands and started to rock back and forth. "Who did this? Oh God. Please no. Mrs. Carroll! Come on, Smoke, don't die, man. Please don't die. Mrs. Carroll!"

The other patients began to shift in their blankets, and those who were able, sat up. Mrs. Carroll rounded the corner full speed and slid to a stop in the aisle when she saw CJ and Smoke.

"Please," CJ cried, "help him."

Mrs. Carroll fumbled for the black box attached to the waistline of her scrubs as she took in the grisly scene. She found the white button and jammed her thumb in it repeatedly, sending a distress signal throughout the prison. The rumbling sound of onrushing boots filled the hallway within seconds.

CJ glared at the frozen nurse.

"Goddamn it," he roared, "do something!"

Chapter 18

Dr. Garvin Ponder sat back in his chair and rubbed his bloodshot eyes. He looked up at the popcorn ceiling of his study. Just above him on the other side of the sheetrock, his beautiful Elizabeth was sleeping in their bed. Alone.

He stood and stretched before walking over to his bookcase. He reached behind the fern on the top shelf and grabbed the pack of Kools. He felt sneaky for continuing to smoke after promising his wife that he'd quit, and to his credit he had cut way down. But occasionally, especially when something was gnawing at him like tonight, a healthy shot of nicotine was just what the doctor ordered. He switched on the oscillating fan and cracked the window, then sat down and fired up.

He glanced at the green folder lying open on his desk and blew a dismissive cloud of smoke in its direction. Dane Baker had been dropping hints for months about his upcoming parole hearing, fishing for a recommendation. Ponder played along for research purposes and, to be fair, some progress had been made, but there was no way he was risking his career and reputation on a thug like Dane Baker. It wasn't because of his beliefs; every race had fringe elements and xenophobes. Racism was not against the law and Ponder was too professional to take ignorance personally. The reason he could not, in good conscience, recommend Dane for parole was because he was a sociopath, capable of killing with the cool detachment of someone buttering a piece of toast.

But it was McCallister who dominated his thoughts. Not Baker.

The brutal stabbing of the old man in the hospital just seemed so out of character for him. So random. All the data he had gleaned regarding McCallister suggested borderline personality issues, anti-social behavior, and of course, his mother's suicide was well documented. There was also psychosis and chemical dependency on his father's side of the family. His genes were far from unblemished and he would never qualify as a poster child for mental health. But murder? Heinous, cold-blooded, premeditated murder? That just struck him as something that fell beyond the scope of McCallister's particular skill set.

A thought hit Ponder. He clamped his teeth down on the filter of his Kool and leaned forward, rapidly tapping a few keys on his computer.

The advent of the Internet was a godsend. Gone were the days where hours were squandered poring over dated microfilm at the local library or waiting weeks for a response from the Division of Vital Statistics. Even the most obscure information was literally a few keystrokes away, and the volume was multiplying exponentially with each passing day.

The face sheet of Ulysses Griffith appeared on the screen. Ponder studied it for the tenth time that week. He was so familiar with it by now that he could see it in his sleep. It was the eyes that got him. Prison life could literally change the bone structure of a man's face. Harden it. Mr. Griffith was no exception. His jaw was set, his chin jutted, and the space between his eyebrows was permanently creased from years of scowling.

But his eyes sang a different song.

Smiling was strictly prohibited when being photographed by the Department of Corrections. Ponder had spent more than a few afternoons over in receiving where the new inmates were photographed. Any sign of a grin, any hint of a smirk, would result in a stern reprimand and a do-over. More than a couple of do-overs usually netted the jovial photographee a trip to confinement. No one smiled there.

He wondered how many times Mr. Griffith's picture had been taken before the photographer finally gave up. It was the eyes. They just . . .

twinkled. Kindness, mirth, and warmth radiated outward from them. They were their own source of light.

Sure that's not the light of insanity you're seeing?

He took a last drag and stubbed out his cigarette on an empty Coke can. He scrolled down. There was still no mention of his death on the website. The system hadn't been updated in almost a week.

Ponder was not a forensic psychologist, and although the field fascinated him, he had no aspirations of changing careers this late in the game. He was not trying to solve a murder. He'd leave that to the Inspector's Office.

It was McCallister's involvement that intrigued him. In spite of the fact that he was found at the scene, covered in the old man's blood, Ponder's gut told him that the troubled young inmate was not responsible. The other men on the wing seemed to share his opinion. When he did a walk-through of the unit to ensure the murder didn't have any dangerous psychological repercussions on the other patients, they were very vocal about McCallister's innocence. They claimed he loved Ulysses Griffith.

Like a father.

He scrolled down further. The information was the same as last night and the night before: *No aliases, no priors, one count of first degree murder out of Alachua County, sentenced to natural life.* He sat back in his chair and rolled his head in circles, feeling his neck crack and pop as the tension ebbed. The dusty monitor looked fuzzy. He was starting to see double. He blinked a couple of times and massaged his eyes in his palms. He was just about to shut it down for the night when a word toward the bottom of the screen made him pause.

Detainer.

There was a small box next to the word with an X inside of it. Ponder reached for his mouse and clicked on the X. He wondered how on earth he'd missed it, then realized it was probably because it was buried in two long paragraphs of departmental jargon in a small font at the end of the page. The crucial information, the data he now knew by heart, was all up by the picture: scars, marks, tattoos, length of sentence, date of sentence, last known address, emergency contact.

This was something different. Something new. It might be nothing, but in March of '75, a detainer was issued for Mr. Griffith. He was wanted in Lincoln County, Indiana.

~

Ruth Carroll was pissed. She had been standing outside the door of the Inspector's Office for at least forty-five minutes. She stared down at the ashtray. Five white cigarette butts, all hers, lay gnarled and bent in the sand. She reached in her pocket for another just as the door opened.

"He'll see you now, sweetie," said the receptionist.

Mrs. Carroll withdrew her hand and marched into the office "Second door on the right, honey," the sweet country voice chirped from behind her.

She stopped at the hallway entrance and turned slowly toward the receptionist, then snatched off her ID tag and stomped back to her desk. She shoved it in her face.

"My name ain't Sweetie," she snapped, "and it sure as hell ain't Honey."

The receptionist winced.

"It's Ruth Carroll or just plain old 'Nurse' will be fine if you can remember that. Got it?"

The young girl nodded profusely.

"Good."

She remained leaning over the desk for a few moments with a lingering scowl. Finally she turned and strode down the hall. When she came to the second door, she rapped her knuckles against the wood. Out of the corner of her eye she saw the receptionist jump. She smirked.

"Come on in, Ruthie," said a voice.

Inspector Chandler Mason was sitting in front of a television holding a remote.

She cut straight to the point. "He didn't do it, Mason."

"Who didn't do it?" the inspector asked.

She rolled her eyes. "Don't play games. You know damn well who. The kid. McCallister. My orderly."

He glanced at her. "I know he didn't. Come take a look at this."

She grabbed a chair. "If you know he didn't do it, then why is he still in lockup?"

He looked at her funny. "I was planning on signing him out sometime this week. If that's agreeable to you."

"Hmmph," she muttered, plopping down next to him.

He aimed the remote at the TV and pressed a button. "Watch."

The picture was grainy black and white with a horizontal line of snow rolling repetitively up the screen. She recognized the location. It was the hallway of Two East. A figure appeared in the doorway of the bedding area. His upper torso and face were concealed behind a stack of blankets.

"This is our guy," said Mason, pausing the video. "Do you recognize him?"

She shot him a look.

"I'm kidding."

"You don't have a better camera angle?"

He shook his head. "This is the best we've got."

She leaned forward.

"See his hands?" asked Mason.

"He's black."

"Very perceptive," said the inspector. "That narrows the pool of suspects down to about seven hundred people. Now I need you to think, Ruthie, have you noticed anyone suspicious on your floor lately?"

She thought about it hard before finally shaking her head.

"He had blankets. Who brings the laundry up?"

"Believe me, that ain't him," she said, jerking her head at the TV. "Our laundry man's about four hundred pounds."

"All right," he said, pressing the power button on the remote. "Well, if you think of anything, give me a call."

She stood and moved toward the door.

"And Ruth."

She turned.

"I can't let McCallister work for you again."

Her eyes narrowed. "Now you listen here, you—"

He raised his hand, palm out. "It's against procedure. He's part of the investigation. I could lose my job."

She slammed the door behind her and stormed down the hall.

"Asshole," she muttered.

~

Dane Baker was in good spirits. Ponder could tell. It wasn't something as easily noticed as a smile. The humongous convict rarely smiled anyway. This was much more subtle and harder to pinpoint. The cumulative effect of body language, speech pattern, and energy. He also understood how volatile Dane was and how rapidly those conditions could deteriorate.

He took a deep breath and discreetly fingered the edge of the distress button clipped to his belt. The game had to stop today. Continuing would be a violation of his own code of ethics. In his defense he had never once promised Dane anything. He just wanted to delve into the dark psyche of the killer. A place that none of his colleagues had been able to explore. But Dane Baker had found hope in his vague, noncommittal responses, and Ponder knew it was wrong to dangle freedom just beyond his outstretched hand. Freedom that, in truth, would never be realized. His own principles were being compromised. How did the quote go? "When fighting monsters, one must take care not to become a monster himself in the process."

Have I become one of Friedrich Nietzsche's famous monsters? he wondered as he stared across his desk at the giant lifer.

Dane stared back.

Ponder cleared his throat. "I have some . . . well, some rather unfortunate news."

Dane leaned forward. "I'm listening."

Ponder broke eye contact and looked at the dirty window behind him, still lightly stroking the panic button on his belt. He exhaled. "Dane, I'm sorry. I can't make a recommendation either way at your parole hearing."

There. He said it. It was out. He felt liberated. He glanced at Dane. A reddish-purple tide had crept from his collar, climbed his bulging, veiny neck, and was spreading across the tight skin of his face.

"Why the fuck not?" Dane exploded.

Ponder flinched. "It's my boss," he lied. "He instructed me not to get involved. I'm sorry."

"Fuck that!" said Dane, trembling with rage and breathing heavily. Ponder kept his thumb on the button but didn't press it. "Dane. Please. Try to calm—"

"What boss? You're the head of mental health."

"My boss is the State of Florida," Ponder said. "That's who signs my paychecks. Listen, I know you're upset. I would be too. But you've come too far to turn back. This is just your first hearing. Everybody gets set off on their first hearing, right?"

Dane stared down at the carpet.

Ponder's thumb eased off the panic button. "You just have to keep doing what you're doing and who knows? Maybe things will be different by the time your next hearing rolls around."

"What if I cooperated?" mumbled Dane.

"I'm sorry?"

Dane raised his head. "I said what if I cooperated? You know, provided assistance. Snitched. Would that change your *boss's* mind?"

He said the word *boss's* with a smirk and offered up the question with the knowing arrogance of a wealthy patron flashing a twenty at his waiter in exchange for a better table in a restaurant. His sudden shift from raging powder keg to calm deal-broker caught Ponder off balance.

"What sort of information?"

Dane folded his arms over his chest and rocked back in the tiny blue chair. "About the murder up in the hospital last week."

Ponder swallowed. *Why hadn't he thought of Dane in the first place? He was only the most dangerous man on the compound.*

"I know what you're thinking, Doc." Dane smiled. "It wasn't me. I'm sure good ol' Inspector Mason has watched the tape a thousand times by now. Those hands holding that stack of blankets were black. Right? Blacker than yours even." He paused and held up two massive fists. "These are still snow white as ever."

"What exactly do you know, Dane?"

"Oh, not much," he said, bringing the front legs of his chair down and leaning forward, "just the name of the killer and the spot where he stashed the knife."

"And how do you know these things?"

Dane smiled. "This is my compound. I've got eyes everywhere. Nothing happens inside this fence without me knowing about it."

"And what exactly do you want?"

"Same thing I've always wanted. Your recommendation at my parole hearing. And maybe a few words on how I helped solve a homicide. Top secret, of course."

Ponder twirled his pen between his fingers as he pretended to weigh the pros and cons of the offer. "Okay," he said finally, dropping the pen on his desk, "tell me."

"Wait a minute now, Doc, shouldn't you run our little deal by your boss?"

"I'll handle it."

"Well then, I at least want your word," he pointed a massive finger, "and no fuckery."

Ponder stared at him. Agreeing to this far-fetched, impossible, naïve deal ran contrary to everything he stood for. It was unethical, manipulative, and an utter abuse of power on his part. It would be morally wrong to mislead a delusional patient regardless of motive.

He slowly nodded his head. "You have my word."

. . . and when you look long into an abyss . . . that abyss also looks into you.

CJ lay on his mat and stared up at the graffiti on the empty bunk above him. For some reason he was fascinated by the nicknames, years, cities, and messages that were etched into the green paint. He wondered about all the people who had lived in the cell before him. Who were they? What had they done? Were they still in prison?

Were they still alive?

He blinked and the image of Smoke's limp, blood-soaked body ripped through his mind, causing him to flinch. He made himself focus on the graffiti overhead. His eyes roamed back and forth over the cryptic scribble. There were at least a thousand markings. Over the last eleven days he had made a game of seeking out the oldest date. The current champ was "Stone '72" down at the other end of the bunk. CJ wasn't even born yet in 1972.

A wheel squeaked down the hall. *Nurses' cart,* he thought. He knew the sound from his time on the slab next door to Hustleman. The nurse used to stop at his door every day. That seemed like another life. Before that he only wanted to die. Before that he only wanted to be home with his mom and dad. Before that he only wanted to be cool or tough or anything besides himself. Before that he was simply drifting. Floating. Letting life happen. Each stage felt like a different lifetime; each era foreign and far off. These were the roles Smoke once asked him about.

"All the world is indeed a stage . . ."

Smoke. His father's death hurt, and his mother's suicide was the single most crushing and devastating event in his young life, but finding the old man mutilated in his hospital bed was so shocking, so surreal that he was still trying to grasp what happened. It was like a callus had been ripped from his soul and at any moment a tidal wave of pain would wash over him, but for now he was caught in the hollow silence between cause and effect. Waiting.

The flap on his steel door sprung open and a familiar raspy voice filled his cell.

"McCallister! Front and center!"

He stood and walked barefoot across the cell. Mrs. Carroll was standing outside the door behind a cart. She turned to the guard who was escorting her.

"Give us a little privacy," CJ heard her say. "I need to see this inmate's backside. Anal warts."

The young officer frowned and hurried off.

She bent and peered through the flap. "How's it going in there?"

CJ shrugged. *What the fuck did she care?*

"Well, listen, I ain't any good at stuff like this, but I wanted you to know that I never thought you was guilty. None of the men did neither."

He was speechless. Mrs. Carroll was at his confinement door . . . *and being nice to him.*

"You should be released any day now. They got the one that did it. Bastard. They should be hauling him over from Mason's office sometime this morning."

CJ nodded.

"Well, I just wanted you to know that," she said, tapping her fingers on the door and watching him through her black framed glasses. "You did a good job up there, McCallister. A fine job. Maybe when all this blows over we can get you back."

"Thanks," said CJ, uncomfortable with this new soft side of her.

She looked around before opening a drawer on the med cart and grabbing a book. She quickly slid it through the flap. It fell to the floor.

"From Ryker," she said as she slammed the flap shut and walked away.

The sound of the squeaky cart faded as she moved down the cell block. He picked up the book and glanced at the cover. Birds were soaring from broken chains. It was *We're All Doing Time* by Bo Lozoff. It belonged to Smoke. It was the book Gina used to borrow all the time.

He sat down on his bunk and opened it. A note was written inside the cover.

Dear CJ,

If you're reading this, it means the chemo didn't work. Ha Ha. If I had an estate to leave behind, I would leave it all to you. Unfortunately all I have is this book. I hope it brings you as much peace as it has brought to me over the years. I'm looking forward to meeting your parents up here and telling them what an honorable man you've grown to be. Hopefully someday our paths will cross again. Until then keep your head up, remember the dragonfly, and know that "to live in the hearts of others is to not die."

God Bless and Go Braves,
Always,
Smoke

His eyes brimmed with tears as he stared at the labored handwriting of his friend. She said that Ryker sent the book. He speculated that Smoke wrote the note inside and gave it to him to hold in case of an emergency.

He read the words again.

Nah, Smoke, the chemo was fighting the cancer just fine, he thought. *It just couldn't stop a knife in your throat.*

He lay back in the bunk and thumbed through the pages, staring blankly at the words and pictures, remembering his friend, wondering who killed him, and why.

A door rolled upstairs in the cell above him and slammed shut.

"Hey, Forty!" a voice called through the vent.

CJ turned a page. He hoped whoever moved in above him wasn't a big talker. The ventilation shaft that ran between his cell and the cell next door also extended up between the two cells above him. One loudmouth on the vent could keep everyone awake at night.

"Hey, Forty! This Big Herb from the northside."

Silence. Then a low voice came back through the vent.

"What's up, Herb."

CJ was only half listening as he skimmed over the cartoon examples of yoga poses in the book.

"What they lock you up for, homeboy?"

"Pussy-ass cracker Dane Baker."

CJ set the book on his chest and stared at the vent.

"Y'all fought?" asked Big Herb.

"Naw. He hired me to slump some old man in the hospital, then snitched so he wouldn't have to pay me."

The conversation went on, but the air-raid siren screaming in CJ's head kept him from hearing any more. His teeth were clenched and his fists were balled tight. He swung his legs over the side of the bunk and sat up. Vomit churned in his stomach as he rocked back and forth.

He was so sick of bullies . . . sick of fear . . . sick of hurting . . . sick of losing the people he loved the most . . . his dad, his mom, and now Smoke. Why was it that good people suffered and died horrible deaths while the Dane Bakers of the world, the Alvorados, the Fortys seemed to live on and even multiply?

CJ walked over to the vent.

"Hey, Forty," he called, his tone ice.

"Who's that?" a voice asked.

"My name is CJ McCallister. Remember it. Because after I kill Dane Baker, I'm coming after you, and I don't give a fuck if I have to transfer to every prison in the state. You're gonna pay for what you did."

There was a long silence before Forty finally responded. "Bring it."

A key rapped on CJ's door, causing him to jump.

"McCallister! Get off that damn vent and pack your shit," said the guard. "You're being released back to the compound."

~

The door buzzed as he approached. He pushed it open and stepped into a secure hallway. A camera mounted on the ceiling tracked his movement. He let the door shut behind him and waited. After a few seconds the door in front of him popped open. He slung the pillowcase containing his few property items over his shoulder and walked out into the sunshine.

The fresh air tasted good. A cigarette would taste even better. He scanned the sidewalk for a familiar face.

Getting out of confinement was like getting out of a prison within the prison. On lockdown there was no TV, no canteen, no cigarettes, and no coffee. Just three showers a week, three trays a day, and four walls to stare at the rest of the time. Twenty-four-hour lockdown. At least on the compound there was rec and work, the freedom to move, and the basic amenities of prison life, as trivial as they were.

CJ didn't mind the Spartan solitary conditions of the box, but he had to admit the sunshine sure felt good on his face. He knew he made a pitiful sight. He was thin, pale, unshaven, and the confinement blues he was given were rumpled and paint-stained. A hot shower and a cigarette were the first two orders of business. Then he was going to find a knife.

"CJ?" called a voice from behind him. "CJ McCallister?"

The voice was familiar but he couldn't quite place it. He stopped and turned.

Because the prison functioned as a medical center for the sick and dying, a receiving unit for new commitments and a drop-off/pick-up point for the thousands of inmates already in the system and transferring from one prison to another, Lake Butler was a notorious meeting ground for old friends. And old enemies.

CJ's eyes widened and blinked. He dropped his pillowcase on the sidewalk and shook his head in disbelief. A smile spread across his face.

"No fucking way," he said. "I don't believe it." He extended his hand.

Rick pushed it aside and gave him a hug.

"Damn, white boy," he laughed, "you smell like shit!"

"What are you doing here?" CJ asked.

"Time," he said, releasing him, "same thing you're doing."

"What happened?"

"Long story," said Rick, reaching down to scoop CJ's pillowcase from the concrete and handing it to him. "Let's go to the rec yard. I'll buy you lunch. You look like you haven't ate in a month, come on."

CJ fell in step beside his old friend. There was something magical about bumping into a familiar face hundreds of miles from home, especially in a lonely setting like prison. Something almost healing.

Rick was more than a familiar face. They had fought side by side, robbed together, got high together, they were best friends. Ever since that first day by the soccer field in juvie.

CJ glanced over at him and smiled. Rick was family A long-lost brother.

~

Happiness is happiness. It can't be legislated, restricted, or banned. Even a sentencing judge has no power over it. It's not limited to mountaintops, fair midways, or the beds of lovers. Sometimes it appears in the most dire of circumstances, in the most hopeless of times.

CJ inhaled the final delicious bite of his microwaved chicken sandwich and licked the crumbs from his fingers, then he chugged the rest of his Coke. He burped loudly and set the empty can on the pavement. Rick was watching him. "I remember when you used to be all polite and shit, passin' me your trays in juvie cuz you didn't like eggs or onions. Now you eat like an animal."

"I've been *living* like an animal."

Rick glanced down at his dirty, wrinkled blues. "I see that."

"Well, I haven't bathed much over the last two weeks, or shaved. I've been in confinement."

"I know. I've been waiting for you to get out."

"You knew I was here? How?"

Rick reached in his pocket and pulled out a pack of Newports.

"Oh man," said CJ, "gimme one."

Rick tossed him the box. "When I first got off the bus, I asked about you. That led me to an older cat outta Orlando. Hustleman."

CJ nodded and fired up a Newport.

"He told me you were here. Then he tried to sell me some hemorrhoid cream and some tennis shoes and a do-rag and some naked flicks."

CJ laughed and blew out the smoke. "Yeah, that's Hustle."

"So how much time you got left?"

CJ looked out across the rec yard. "I don't know. Eleven, twelve, something like that. Could be a lot more if I fuck up and lose my gain time." Dane Baker was on the pull-up bar. He watched him a moment before turning to Rick. "How about you? How long do you have?"

"They gave me ten mandatory, but I'm appealing it."

"What happened?"

"Police kicked in the door, lookin' for Kane."

"Wait, Kane got out?"

"Yeah. He beat it in trial. No murder weapon and the only witness disappeared before jury selection. State attorney was thirty-eight hot, been fuckin' with us ever since."

"Damn."

Rick took a drag from his cigarette. "Kane's still hiding out, as far as I know, but they got all us. Found a brick and a half in the freezer, and Ty had a forty-five in his wheelchair. Even Mario got fucked up."

CJ's eyes widened. "I thought he was playing football."

"He was. He got drafted in the second round by the Seahawks. Thirty-fifth overall. But he tore three ligaments in his knee during training camp and got put on I.R., came home with that fat signing bonus, and Ty talked him into investing in the family business. He never went back."

CJ flicked his cigarette out into the grass and shook his head. In his mind, he could see the old house in Perrine. He could picture the people that Rick spoke of and the guns and the coke and the cops. What he could not imagine was himself in that life. Not again.

He glanced over at the pull-up bar. Dane Baker and his cronies were laughing about something. *Laugh while you can, you murdering piece of shit.*

"Do you remember April?" asked CJ.

"Your little girlfriend? From Peaches? Course I remember her."

"Have you seen her?"

"Once. She was workin' at a club out by the airport, dancin'."

CJ sat up straighter. "Naked?"

Rick smirked. "Come on, CJ. What bitch you know dances with her clothes on? Yeah, she was naked! Fine, too."

A pang of yearning flared within him at the memory of April.

"Don't worry," said Rick, "I threw a couple dollars at her for you."

CJ was silent.

After a few moments Rick spoke again. "CJ, I . . . I'm sorry for not keepin' in touch with you—"

"Aw, man, I don't care about that."

"No. I was dead wrong and I'm sorry. I coulda at least sent you some money. It's just that when you were in the county jail, you know . . . I was *with* you in that cop's house. We just thought it would be better if there was no contact. Know what I'm sayin'? Then, one thing led to another and Mario came home, and Kane—"

"It's cool. Plus don't forget you did tell Kane to look out for me."

Rick laughed. "Yeah, that's right. I almost forgot. He told us he had you in there fightin' crackheads and bums."

CJ laughed too. "So are you gonna be a permanent here?"

Rick shook his head. "The paper I got at South Florida said I was classified to go to Century Correctional. I heard my dad is there."

CJ looked at him. "Your dad?"

"He was already locked up when I was born. Where is Century anyway?"

"Panhandle, damn near Alabama. Twelve hours from Miami. That bus runs on Wednesdays."

"Tomorrow."

CJ didn't respond. He was watching Dane Baker head straight toward them from across the yard.

"You all right, man?" Rick asked.

CJ nodded but kept his eyes trained on his enemy. Dane's shirt hung from his back pocket and his massive upper body rippled as he moved in their direction. He was covered in tattoos, but the one that stood out the most was scrawled across his stomach in dark bold letters. It said UNKILLABLE.

We'll see about that, thought CJ.

If a smile could ever be hostile and loaded with unbridled hatred, that was the expression fixed on Dane's face as he approached them. His mouth was pulled tight against his sharp yellow teeth, and his eyes glowered from beneath the overhang of his heavy brow.

"What's up with this?" Rick asked as Dane stomped through the grass to the edge of the pavilion where they were sitting.

He didn't stop. He marched right between CJ and Rick and disappeared into the shuffling throng behind them, like an imminent threatening storm that blew over without even a drop of rain.

CJ reached for another of Rick's cigarettes, his heart pounding in his chest like a speed bag.

"Friend of yours?" asked Rick.

He hated his hand for trembling as he struck the lighter.

"Cee, who was that?"

CJ blew a stream of smoke at the sky. "Remember Duke?"

Rick nodded. "I remember."

"Same shit, different dude."

~

His eyes were shut. The thin skin of his throat was pulled tight. He could feel the buzzing motor vibrating all the way down in his toes as the needle jabbed against his Adam's apple.

"You wanted this," said Bones, pausing to wipe the blood with an ink-stained rag.

CJ felt a shadow hovering over him. He opened one eye.

Hustleman.

"Oh, *now* you wanna come kick it with Hustle and Bones, huh?" said Hustle in his exaggerated manner of speaking.

"Just Bones," said CJ, smiling.

Hustle laughed. "Your homeboy ride this morning?"

"Yeah."

"Well, least you got to see him."

CJ didn't respond. A long, painful line was being shot into his throat as he clenched his teeth and unconsciously pulled away from the insistent needle.

"Stop that!" Bones scolded him.

Hustle sat down on the locker next to the bed. CJ could tell he had something on his mind, even with the painful distraction of Bones's merciless needle puncturing his flesh.

"I think I fucked up," said Hustle.

CJ kept his head still while focusing his eyes on Hustle.

"Almost done," said Bones, "don't move."

"That cat, Forty," said Hustle, "the one they locked up for killin' your friend."

CJ's eyes narrowed.

"That's the same one I sold the knife to," said Hustle. "I'm sorry, man."

CJ tensed. A bolt of memory flashed in his mind. He was rocking Smoke's lifeless body, yelling for help. The room was spinning. There was blood. Then, the scene faded. He relaxed and glanced over at his friend.

"It's not your fault," he finally said. "There's no way you could have known."

Bones paused and dipped the needle into a toothpaste cap full of black ink.

"But I do need a favor," said CJ as the motor began to hum again.

"What's that?" asked Hustle.

"A knife," said CJ, shutting his eyes as the needle returned.

"Aw shit," said Hustle, "here we go again."

"I will pay you," CJ said through his teeth.

"No way," said Hustle. "It ain't happenin'."

The motor shut off and Bones wiped the excess ink and blood from his throat.

"Voila," he said, inspecting his handiwork.

CJ sat up. "Look, those motherfuckers killed my friend. I'm the one who found him. I saw what his body looked like—"

"They already got the one who did it," hissed Hustleman.

"He was a fucking pawn."

Hustle looked up at the ceiling and slowly shook his head. Bones dug a small scratched mirror out of his locker and passed it to CJ, who used it for emphasis as he spoke.

"What if it was you they stabbed?" He pointed the mirror at Hustle. "Wouldn't you want some get-back? Some revenge?"

Hustle was quiet.

"Well, it wouldn't matter what you wanted," said CJ, "cuz there's no way I could smell myself if I let that slide. I'm doing this. With or without your help."

They locked gazes. CJ could feel the blood from his fresh tattoo streaming over his collarbone and down his chest. He made no move to wipe it. He continued staring stubbornly into the face of his closest confidant and friend until Hustle finally exhaled and looked away.

"Damn, you a stiff-necked white boy!" he said.

CJ didn't budge.

"Okay," said Hustle, nodding. "If you sure this what you want, I got you."

"Thanks."

"But hold up," said Hustle, raising a palm, "you can't just go buck-wild in the yard chasin' people 'round with knives. We do this *my* way. Understand?"

CJ nodded at his own reflection as he held up the mirror and examined his newest tattoo. Beautiful and ominous, it spanned the entire breadth of his throat. He raised his chin to see it better. A smile lit his face.

"What the hell is that thing anyway?" asked Hustle.

"A dragonfly," said CJ.

Chapter 19

The coffee was black and strong. Its rich aroma filled the small study as steam poured off the rim of the mug. Ponder reached for it and attempted a sip while staring at his computer screen. Still too hot. He set it back down. The Department had finally updated the website and there was now a red "Deceased" stamp over the face sheet of Ulysses Griffith. The red word slashed diagonally across his face like a laceration.

Although McCallister was no longer a suspect and had been released from confinement, there were still some nagging questions revolving around the murder on Two East. Marcus Reed, or "Forty" as Dane called him, was the killer. There was little doubt of that. But why? Where was the motive? The Inspector's Office didn't seem to care now that they had a weapon and a suspect that matched the tape, but Garvin Ponder was not satisfied. The more he thought about it, the more convinced he became that Dane Baker was involved. He was not buying Dane's explanation that his intimate knowledge of the murder was based on his "eyes all over the compound." The problem was that there was no evidence that Dane had a motive either.

If only Reed would talk, thought Ponder as he scrolled down through the information under Griffith's photograph. His cursor settled near the box marked "Detainer." He clicked on the X. *Lincoln County, Indiana.* He reached for his coffee again.

Suddenly a snippet of conversation from a session with Dane Baker months ago played in his head.

"I think that I was eight at the time, might've been seven though, I'm not real sure."

"Here?"

"Crystal River. We moved down from Indiana maybe a year before."

Ponder almost spilled his coffee in his lap. He sat up straight and scrolled back to the top of the screen. The picture stared back at him. He remembered the scar Dane showed him, the cigar burns, the neighbor's dog, the horror stories of his childhood. He cocked his head to the side and searched the photo for resemblance.

"We moved down from Indiana maybe a year before."

He looked at the face behind the red "Deceased" stamp. *Could it be?* The last names were different, but that didn't matter. People changed names all the time. He glanced at the old man's date of birth and did some quick math in his head. Dane Baker was eighteen years old when he was charged with murder in 1971. He was now almost forty-three. Ulysses Griffith was born on November 5, 1928. The ages definitely lined up.

He knocked his chair over as he rushed to the file cabinet in the corner. He kept a personal folder on Dane Baker in his study with a running commentary on his progress. Stacked in the front and back pockets of the file were twenty-five years' worth of his colleagues' notes on the killer, as well as every bit of data he could find regarding his trial. There wasn't much of the latter, but he distinctly remembered a few laminated newspaper articles that he inherited from his predecessor. He tore through the file in search of them now.

There were three in all, but only two of the articles included a picture. One was of Dane Baker in cuffs and shackles being escorted by deputies across a parking lot. The other was a shot of the courtroom audience. This was what he was looking for. He scanned the faces along the front row, then paused and shook his head in wonder.

He ran back to his computer and held the newspaper photo next to Ulysses Griffith's D.O.C. mug shot. There was no question. The man sitting on the front row at Dane's murder trial and the old man who was stabbed to death on Two East were one and the same. And he just happened to have an outstanding warrant in Indiana, the same state Dane Baker's father was from. *There's your motive,* thought Ponder, *revenge. For eighteen years of abuse.*

He picked up the phone and dialed information. "Can I get the number of the Lincoln County Indiana Sheriff's Department?"

~

CJ and Hustle sat on the edge of the concrete at the far end of the pavilion, a couple of feet from where he and Rick sat a few days before. CJ glanced over at the exact spot.

Did that really happen? That day had an otherworldly, dreamlike quality about it, like two people from parallel universes meeting briefly on an astral plane. Actually the entire month had been surreal, beginning with the murder of Smoke.

He flinched. The powerful memory of finding his friend butchered and bleeding in his hospital bed tore through CJ with all the force and clamor of a runaway freight train. Gripping, consuming, thundering in his ears. Then just as quickly, the roar faded into a distant tremor and the clanging died away. Then silence.

A bird chirped from the roof of the pavilion.

"You watchin'?" asked Hustle.

"Yeah," CJ said, glancing over at the two guards by the basketball court.

"Not just them," said Hustle, "don't let nobody walk up on me. These snitchin'-ass inmates are just as poisonous as the police."

The abrasive sound of metal rubbing concrete filled CJ's ears. He reached in his pocket for the yellow pouch of loose tobacco and slapped it against his knee.

"Roll two," said Hustle as he continued to sharpen the knife.

CJ leaned forward and looked at the weapon. It was more like an ice pick than a blade, a thin metal rod that was filed to a point, long enough to go through a man. He shivered and gulped as a tide of doubt swelled within him. *Could he really do this?*

He thought of Smoke.

Damn right, he could.

He lit a cigarette and passed it to Hustle, who stopped long enough to take a drag before sticking it in the side of his mouth and getting back to work.

"Almost done," he said.

CJ didn't respond. He fired up his own cigarette and surveyed the yard. The fresh ink on his throat itched. He brushed the back of his finger against it. The dragonfly was his most visible piece. All his other work was hidden beneath his shirt. For a while he had harbored the hope that maybe, *just maybe,* he could get out and do something with his life. He still had the letter from Mr. Ramos promising him a job. He opted not to get a tattoo beyond his elbows for that reason.

Smoke's murder changed everything. The dragonfly tat was not only a tribute to a dead friend, it was a middle finger to the world. His last line of defense had fallen. The transformation was complete. This was his life. Prison. He was a convict.

"You spacin' out again," said Hustle. "You sure you wanna do this, man?"

CJ looked him in the eye and nodded.

Hustle ashed on the concrete. "You remember where to hit him?"

"Throat, chest, ribs, stomach."

"That's right," said Hustle, "but watch out for the chest. Lotta bone up in there, hard to get through, but if you do, make sure you go in on his left side. There's a spot 'bout six inches down from his armpit, straight shot to his heart, like butter."

CJ glanced down at the knife. Hustle was holding it low, on the side of his leg. The sun glinted off the metal.

Hustle's voice hardened. "After you stick his ass, you twist and rip, you hear me?"

CJ nodded.

"Here," said Hustle, sliding the knife across the pavement.

CJ stuck it under his shirt.

"All right, so let's say you do this, and you joog his ass ten, twenty, fifty times. He's layin' over there in the dirt, bleedin', dyin', whata you do next?"

"I find you."

"It won't be hard. I'll be right there. Try to pass me the knife as smooth as you can, but don't sweat that too much. Just get it to me. I'll take it from there."

CJ nodded.

"Then what?"

"I go to the bathroom under the pavilion and find the bleach—"

"Under the second sink."

"I wash up real good, strip off my blues—"

"And leave 'em anywhere," said Hustle.

"And I walk out wearing shorts and a t-shirt."

"There'll be an extra shirt under the sink with the bleach, in case yours has any blood on it. Make sure you go straight to the track when you come out. Try to blend. Start walkin', or jog if you can. You'll just be another white boy on the rec yard exercising."

CJ took a last drag from his cigarette and exhaled heavily.

"You know," said Hustle, "you don't have to do this. Ain't no shame in changin' your mind." He paused and looked sympathetically at CJ. Then his features hardened. "But once you poke him with that steel, you can't turn back. Ain't no sayin' 'excuse me' and runnin' off. You gotta finish the job. Then you gotta live with the fact that you killed a man for the rest of your life."

CJ stared down at the ground for a moment before slowly turning to Hustle.

"No problem."

~

The static roar of the crowd at Joe Robbie Stadium droned from the speaker on his TV. The Dolphins were blowing out the Jets. Marino had been pulled and was smiling on the sideline. Garvin Ponder's eyes fluttered shut and his breathing deepened as he nodded off on the couch.

The phone rang. He reached back over the arm of the sofa and groped blindly for the phone on the end table.

"Hello."

"Is this Garvin Ponder?" a gruff southern voice asked.

"Yes it is," he said with a yawn. "Who's speaking?"

"What kind of name is Garvin anyway?"

He frowned and glanced at this watch. "I'm sorry, sir, I didn't catch your name."

"Fred Burnett, Lincoln County Sheriff's Department, Warrants Division. You left me a message last week."

Ponder sat up so fast that he nearly snatched the phone jack from the wall.

"Good afternoon, sir," he said, reaching for the pen and pad on the coffee table. "I just have a few questions."

"Are you some type of reporter?"

"Not at all," said Ponder. "I'm a psychologist. I work at the prison down here in Lake Butler, Florida."

"A psychologist? Hell, that's worse than a reporter!"

Ponder laughed. "Thanks. Listen, I was calling about an old warrant you guys issued."

"How old are we talking about?" There was a smile in the man's voice. "I've only been working in this basement for the last thirty-seven years."

Ponder gave a low whistle. "Sounds like I may have found my man then. We had an inmate down here who had a detainer in your county. Ulysses Griffith."

"Whoa, what do you mean *had?* That warrant is still active."

Ponder looked at the phone. "I take it you're familiar with the case?"

"Hell, who ain't? It's not often that our little town has a beheading. In fact, I can't remember one before or since your Mr. Griffith came along. You didn't release him, did you?"

"Not exactly. He was murdered."

"I figured that was coming. It's a miracle he made it this long."

"I was wondering if you had any aliases or AKAs listed on his file."

"I can check for you, but your own agencies probably have more info on him than we do since he was from down there. He's never even been arrested in Indiana."

"Actually, he was originally from Indiana."

"If you say so. Is there an alias you think he may have used in the past? I can check that for you."

"I believe his real name may have been Baker. He was the leader of some sort of white supremacist group."

The phone went quiet.

"You're kidding, right?" asked Burnett.

"Not at all," said Ponder.

"Well, then you're confused. Floyd Baker *was* the leader of an Aryan splinter group. 'The Confederate Front' they called themselves. You got that part right. There are still a few members around town, I suspect. But Ulysses Griffith ended Baker's life with the blade of an axe. That's what the warrant was for. Murder. As far as I know Griffith never tried to steal his identity."

Ponder struggled to process this new information. He couldn't quite get his mind around what the old cop was telling him. He aimed the remote at the TV and silenced it with a swift jab of his thumb.

"Did this Floyd Baker have any children?" Ponder asked.

"Seems like he might've had a boy, but I can't say for sure," said Burnett. "He spent a lot of time out of state."

Ponder was scribbling furiously on his pad. After a few moments of silence Burnett finally spoke. "Well, if there's not anything else I can help you with . . ."

Ponder underlined a final word and grabbed the phone from the crook of his neck. "Listen, Mr. Burnett—"

"It's Fred."

"Fred, thank you. May I contact you again if I have another question?"

"Anytime, Dr. Ponder."

"It's Garvin."

He laughed. "Anytime then . . . *Garvin.*"

They exchanged good-byes and hung up.

Ponder still felt as if he'd been punched in the temple. Then slowly, his scrambled brain began to regroup and organize itself. He stared down at his notes.

So Griffith was not Dane Baker's father after all, he thought. *He was his father's killer.*

~

Although breakfast was served before dawn, CJ didn't go back to sleep when his dorm returned from the chow hall. Instead, he removed his shorts and t-shirt from his locker along with the paint-stained blues he was given when he was released from confinement and quickly changed clothes. After tying his shoes with double knots, he grabbed the book Smoke had given him from under his pillow and lay back to read as the sun came up.

Out of all the prisoners featured in the letters section of Bo Lozoff's *We're All Doing Time,* CJ's favorite was Maury. Maury was a big, mean-looking convict from the Oklahoma prison system in the 1970s. CJ laughed at his rants, shared his distrust of the human race, and thought his artwork was badass. It was obvious from his letters to Bo that Maury took zero shit and feared no one. Sadly there was no happy ending for him. No transformative spiritual awakening. He died in a prison shower, stabbed to death. *Just like Smoke.*

The sun shone through the slatted windows across the dorm. Some of his neighbors were beginning to stir. He set the book down and reached over the head of his bed, removing a square of baseboard from along the wall and fumbling around in the space behind it. After a moment of groping blindly, his fingers finally found what they were seeking and wrapped around the handle of the shank. A remnant of a conversation he had with Smoke not long before he was killed, echoed through his memory.

"Promise me that after you return that to your buddy, you'll never touch another knife."

"I promise."

He hated breaking his word, especially to Smoke. But this had to be done. People had missions in life. Destinies. His was to scrub the earth clean of the festering sore that was Dane Baker. He was no longer running from that truth. If anything, he embraced it.

~

Ponder couldn't see the inspector's eyes, but he sensed the controlled burning of contempt flickering behind the dark lenses of his Ray-Bans as he approached. The feeling was mutual. Chandler Mason was a pretty boy. He favored pastel shirts and ties, his hair was perpetually moussed, and his teeth were a brilliant white. Ponder held that if Mason spent as much time pursuing predatory inmates and crooked guards as he did plucking his flawless eyebrows, the prison would be a much safer place.

Ponder had been waiting outside his locked office for twenty minutes.

"Morning, Garvin," he said, reaching for his keys. "What brings you down here so early? Shouldn't you be off somewhere trying to *understand* our murderers and pedophiles?" He pronounced the word *understand* with disdain as if it were a crusty sock or a dead fish rotting in the sun.

Ponder resisted the urge to fire back with a cocky response. "Good morning, Chandler," he said, following him through the empty waiting area and down the hall to his office. "Actually I've got some more information on the Griffith murder I thought you might want to hear."

Ponder remained standing in the doorway as Mason tossed his briefcase in an empty chair and sat down behind his desk. He removed his sunglasses and glared at Ponder.

"More classified information from your confidential informant?" he sneered. "This guy's got the inside scoop on everything. Maybe he knows where Hoffa's buried too. Hell, you need to ask him who killed JFK next time you talk with him."

A tiny muscle in Ponder's face began to twitch as he stared back at the inspector. This was all about pride for Mason. He was pissed because Ponder wouldn't reveal his source, because the killer and the murder weapon were found before he barely began his investigation. By a psychologist, no less.

Ponder couldn't resist a small barb. "Let's not forget that without my confidential informant, you'd have nothing right now."

Mason's voice was cold. "Say what you have to say and get the fuck out of my office."

Ponder crossed his arms and leaned against the doorframe. "You've got some anger issues, Mason. Ever thought about talking to a psychologist?"

He pointed a manicured finger at Ponder. "You're pushing it, Doctor. You hear me? Believe me, you do not want me for an enemy. I can have you transferred so deep in the panhandle you'll need a John Deere to get to work. Now if there's something you have to say, then say it, but if you're only here to gloat, I'd be careful if I were you."

Ponder nodded and took a step inside the office. "Well, in order for this to make any sense to you, first I guess I need to tell you the name of my informant."

Mason raised an eyebrow. "I'm listening."

"Are you familiar with Dane Baker?"

"Sure," said the inspector, "highest ranking member of the Aryan fold. I've got a file on him, been quiet for the last few years."

Ponder was silent.

The inspector's eyes widened. "Are you saying that Dane Baker is your snitch?"

"Yes, I am. He is. But there's more. I think the reason that Baker knew so much about the murder is because he was behind it."

"And why would you think that?"

"Because the old man that was stabbed to death had a detainer in Indiana. A warrant for the murder of a man named Floyd Baker, Dane Baker's father."

The inspector's face went pale. "I'm not . . . understanding you."

Ponder leaned over his desk. "Know what I don't understand? I don't understand how the Inspector's Office at this prison could overlook such a crucial fact and allow two mortal enemies such as these to live on the same compound."

The inspector was visibly flustered. "Ah . . . well, Griffith wasn't actually a *gain.* Technically he was classified to another prison. He was just here as a patient."

"I see. And how'd that work out for him?"

Mason was quiet.

Ponder smiled. "So it looks like we may both be needing those tractors, eh?"

"He needs to be removed from population now," said Mason, standing and retrieving his radio from the battery charger. "I'll get the captain."

"I'm going with you."

~

The inmates filed out of their dorms and merged into a slow-moving line on the sidewalk where they were herded along like cattle by grim-faced, tobacco-spitting guards. The line bottlenecked through a narrow gate, then dispersed out into the wide-open rec yard. CJ, Hustle, and Bones glanced briefly at one another before heading off in different directions.

CJ walked under the pavilion. The sound of slamming dominos, the blaring television, and hundreds of voices competing to be heard engulfed him. The roar was constant, a sustained crescendo that bounced off the pavement and echoed from the rafters. He wove his way between the card games and cliques, around wheelchairs and gospel quartets, through the small crowds that bounced around would-be rap artists and the Bible-waving prophets who shouted their condemnation from nearby tables.

"Hey, young thing," a voice breathed in his ear, "you looking for a daddy?"

CJ ignored it and pressed through the crowd.

"Hey, bitch!" the voice shouted behind him.

Suddenly he was snatched backward and almost fell. He spun and pulled the knife from his pocket. Ready. The man was probably in his late forties, blacker than Hustle, with a scar that began over his eyebrow and slashed down through his eyelid, across his nose, and ended on the other side of his mouth. He backed off when he saw the knife.

"My bad," he stammered. "I thought you was someone else."

CJ watched him melt back into the crowd before finally turning away. His heart was racing as he slid the knife back into his pocket. The few people who were paying attention to the altercation stepped aside to give CJ a wider berth as he passed.

The crowd thinned as he neared the far end of the pavilion. He looked back once to check if Scarface was following him, then he stepped off the pavement into the grass.

The yard was packed. The sound of basketballs pounding concrete filled the air. The bleachers by the softball field were lined with spectators as a game of transients versus permanents was going full swing. Mexicans and other South and Central Americans were kicking around a soccer ball. Barefoot white boys played beach volleyball in the dirt, while the track that encompassed the sprawling yard was alive with joggers and power walkers.

There were probably eight hundred people outside, maybe more. But seven hundred ninety-nine of them didn't matter. CJ sifted through the faces, discarding groups and entire sections as he walked. He never had to squint or double-take. The man he sought was not easily confused with anyone else. He towered over most of the other inmates and was covered in tattoos.

CJ caught sight of Dane Baker over by the pull-up bars, barking orders as he assisted one of his henchmen who appeared to be struggling. His fingers curled around the knife. His knees began to tremble as fear and adrenaline flooded his bloodstream. He conjured an image of Smoke's dead body and held it in his mind. His friend and teacher lay broken and leaking on the sheets of his hospital bed. Rage came howling, chasing away the fear and blowing through his mind like a whistle of red steam. Distant shouting urged him on. The pounding basketballs were native drums. His face twisted. He took a step forward.

"Promise me that after you return that to your buddy, you'll never touch another knife . . ."

"I promise."

CJ silenced the memory with a mental backhand.

Fuck that.

Dane Baker was no longer just Dane Baker. He was Duke and the Barocela twins. He was Greedy Greg from the county jail. He was Rudy making out with Andrea Marcos. He was April turning her back on him. He was Kane punching him in the stomach. He was Alvorado and Lozano and Judge Blevins. He was the heart failure that killed his father, the suicide that took his mother. He was that asshole under the pavilion with the scar on his face.

The rage boiled over. CJ was running. Dane Baker hung from the pull-up bar. His tattooed back was coated in a sheen of sweat. Heads turned as CJ ran by.

"Dude! What the fuck?" someone shouted as he sprinted under the volleyball net, disrupting the game.

Faces blurred as CJ flew across the grass. When he closed in on Dane, he leaped into the air and sent a foot crashing into his lower back, ripping the bully from the bar and sending him tumbling end over end in the dirt.

Movement from the corner of his eye caused him to turn just as Dane's crony rushed him. His face was a mask of hatred. CJ remembered his greasy black hair and broken teeth from the breezeway under I-Dorm. He met him with a fist, dropping him easily and knocking him out. The gathering crowd roared their approval.

CJ turned quickly back to Dane, who was struggling to his feet. He took three decisive steps and kicked him in the face. The bully flopped backwards and attempted to roll to safety, guarding against another shot. CJ didn't relent. He continued the torrent of vicious kicks until Dane stopped rolling. Then he straddled his chest and began raining blows on his face, steady and constant, one following the next, penetrating his guard, smashing his chin, splitting his eye.

Dane gave up trying to fend off the blows and reached for the collar of CJ's shirt, clutching it in his massive fist. CJ swung harder, faster, refusing to let up. He was still swinging as Dane released a Viking roar and slung him back over his head like a rag doll. CJ's face slammed against the packed dirt, the impact momentarily short-circuiting his brain and dazing him. He used the pull-up bar to help himself up. A crowd was watching him. They were shouting something. Their faces were contorted and their mouths moved, but he couldn't hear. He shook his head. Hustle was there. He blinked. Hustle was pointing. The sound came back on.

"Behind you!" he yelled.

CJ turned. Dane was standing. He brushed the dirt from his ass and rolled his neck. A stream of blood trickled from his eye down the side of his face. He spat a bright red clump in the dirt and stared at it a moment. The crowd was silent. He looked at CJ and smiled. His yellow teeth were coated in red.

"You're dead," he said, raising his fists.

CJ responded by raising his own.

Dane moved in quickly. CJ didn't even see the punch, but fireworks exploded in his head and he was suddenly on his hands and knees staring down at the dirt. Then a boot slammed into his stomach, lifting him off the ground.

"Get up," said Dane.

CJ struggled to his feet and threw an off-balance hook. Dane weaved it easily and punched him in the stomach, then held him up long enough to spit a mouthful of blood in his face. The crowd began to murmur.

"Come on, you little pussy!" Dane bellowed. "Fight me!"

The slap was a bolt of lightning, sending him crashing to the ground. He landed on his side. There was something under him, something jagged.

The knife!

"Get up and fight, bitch!" Dane snarled from above him.

CJ abruptly rolled backward and jumped to his feet, gripping the knife and holding it in front of him.

The crowd reacted.

Dane's eyes widened. "For me?"

He then feinted high with a left jab and easily swatted the knife from CJ's trembling, inexperienced hand with his right. It fell harmlessly to the ground.

"You're gonna wish you woulda used that when you had a chance," said Dane before stepping into a knockout punch.

CJ ducked and shot between his knees, scurrying to his feet behind him. He glanced over at the knife glimmering in the sun.

"Don't even think about it," said Dane.

CJ backed up and raised his fists. He knew he couldn't beat Dane in a boxing match. He had one chance, maybe.

"That's right, pussy," Dane sneered at him. "Fight me like a man."

They squared off in the dirt, hands raised, fists clenched, eyeing each other warily.

CJ leaped in the air and brought both feet down on Dane's kneecap. The bone cracked like a gunshot and bent sickly backward. Dane fell to the ground writhing in agony.

CJ walked over to the grass and scooped up the knife. The crowd was in a frenzy.

"One time!" someone shouted. "The man's comin'. Whole gang of 'em."

CJ straddled Dane and leaned over his face.

"Why did you kill him?"

"Fuck you."

CJ reared back and slammed his head into Dane's nose. It exploded like a tomato.

"Why?" CJ demanded.

"I didn't kill no one, asshole."

The crowd began to murmur.

"One time, CJ," Hustle called, "they comin' through the gate."

CJ pressed the tip of the shank against Dane's throat. He began to squirm.

"Why did you kill Smoke, you motherfucker?"

Dane's eyes were rolling around in his head. His face was smeared with blood and dirt. "I don't know what the fuck you're talking about."

CJ nodded, then slammed his head down into the bully's broken nose. Again.

"Goddamn it!" Dane roared "You better fucking kill me!"

"CJ!" Hustle shouted. "Police!"

He ignored the warning. "Why?" he growled.

Dane began to writhe and thrash beneath him. CJ twisted the knife deeper into his throat. Blood trickled down the side of his neck.

"Why?"

Dane finally broke. "Because he killed my father!"

"Why would Smoke kill your father?"

"Because I drowned his faggot-ass son in the river. Now get the fuck off me."

"CJ!" called Hustle. "One time, man!"

CJ raised the knife and stared coldly into the eyes of the man who ordered the killing of his friend. Had he really killed Smoke's son?

A memory flashed through his mind. He was sitting on Smoke's hospital bed.

"What about the other one?"

"The other murder? That one," said Smoke, "was pure revenge."

CJ lifted the knife higher. He placed his left palm over his right fist and brought it straight down with every ounce of force his body could summon, hollering as he fell forward. The steel cut through the hushed air in a vicious slash and slammed down into the ground an inch from Dane's ear.

Hustle came running up and pushed him aside. "Man, you deaf or what?" He pulled the knife from the ground. "Police comin'! Now get your ass outta here!"

CJ staggered to his feet and walked away. When he looked back he saw Hustle slide the knife to Bones, who passed it off to a jogger, who dropped it in a wheelchair. He lost it after that. He was distracted by all the guards circling Dane Baker and his homeboy, who was still knocked out over by the pull-up bar. Dr. Ponder and the inspector were with them.

He kept his head down as he hurried to the pavilion bathroom. He ripped off the bloody blues he was wearing and tossed them behind a toilet. He then reached under the second sink and found the bleach and the t-shirt. He snatched off the t-shirt he was wearing and used it to wipe his face. It came away bloody. He doused his head and hands with bleach before washing off and slipping on the clean shirt.

He exited the bathroom in a hurry and stepped out on the track. People were watching him. Some subtly raised their fists, while others smiled and shook their heads. A few made brief eye contact and quickly looked away.

Uncomfortable with the attention and aware of the growing number of guards surrounding Dane, he decided to jog. The wind and sun felt good on his face. Other joggers passed him. He watched them sprint down the straightaway and round the curve. He didn't alter his pace. He wasn't in competition with anyone.

Across the yard a nurse was pushing an empty wheelchair through the rec gate. He thought of Dane's leg snapping beneath his feet. A slow smile spread across his face. He could have killed Dane Baker. He knew it. Dane knew it. Everyone watching knew it. The wheelchair coming across the yard could have easily been a gurney and a body bag instead. The difference was a couple of inches. That's how close Dane was to death and how close CJ was to having a murder on his conscience. Maybe on his record too.

For the second time that day, the people from his past paraded through his mind. The twins, Duke, Rudy, Andrea, April, Greedy, Kane. What was he trying to prove and who was he trying to prove it to? His family was gone. His freedom was gone, yet he was still on the hamster wheel. Still fighting the same old uphill battle of trying to be something he was not.

He rounded a turn. His breath, his heartbeat, and the crunching gravel beneath his shoes were the only sounds he could hear. The rest of the yard ceased to exist. It was just him and the track.

Behind him was a crossroads. He could have just killed a man. A man who probably deserved to die. The world would be a better place without Dane Baker. Or at least the prison would. But killing a man would also be a new low in his downward trajectory, entangling him deeper in the web and hastening the descent of the bounding snowball that was his life. He thought of Smoke and their conversations on roles, appearances, hate, fear. Smoke wouldn't have wanted him to kill anyone. He was about forgiveness, not revenge. Smoke didn't even want him touching a knife. He made him promise.

But why didn't Smoke kill Dane? Maybe they were never at the same prison. Maybe Smoke considered vengeance served after killing Dane's father. An eye for an eye. If Dane was even telling the truth. Or maybe Smoke just gave up the vendetta when he found God. CJ doubted he would ever know the reason.

Up ahead Dane Baker was handcuffed and being rolled off the yard in the wheelchair.

"Murder?" he bellowed, ignoring his disfigured leg. "You're locking me up for murder? Who the fuck'd I kill?"

A gust of wind blew the inspector's turquoise tie over his shoulder. "You tell me."

Dane spotted CJ. "Hey! That motherfucker's got a knife! He's the one you should be locking up. He broke my fucking leg!"

The inspector nodded to a nearby guard.

"Stop right there!" the guard ordered as CJ was jogging by.

CJ slowed to a stop and turned around. Dane's face was a purple grimace. His left leg was still bent at an awkward angle. He was surrounded by officers, while Ponder and the inspector held a private discussion off to the side. His underling, the one CJ laid out, was already being escorted through the gate in cuffs.

CJ breathed heavily. His face was red and covered in sweat. "Sir?"

The guard glanced over at the inspector.

"Shake him down," called Mason before saying something else to Ponder.

"Turn around and place your hands over your head," said the officer. CJ complied.

The guard gave him a thorough pat-down before turning back to Mason. "He's clean."

"Well then, he hid it somewhere!" Dane shouted.

Mason and Ponder rejoined them.

"So you're saying this is the man who broke your leg?" asked the inspector.

"And tried to stab me!"

"Well then, who's that?" asked Mason, nodding over at Dane's homeboy with the swollen eye, standing outside the rec gate in handcuffs.

"He was with me," said Dane, pointing at CJ. "He knocked him out."

"Knocked him out," Mason repeated, looking over at CJ. "Right. So let me get this straight, Mr. Baker. You're telling me that this . . . *boy* over here singlehandedly beat the living shit out of you, breaking your leg with his bare hands, and then, if that wasn't enough already, he goes and knocks out your comrade over there too?"

A few of the guards chuckled. Dane shut his eyes tight and began to rock back and forth in the wheelchair. "Fuck you," he growled, "fuck all of y'all."

The nurse looked concerned. "I really need to get him over to the hospital."

The inspector studied CJ a moment longer. "Nice tattoo," he finally said. "Get out of here."

CJ glanced at Ponder. The doctor nodded. He felt a thousand eyes on him as he walked away. Behind him he heard Dane Baker roaring in anguish, whether because of the pain of a broken limb or the fact that he had gotten away with it, CJ wasn't sure. The sound faded as he took off down the track.

A feeling of exultation swept over CJ as he ran. Two lives had been spared that day. Dane Baker's and his own. It seemed like he'd been letting life happen since junior high, wandering aimlessly, reacting, desperately trying to be anyone but the scared little kid that was bullied by Joey Barocela, cheated on by Andrea, betrayed by Rudy. It was time to find his way back. To himself.

The back stretch of the track was unoccupied save for a lone jogger way ahead of him and an old-timer limping along in a straw hat. CJ looked up into the blue sky. He imagined his mom, dad, and Smoke looking down on him. He raised his fists in triumph as pride swelled within him. For the first time in forever, CJ McCallister was free.

Epilogue

JUNE 2005

The Greyhound rolled down the two-lane highway, winding its way through the endless orange groves and farmland of Central Florida. The blazing noonday sun was reduced to a twinkling white star outside the dark tinted windows of the bus. Many of the passengers were lulled to sleep by the hum of the diesel engine, by the AC blowing from the side panels, by the relentless sameness of the passing landscape. A truck sped past in the other direction. Air brakes hissed. A baby cried. The normal mundane sights and sounds of life being lived were everywhere. CJ was mesmerized.

Who but a climber can know the feeling of scaling Everest? Who but a mother can know the feeling of childbirth? The same can be said for the unparalleled rush of walking out of prison after serving multiple years. Only a small fraternity of men and women ever get to experience this particular brand of exhilaration, of hope laced with wonder and fear. Of life restored.

After fourteen years, seven months, and twenty-one days, the Department of Corrections gave him a check for a hundred dollars and a Greyhound ticket to anywhere in the state. He kept the check folded in his pocket with an old letter from his mother's boss. The only other property he carried was the book Smoke had left him. He absently fingered the yellow dog-eared pages as the pastures and cattle and silos streamed by.

The bus began to slow and eventually came to a full stop before turning off onto another road, a four-lane highway. CJ stared across the median at the passing cars. Everyone seemed to be talking on phones while they drove! The world he exited in 1991 and the world he was reentering in 2005 were two different planets. The sun had risen and set thousands of times while the earth spun on its axis. Whole calendars fluttered in the wind behind him, as if sucked from the window of a speeding car. Nations warred, babies were born, Rodney King, Kurt Cobain, the Internet, Oklahoma City, Waco, Monica Lewinsky, Peyton Manning, Eminem, Y2K, LeBron James, George W. Bush, 9/11, Afghanistan, Columbine, Super Wal-Mart. Yet in the time capsule of prison life, nothing changed. Each passing day was the same as the last: work out, read, eat, and sleep. The routine rarely varied as the years melted away.

His reflection stared back from the moving backdrop of traffic, telephone poles, and single-story buildings that dotted the highway outside the tinted window. He saw tattoos and muscles. He saw lines etched into the skin of his face. He saw a fourteen-year-old boy, a twenty-year-old jit, and a thirty-one-year-old man. An overcomer, a survivor, a warrior.

"Lakeland," announced the driver as the bus turned down a side street and into the Greyhound terminal. "Departure time, 1:15 p.m."

The brakes hissed as the passengers stood and began filing off the bus. CJ didn't move. Beyond his reflection was an empty, gravelly bus station parking lot. Beyond that was a meadow. Surrounding the meadow were towering oaks, and above the oaks stretched a blue, cloudless sky, as vast and infinite as his own possibilities.

A summer gust blew through the meadow, causing the tall grass to bend and ripple. Something stirred. He looked closer. A dragonfly was circling the field, then two, then twenty. Suddenly one left the meadow and flew across the parking lot, like a tiny fighter jet aiming straight for the bus. CJ's eyes widened as it braked in midair, hovering just outside his window for a moment before shooting straight up into the sky and disappearing.

"Sir?" came a voice from behind him. "Excuse me, sir?"

He turned. She was no older than twenty-seven and obviously Hispanic. Her dark pretty eyes were hooded and a loose strand of hair was stuck to her cheek.

"Do you know what time it is?" she asked.

A smile tugged at the corners of his mouth.

"Now," he said, "the time is right now."

Other Novels by Malcolm Ivey

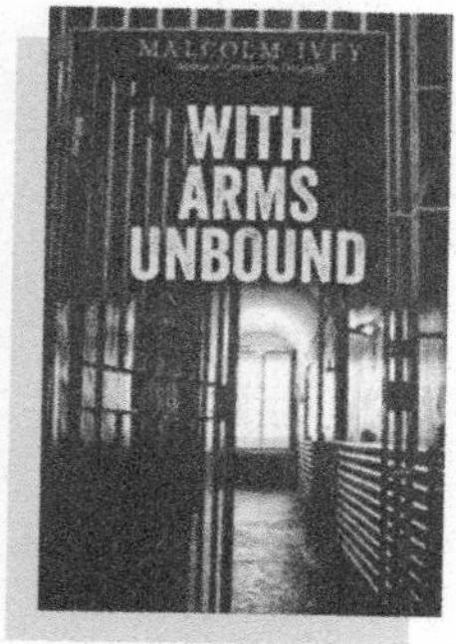

2014 Edition

A stark tale of forbidden love, domestic violence, and crystal meth, *With Arms Unbound* charts the interlocking destinies of a woman trapped in a toxic marriage, the man who would die to set her free, and the husband who would kill before he let her go.

2016 Edition

On the Shoulders of Giants chronicles the intersecting journeys of a foster kid and a projects kid as they battle their way through adolescence into adulthood. An exploration of race, part memoir, part coming-of-age, part thriller, part love story, this transcendent novel defies genre.

2018 Edition

Released after years in prison, Mason Foster now clings to the solitude of his boyhood home, until two neighborhood children barge into his life. Their widowed mother is dating a man she thinks she knows, but does she, really? Hearts will be broken, lives shattered, tables turned in *Sticks & Stones*, an unforgettable story of neighbors, lovers, and friends.